FATAL SHADOW

CHAMPIONS OF FATE: BOOK 1

NOEL COUGHLAN

FATAL SHADOW

Copyright © 2020 Noel Coughlan

Cover Illustration by MiblArt (https://miblart.com/)

Edited by Proofed to Perfection (http://www.proofedtoperfection.com/)

Published by Photocosmological Press (http://photocosm.org/)

Paperback Edition: ISBN:978-1-910206-17-1

For Evan.

1

____

Seven assassins, foiled by the watchfulness of the princess's retinue, had previously failed to kill Drinith of Kaplar. Now, somewhere in the palace of her host, the Aether Emperor, an eighth crept unchecked toward her bedchamber. In a premonition, Quiescat had seen the man flitting between shadows in dimly lit corridors as he moved inexorably nearer her door, his bland, blue-black countenance rigid with concentration, the blade of his dagger as black and cruel as his purpose. Quiescat had already witnessed every blow of the impending struggle. He had seen her standing blood-spattered over the corpse of her would-be killer. But the vision gave Quiescat little comfort. The child he had raised from a baby was about to face a consummate killer in single combat, and the exiled Oracle of Godsdoor could do nothing but wait and pray his prescience proved true.

Slouched in his seat, wringing his sweaty hands, he stared at the dragon amber tiles covering the bedroom floor. He was only vaguely aware of the Crevast, the void between worlds, howling for his attention beyond the long windows. The aging warrior, Gelasin, couldn't be ignored so easily. Quiescat kept glancing up at that tense knot of bone and sinew wrapped in drum-tight green-black skin and battered armor. His lean mouth always verged on an insolent smile, owing to the rugged, matte black scars in his cheeks where his honor tattoos should have been. Leaning against the wall, his arms folded, he appeared to be the very embodiment of smug indifference.

"How can you stay so damnably calm?" Quiescat whispered. "Our princess's life is in danger."

Gelasin arched an amused eyebrow. "I have faith in you," he said with a whiff of sarcasm. "And I've faith in her. She must prove to her prospective subjects and allies that her right to rule extends beyond an accident of birth. Thanks to you, she's ready for the assassin's every move. She faces more of a dance than a battle."

Quiescat snorted. "Don't thank me. I never should have agreed to this escapade."

Gelasin's eyes narrowed. "You're not questioning your vision, are you?"

"No." Quiescat massaged the aching stiffness in the back of his neck. He knew his prevision was true.

Unfolding his arms, Gelasin straightened. "Are you certain she's safe this time? The sequence of moves I worked out with her is specific to the attack you described, down to the wielding hand that the assassin favors. She's not wearing her mail shirt precisely because, according to your vision, it was an unnecessary burden. If you're wrong..." He gripped the hilt of his sheathed dagger and stared at the door. His whole body compressed as if ready to pounce toward it.

The sudden tension in his demeanor tempted a smile from Quiescat. The renegade, having so often pooh-poohed his misgivings in the past, now turned to him for reassurance. "She will win. The vision is certain."

Relaxing, Gelasin folded his arms and rested back against the wall, but he kept glancing at the door. "It wasn't just symbolic or something?"

"It wasn't allegorical," Quiescat said wearily. He missed the ambiguity of cryptic dreams, but such things were the poetry of youth. His prophetic glimpses had turned prosaic long ago. Since

Godsdoor's fall, his visions had become limited to fixed points nailed into a dark and uncertain future. After tonight, only one would remain: the moment of his death. It, too, drew close. He had replayed it so many times, it no longer inspired fear, but only a gnawing sense of loss and failure. He could see nothing beyond it. It might be a blessing. Never mind the recovery of her throne; the odds were stacked against Drinith's very survival, and he didn't want to contemplate her death.

Could his prophetic insight fail? Could she die tonight? Prescience was a fickle gift, prone to misinterpretation. No, he couldn't be mistaken. She still lived in his final vision. Unless her presence was an illusion, a trick of some kind, the sort Fate loved to play.

Gelasin pursed his lips. "She's not alone. Jarma's in there with her. Between the two of them... You saw Drinith kill him."

Quiescat winced, nodded.

"I slew my first man when I was fourteen," Gelasin said. "Drinith's almost nineteen."

Quiescat shook his head in disgust. "I'm nearly fifty and I've never killed anyone." *That is, not in hand-to-hand combat.* Quiescat had caused far more deaths than the warrior ever had or would. His prognostications had divided families, started wars, pitted kingdoms and empires against each other. Yes, his words had possessed the power to kill until the tyrant Magian the Infinite had driven him from his temple.

Gelasin gestured with his forefinger and thumb at the pits in his cheeks. He smiled. In the dull light, they became two jagged black holes in his face. "You didn't get what once adorned these cheeks until you had killed in the service of the Emperor of Kaplar."

When Quiescat first encountered Gelasin, the warrior had scorned that same emperor. He had deigned to join Drinith's retinue only because his detestation of Magian eclipsed even his hatred of her father, Hemrath. The subsequent years as her protector had inspired a change of heart, a nostalgia for the life he had forsaken, and a fierce loyalty to the heir of his former liege. It made his reckless urgency to thrust her in harm's way even more infuriating.

The fault didn't lie with Gelasin. He acted according to his nature. Quiescat could have stopped this. He should have. He still could.

"I weary of this," he declared, slapping his hands on the armrests.

A sudden clamor from the neighboring bedchamber transfixed him mid-rise. His fingers dug into the padded leather, but he remained frozen in a pained hunch, terrified that anything he did, no matter how slight, might sabotage his vision as his princess fought for her life.

2

———————

The clamminess of the dagger's hilt made Drinith's palm itch as she waited behind the door for the man coming to murder her. She felt none of the readiness Gelasin had claimed to see in her. Stripped of her mail shirt, her tunic felt flimsy. Her heart leapt wildly at every swoop and swoon of the wind beyond the palace.

Another young woman with a cloud of red and gold hair, her living reflection, lay in her bed, creating an eerie sense of disembodiment. The candlelight made the cyan gem shine like a star against the green-black night of her forehead. A sheet of red silk molded around her sprawled body, drawing the eye with its vulnerable nakedness. Beneath the massive pillows, however, the girl held an axe.

How could her handmaid, Jarma, display such remarkable calm knowing all the while an assassin drew near? She had disguised herself as Drinith so that the assassin would assume it was she who lay in the bed. If only Drinith could check her nerves as easily as her friend did and quell the flutter in the pit of her stomach. If she failed this test, both of their lives would be forfeited. It would have been easier to face the assassin alone.

This scheme was the height of folly. She should have never agreed to it.

But it was too late now to send Jarma away. The bright yellow light spilling through the long windows had already darkened to the burnt orange gloom of a Crevast night. The assassin could arrive at any moment.

Her whole body reverberated with the urgent throbbing of her heart. She needed to calm down. She practiced her moves—her dance, as Gelasin dubbed it.

Something flickered in the corner of her eye; a pair of curved shadows bit into the stripe of light beneath the doorway before it disappeared. She held her breath as the handle silently rotated downward. She stepped back as the door gently swung open with nary a creak. Her heart thumped so loudly in the silence an absurd panic gripped her lest her would-be murderer should hear as he drifted into the room with all the softness of a shadow. Hunched and cowled, he raised a stiletto in his left hand, its needle-like blade pointing downward, ready to strike the sleeping girl.

The multiple shifting shadows of the dagger cast by the encircling candles crept up the blood-red silk to close on Jarma's chest like the hooked fingers of a massive claw. Still feigning repose, she shifted slightly and emitted a soft sigh. If Drinith didn't strike now, it would be the last sound her friend ever made. Tightening her damp grip on her knife, she plunged forward.

Alerted by her soft intake of breath, the assassin swerved around. His knife flicked upward as he swallowed the gap between them in a single precise leap. He stabbed twice with the whole force of his body where her torso should have been, but she had already swerved clear. He swept the blade after her, but she had stepped inside its arc and clamped her arm over his elbow. She had no time to savor the chagrin, briefly betrayed by the candlelight, on his blue-black face. His second dagger flicked out at her from beneath his arm like a striking snake, but she was ready for it. He yowled as she drove her knife through his hand, impaling it into his forearm, forcing him to drop his weapon. Her blade had penetrated deeper than she had intended; she had only meant to cripple his hand. She yanked her knife free and drove it at his neck, chasing the moment of victory Quiescat had foreseen. The assassin slapped at her with his wounded hand. He twisted clear and jammed his knee into her stomach. Winded, she lost hold of his arm, but she fastened onto it again before it could slip free. Bright pain jabbed her side. Ignoring his bloody slaps, she stabbed his arm three times, cracking bone, snapping the tip of her blade. She threw herself upon him with a violent roar. Her dagger made a loud crunch as it rammed into his chest. As he flopped back, the blade pulled her forward and she toppled with him. The floor slammed her blade deeper, sinking it all the way to the hilt. She rolled off him as Jarma dropped her axe on him. Blood spurted from the assassin's neck as his severed head rolled across the floor. It came to a stop at an awkward angle, eyes gazing up at Drinith in bewilderment until the last vestige of life drained away.

Warm blood greased Drinith's tunic. She assumed it was all her assailant's until a sharp pain in her side reminded her otherwise.

3

———

A high-pitched cry pierced Quiescat's heart. In the instant he took to react, Gelasin had dashed out of the room. Quiescat stumbled after him into the corridor.

Anxious faces peered through opening doors. A stranger, claret-skinned and yellow-eyed, stepped into the hall, naked save for his rapier. Another assassin. Quiescat froze.

The man arched a hairless eyebrow. "It's me, Halyard." He pointed to a pair of interlocked emblems tattooed in yellow on his chest. One of them, an alerion taking flight, belonged to his lover; the other, a peridexion tree, must be his own. Below them was a straight, bright scar. Stripped of his fine clothes and makeup, the courtesar was all but unrecognizable. He looked a much older man, particularly with his cropped pate. His signature feathery coiffure was clearly a wig. The absence of his platform shoes was likewise telling, robbing him of both real and figurative stature.

The gray-blue lowlander, Zin, burst from the opposite room in full armor, sword in one hand, dagger in the other. A murderous grin was set in the diamond of laughter lines between the sharp nose and prominent chin of his long, scrawny face. His black hair was even neatly tied back. Gelasin must have forewarned him but not the courtesar, for some reason.

The far end of the corridor filled with the echoey thuds of rushing palace guards, arrived much too late.

"You all wait here!" Gelasin growled as he dashed into Drinith's room. Zin's grin slid away as he staggered to a halt. Quiescat slipped between him and Halyard and followed Gelasin inside.

The fault for this debacle lay with Quiescat, not Gelasin. Quiescat shouldn't have let the warrior sway him. Fighting and killing was the limit of Gelasin's understanding. He respected only killers like Zin and couldn't countenance following anyone who didn't share his infatuation with violence. The supposed wiser man had heeded the counsel of a bloodthirsty old fool.

Jarma stood by the bed, her face stretched with horror, a bloody axe dangling from her hand. Quiescat followed her dazed stare to where the princess lay. Gelasin's crouched back obscured everything except her bare feet. Quiescat seized the warrior's shoulder to pull him out of the way. Gelasin swung around and punched him so hard he flew backward across the room, smacking the wall. He kept upright despite his stupefaction. His nose throbbed with raw pain. Rivulets of blood tickled his lips and chin.

"You damned lunatic!" Quiescat spluttered.

"Sorry," Gelasin said with a casual shrug. "Force of habit. My reflexes are honed to react instantaneously to uninvited contact."

Scowling, Quiescat sought his handkerchief and delicately pressed it to his nose. "I'm sure it's broken," he observed sullenly.

"Shall I just let Drinith bleed while I set it for you? A simple procedure. I'll just hold your beak between my hands and twist—"

"Of course not," said Quiescat, taken aback. Trust Gelasin to make him feel contemptible despite being the victim of his fist. "How bad is she?"

Gelasin examined the wound for an unbearable length of time before he set about treating it. "She's fine. The cut's superficial." He shifted to reveal the princess's blood-spattered face. Too weak to speak, she wore a brave grin to confirm Gelasin's assertion—and to conceal her distress from her companions. Quiescat's relief numbed the sting of his injury.

Gelasin picked up the assassin's blade. "Yeah, she's fine—as long as the blade was clean. He looks like he's from our home shard."

Still holding the handkerchief to his stinging nose, Quiescat strode over to the headless corpse. Kneeling stiffly, he examined it. He turned one hand over to discover a tattoo on its palm: five white stars arranged in a circle. "His order doesn't resort to poison." The pentaculars never needed to. They always killed their quarry by dint of sheer determination and brute strength. "And they're not from Rhumgad. They're local." He warned Gelasin off interrogating him with a shake of his head. The motion made his nose hurt worse.

An officer pushed his way through the onlookers walling the doorway. Beneath his massive finned helmet, his face blushed violet. "Is the princess injured?" he piped.

"She'll live," Gelasin sneered.

"The Aether Emperor must be informed."

"Disturb your master's sleep if you must, but the princess has already dealt effectively with the threat—as any fool can plainly see." The officer, top lip twitching, let the effrontery pass.

"We'll need a new bedchamber for her, obviously," Gelasin added. "Take care of that, won't you?"

The officer spun on his heels and elbowed his way through the sea of gawkers. Gelasin bounded after him and herded them across the threshold. Quiescat's acolyte, Abecedar, squeezed inside before the warrior slammed the door, his dark eyes bugging more than usual as they darted about the room.

"Master, you're hurt! How?" He reached for the bloody handkerchief Quiescat pressed to his nose.

"No need to concern yourself." Smiling, he gently brushed Abecedar's hand away. "It was an accident. Right, Gelasin?" He shot his rival a condemning glance.

"Hey, I said I was sorry."

Clutching a bedsheet around her with one hand, Jarma still held the axe in the other. Her red and gold wig leaned precariously to one side. A shred of dried glue marked her forehead where her paste jewel had been located. She looked lost and a little annoyed. She had reason to be. Distracted by Drinith's injury, everyone had forgotten the poor girl.

"Are you okay?" Quiescat reached out to reassure her, but she flinched from his touch. The axe slipped from her fingers and clattered against the floor. Abecedar stumbled over it and threw his arms around her. She didn't hesitate to reciprocate his consoling hug. Quiescat did his best to suppress a smile. Would she be so eager for his attention after Abecedar succeeded him? Many people dreaded the Oracle of Godsdoor more than any assassin. They feared the truth he possessed, even those who sought to learn it. His temple had been razed during Drinith's infancy, and the only future he could now glimpse was his end, but the mystique of his position still daunted most folk—except Gelasin. To him, the oracle, like the princess, was just another weapon to wield in his personal war against Magian the Infinite. But then, the warrior appeared to fear nothing, not even death.

"You never said she'd be wounded," Gelasin carped.

"I warned you of the dangers."

The rawness of Quiescat's indignation surprised Gelasin. Quiescat hadn't foreseen Drinith's wounding and his unease about Gelasin's scheme had been vague at best. As his powers waned, the seer clung even tighter to the illusion of omniscience. Yes, the great Oracle of Godsdoor had degenerated into a petty street conjurer dependent on deception and sleight of hand to keep a step ahead of the other vagrants.

Gelasin pressed: "You never said—"

"If I had, would you—"

"Enough." The disconcerting faintness of Drinith's voice silenced him. Her feeble effort to rise drew everyone to her. Even with Gelasin and Abecedar supporting her, she looked as though she might collapse at any moment.

"Sit on the bed," Gelasin urged.

She shook her head as she pressed a hand to her bandaged

wound. "Take me from here," she said, desperation edging her voice. "Somewhere I can wash away this bloody mess."

"You're crying." It took Quiescat a moment to realize Jarma was talking to him. "I've never seen tears shine so," she added. Gelasin and Drinith likewise looked upon him with keen interest.

Abecedar, meanwhile, regarded his master with a predatory leer. He knew what these tears meant: another prophecy had come to pass, another step nearer Quiescat's end—and, with it, the passing of his oracular power to his sole acolyte. Poor misguided fool! It was too late to warn him. He had already committed his life to the pursuit of the gift. He wouldn't listen any more than Quiescat had in his day.

"Don't weep for me," Drinith said. "I'll be fine."

Quiescat mirrored her wan smile and wiped the tears from his cheeks. He must relinquish his ability to his acolyte, or it would die with him. Drinith needed oracular protection and Quiescat was spent, a husk of a man who couldn't see beyond his impending death. But was Abecedar ready for this terrible burden?

4

Drinith's wound prodded her awake. She shifted in the bed and regretted it instantly as the pain redoubled. The drug that Quiescat had given her must be wearing off. Her head felt like someone had stuffed it full of burlap and nettles, perhaps a lingering side effect of the medicine. She groaned for help. Something moved at the end of the bed. Panic gripped her. Could it be another assassin?

Jarma's face, drawn with worry, popped into view; she had been adjusting the bedclothes, and now sat at the end of the bed with easy familiarity. "How are you, Your Imperial Majesty?" It wasn't her habit to speak so formally in private, but they appeared to be alone in the room. Nobody aside from Jarma ever bothered to use the proper etiquette in addressing Drinith. Most of her retinue referred to her as Her Highness. Gelasin alternated between that and Princess, the latter generally when in a sarcastic or peevish mood. Quiescat never addressed her by anything other than her first name.

Drinith relaxed. "I'm fine," she tried to say, but she managed only a low moan.

"I'll get Quiescat," Jarma said, leaping from the bed. The jarring motion aggravated Drinith's wound; she bit her lip to stifle the pain.

Jarma's bare feet pattered across the tiled floor. The door squealed open and slapped shut on Drinith's plaintive mumble for her to stay.

She shut her eyes as she waited for Jarma's return. The memory of the assassin came unbidden—the surprise on his face, the fear. Drinith had reveled in the swelling terror in those dark eyes. For that instant, she had imagined herself soaring above him and the other assorted killers Magian of Javlohm had dispatched to hunt her. Her realm, the Kaplar Empire, everything she had lost, had been hers for the taking. His blade had punctured that illusion.

Gelasin's scheme had nearly killed her. Quiescat had been reluctant to rely on his vision to protect her, but Gelasin had argued down his objections. Even then, Quiescat had doubted the wisdom of the enterprise despite his assurances to the contrary. His enigmatic crystal eyes never betrayed his feelings, but he couldn't hide the apprehensive quiver in his voice. She shouldn't have let Gelasin persuade her.

The door opened; Quiescat, Gelasin, Abecedar, and Jarma filed inside. Their grins had a suspect uniformity. Pain wracked Drinith's side as she attempted to rise. Jarma quickly slipped her arm beneath her uninjured shoulder, helped her drag herself into a sitting position, and propped her up with pillows.

"How do you feel, Your Highness?" Gelasin asked, gently patting her hand. Too angry to answer, she glared at him. Oblivious to her ire, he pulled up a high-backed chair and sat beside her. The craters in his cheeks reminded Drinith of a grinning death's-head as he beamed with pride. "The Emperors of Kaplar vanquished many foes, but they had slain none with their own hands in generations."

"Jarma dispatched him, not I—and quite handily, I might add. If she hadn't, I would be dead."

Gelasin took no notice. "Already, news of your triumph echoes through the palace." He winked. "Our host and his co-emperors cannot ignore this."

Quiescat's smile faded, revealing the anxiety it had hidden. "I hope you're correct."

Gelasin sneered at him. "The Elemental Pentarchy of Thirring takes great pride in its hospitality. An assassin injuring one of its guests is a grievous humiliation. The Aether Emperor must recompense the princess for his failure to protect her." He spread his hands. "That's a perfect opening to enlist his support against Magian."

All the schemes Quiescat and Gelasin had set in motion to win foreign rulers to their cause had come to naught. They had only succeeded in burning through Quiescat's fortune and putting all their lives in danger. A few times, only Quiescat's gift had saved them from catastrophe.

The oracle bowed his head and rubbed the back of his neck. "You assume too much. There are other ways for the Aether Emperor, Dariffon, to rid himself of the stain on his honor."

Gelasin stiffened to attention. "What do you know you're not telling us?"

Quiescat lifted his head, shot him a withering glance. "Nothing," he growled. He massaged his forehead. "Nothing," he repeated softly.

"If you know something—"

"Stop it!" Drinith snapped. The relationship between the oracle and the warrior had been frosty for as long as she could remember, but lately, as Quiescat's powers dimmed, they quarreled often. Too often.

Quiescat's hollow chuckle sent a shiver through her. "I'm as blind as you are, Gelasin. Almost."

The warrior's exasperated glance pleaded for her to take his side. His head joggled as though it might explode. "Then pass on your power to Abecedar before it dies with you."

Abecedar concealed a blossoming smile behind his hand. His reaction might be understandable, given he had sacrificed his entire life for the chance to become the Oracle of Godsdoor, but his eagerness disgusted Drinith. She loved Quiescat too much to lose him.

Quiescat straightened and craned his neck to look down haughtily upon the warrior. Drinith had become so accustomed to his crystal eyes, she rarely noticed them, but his indignation made them glitter inhumanly. "You don't appreciate the sacrifice that you ask."

Gelasin drew his dagger, pointing it at his own chest. "I'd give my life to protect the princess. Would you not do the same?"

Drinith bolted upright in the bed, hiding the pain that ripped through her side. "Enough! This bickering must cease."

A knock at the door stilled everyone. At Drinith's nod, Jarma opened it and slipped outside. Drinith strained fruitlessly to make sense of the murmured conversation in the corridor.

Jarma re-entered. "Your Imperial Majesty, the Aether Emperor's physician begs an opportunity to examine your wound."

Leaning back onto the pillows, Drinith looked to Quiescat for his counsel.

"Dr. Aerwig is a fine physician," he said, rubbing his chin. "Better than me, I dare say."

"High praise indeed," Drinith said. "Jarma, permit him to come in."

Aerwig entered, a smile flickering beneath his silver mustachio. "Good evening, *Your Highness*." He gave Jarma a sour sidelong glance, as if he found her use of *Your Imperial Majesty* somehow offensive. His exaggeratedly graceful bow bespoke derision for the derelict royal he had been dispatched to treat. Cold anger lurked in his silver-blue eyes. "The inspection of your wound requires privacy. Would you mind dismissing your retinue?"

Gelasin and Quiescat exchanged glances. "Jarma can stay," said the warrior, smirking. "I'm sure she'll see nothing she hasn't seen before. Wait here. I'll be back in a moment."

He strolled back in swinging the axe dangling from his hand. Jarma grimaced as he passed it to her. He winked at the doctor. "Be forewarned: she knows how to use it."

"What are you implying?" Aerwig spluttered. "I am a physician, sir!"

"I'm just being friendly," Gelasin tossed over his shoulder as he sauntered out of the room. "If I wasn't, I'd be wielding the axe myself." Quiescat and Abecedar followed him.

"Are you in pain, Your Highness?" Aerwig asked coolly.

She nodded; the pain made her wince.

"I shall take that as a yes." Aerwig's smile failed to warm the coldness in his eyes. He produced a small red lozenge from one of the many pocket slits on his padded velvet tunic, proffering it between thumb and forefinger. "Please swallow this. It will numb the pain."

She hesitated. "What is in it?"

He smiled. "Its exact formulation is a secret known only to my order."

She glanced at the closed door, yearning for Quiescat's advice. She'd have to make up her mind or look like the oracle's puppet before one of Dariffon's servants. Quiescat had already declared his admiration of the doctor's expertise. "Jarma, please get me some water."

"Pardon me, Your Highness," Aerwig said. "The lozenge will dissolve into a liquid naturally. You need only place it on your tongue, like so." He mimed an unsavory demonstration.

Drinith snatched the pastille and, turning her head in modesty, did as the doctor asked. It melted instantly. The liquid tasted sweet without being cloying. "It's nicer than I expected."

"Medicine doesn't have to taste awful to work," Aerwig said solemnly.

Almost instantly, the pain evaporated.

"Feeling better?" he asked.

She nodded.

At Aerwig's insistence, Jarma removed Drinith's nightshirt. He unwrapped the bandages with surprising speed and lightness of touch and scrutinized the wound. "Very nice work. Exceptionally clean and neat. Who is responsible?"

"My adviser, Gelasin."

"He's certainly adept at stitching. Must have had a lot of practice. And the salve?"

"The oracle had it."

"The very one I planned to use myself. I recognize the scent. I'll apply more." As soon as he finished, he wrapped up the wound again. "You should suffer minimal scarring if you continue to apply it every day until the wound has fully healed." He nodded to himself. "I'll report to His Elemental Majesty that you should make a full recovery."

He bowed curtly and departed. Moments later, Abecedar and Gelasin tramped back in. Through the open doorway, Drinith glimpsed Quiescat remonstrating with Aerwig.

"He's a bit annoyed with the doctor," Gelasin said, jerking a thumb over his shoulder at the two men. "That pain medicine he gave you is addictive in large doses. And awfully expensive. Some of the ingredients come from the wrong side of Empyr, if you know what I mean." He chuckled. "The demon side."

"I'm afraid I don't understand your meaning."

"Never mind. Aerwig said it was too low a dose to addict you. Frankly, you're not rich enough to afford a habit like that." He patted her hand. "You'll be fine."

Quiescat stalked inside and slammed the door. "That insufferable old fool."

Gelasin furrowed his brow. "The doctor has fallen in your estimation, it seems."

Quiescat rushed out of the room again.

"Do you know what he's doing?" Gelasin asked Abecedar. The young man shrugged.

The oracle returned and unstoppered a vial of black liquid. "Jarma, get a basin." He thrust the vial at Drinith. The tarry reek made her stomach roil. "Drink it."

"What will that do?" Gelasin asked.

"It'll purge that narcotic."

Gelasin rolled his eyes. "You're overreacting. Drinith doesn't want—"

"Give it to me!" Drinith took the vial and tipped the potion into her mouth. She gagged as she tried to swallow it. The spewed contents of her stomach splashed into the silver bowl Jarma shoved under her chin. She continued to gag even after nothing remained for her to vomit. Her throat and mouth burned. She pushed the bowl away.

"Was that necessary?" Gelasin asked. "The doctor said he had given her a very low dosage."

Drinith drank some water Jarma passed her to wash away the awful taste in her mouth.

"We have only his word for that," Quiescat said. "That inflammation around the Aether Emperor's mouth matches a symptom of addiction to Devil's Dew. There's no telling what chicanery the good doctor might employ to cure his patron of his current embarrassment."

Gelasin bobbed his head. His mouth compressed into a grim line. "Do you really think Aerwig tried to addict the princess?"

Quiescat sighed. "I don't know for certain."

"So the doctor might be simply doing his best for his patient."

"The point is," Quiescat spat, "we can't trust Dariffon or his servants."

Gelasin frowned. "You were singing Aerwig's praises earlier."

"That was before he gave her Devil's Dew."

"I shouldn't have taken it, but the pain was nigh unbearable," Drinith said. "I'm sorry."

"It's not your fault, princess," Gelasin said.

"No, of course not," Quiescat said.

"The oracle's to blame." Gelasin turned and fixed his smoldering gaze on Quiescat. The latter straightened and, scowling, defiantly puffed out his chest.

Drinith smothered a sigh. As a child, she had admired both men. No, she had worshiped them. Now, their bickering and posturing put her in mind of bratty children. They both doted on her, she knew, and each was fiercely loyal, but she must end their rivalry before it brought calamity on them all.

A knock summoned Jarma to the corridor. She returned, nervously biting her lower lip. "Your Imperial Majesty, there's a herald outside. You are cordially invited to breakfast with the emperor on the grand balcony tomorrow morning."

Gelasin exulted: "So that's why the physician came—to mend Drinith so she may attend!" He sneered at Quiescat. "I told you my plan would work." The oracle's dismissive snort only amplified his elation.

"Jarma, inform the herald we would be happy to accept his invitation," Quiescat said morosely. The warrior approved with a firm nod.

Their presumption irritated Drinith. She was no longer a child who must be led by the hand by her guardians. But it would be churlish, and appear weak, to challenge a judgment with which she could find no fault. "I agree. Jarma, please inform the herald."

The maid squirmed. "Pardon, Your Imperial Majesty," she said, with an apologetic glance at her advisors, "but the Aether Emperor extended his invitation to you alone."

"The effrontery!" Quiescat muttered. Gelasin worked his jaw muscles in mute fury.

Drinith smiled wryly at the consternation on their faces. They had shown less alarm when sending her to fight the assassin. She declared with a ferocity that brooked no debate: "If that is our host's will, then I will go." It felt good to take charge.

5

———

Sitting in his favorite chair, Quiescat stared at the flooring's amber tiles, doing his best to ignore Gelasin as he paced the bedchamber like a caged animal.

"A fortune lies beneath our feet," he remarked dreamily. "It's a pity we can't pry a few dozen dragon amber tiles off the floor. Our financial woes would be staved off for some time."

"Leave managing the finances to me. Focus on Drinith's safety."

The *clack-clack-clack* of Gelasin's heels kept up their monotonous song. Quiescat said through gritted teeth: "You damnable nuisance, I should never have let you into my room! Drinith will be fine. It's a breakfast, not another assassination attempt."

Gelasin stopped dead in his tracks. "Yeah? You assured me she'd be safe with the assassin."

Quiescat ignored the jibe. "I wish I could give you some insight into what will happen, but I can't. Sorry."

Gelasin hesitated. "An oracle who can't see the future isn't much help."

"After last night, the only vision I have left is of my death," Quiescat said. "You know that."

"But you've shared nothing about that last vision with me."

Flushing, Quiescat rose from his seat and, clasping his hands behind his back, drifted over to the window. He peered through it at the vast sepia emptiness beyond, the dim necklace of jagged stars on its imaginary horizon, each a neighboring shard, as immense and real as Thirring. Practice made it easy to pick out his home shard, Rhumgad. He eclipsed it with a finger on the pane. This was as close as he'd ever be to touching it again. "The moment of a man's death should be a private matter, at least until it happens," he croaked, coughing to clear an uncomfortable tightness in his throat. "My death poses no threat to Drinith's safety."

"No threat?" Gelasin growled. "No threat when the power that has kept her alive since her infancy could be lost?"

The sharp, whistling inhalation stung Quiescat's nose, which, as it turned out, Gelasin hadn't broken after all—although it still hurt like a demon's slap. His sigh fogged the pane. "I'll pass it on to Abecedar in plenty of time. I didn't protect Drinith all these years only to become the instrument of her destruction."

"But if the power is useless to you, why delay? You told me before it takes a new oracle two red months to have his first vision."

"It can take two red months," Quiescat said, "but one red month is the norm."

"You say it like that's an instant." Gelasin chopped the air with his hand as he spoke. "That's a very long time to lack the one thing that has saved Drinith again and again."

Quiescat bowed his head. "True."

"We've never been friends," Gelasin said in a more conciliatory tone. "Your visions may have led you to me, but I'm well aware you've suspected my motives from the very start."

"My motivation extends beyond the political." Quiescat turned to Gelasin to gauge his reaction. "Or the divine. I promised a better man than I to protect Drinith, and I love her more than the gods I serve—"

An amused snort cut him off. The warrior pounded a fist against his chest. "Do you truly believe I care so little about the girl? I've devoted a dozen years of my life to protecting her. I've served her longer than her father."

Quiescat gasped. "Is it really that long?"

"Yes. Twelve long years of wandering across the Crevast from shard to shard, begging for help. But for her, I'd have returned home years ago to bring the fight to the Javlohmers. I've learned a healthy dislike for monarchs, but Drinith's different. She lacks her father's overbearing pride and cruelty. She'd make a good *peacetime* ruler, thanks to your tutelage."

So says the man who sent her to fight an assassin. Quiescat let the criticism implied in the warrior's compliment pass without comment.

"I guess your power knew what it was doing when it nudged you to recruit me," Gelasin went on, "even if you didn't."

"Is that a question or an observation?"

"Make of it what you will." Gelasin pointedly plopped himself down in the armchair Quiescat had vacated and stroked the silk damask upholstery. "You don't mind if I sit here, do you?" He hoisted his filthy boots on the matching footstool and crossed his legs at the ankles.

The oracle essayed a tiny smile. "Make yourself at home. You seem to be in an uncharacteristically garrulous mood, my laconic friend. Perhaps you won't mind telling me why you were expelled from the Warserks."

Gelasin chuckled grimly. "I wasn't expelled. I quit." He stroked his ruined cheeks. "I cut off my honor tattoos with my ceremonial dagger. There are still scars on my fingers where the blade sliced them as I broke it. The other Warserks could imagine nothing beyond their honor. They worshiped Hemrath of Kaplar with all the dull devotion of a herd of cattle, and he led them to the slaughter. Where's their honor now? Forgotten like their names."

"Their sacrifice will be remembered always," Quiescat insisted.

Gelasin's ugly grin derided him. "Their sacrifice perhaps, but not their names. Tell me, do you remember the name of the one who entrusted you with our princess?"

Wincing with embarrassment, Quiescat shook his head. "He never told me, much to my regret." He couldn't remember the man's face, not even the words tattooed on his cheeks, but the love in his eyes as he handed over the infant still haunted him. It was a father's love.

Gelasin threw up his hands. "See? I bet he left Godsdoor grinning from ear to ear, delighted that he had done his duty and he could throw his life away against the Javlohmers in some vainglorious gesture. Every Warserk was half in love with death."

"His sacrifice wasn't in vain," Quiescat insisted. "It saved Drinith's life."

Gelasin studied the floor. "Well, perhaps your mystery man was the exception." He looked up. Quiescat shied from his forceful stare. "But the rest, they threw away their lives for nothing."

"They died protecting your people."

"They died defending one tyrant from another. And they lost, so they died for nothing."

Quiescat trembled with indignation. "Coward! You dare to so callously dismiss Warserks of far nobler valor than yourself? They won't be forgotten, not Harkon Battlehone nor Dizar the Grim nor Jaster Quake nor Perseveer."

"They've all been dead for a thousand years."

"What about Kragan the Staunch?"

Gelasin roared with laughter. "It turned out he wasn't. He forsook his emperor after the Battle of Gway."

"But Kragan died in that battle."

"He survived it, but he sacrificed almost every man under his command to win it. Watching his friends' corpses being tossed in a hole with their dead foes taught him the true value of the Warserks' honor." Despite his eyes' sentimental luster, the steeliness remained. "While Hemrath raised a monument over their grave to celebrate his victory, I slipped away, renouncing everything that connected me to his service, including my name."

Quiescat gasped. "*You* were Kragan? Impossible! You're too young."

The warrior arched an eyebrow. "Battles, not years, forge Warserks' reputations. Did you really think my birth name was

Gelasin?" He stroked his ruined cheeks. "I adopted it afterward as a joke on account of these pretty dimples."

The revelation left Quiescat aghast. He had always assumed that the warrior had been a rogue, but somehow discovering that the great Kragan had betrayed his legend made his dereliction of his duty a hundred times worse. "I'm supposed to leave Drinith in the hands of a—"

"Choose your words carefully," Gelasin growled. "I won't stand for being slandered. I'm not a traitor."

"No, you're not," Quiescat realized. The sincerity of his newfound sympathy for his rival surprised him.

"If anything, I was too loyal," the warrior muttered to himself.

But sympathy wouldn't protect Drinith. Having already abandoned one liege, Gelasin might find a reason to forsake another. This whole business with the assassin had been a test, whether the warrior realized or not. He had needed Drinith to prove she was worthy of his fealty. If she had failed...

Gelasin sneered at Quiescat's quiet panic. "I can see things too, Oracle. You're asking yourself, can I be trusted with the daughter of the emperor I came to despise? Would I really help put her on the throne? Well, why don't you peek at what lies ahead? Oh, right, you can't. You're as blind to what happens after your death as any other man."

Quiescat walked silently to his bedchamber's door and held it open. "I have abided your company for as long as I care to. Please leave!"

"As you wish," said Gelasin, taking his sweet time.

When he had gone, Quiescat collapsed into the chair. As he stared at the black marks Gelasin's boots had left on the footstool, a breathless hysteria overtook him. He had to lift the black shroud over Drinith's future. Gelasin was right; he had delayed too long. He must find Abecedar, without delay. Throwing on a cloak, he swept into the hall.

6

———

Drinith studied herself critically in the full-length mirror in her new bedchamber. The gold highlights in her red hair were intended to be a subtle reminder of the lost blood crown that was her birthright. She wore her best dress. Embellished with ornate goldwork, its color was supposed to be Kaplar cyan. It didn't quite match. The true dye was prohibitively expensive, so her dressmaker had to use a cheaper alternative. Like everything else she owned, it had seen better days. Hopefully, the Aether Emperor wouldn't observe the frayed seams and loose threads here and there, particularly where the hem brushed the ground. She noted with dismay that the bandage around her midriff combined with her mail shirt to create a noticeable bulge. The jewelry she wore were fakes, convincing but worthless. The teardrop cyan emerald on her forehead was all that remained of her dynasty's treasure.

"You look lovely, Drinith," Jarma remarked.

Drinith whirled around to face her. "Kind of you to say so," she said, smiling. "I feel rather like the ragman's daughter in these make-do habiliments, but thanks to your skill, I suppose I'm presentable."

Princess and maid turned toward the sound of polite rapping on the door.

"I had better go," she said to Jarma. Her escort had been waiting outside for some time, and she couldn't afford to vex Dariffon with her tardiness. "And thank you, Jarma."

Perplexed, Jarma shrugged. "Your Imperial Majesty, I'm employed to attend you."

Her unnecessary formality made Drinith smile. She placed a hand on her shoulder. "I'm not talking about this. I meant last night. Putting your life at risk like that shouldn't be your job."

Jarma's eyes glistened. "It mightn't have been my job, but it was my honor, Drinith."

More rapping, louder, more insistent.

"You should go," Jarma said. Gently drawing away from Drinith's hand, she opened the door. Drinith stepped into the hall. The captain gave her a perfunctory nod before strutting down the corridor. She followed him, the dozen guards standing to attention along the wall falling in either side of her. The Aether Emperor had determined to take no further chances with her safety.

A nervous butler in unfamiliar red and orange livery awaited her in the anteroom to the balcony. The shut doors and his apologetic manner filled her with silent consternation. Had her host, growing impatient of her arrival, canceled her audience?

"I'm sorry, Your Highness," the butler said. "It is the custom to remove footwear before entering the presence of an elemental emperor." He didn't mention that royalty was generally exempt from such indignities. Previously, the Aether Emperor, in a subtle nod to her heritage, had extended that honor to her. Obviously, she was being punished for her lateness.

She had assumed her dress would conceal the poor condition of her embroidered silk shoes. Fuming silently, she kicked them off.

The butler, evidently relieved that she had chosen not to make a scene, smiled sheepishly and nodded. He pushed the doors open and, standing aside, invited her to pass through with a flourish of his hand.

A warning pain prodded her side as she slowly approached the grand balcony. She paused at the threshold, daunted by its perfect transparency. The rumors that it had been made from crystallized air must be true. No reflection marred it, not even hers, as she looked down upon it. Far below, the sepia and orange clouds shrouding the inner sun tossed and stirred as though excited by the prospect of her impending plummet.

The two marbled moons, red Ruis and white Neor, hovered just above the dragon-claw throne floating in the distance as if attending the man—most definitely not Dariffon—who sat upon it. As he shifted, the red and gold of his raiment danced on the fabric. On his head rested a crown of vitrified flame. This could only be the Fire Emperor, Garsid, in all his glory.

A long table stretched before him, overflowing with enough delicacies to feed several dozen guests, although Drinith was the emperor's sole breakfast companion. Twenty guards formed an arc behind his throne. Arranged by height, they gave the impression of two gigantic wings outstretched. A three-legged stool awaited Drinith at the near end of the table, its plainness incongruous amid all this dramatic splendor—another less-than-subtle reminder of her destitution.

The guard on the Fire Emperor's immediate right beckoned her with an impatient wave. She stepped forward. Panic gripped her as she could feel nothing beneath her bare feet. The natural expectation of plunging into the void below made her body riot, but she fought the dizzy fear threatening to knock her down. She mustn't stumble or get sick. She couldn't afford to show weakness. She was a royal like the Emperors of Thirring, albeit one of straitened circumstances. Forcing what she hoped was a convincing smile, she focused on him and continued onward, step by quivering step.

Garsid's puffy face was the color of congealed blood, but his black eyes regarded his guest with inscrutable coolness. The lower lids of his eyes sagged to form two black crescents, creating the unnerving impression of a mask. He invited her to sit with a languid wave of his hand. As Drinith gingerly planted herself on the stool, the pain in her side made her wince. Despite the discomfort of her seat, its sturdiness reassured her. She scanned the dishes on the table, delicacies from a dozen other shards seasoned with spices from a dozen more. A stink of putrescence came from one, she couldn't tell which, overpowering the rest. Leaning forward, the Fire Emperor violently jammed a silver knife into the split ventral shell of an upturned arthropod. The sound of tearing flesh wrenched her stomach as he pulled the two halves open like stiff doors. It took all her effort not to vomit as the stench intensified. Spooning a lump of pink jellied flesh from inside, he held it up, regarding the delicacy lustily. A long purple tongue lolled out and hung in the air expectantly. Feeling Drinith's eyes upon him, but oblivious to her disgust, he turned toward her, his tongue hastily slithering back into his mouth.

"Where are my manners? The honored guest should take the first bite. Please, eat, enjoy!"

Drinith didn't see how that was possible. She focused on the dishes immediately before her: piled worms in blood-red sauce; a splayed lizard, its shriveled organs coated in blue crumbs; a pie that quivered as though something lived beneath its crust; varicolored brain segments in a jelly dome; a boiled sheep's head; and a bowl of what looked like iridescent rotted fish. She picked up her fork, uncertain where to stick it. A plate of two-moon cakes was the lone toothsome dainty amid this gastronomic horror; the treat was her especial favorite, but to reach it she'd have to rise from her seat. Would that show weakness? Displeasure already ripened in the Fire Emperor's stare as he continued to hold his fork aloft, his purple tongue poised like a prehensile whip.

She lunged for the red and white disks and, snatching one, nibbled it delicately. Its familiar sweet and spicy taste delighted her. With a scornful smile, Garsid swallowed the content of his fork. It squeaked softly as he chewed. The guards filed by both sides of the table back toward the entrance. Following them with her eyes, Drinith beheld the astonishing immensity of the palace. A statue of an armored warrior stretched above the top of the precipice, his legs disappearing into the cloud below. A monstrous dragon, as colossal as any living one, sat atop his helm. The crystal air balcony formed an invisible platter in his monstrous hands. The panorama held her attention until her host's gravelly voice broke its spell.

"Before my brother emperor, Dariffon, killed himself to expunge his great shame, he asked me to pass on his heartfelt apologies. His failure to safeguard you while under his roof was inexcusable." He pulled a face. "I have taken over his duties until a new Aether Emperor is installed."

The revelation cut deeper than the assassin's blade. Gelasin's plotting had cost Dariffon his life. "The assassin is dead, and I have suffered no grave harm." The twinge in her side contradicted her, but she managed not to wince.

The Fire Emperor fenced away her reassurance with his fork. "Honor is intrinsic to the deed itself. The outcome is inconsequential. Otherwise, the evil or goodness of a deed would hinge not on its intention but its consequences, however unforeseen. Hospitality is something we hold as sacred in Thirring and the safety of guests is paramount. My brother proved negligent in his obligations as a host." Hoisting a crystal goblet, he slurped down a long draught and licked the purple droplets on his upper lip with his impossibly long tongue. "He knew your history. He understood the forces bent on your destruction better than you—"

"Magian."

Garsid plucked a grape from a heaped centerpiece and rolled the fruit between his fingers. "And others. You're a ruler searching for somewhere to rule—a threat to the weak; to the strong, an unnecessary irritation."

Drinith pulled a face. Why should Magian or anyone else consider her a threat? Her entire life had been a succession of empty promises and dashed hopes.

Garsid's smile broadened. "It's the oracle, you see. Everyone— including, I'm sure, Magian—is keenly aware of his reputation. If he let his temple burn for you, if he has suffered nearly two decades of exile on your behalf, he must have a compelling reason—some insight into your future."

If Quiescat had, he had never shared it with her.

"If he hadn't been so tight-lipped on the subject, if he had shared some discreet hints with those rulers he canvased on your behalf, his efforts might have met with more success." Garsid popped the grape in his mouth. "What do you know about your assassin?"

"He's dead."

"The tattoos on his palms identify him as a member of a sect of assassins well known to us here on Thirring. They refer to themselves by a convoluted and pompous title that I can never remember"—he snorted and belched—"but everyone just calls them pentaculars because they hunt their quarry in groups of five. Many of their victims, like you, survive the first or maybe the second assault, but I've never heard of anyone surviving the fifth." He munched down another spoon of the pink flesh. Squeak. Squeak. Squeak. Drinith clamped her mouth shut to dam her growing anger at his detachment from her plight.

"We have an agreement with the pentaculars," the Fire Emperor said. "A treaty if you will. We leave them alone and they refrain from meddling in local politics. Unfortunately, since you're not local, they considered you fair game."

He slurped more wine. "That assassin you killed last night, remember his face. You'll be seeing it again. That face belongs to the man who hired them to kill you."

"But who would expose their identity in such a blatant manner?"

Garsid grinned as he squeaked through another mouthful. "Primarily, the rich and vengeful."

"Then that assassin bears Magian's face." The notion discomfited her, but at least she had seen her enemy, in a fashion.

The Fire Emperor shrugged. "Not necessarily. They take the face of the man who hires them. By all accounts, Magian the Infinite is quite a recluse. If it was him who enlisted the pentaculars, he would have likely used a middleman."

Drinith couldn't help being disappointed.

"There's something else you should know about the pentaculars. In bonding to form their little team, the pentaculars sacrifice their individuality and blend their souls. They attack one at a time, each taking his turn to confront their target. When an assassin dies, his strength disperses equally between the remaining members of his circle. Thanks to your dispatching of the first assassin, his four comrades became one fifth stronger. Kill the second, and the three survivors become more powerful by one third, and so on. If the first four assassins are dispatched, the fifth will fight with the strength and speed of five men."

Gelasin and Quiescat must have known this, and yet they had kept it from her. For all their talk of her wearing the Blood Crown of Kaplar, they treated her like a child. Drinith's hands balled into fists beneath the table as the Fire Emperor chewed another squeaky mouthful.

Her host dabbed his mouth with a satin napkin. "I'm afraid your days are numbered if you stay here. I must ask you to leave Thirring before more unpleasantness occurs."

Drinith shot to her feet and pounded the table with her fists, rattling plates and cutlery, collapsing the fruit centerpiece. "So you drive me out like an unwelcome pest that has crept under your roof? So much for the vaunted hospitality of Thirring."

Garsid's amused smile taunted her. "You came here to seek allies against Magian of Javlohm. My deceased brother never intended to help your cause. He merely sought to keep you in the gilded cage of his prevarication."

He gestured for Drinith to be seated. Trembling with shock and indignation, she did so.

She belonged to a line of emperors and kings stretching back to when the world was whole and one. How dare the Elemental Pentarchy inflict this extraordinary humiliation upon her! The whole universe appeared to conspire against her.

"I met him only twice briefly," Drinith said.

Garsid dug between his teeth with his fingernail, extracted a quivering morsel of pink meat, and sucked it into his gullet. "But he watched you. Only the strict mores of hospitality prevented him from venturing beyond distant study."

"It was lucky for him he didn't, or he'd have joined the assassin in death," she growled.

A flicker of fear briefly animated the Fire Emperor's pudgy countenance. "Your presence killed him in any case," he said, quickly regaining his composure. "And for that, I must thank you. I wouldn't be here with you enjoying this delightful feast. And to be honest, I never liked Dariffon. Too greedy. Too many foreign ideas." He steepled his fingers, smiling unctuously. "That's why I've arranged at some expense for a dragon to take you anywhere in the Crevast—any shard where you might find sanctuary."

Where could she go? Thirring had supposed to be their last, best hope. "And to fulfill your obligations as my host."

"Of course," he said. "When a guest has to leave, a host must ensure they do so safely." He raised a finger. "Oh, I almost forgot. I have a present for you." His nod summoned a waiting guard, who approached carrying a covered silver platter and halted beside Drinith. At the emperor's signal, he lifted the silver cloche. Drinith recognized the severed head beneath it as the assassin, the bland visage curiously more dynamic in death than in life with mouth agape, wide eyes staring. The neck appeared to have been cauterized; the scorched flesh, muscles, and veins stood out in sharp relief against the blue-black skin of the face. Its similarity to the gawping sheep's head made her shudder.

"Thank you, but I have no desire for such a trophy," she said.

Garsid threw back his head and shook with laughter. "You misunderstand. The head doesn't belong to the assassin you so ably dispatched. It's his successor."

She searched in vain for a reason to be thankful. Garsid seemed to regard this second pentacular's elimination as some personal triumph, but Drinith found nothing reassuring about it.

Garsid's self-satisfied grin gave way to a frown. "You seem unimpressed with my gift." He nodded at the grisly head. "That leaves only three to hunt you."

"If I understand you correctly," she said, seething with anger, "every pentacular who dies adds to his successor's strength. Therefore, each assassin that is slain brings my death a step closer!"

Garsid shrugged. "That is a most pessimistic way of looking at it, my dear. And if I may say so, quite ungrateful. I only acted as a good host should. Now, won't you have some more victuals? What we don't eat will have to be thrown out. Perhaps some lizard..." He twisted off a hock and gnawed it. "Cold now, but still delicious."

Drinith's gaze swept the table; she felt her gorge rise. "I believe I've had as much of your hospitality as I can stand." She stood and made a point of kicking over the stool before heading for the exit with a flounce.

"The girl has no manners," Garsid mumbled, sucking a lizard tail down his throat.

7

———————

Silence answered Quiescat's pounding on his acolyte's door. He kicked it in frustration. Gods damn Abecedar! The lowlander had coveted Quiescat's gift for most of his life, and now that the moment was at hand, he'd disappeared. Where could he be? Quiescat had a good idea: probably trysting with Jarma. His prophetic ability wasn't the only thing the young fool lusted after.

Quiescat stalked up the corridor to Drinith's bedchamber. Abecedar naively assumed Quiescat hadn't noticed his dalliances with Drinith's maid. Perhaps he believed his master too wizened and aloof to detect their lingering glances and furtive whispers. Back in Godsdoor, where dozens of acolytes competed to become oracle, Quiescat would have barred Abecedar from succeeding him for such amorous toying, but now no other viable candidate existed. Quiescat's only consolation was that Abecedar would soon abandon his flirtation. The gift would change him once he accepted it.

Quiescat's predecessors had easier ends. They'd passed away gently in their beds, whole until near their last breath. They hadn't to deal with the messiness of a violent death.

Not bothering to knock, he swung open Drinith's door. Jarma

gasped and stared at him with frightened eyes. Quiescat had half expected to surprise the youths in each other's arms, but the girl was alone, mending one of Drinith's dresses.

"Where is he?" he demanded. Irked by her perplexed silence, he added, "Abecedar."

"He's in Versifer's room, I think."

Versifer—the foppish poet who had been moved by Drinith's beauty to forswear his trade. Gelasin's intense distaste for him had gone some way to endear him to Quiescat, but the oracle could brook no obstacles to his plan. Slamming the door shut, he hastened back down the hall.

Quiescat pummeled Versifer's door with both fists. Finally, he heard the poet's irritable "I'm coming, I'm coming!" rising above the sounds of merrymaking within. Versifer's smooth, plump face timidly peeped through the doorway. His dashing waves of silver-blue hair were parted down the middle. The smell of alcohol wafted from the room and was no less strong on the poet's breath. His heavy eyelids peeled open with surprise. "This is an unexpected honor—"

"Is my acolyte within?" Quiescat demanded, attempting to peer beyond him.

Versifer stepped out of his way, revealing four members of Drinith's retinue hunched over a low table covered with goblets, stacks of base coins, and patterns of triangular tiles. Quiescat recognized the poet's battered, broad-rimmed leather hat slung over one ear of a fifth empty seat. To its left sat Zin, Gelasin's henchman, looking even more murderous than usual, perhaps due to the paucity of coins in front of him compared to the other gamblers.

To the right, Halyard, in all his gaudy finery, glanced up from his tiles. His makeup made him look ten years younger. His mistress, Epmar Hax, funereal in her accustomed drab black, sat behind him like a shadow, cradling her drink. She never made any effort to conceal the lines and wrinkles on her rust-red face that made her look much older than her lover. The gray braid ringing her head defiantly proclaimed her advanced years. Quiescat wished he could be so sanguine about growing old. Her silver eyes regarded him coolly. She always hid her antipathy toward him behind brittle politeness. She chafed at taking orders from anyone other than Drinith.

In front of them sat a green-black highlander, Prosper Destil, a slender older man with receding dyed black hair. He wore a white apron over an expensive, snug-fitting floral jacket, a memento of better days as the richest man in Rhumgad. Gelasin had rescued him from penury, anticipating his former connections on the shard might prove useful. When that hope was dashed, the warrior had wanted to be rid of him, but Drinith had insisted on retaining him as her chef and food taster.

The fourth player, Abecedar, looked so like an errant child fearing chastisement that Quiescat had to repress a mirthless chuckle. "We're playing a game of triples," the young man explained sheepishly.

"You've no time for games of chance," Quiescat said. "Come with me."

The oracle and his acolyte headed back to Quiescat's chamber. No supernatural intuition was required to read the dread on Abecedar's face as Quiescat shut the door behind them.

Quiescat waved at a chair. "Sit." Abecedar hesitated. "Please." As Abecedar complied, Quiescat seized on his distraction to bolt the door. No one else must witness what was about to occur.

Quiescat moved to the seat across from Abecedar, but instead of sitting, he stood behind it and, bowing his head, gripped its back. "The time has come." His softly spoken announcement sounded thunderous to his own ears. Now committed, he had no choice but to follow through. Not that there had ever been any alternative, only the illusion of one, but now he had been stripped of even the comfort of that pretense.

Abecedar's silence disconcerted him. Had he nothing to say? Quiescat looked up. The boy's vacuous expression made him squeeze the crest rail so tight it hurt. Could he entrust his gift to such a dull intellect? Drinith's life and the survival of the oracular power itself depended upon the astuteness of its wielder.

No, Abecedar didn't deserve such scorn. He wasn't the cause of this anger building within Quiescat, threatening to overwhelm him. The sense of impending loss stung deeper than any physical wound. The surrender of his power might be both inevitable and necessary, but it would reduce him to a blind husk. Maybe that was all he had ever been, a physical and mental carapace for his ability.

The thought, coming after a lifetime of contemplation on the subject, intrigued him. There had always been a vaguely sentient quality to his power, a purposeful mulishness. He had always struggled to direct it, while it had forced upon him unbidden and sometimes unwanted glimpses of the future. His temper dissolved in newfound humility.

He released the crest rail, his palms and fingers tingling with the imprint of the carved wood. Noticing Abecedar's incomprehension slipping toward vague dread, Quiescat forced a stiff smile. "My time as oracle has reached an end. The gift requires a new host if it is to survive."

The revelation only made Abecedar more anxious. It was as if, after coveting the Tear for most of his life, a horror of it suddenly struck him, now that it was within his grasp. He cleared his throat and glanced at the door. "I need to talk to someone first."

"What!" Quiescat exclaimed. He couldn't have heard correctly.

The young man blushed. "I'll do my duty, but I need to speak to Jarma first."

Quiescat's stomach churned. "Do you think this is a joke?"

Abecedar raised a conciliatory hand. "No. Far from it. I take this extremely seriously. That's why I must speak to Jarma. She and I..." He shrugged.

"You can talk to her all you want afterward," Quiescat muttered.

Abecedar bowed his head. "I won't be the same person then. When she looks into my eyes, she'll see a stranger. I'll be a stranger, even to myself. I have to say goodbye to her."

Quiescat plodded over to the door. He sighed as he undid the bolt. "Go," he said without glancing around. "Be quick."

The clatter of Abecedar's sandals halted abruptly at the doorway. Quiescat felt the youth's hand on his shoulder. "Thank you, master."

A knot of emotion robbed Quiescat of his voice. By the time he acknowledged his acolyte's whisper with a nod, Abecedar was racing down the hall.

Quiescat heard the echo of his footsteps, the urgent knock, the creak of an opening door, the mumble of distant voices. Determined not to overhear their conversation, Quiescat shuffled over to the bed and sat down.

The open door teased him with the possibility of escape. The temptation made him smile. He was going nowhere...but what about Abecedar? What would Quiescat do if he didn't come back?

Leaden steps in the hall drew Quiescat to the entrance. A jittery Abecedar stamped by him. He plopped down on a chair and heaved a sigh of resignation. "I'm ready."

"It's okay," Quiescat assured him. "I had some misgivings myself when old Lexasis told me my turn had come." It was a lie. Not even a scintilla of doubt had troubled his craving for the gift. It was different back then. Everything had seemed so unequivocal, so ordered, as solid as the walls of Godsdoor itself.

"What was it like to foresee your death?" Abecedar asked.

Checking his exasperation, Quiescat sat down so that master and acolyte might face each other. "The first time, it shocked me. But it lost its potency with each repetition." He shrugged. "I've come to accept it. You can't fight the course Fate has set for you."

Abecedar smiled feebly. "Most of the time."

Quiescat was encouraged by the hint of courage lurking deep in his acolyte's apprehension. "True, but such transgressions always come at great cost. Greater than most mortals can take."

"Ironic given that our oracular power exists only because of a transgression." Abecedar's sneer quickly faded. He tilted his head, stroked his neck. "I didn't mean to impugn—"

"Impugn? You merely spoke the truth. The first oracle was a thief and possibly a murderer. But for generations, his crime has led to much good—not least, the survival of our princess."

Abecedar nodded. "If her father had heeded your warning and stepped aside, Kaplar wouldn't have fallen."

"Don't judge Hemrath too harshly," Quiescat said. "He didn't ignore my warning. He misinterpreted it."

"For his own benefit."

"Ultimately, it wasn't. Potentates aren't usually receptive to the revelation that Fate shapes them and not the other way around. They are mortal men, wont to trumpet their victories and deny their failures. It's a wonder he even heard my warning over the sycophantic clamor whirling about him." That day, Hemrath had sworn to raze Godsdoor if he triumphed against Javlohm. His screaming indignation would have terrified Quiescat, but for the certain knowledge he wouldn't survive to make good on his threat.

Abecedar leaned back in his seat, knitted his fingers and studied them absently. "Fate treats the dreams of kings and beggars with equal disdain, but only the beggars notice."

The adage applies equally well to prophets, Quiescat mused. He rose from his seat. "Let's do this," he declared with artificial confidence —*before I lose my nerve.* "Lie down there," he said, pointing to the bed.

Thank the gods, Abecedar obeyed. The only problem was, he lay in the wrong direction.

"Turn around," Quiescat said, making a circular motion with one finger. "Your head needs to be at the foot. Otherwise I cannot reach you."

As Abecedar settled into this new position, Quiescat bolted the door again. He approached the bed. Every step felt so momentous, he counted them. One. Two. Three. Four. Five. He gazed down at Abecedar's face, its familiar features made alien and enigmatic by their upside-down orientation. What was writ upon them? Resignation? Fear? Expectation? Quiescat couldn't read his expression.

"It will take a few minutes for me to prepare," he said. "When the transfer begins, you must keep your eyes open, however great the pain. Understand?"

Abecedar nodded.

Glancing around the room, Quiescat caught sight of his reflection in a long mirror on the wall. The years since his flight from Godsdoor had gnawed away the soft flesh, leaving a gnarled stick of a man with receding blue hair. His glassy eyes remained unchanged, but soon they would be gone.

He drew reluctant eyelids over them and sought the emotional leverage he needed. The gift had been born out of grief. The lenses through which he and his predecessors glimpsed the future were the crystallized teardrop of a far more powerful entity, a divinity in all but name. Only their bearer's sorrow could dissolve them for their transfer.

But what could move him to weep? The destruction of Godsdoor had been a mixed curse. The shame of his failure as its custodian was blunted by the world its fall had opened up to him, the wonders beyond Rhumgad he might have never known. Even the loss of his power, however much he disrelished it, couldn't draw a tear. He had become inured to his impending death. It could have been much worse. Better to die, for example, than to witness Drinith's end.

Surely, she must die. Every shard she had turned to for help had spurned her while Magian's assassins closed in. The pentaculars never failed to claim their victims. True, thanks to Quiescat's powers, she had cheated an equally certain death on previous occasions. But the gift was only as strong as its wielder. Poor Abecedar had no time to grow into the role about to be thrust upon him.

Without Quiescat's help, Drinith was doomed. Unbidden, her image filled the darkness, not as an adult but as a small child. Her personality had blossomed around the age of three, or at least his awareness of it. He thought of her as his daughter, and she had made him more human as a result. Now, all that was in danger, because this one time, he couldn't cheat Fate.

He began to cry. A tear smacked Abecedar's face; he gave a soft yelp of surprise. Another tear struck, and then another. The patter became a downpour.

For the briefest moment, Quiescat saw the world anew through the warping crystals. The room, and everything within it, bowed and stretched as they softened and oozed from his sockets. From the bottom of this well of distortion, Abecedar's eyes stared in terror. The skewed panorama snapped into a perfectly spherical perspective before plummeting toward the acolyte. It smashed into myriad competing, refracting vistas. They quickly dimmed to impenetrable darkness. And somewhere beyond it, Abecedar screamed.

8

A line of guards awaited Drinith in the anteroom after she stalked away from the Fire Emperor's table. She almost missed Gelasin leaning against the wall behind them. Skirting around them, he smiled and shrugged. Curious as he was, he knew better than to quiz her in front of this audience.

"Thought I'd come and collect you," he said, "and save these fine gentlemen a trip."

An officer stepped forward. "We will escort her back to her quarters," he insisted.

Gelasin waved his hand. "There's no need."

"The Fire Emperor's *orders*."

Frowning, Gelasin looked to Drinith.

"Dariffon is dead," she said, "I'll explain everything later. Let these good men do their duty. Frankly, I feel safer wandering the palace in their company."

The officer and two of his men accompanied them through labyrinthine corridors and stairs back to their familiar little corner of the palace.

"We'll talk in my room," she murmured as they shed their escort.

Jarma stood outside Quiescat's chamber, pounding on the door.

"Someone was screaming in there," she said breathlessly. "I think something terrible has happened."

Wailing and banging of furniture came from inside.

Gelasin waved Jarma out of the way. He rammed his shoulder against the door so hard, he bounced off it and would have toppled backward but for Drinith's steadying hand. "Only the best workmanship in the Aether Emperor's palace," he muttered through gritted teeth. He tried again. The door didn't budge, but the jamb crunched under the splintering blow. Backing up to the far wall, he charged with the force of a battering ram. The door banged against the interior wall as Gelasin hurtled across the threshold. Drinith followed far less dramatically.

Gelasin stood doubled over, catching his breath. "He predicted his own death," he gasped. "I never thought…"

Abecedar, clutching his hands to his eyes, staggered around the room. Quiescat lay on the floor. Drinith knelt by his side. His eyes had shrunken. The slits under the slack eyelids gave a glimpse of the hollows beneath. A soft sigh, barely audible. Thank the gods he lived.

Drinith looked around for help. Jarma cradled the moaning Abecedar on the corner of the bed. Gelasin straightened. Rubbing his shoulder, he hobbled over to Quiescat.

"He's alive," Drinith said.

Prosper peeped through the doorway. Gelasin beckoned to him, saying, "Help me lift him onto the bed."

Quiescat's head lolled about grotesquely as Gelasin heaved him up by the shoulders and Prosper lifted his legs. Drinith pulled back the blankets and they laid him on the sheet. Pulling the blankets back over him, she propped up his head with a pillow.

Gelasin had crouched beside Jarma and Abecedar. Curiosity drew Drinith around the side of the bed until she could see Abecedar's face. Gelasin had lifted it with a finger. "Open your eyes," he said.

Tears drizzled down Abecedar's cheeks as his eyelids fluttered open to reveal the spherical transparent crystals beneath.

"I guess we have a new oracle," Gelasin said, looking entirely too pleased. "Of course, according to Quiescat, it will take about two red months for his powers to manifest. In the meantime, we'll have to do our best without its help."

Drinith's gaze turned to Quiescat. *Don't die on me. I need you.* "Gelasin, we need to talk. In private."

Jarma and Prosper helped Abecedar out of the room. Drinith propped a chair against the broken door to keep it shut. Gelasin sat in the other, doing a bad job of not smiling. "We could have moved to your room."

"I'd rather stay here," she said, sitting on the edge of the bed. She couldn't abandon Quiescat even to the care of her retinue. Besides, she found comfort in his presence, however incapacitated. "You look happy," she said pointedly.

Gelasin's eyebrows arched. His demeanor turned grave. "I don't revel in Quiescat's misfortune if that what's you're implying. We mightn't have been particularly close, but I respected him, admired him even. The only consolation I can find is that the oracular power has been secured. It's what he wanted. It's why he passed it to Abecedar. His paramount concern, and mine, is your safety."

Somewhat assuaged, Drinith said, "We have been asked to leave Thirring."

Gelasin bolted upright. "What!"

"Our host took his life because he failed to protect me. His fellow emperors want us gone before we bring any more calamities upon them. We must leave tomorrow."

"Humph! I suppose we have to leap off the shard and flap our arms like wings until we reach another."

"They've provided a dragon, apparently. By the way, what do you know about the pentaculars?"

"Assassins, local to here." He shrugged. "But this shard is the one place in the Crevast where you're safe from them."

"My attacker was one."

Gelasin directed a venomous glance at Quiescat. "He knew. He recognized the symbol on the assassin's palm. I'm certain of it." He tapped a forefinger against his lower lip. "The next one who comes will be stronger. And we're unlikely to have the advantage of prevision this time. But the third will only come after the second's dead. If we can capture—"

"The second assassin is already dead. Another gift from Thirring's rulers."

Glancing at the ceiling, Gelasin shook his head. "Then, when the third assassin comes, we must take him prisoner. While he lives, his successor can't strike." If only that was as easy as he made it sound. "Where will this dragon take us?"

"Wherever we want. To Empyr if we so wish."

Gelasin grinned. "The Dual City? I doubt the dragon's captain would be so accommodating. Besides, the angels and devils of Empyr are too preoccupied with their perpetual war to take any interest in our cause." Drinith hadn't intended her suggestion to be taken seriously, but she didn't bother to correct him. "They're so far away. Rhumgad is probably just a name to them, if even that. The same is true even for nearer shards like Sgard and Magmel. We've already tried most of Rhumgad's neighbors capable of taking on Magian. We're left with three states, all rivals on the shard of Noster. The necromancers of Laxur are only interested in corpses. The Shopkeepers of Ophigee would pry Rhumgad from Magian only to sell it to the highest bidder. That leaves the Halcyon Republic of Gyre."

Drinith's gaze drifted to her unconscious adviser. "Quiescat has been against going there."

Gelasin leaned forward conspiratorially. "I don't mean to speak ill of the, er...ill, but on his advice, we went to the Ethereal Republic of Numenal. Of course, you remember what happened there. They came awfully close to stealing your soul and enslaving you."

"He was the one who saved me," Drinith said, annoyed on Quiescat's behalf.

"He should have never put you in that position in the first place!" Gelasin stabbed the air with his finger. "And then he brought us here, to Thirring, only to draw the pentaculars on you. And all the while he had his prevision to lean on." He added more sympathetically, "Understand, I'm not calling him a fool."

You've come close to it, Drinith thought bitterly.

"I'd be a fool myself to do so," Gelasin said. "I'm just trying to make the point that his great wisdom didn't make him infallible. He could be as wrong as any man." He grinned. "Like me, for example. And we can't be sure what he might have advised if he knew our current circumstances. Let me get Halyard or Epmar. They're from Gyre. Their insight would be invaluable."

Drinith nodded wearily and Gelasin hurried to find them. He soon returned with Epmar. It wasn't a surprise. Epmar generally did most of the talking for the couple.

"We have to leave Thirring in a hurry," Gelasin explained. "What can you tell us about Gyre? We're thinking about going there."

"You could try there," Epmar said sadly. "Its rulers, the meritocrats, being predominantly women, might have some sympathy for the princess's plight. But if you go there, Halyard and I won't be traveling with you."

The veins on Gelasin's temples popped. "I can't believe your utter ingratitude. You live off our largesse and now, when assassins stalk the princess, you turn your backs on her."

Epmar folded her arms and lifted her chin. "Halyard is paid a wage for his service, which you agreed to."

Gelasin stroked his scars.

"My help comes free aside from my board," Epmar said. "And most of the time, whatever ruler hosting the princess provides that. We'd be delighted to accompany you to any destination other than Gyre. I made that clear to you that when we first joined you."

"You didn't tell me," Gelasin groused.

"I told Quiescat."

Gelasin glowered at the man lying in the bed. "We need both you and Halyard. At least until we have found replacements."

"We'll be happy to follow you anywhere. Even to the bowels of the undercity of Empyrosis if need be. Anywhere except Gyre. Let us know what you decide." With a parting nod to Drinith, she strolled out the door.

Gelasin slammed it shut only for it to yawn open again. "That insufferable woman. Halyard might be a strutting peacock, but he's loyal. He'd never forsake us at this precarious time. This is her fault. And Quiescat's."

Gelasin's whining was tiresome, but getting into an argument with him wouldn't help. "Epmar and Halyard have both served me with honor since joining my retinue. They must have a compelling reason for avoiding Gyre."

"Perhaps you're not fully aware of how desperate our situation has become. Aside from our two friends from Gyre, your retinue includes Quiescat and Abecedar. Neither of them is in much of a state for fighting, if they ever were." He pulled a face. "Then there's Jarma, who is hardly a warrior—"

"She killed an assassin last night."

"She swung an axe once. If that hadn't killed him, she'd be dead now. Then there's that failed usurer, Prosper Destil, whose cooking is deadlier than any weapon." He snorted. "What cook can't even fatten himself?"

"Prosper's a good cook," Drinith muttered.

"But not a warrior. Neither is Versifer. I know as much about poetry as he knows about combat. That leaves me and Zin. I'm past my best. Zin's good, a real killer. To be honest, he's a bit too good at it."

At last, something they could agree upon. Zin's presence always put Drinith on edge. His gaze lingered on her; she always had the disconcerting feeling he was undressing her with his eyes.

Finally taking notice of Drinith's quiet exasperation, Gelasin raised both hands. "It's not my intention to belittle or insult anyone," he said, "but if I must speak bluntly to protect you, then so be it. We can't afford to lose Halyard. We don't have the coin to recruit a replacement of his caliber."

"Then we must avoid Gyre to keep him," Drinith said. "We should go somewhere else. Laxur, perhaps."

Gelasin's lips tautened into an angry line. "We won't find much help in Laxur. They'd have more use for our corpses than our cause."

"Laxur's better than Gyre."

They both turned to the speaker—Quiescat. Drinith threw her arms around him. "Thank the gods."

Gelasin snorted behind her. "Welcome back," he said without warmth.

"Abecedar?" Quiescat asked.

"We moved him to his room. Jarma's minding him. He's...disoriented."

"That's natural," Quiescat said. "It will pass in time."

"How much did you hear?" Gelasin asked warily.

Quiescat smiled thinly. "Enough."

"Aside from losing Halyard and Epmar, have you any other reason for not going to Gyre?"

"I have," Quiescat said.

"And that is?"

"My business."

For a moment, Drinith feared that Gelasin would lose his temper and say something they'd all regret, but after glaring at the floor for some time, he looked up and smiled. "Not good enough," he said, shaking his head.

"The archipelago is riddled with dreameries," Quiescat expounded. "The crystal spheres exert an attractive force on the Tear of Fate. If Abecedar drew too close to one, the Tear might be ripped from his sockets, or worse, he might be dragged into the clutches of the Fate Healer within."

"How close is too close?"

"Of course, the danger was theoretical back on Rhumgad given its peculiar lack of a dreamery. However, my predecessors believed that keeping half a continent between them and any dreamery was advisable."

Gelasin grimaced. "What utter rot! You've visited tiny shardlets before without coming to harm."

"I was careful to never go anywhere the pull of the local dreamery could overwhelm me. Abecedar is inexperienced—"

"You were inexperienced once. You managed to negotiate this danger."

Quiescat pursed his lips in stubborn silence.

"What about Halyard and Epmar?" Drinith asked.

Gelasin waved an arm at her. "Leave them to me. I'll see if we can come to some *compromise*." He spat the word as he disappeared into the hall.

"How's your side?" Quiescat asked Drinith.

"It twinges a bit," she admitted. "But it's nothing I can't handle. Never mind me. How are you?"

"I've been better." A shudder wracked his cadaverous body. "Is Gelasin gone?" he whispered.

"Yes," Drinith said.

"Tell me everything that's happened. Leave nothing out."

9

Lost in sepulchral darkness, Quiescat clung to Drinith's hand, a precious tether connecting him to the living. He had to be brave for her. Perhaps he couldn't help her, but he must be her smallest burden until his death. At least that release would come soon.

He placed his other hand on hers with surprising ease and smiled to reassure her.

"Do you want a drink?" she asked. "Or something to eat?"

He answered with a headshake. "I'm fine."

Perhaps he had been rash to scupper Gelasin's plan to go to Gyre, but the risk its many dreameries posed was too great. If Abecedar stumbled into one and encountered the being from whom the Tear had been originally stolen, the result could be catastrophic. The Fate Healer did not forget or forgive.

Someone cleared their throat. "Hello, Oracle," Dr. Aerwig said. Trust him to enter with the stealth of an assassin.

"Please, don't call me that," Quiescat pleaded.

"Sorry. Force of habit. How should I address you?"

How does one address an empty shell? "Quiescat will do. I have no other name or title."

"Very well. Quiescat." He said the name as though testing its heft. "If you wouldn't mind, I'd like to examine your eyes."

You mean the holes in my face. "If you must."

Aerwig took a deep breath. Quiescat's eyelids fluttered like frightened butterflies. Aerwig pinched one and lifted it back. "Remarkable. Truly remarkable. Everything is intact and present except the eyeball itself. Astounding."

Quiescat didn't bother to point out that his natural eyes had been removed three decades earlier. Why did he let this scavenger pick at his carcass? This examination had no purpose beyond satisfying Aerwig's curiosity.

"Enough," Quiescat murmured.

The doctor's fingers maintained their pincer-like grip.

"Enough!"

Aerwig withdrew. "How do you feel?" he asked.

Quiescat hesitated to answer. Even if he convinced the doctor he was too sick to travel, the Fire Emperor would never permit a delay to Drinith's departure. He might hold Quiescat here, separating him from her. "Aside from the obvious, I feel fine."

"No pain?"

"No."

"No dizziness or headaches?"

Only the one you're giving me. "No."

"Good good good. But take it easy for the next day or so. No unnecessary exertion. I don't pretend to understand the physical change you've undergone, but I imagine it has impacted more than your eyes, at least in the short term."

Quiescat smirked. For him, the long term didn't exist. His own afflictions didn't matter. Drinith needed the guidance of her new oracle to have any hope of surviving. "But what of my..." He stopped himself from referring to Abecedar as his acolyte. "What of my successor?"

"He's still adjusting. Don't worry about him. I'm more than capable of managing his condition."

The temerity of this patronizing charlatan! Aerwig knew less than nothing. Quiescat threw off his blankets. "I must go to Abecedar."

"I really think you should rest," Aerwig shrilled.

Quiescat tried to swing his legs out of the bed. "Drinith, help me up."

She gently guided him to his feet, steadied him as he adjusted to standing.

He looked toward where he guessed Aerwig stood. "You may leave, doctor. I'm sure somewhere in the palace there's a guard with a boil on his buttocks in need of lancing. If we require your services again, we'll be sure to call."

"As you wish," Aerwig said with strained politeness.

Quiescat listened to the doctor's steps melt away.

"There's a few things I must discuss with you," Drinith said with alarming reticence. "I haven't quite told you everything the Fire Emperor said."

"Oh?" Quiescat tensed.

"Have you any idea what will happen to me? After…"

"I can't see beyond my own end. You know that."

"You won't tell me how you die."

His throat tightened. "My death is already set. Neither of us can change it. All I can tell you is that it will be gentle." The lie discomfited him, but the truth would only hurt her. "I won't suffer."

"If it's so gentle, why won't you tell me? You're concealing something. You didn't tell me the assassin was a pentacular either."

"I didn't know he was one until I checked his hand. I wanted to stave off burdening you with that knowledge until it was necessary."

"I'm no longer a child to be protected from the truth."

"I know," Quiescat said. "But I no longer have truth to offer. That burden has passed to my successor."

Drinith squeezed his hand reassuringly.

"Abecedar will have the answers you seek in time," Quiescat said. "A new oracle will bring new visions and a new perspective."

"Good news!" Gelasin stomped into the room. "I've found a solution that should satisfy everyone. Halyard and Epmar will accompany us as far as Gyre and then continue on with the dragon to Laxur."

"Who agreed we were going to Gyre?" Quiescat spluttered. "The floating archipelago poses an especial danger to a new oracle. Laxur is safer for Abecedar and as likely as Gyre to aid us."

"That's where you're wrong," Gelasin crowed. "Epmar will write letters of introduction on the princess's behalf to certain meritocrats of her acquaintance."

"Indeed! Coming from an exile, such letters are scarcely worth the parchment they're written on."

"You would take that attitude, Quiescat," Gelasin sneered. "They're certainly better than pounding on random oligarchs' doors begging for an audience."

"Gelasin has a point," Drinith said. "Is the threat the dreameries pose insurmountable?"

"I suppose not," Quiescat admitted.

"Abecedar won't be alone," Drinith said. "He'll have you to help him."

Unable to bring himself to lie, Quiescat nodded. He'd not survive long enough to reach Gyre. "You've won the argument, Gelasin, it seems." The memory of the warrior's pitted grin came unbidden to his mind.

"Hopefully, we've all won," Gelasin said in a rare moment of magnanimity. "I'll go see if I can find our dragon and inform its captain of our plans."

"Make sure he keeps our destination to himself until we are on the wing," Quiescat said.

"Of course!" Gelasin's steps bounded away.

Quiescat squeezed Drinith's hand. "Please take me to Abecedar," he said, adding ruefully, "I'm afraid you'll have to be my eyes, my dear."

"It shall be my pleasure."

Drinith guided him carefully down the corridor. It took far longer than he expected for her to stop him at Abecedar's door. Someone quietly sobbed outside it.

"Versifer's inside trying to talk to him," Jarma said, her voice brimming with resentment. Indeed, the poet's muffled prattle could be heard beyond the room. Drinith rapped and, not waiting for an answer, stepped inside, gently drawing Quiescat in after her.

Versifer paused mid-platitude. "Abecedar, Quiescat's here to see you," he announced.

"Would you all be good enough to give me a moment alone with the oracle?" Quiescat asked.

Versifer and Drinith steered him onto a chair and departed, shutting the door behind them. Quiescat gave Abecedar the opportunity to speak first. But Abecedar said nothing. Only the regular sound of his breathing betrayed his presence.

"How are you feeling?" Quiescat asked at last.

"My eyes hurt," Abecedar groused.

"The pain will pass," Quiescat assured him. His hand trembled with the urge to pat Abecedar's hand, but the occasion was too solemn for him to be fumbling about like a fool.

"I don't feel human anymore," Abecedar said, his voice edged with fear.

"I won't lie to you. That feeling will remain with you, but you'll become inured to it in time." *It will even become part of you, and when the day comes that you, too, must surrender the gift, you will miss it.*

"It's easy for you to say that!" Abecedar raged.

Quiescat guffawed. The charge was so far from the truth, it was ridiculous! Abecedar burst out in desperate laughter too. Shaking with mirth, Quiescat tilted forward to drain the pools of tears gathering in his ocular cavities. It took both men, the old oracle and the new, some time to regain their composure, but the hilarity proved a tonic for Quiescat. The darkness weighed a little less on him.

"I've been such a fool, such a blind fool," Abecedar said. "Sorry. I meant no offense."

"None taken," Quiescat said. "If you're a fool, then so am I, as are our predecessors all the way back to Agebor the Larcener. But our sacrifices are not without purpose. While Drinith lives, hope remains for Rhumgad."

"You've seen that for certain?"

Quiescat winced. "No. Remember, I can't see beyond my death. But we are entitled as any mortal to hope. Nothing unwitnessed is certain."

"I've had a vision."

"Oh?" Previously, it had taken a red month or more of acclimatization for the power to manifest in a new oracle. Abecedar's revelation should have been a tremendous relief, but it filled Quiescat with trepidation.

"Some things can't be shared," Abecedar said. "As you've said in the past."

Quiescat nodded in agreement, though the rebuke stung. He had no right to question Abecedar. The future belonged to him, and nothing remained to Quiescat but the scraps of the past. And his own death.

"Versifer tells me we have to leave tomorrow," Abecedar said.

Quiescat nodded. "Hopefully, Gyre will prove more willing to aid us than the Elemental Pentarchy of Thirring."

It might well be a mercy that Quiescat wouldn't live long enough to find out. His final vision had revealed he'd die on the trip. He would physically see his death as well. An aftereffect of the gift would briefly grant him sight shortly before the assassin killed him—a dubious boon.

The only consolation was that Quiescat would die well.

10

———

Drinith and her retinue ambled through the palace, encircled by a dozen guards. The Fire Emperor was determined that his guests should reach their dragon without incident. Behind them, a similarly sized complement carried their luggage. Gelasin alone resisted the porters' help. He had developed a fierce attachment to his fat knapsack and refused to surrender it.

The escort moved no faster than Quiescat. Gelasin, used to a more rapid pace, kept having to slow to a stop to avoid crashing into the two guards ahead of him. Several times, he glanced up at the ornate ceilings in frustration. In the center of the group, Drinith held Quiescat's arm, murmuring instructions whenever they passed through a door or changed direction.

"To think I held your hand when you were a child and now you must hold mine," he whispered sadly. "How's your side?"

"Good," she said, despite its dull ache. "The medicine you gave me appears to be doing the trick."

Stairs proved to be the most formidable obstacle. After he stumbled on the first step, nearly plummeting headfirst down the rest, Epmar took his other arm, and she and Drinith helped him descend. Quiescat's breathing quickly became labored.

"We can pause if you're tired," Drinith said. Pain needled her side.

Quiescat shook his head. "Every step feels like leaping off a precipice."

Terrible sadness pressed on Drinith's chest. To think this great man, this hero who had sacrificed so much to protect her, had been brought so low. He was in no fit state for this arduous journey and yet who else could look after him but her?

"I promise we won't drop you," Epmar said. "We're nearly there. Just a little way to go."

All the while, Gelasin had tapped his foot impatiently at the bottom. "I hope the dragon doesn't leave without us."

"That won't happen," the officer assured them. "Even if we must carry him." Despite the absolute solemnity of his statement, Gelasin's horselaugh echoed through the palace.

Quiescat picked up his pace.

"Well done," Epmar said as he reached the bottom.

"Fantastic work." Gelasin thrust an upturned thumb before Quiescat's blind eyes in mock appreciation of his effort, then stomped on. Drinith's jaw clenched. How dare he treat Quiescat with such blatant condescension! Now was not the time to confront him, with this crowd as an audience. She'd do it in private later. Quiescat had suffered enough embarrassment already.

It took a long time to reach the entrance to the dragon perches. The officer waved at the massive double doors, and they groaned open as if by magic. The violent breath of the Crevast spilled inside, carrying the hisses and growls of dragons on it as if the void itself made them.

They proceeded down a tubular tunnel to the harbor. Circles of barbed spikes protruded at intervals along its length like open jaws. The harbor itself comprised a vast lattice of interconnected platforms, cranes, and perches in several of which dragons rested. Everywhere, dockhands worked with the beasts' crews to load and unload them.

In comparison, the ornate forked pier stretching before Drinith's party was eerily vacant. Their transport was perched between its prongs, but only the three masts were visible. Curiosity drew Drinith to peer over the edge. The saddledeck with its raised quarterdeck and sterncastle might have been part of a ship, but it traveled not on the sea but the air. Hidden beneath it was the living mountain of muscle, bone, and scale that would carry it across the void. The breeze failed to dispel the redolence of burning sulfur emanating from the dragon tucked under the pier.

A short, compact man climbed up the gangplank to greet them. He had bright silver eyes and dusky blue skin. Two curved spikes of lacquered silver beard jutted from his cheeks like tusks. Gelasin met him at the top and they shook hands.

"I trust everything is in hand for our trip, Pinchel," Gelasin said. They had already met to finalize the details of their journey.

"We'll be away before noon," Pinchel assured Gelasin, peering beyond him. Spotting Drinith, he strode over to her and bowed so low she feared he might bang his forehead against the platform. "Welcome, Princess, to the *Surly Bonnacon*. I'm her captain, Pinchel, born a draker, and no doubt destined to die one." He winked, his beards shifting apart like mandibles as he smiled. "But not on this trip. No, gentlefolk, no." He glanced around and gave them a conspiratorial wink. "We'll get you to your destinations as hale as you are now. Perhaps even more so. The winds of the deep Crevast have curative properties, they say."

After the guards dumped the luggage in a pile on the pier, the officer gave Gelasin a curt nod and marched his troop back into the palace.

"I'll get some of my crew to bring your bags on board," Pinchel said. "Don't worry. Nobody will touch them. This is one of the emperors' private berths."

They followed him down the steep gangplank. Too narrow to walk two abreast, Drinith descended ahead of Quiescat, one of his hands resting on her shoulder, the other feeling its way along the guide rope. Her throat tightened as he wobbled behind her, but he gently batted away hands eager to help him. "I won't fall. I promise." Alerted by the others that he had reached the bottom, he let Drinith take his arm and stepped slowly onto the saddledeck.

"Where is the rest of the crew?" Gelasin asked, eying the empty deck.

"They're down below, loading the cinchdeck," said Pinchel. "Except for the whisperers on duty, of course. They're up on the headstall, the compartment around the dragon's head." The draker opened a crate beside the end of the gangplank and pointed to the harnesses and lanyards within. "I want all of you to put these on. If you look about, you'll see a lot of anchor points and guidewires. Use them. And don't forget to strap into your bunks at night. I'm expecting a smooth journey, but if we hit a bit of turbulence, I don't want any of you bouncing around your quarters or, worse, falling off."

"You don't wear them yourself," Gelasin observed.

Pinchel threw back his head and cackled. "Dragons, no! I've a good intuition for knowing when to hold on. The same is true of every draker. Only landlubbers need to tie off. No offense."

"When I previously traveled on other dragons, I rented a parachute," Prosper Destil said nervously.

Pinchel swatted the suggestion. "A scam. A waste of money. If you fall off a dragon in the Crevast, the only thing you'll hit is the inner sun. You'll burn to a cinder, and all a parachute would do is prolong your suffering. Anyway, they probably didn't even give you a real parachute, just a bundled sheet stuffed in a bag." Noticing the mounting horror on Prosper's face, he added, "Not that it's likely to happen." He winked. "Never lost a passenger yet. Now, let me show you to your quarters."

As Pinchel led them toward the quarterdeck, he appeared oblivious to the sudden tremble beneath their feet. Drinith halted, mesmerized by the scaly mountain rising above the manmade structure. As the dragon's neck craned upward, jutting spines crested it, followed by its massive head. Two small horns protruded from its chin like a goatee. The little wooden headstall tucked under its spiked frill looked so flimsy. A wooden strip extended from the headstall across its forehead. It was hard to credit that the captain could steer this gargantuan beast from the glass bauble at the center of this headband—the so-called pineye. The dragon's huge red eyes glared down at the saddledeck for a breathless moment before it looked away. A black forked tongue whipped from its lipless mouth as it emitted a deafening hiss.

"What's that noise?" Quiescat demanded. "What's happening?" The others' awed silence left him perplexed.

This wasn't the first time Drinith had traveled by dragon, but the creature's immensity still daunted her. She glanced at her companions. Awe was writ large on every face, even Gelasin's.

Pinchel lurched to a stop. "Don't worry," he said with a bemused smile. "When Surly's perched, she makes that sound a hundred times a day. The old girl's just living up to her name. After a while, you won't even notice."

He opened the door and, with a flourish of his hand, indicated they should descend the narrow steps. "Your quarters are through the door on the left."

Gelasin waved the others back. He descended the steps with knife drawn and entered the cabin.

"Not a very trusting soul, is he?" Pinchel said with amusement.

"I apologize if his behavior seems extreme," Drinith said.

"Don't worry about it. He's just doing his job, like me."

"It's clear," Gelasin said, bounding back up the steps. He added with a smirk: "It's a bit small for the lot of us."

"I'm afraid the cabin is only large enough to accommodate the princess and her maid," Pinchel said. "We must berth the rest of you below deck."

Drinith held her breath as Gelasin loomed over the little man. "Unacceptable! We must stay together, at least for the present."

Pinchel's bushy eyebrows twitched like caterpillars over a flame. "Well, I don't know—"

"The oracle and his...predecessor can take the cabin up here," Gelasin said in a more conciliatory tone. "The princess will stay with me and the rest of her retinue."

Drinith exhaled.

Pinchel inclined his head deferentially. "If you're sure..." Drinith answered his inquisitive glance with a firm nod.

"We are," Gelasin said.

Pinchel shrugged. "That's your business."

Gelasin stroked his cheeks. "Tell me, Captain, have you taken on any new crew since you perched?"

"We've the same crew we arrived with."

"What's your view of stowaways?"

Pinchel's eyes narrowed. "I doubt you're talking about some starry-eyed youth captivated by the romance of life on board a dragon—never any shortage of that dreamy lot. Methinks you mean someone more unsavory."

"I'm talking about a criminal intent on murdering our princess."

Drinith cringed. However warranted, this fuss embarrassed her.

Pinchel sucked in a breath. "Are you certain such an individual is on board?"

"The emperors guaranteed our princess's safety," said Gelasin, shrugging, "but here, we're no longer in their domain. I can't be certain if an assassin's on board until we've conducted a thorough search. There's no point in looking until we're away from the perches."

"Agreed—a wasted effort if our quarry sneaks on board after we've finished our search. We'll conduct a full inspection after we've taken flight. The Draker Articles are plain about assassins. Toss them into the void."

"I'm afraid you mustn't do that," Drinith said. "If he's on board, we need him alive."

Gelasin smirked. "True. If we find him, though, he'll consider burning in the inner sun a gentler punishment."

11

—————

Quiescat sat in his new quarters in vexed silence. Blindness weighed heavily enough without his former acolyte's stubborn silence further isolating him. The lingering memory of Abecedar's smug grin haunted him. Had the oracle no pity, leaving him to wallow in this numbing darkness, anchored to reality only by the hard wooden seat pressing against his bottom?

Clearing his throat drew no reaction. Either the oracle didn't notice or didn't care. Perhaps a vision distracted him. A pang of jealousy gripped Quiescat, now double-blind and useless, waiting only for death to fulfill its promise. He sank into a profound melancholy as the minutes ticked by and the black silence deepened.

"I envy you."

Quiescat flinched. "Eh? What's that you said, Abecedar?"

"Sorry, I didn't mean to startle you. I said I envy you."

"Why?" Quiescat asked, sounding harsher than intended.

"You face your death so calmly."

"What do you know of my death?"

"I know more than you imagine."

"Is there something you wish to tell me?"

"I've had...a second vision," Abecedar said with noticeable reluctance. "I can't share the details."

A surge of jubilation quickly passed. Quiescat tensed. "Does it involve Drinith?" he couldn't help asking.

"In a way. I really can't tell you. And yet I need your advice."

"I understand." Quiescat meant it. He appreciated the loneliness of glimpsing the future and being unable to share it. "Then let us discuss the nature of your visions without trespassing on their details." He considered how best to put his question. "Forgive me for asking, but are you sure both of your visions were truly prophetic and not idle dreams?"

"They were both visions." His voice held a note of annoyance. "I'm sure of it. They came to me while awake and they...had a tangible quality."

"Yes," Quiescat said, nodding. "There's a solidity to true visions that sets them apart. They bear the heft of reality. Am I right that these visions were of actual events and not allegorical?"

"You're correct," Abecedar said wearily.

"Then they're fixed points in time. They cannot be altered without great cost. The best you can do is prepare for their aftermath."

"Like your death."

The reminder stung. Quiescat heaved a deep sigh. "Indeed."

"You've often mentioned this great cost, but you've never told me what it is."

"I've never meddled with the future to find out. It's received wisdom passed down from one oracle to the next. Probably came from Agebor himself. If anyone dared to attempt such a feat, it would be the Larcener."

"So the edict might be rooted in little more than spurious assumption."

Quiescat flinched. He must scotch this dangerous line of reasoning before Abecedar did something foolish. "Don't make the mistake of presuming you know better than our predecessors. The gift isn't some trifle to be played with. It has crowned kings and toppled them. It has built and ruined empires. Its predictions spared Rhumgad innumerable calamities—"

"Except Magian. It failed to foresee the threat he posed."

"Magian appears to be a blind spot," Quiescat admitted reluctantly, "but his minions aren't. We can see them when the gift permits."

"The Tear has never given us a glimpse into the plans of the greatest conqueror in Rhumgad's history. Have you ever wondered why?"

"There's a lot about the gift we don't understand. But we know enough to appreciate the danger of its misuse. Don't we?"

"But..."

"But what?" Quiescat snapped.

"If a vision is fixed, and we can't break it, maybe we can bend it a little."

"No no no! You mustn't!" Quiescat felt cold and hot at once. His stomach roiled. Had the gift driven Abecedar insane? His arrogant streak had blossomed into a monstrous narcissism that would destroy not only him but also Drinith and countless others. Somehow, Quiescat had to make him see his conceit for what it was before he unloosed a terrible catastrophe upon the world.

"You've no right to lecture me," Abecedar said coldly. "I'm the oracle now, not you."

"Then act like one. Treat your power with the respect it deserves, not like some brattish princeling playing king with his father's crown! I blame myself. I should have done a better job of mentoring you. Taken you into my confidence more often. I fear I've created a monster..." His voice trailed off.

Abecedar's silent rage hung in the air like a pall. Quiescat knew he had gone too far. "I'm sorry. That was unfair."

But Abecedar still didn't answer.

"Abecedar, please pity an old fool and forgive him." But no absolution came. "Abecedar?" Breathless fear made him whisper it. Dropping from his chair onto his knees, he groped for some fragment of Abecedar—a hand, the hem of his cowl, a boot, anything. Steps, retreating. He crawled toward their sound. Something seized him around the shoulders and midriff, arresting his pursuit with a loud snap. He had forgotten about the damn safety harness. The door screeched open.

"In time," Quiescat said, "I've no doubt you'll outstrip me and the rest of your predecessors, but be patient. Learn to walk before you run."

"There's no time for patience," Abecedar murmured.

The door banged shut.

12

Pinchel assigned Drinith and her companions two compartments on the lower deck. Bare except for the anchor points affixed to the floor and walls and an ominous lidded pail, they might just as easily have accommodated cargo. Judging from the faint odor of stale dung, they must have recently housed livestock. Along with Jarma, Drinith found her section crammed with Gelasin, Halyard, and Zin, the most accomplished warriors in her retinue. For her protection, Gelasin explained.

The weak light from the single lampstone barely pierced the gloom. The cramped conditions, the incessant chatter about who slept where, when, and how, and Zin's lustful glances combined to inspire in Drinith an oppressive claustrophobia. She longed to be alone, or at least be free of Zin. It was hard not to envy Quiescat and Abecedar in their relatively well-appointed cabin, but having witnessed firsthand the conditions her other companions had to endure, she wouldn't have felt right abandoning them. Still, it would be nice to stroll the decks alone for a while. For now, until they had scoured the dragon from top to bottom for potential threats, she had no choice but to suffer this prison of good intentions. Gelasin would never countenance her safety being put at risk.

He and Zin exchanged furtive whispers and chortled as they peered into Gelasin's stuffed knapsack.

"What is so amusing?" Epmar, who had lingered to chat with Halyard, peeked over their shoulders.

Gelasin shut the bag. "Nothing that concerns you."

Epmar frowned. "They looked like the floor tiles from the palace bedrooms."

"It was Quiescat's idea," Gelasin said, glancing at Drinith. "They'll never be missed. We pried them from under our beds." He picked a square-foot tile out of the bag and thrust it at Drinith. Bits of adhesive were still attached to the underside.

Drinith stared at him in disbelief. "Quiescat would have never condoned such theft, much less instigate it."

Gelasin studied the tile. "He may have mentioned it only as a hypothetical, it's true, but once he put the idea in my mind, I couldn't pass on it."

"And why would you take them?" Epmar asked.

"They're dragon amber—worth a small fortune."

Zin's head bobbed in agreement.

"Really?" Epmar arched an eyebrow. "Do you imagine the Pentarchy is so rich that it can afford to furnish guest bedrooms in dragon amber? They're reproductions. Not cheap but not real dragon amber."

"No, you're wrong," Gelasin insisted.

"Give it to me," Epmar said.

Reluctantly, Gelasin passed the tile to her. She tossed it to Halyard. "Try to break it." Zin and Gelasin lunged toward him, but she waved them off. "If it's true dragon amber, it shouldn't fracture."

He propped the tile at an angle against the wall and stamped on it. It shattered into a dozen pieces.

"See, not dragon amber," Epmar said. "I had something similar in my bedroom in Gyre."

Zin's grin vanished. "Empyrosis's burning bowels! I was up the whole night pulling them up. What a waste!"

"The Aether Emperor's servant told us it was dragon amber!" Gelasin moaned.

"I've learned it's best not to listen to domestics on the value of furnishings," Epmar said. "They tend to exaggerate."

"Are they really worth nothing?" Gelasin asked.

"Maybe if you had enough to cover a floor, someone might buy them," Epmar said.

"No," Zin sighed. "We only took the tiles under our beds, remember."

Epmar shrugged. "Maybe someone might want to tile a closet."

Zin grabbed some tiles from the sack and dashed them into smithereens against the wall. "Bah!"

"I hope you realize you'll be picking all those bits up," Gelasin said.

"You shouldn't have taken them anyway," Drinith groused.

Gelasin threw up his arms. "A moot point, *Princess*. You do realize we're broke, right?" He glanced guiltily at the others. "Close to it, anyway."

"Better to be a beggar than a thief," Drinith retorted.

"Empty words, if your belly's empty," Zin snarled.

Epmar smirked. "You never struck me as a man who's ever gone hungry."

Zin's eyes narrowed. "I starved plenty as a child, but I swore after I crawled out of the gutter, I'd never go hungry again." Drinith shivered as his gaze fell on her. "Of course, food doesn't sate every hunger."

A young draker swaggered in, cutting short the bickering. Tall and lithe, he had to stoop to avoid his ornate dragon claw helmet hitting the head jamb. He wore a red velvet waistcoat over a loose blouse. A bullhorn hung from his leather belt.

"You bear an uncanny resemblance to the captain," Gelasin observed conversationally. "Except for the absence of whiskers."

"That is no coincidence; he is my father," said the draker proudly, in a fluty voice. "I'm the saddlemaster, Antonben."

"Ah, keeping it in family," Zin chimed in. "Dear old dad made his son his second-in-command."

Antonben's silver eyes blazed. "I am his *daughter*. And I *earned* my place on the crew, just like everybody else."

Zin appraised her coolly from head to toe, noting the boyish face and flat bosom. "Honest mistake." A thump from Gelasin cut his snicker short.

"Take no notice of him," Gelasin said sternly. "He's not long out of swaddling."

"I apologize, Antonben," Drinith said.

The draker answered her with a warm smile. "You've no need to apologize, Princess. If anything, I should be commiserating you for being stuck with him. I should warn you though, if I begin to find him irksome, I may toss him overboard."

"Yeah? You and what army?" Zin growled.

Antonben made great play of examining him. "I'm sure the three dozen drakers I command should suffice."

Almost everyone erupted in laughter, but Zin's menacing glower filled Drinith with a sense of foreboding and she could only muster a wan smile.

"The captain sent me," Antonben said. "He thought you might enjoy a visit to the whereabout atop the quarterdeck to observe the *Surly Bonnacon*'s departure."

"I'd be delighted," Drinith blurted before Gelasin could decline.

"We'll all go," he said morosely.

Prosper peered through the door. "May I be excused? I feel rather queasy."

"You'd be better getting some air topside," Antonben said.

The chef winced. "I'd rather not be reminded I'm not on a dragon's back. No offense."

"None taken," Antonben said, grinning, the gold incisors and canine on the left side of her mouth glinting. "But I strongly advise you don't get sick down here."

"I'll make sure if I retch to do it into the slops bucket."

Antonben stood with arms akimbo; her nostrils flared. "Your choice. But it smells bad enough down here as it is."

"Prosper, you're coming with us," Gelasin said.

"But I'm nervous around dragons," Prosper pleaded. "And the Crevast frightens me."

"Then find somewhere upstairs to sit down," Gelasin snapped, "and close your eyes."

Antonben released a tinkling laugh. "Landlubbers."

Drinith inhaled the sweet, whistling breeze when she finally climbed out the hatch onto the top deck.

"It's fresh up here," Gelasin observed.

"Wait until we are beyond the shelter of the docks," Antonben said. "You'll know all about wind then."

Several of the crew huddled together, chatting and laughing. Behind them, Abecedar stood hunched over the bulwark. Drinith wondered what he was doing here when he should have been minding Quiescat. Perhaps he also felt unwell. He must be struggling to come to terms with his new eyes. She turned to Prosper. "Would you mind offering Abecedar some company? He looks as though he could use it."

Sighing, Prosper did a passable impression of a deflating balloon. "Very well."

Versifer's hand gently stayed him. "If you don't mind, I'll go."

"Of course," Gelasin said, contempt staining his smile. "Make sure he's tied off. Oracles can fall off the backs of dragons like any mortal."

Versifer exchanged a subtle nod with Jarma and sauntered over to the lonely oracle.

"I'm sure he has the perfect poem for the occasion," Gelasin muttered.

"Oh dear, oh dear! Can't hold it!" Prosper's hand shot to his mouth as he bolted to the other side of the saddledeck.

Gelasin rolled his eyes. "We haven't even left the perches yet."

"Jarma, perhaps you would be good enough to keep Quiescat company?" Drinith suggested.

"Epmar can go," Gelasin snarled, overriding her without the slightest hesitation.

"Has your arrogance no bounds?" Drinith hissed. "Don't you think *I* ought to be consulted in such matters?"

Gelasin dismissed Drinith's cold fury with a pitted grin. "Merely a precaution, *Princess*. You and Jarma look so alike, an assassin might mistake her for you."

Epmar gave him a disdainful glance and smiled at Drinith. "What are your orders, Your Highness?"

Drinith bowed her head and studied her shoes to hide her violent flush, but the fact that Gelasin was right made his insolence even more infuriating. "Epmar, go, please."

While Epmar descended the steps to Quiescat's cabin, Drinith and the others followed Antonben up external stairs to the windowed whereabout. Inside, Pinchel stood, leaning over a table. On it lay a large map and various complex brass instruments. To one side of him, on a cylindrical pedestal, stood a large brass dome girdled by a graduated ring. The arrow notched into the hemisphere gave it the appearance of a demonic eye. Drinith shuddered as it twitched suddenly. The captain also took notice. With an exasperated growl, he struck it with his fist, causing the two drakers staring out of the main window to look back inquisitively at him.

"The damn attracton has been fluttering all morning," Pinchel said, stroking the prongs of his beard. "Nothing serious but annoying all the same. Like something's pulling on it."

Antonben scratched the back of her neck. "Captain, the princess is here."

Pinchel looked up, delighted. "How lovely to see you, Princess." He swept around the table. His grin slipped a little as the crowd shuffled behind her into the whereabout. "I didn't expect so many of your retinue to accept my invitation. I'm sure there'll be enough room to accommodate...everyone. The launch is usually a smooth process, but you all should tie off your lanyards just in case."

Drinith looked around in vain for an anchor point. Pinchel's cough drew her attention to his finger pointing upward. She clipped on to the nearest wire on the ceiling. "I've traveled on dragons before, but I've never had the privilege to be in a whereabout."

"The privilege is all mine, Princess." Pinchel pointed to the metal hemisphere. "You might find this of interest. It's our attracton. There's a metal rod within it that's drawn towards shards, great and small." He jabbed a stubby finger on the map. Arrows packed the space between the shards as if the great landmasses were locked in some terrible war. "The arrows are attracton positions. If you know your starting point, it's easy to use them to plot your course."

"And if you don't know your location?"

Pinchel grinned, impressed by her shrewd question. He waved at the brass contraptions on the table. "That's what these other instruments are for. You must work out your position based on the shards and stars. Of course, clouds might hamper your visibility, in which case you'd have to fly blind and depend on Surly's acute senses to prevent her crashing into anything."

Beckoning Drinith to follow him, Pinchel circled the desk and approached the drakers at the window. At his insistent wave, they stepped aside. "While the dragon's in flight, the headstall is isolated at the far end of the dragon's neck. These two gentlemen manage communications between the whereabout and the headstall. This fine fellow here with all those levers arranged like a giant brass knuckle in front of him sends signals, and the other man holding the spyglass, the spotter, notes any signal from the headstall."

Gently taking Drinith by the elbow, Pinchel directed her attention toward a cluster of brass pipes just behind them. She glanced back at Gelasin. Fingering the hilt of his dagger, he looked ready to pounce across the room to her side. Paranoia must have overpowered his reason for him to regard Pinchel as a danger to her. She hoped her urgent headshake would be enough to dissuade him from a rash action they'd all regret.

"These tubes allow us to communicate with the sterncastle and the cinchdeck on the underside of the dragon." Pinchel grinned. "The saddlemaster carries a bullhorn to communicate with the rest of saddledeck. Not that she needs it most of the time. She has a good pair of lungs, dragons bless her." The drakers chuckled appreciatively.

Three more drakers tramped into the whereabout and nodded at

Pinchel and Antonben. One stationed herself by the tubes. The other two readied spyglasses by the side windows.

"It all seems rather complicated," Drinith said tentatively. "Could this navigation equipment not be placed in the headstall?"

"Nay, Princess, the headstall bobs too much and it's cramped as it is. At least a dozen people live at close quarters over there, including four whisperers, and they're a breed unto themselves. If drakers are mad, then whisperers are doubly so. Comes from spending most of their time crawling in a dragon's ear hole."

"Beats hacking danglebergs off their—"

"Hosfat, please! We have a lady of royal blood present."

The new arrival was a short, reedy, pale man with striking orange eyes. Tattoos of interlocking dragon claws covered his smooth pate. He wore a dozen gold chains over his black coat, each of which carried a dozen or more rings. He smelled of sulfur and wax.

"This is Hosfat," Pinchel muttered. "He's our senior whisperer."

"Pleasure to make your acquaintance, Your Ladyship!" Hosfat boomed. He essayed a ridiculous little curtsy. "I didn't mean to speak out of turn, but back in the day, I was never so happy to apprentice as a whisperer and leave the care of ole Surly's posterior to others. Them danglebergs—"

"You must pardon my garrulous crewman, Princess," Pinchel jumped in just in time. "He's more used to dragons than people."

"Aye, dragons have a better sense of humor!" Hosfat bellowed. "Why else would they pretend we're in charge?" He curtsied again, this time tucking a finger under his chin. "Pardon me, Princess, if I offended your sensibilities! Not much call for royal etiquette, where I come from!"

"Or manners in general," Antonben chipped in, but Hosfat reacted to the jibe with a thunderclap of laughter. Drinith, herself, was powerless not to titter at the whisperer's antics, which did much to curb everyone's jitters, even Gelasin's.

In the distance, the dragon's massive head rose. Green and red lights blinked from beneath the shadow of its frill.

"The headstall asked permission to approach for final boarding," the spotter said.

"Is everyone up on the springboard?" Pinchel asked Hosfat.

"Everyone except you and me! I checked the provisions too! All correct!" His relentlessly booming voice began to grate on Drinith. She withdrew beside Gelasin, relieved her tour had ended without incident.

"Very good," Pinchel said. "Signal the headstall we're ready."

The signaler pulled two of the levers back and forth. The long neck of the dragon folded back on itself as its head loomed ever closer.

"I'm afraid I must leave you in the capable hands of my saddlemaster, Princess," Pinchel declared. He spotted Drinith and, approaching her, pressed his hat to his chest and bowed. "Until we meet again at our destination." He strode out of the whereabout, Hosfat ambling after him. The shadow of the dragon's head plunged the room into darkness.

The gloom lifted remarkably quickly as the head glided into the distance. The shadow under its frill pulled back to reveal the headstall, like a wooden fortification hanging off a precipice.

Antonben rapidly rubbed her hands together. "We'll be off soon."

"Do you not offer any sacrifice to the gods before you set out?" Jarma asked.

"We have no truck with landlubber gods. You're standing on the only god we pray to," Antonben said with a wink. "You might like to watch her lift off through that window to your left."

Drinith slid along the guidewire to join the clustering spectators and peered out expectantly. The pier slipped away, and a monstrous leathery wing rose in its place. She glimpsed white symbols in complex coiling patterns covering its green surface briefly before they melted into the outer sun's reflected glare. Hurt by the painful dazzle, she shielded her eyes.

Sharp tremors passed through the floor as the dragon jolted forward. Drinith yelped and seized her lanyard, as did her companions. The towering shadows of the docks flitted by and disappeared. Drinith wobbled across the trembling floor over to one of the rear windows. Above the harbor and its crude cubic thatch of docks and piers, the massive statue that was the Aether Emperor's palace stood against the cliffside casting its disdainful gaze upon the departing travelers. Below, on the deck, the crew had begun to raise the sails as the dragon's wings languidly soared and dipped.

"We're underway," Antonben declared.

"The headstall signals," the spotter said. "Our destination's Gyre."

"So we finally know where we're going," Antonben glanced at the attracton and hunched over the chart on the desk.

"It appears the good captain kept our secret," Gelasin murmured. "And now our work begins. Zin, get Versifer and Epmar back here."

"What about Prosper?" Zin asked.

Gelasin scowled. "What about him? Leave him alone until he gets his air legs. Saddlemaster, we need to borrow some of your crew. We have some searching to do."

Antonben nodded. "I'll get right on it."

Gelasin formed two parties to search the saddledeck. Over his objections Drinith insisted on participating, so he teamed her with himself and Halyard. He put Zin in charge of Versifer and Jarma. Antonben added two drakers to each group. She instructed the crew of the cinchdeck by voicepipe to carry out a separate inspection of their section.

Even working in two groups with the full cooperation of the crew, the investigation proved painfully slow, dragging through the day and into the night. No nook or cranny went unexplored. They scrutinized every casket, bale, bundle, and crate for air holes, suspicious weight, or other hints of tampering.

"We can relax at least until we reach our destination," Gelasin said when everyone had confirmed they found no trace of a pentacular, but he didn't look relaxed. If anything, he had grown tenser. As the others headed for their bunks, Drinith seized the opportunity to confront him. "I'd like to speak with you if I may."

He smirked. "What's wrong, *Princess*?"

"You needn't take that derisive tone with me." Drinith glanced behind her to confirm no one was in earshot. "I'm unhappy about how you've been behaving toward Quiescat."

A tiny smile played on his lips. "How so?"

"You know very well," she murmured. "I saw you grinning as he struggled down the stairs. You sniped at him at every opportunity on the way to the dragon. The final straw was the insolent thumb you brandished in his sightless face."

Gelasin snorted. "I admit to being exasperated by his slowness. I didn't feel safe in those corridors. Too many dark nooks, too many unfamiliar faces in matching uniforms. Venting my frustration through humor seemed to me like a good way to ease the tension. I'm sorry if you feel I went too far." He hesitated. "I'll apologize to him at the first opportunity. I never intended to embarrass him. I'm sure you're aware, we've never been close, but it breaks my heart to see him so humbled. My mortality has been on my mind a lot recently. His...degeneration reminds me I'm getting on, too. I'm not as spry as I used to be. I won't be able to fight forever. I'll lose my purpose, just like him."

His raw honesty was revelatory. He had always behaved as though hewn from rock, never hinting at such vulnerability.

"It seems I've judged you too harshly," Drinith said.

Gelasin forgave her with a chuckle. "To be honest, I'm more worried about the pentaculars. I wish we had found something. They had plenty of time to get one of their colleagues on board."

A cough drew their attention to Abecedar. "I need to talk to both of you," he said, crossing his trembling arms only to drop them to his sides. "I've had a vision."

Judging from his fevered demeanor, it hadn't been a good one.

13

———

Quiescat's eyelids fluttered open. He stared up at the wooden ceiling above him, confused by what he was seeing. Was he dreaming of his death again? He pinched the back of his hand. The pain felt real, immediate. This sight he experienced was an afterimage of his gift, the product of living his final day countless times before. This would be the last time he'd see. He would die today.

He threw off his blanket and tried to rise, but the straps securing him to the bunk held him down. He always forgot that in the dreams, too.

The noise, fortunately, did not wake his snoring companion, nor did the light streaming through the open shutters. Gods, every rattling breath from Abecedar sounded so smug. For all Quiescat knew, the new oracle might have just returned from his self-imposed isolation. Quiescat carefully undid the buckles and slipped off the harness. He didn't need it. He knew exactly how he'd die, and it didn't involve falling off a dragon.

He picked up a mirror from a shelf and studied his reflection. Despite the many times he had seen his image with its strange shrunken eyes, the blind man staring back at him remained a stranger.

He could stay in his room and never put himself in the way of the assassin's blade awaiting him on deck. He could go right now to Gelasin and warn him that his final vision had revealed that a pentacular was on board. No, he must follow through on the vision. Doing anything else put Drinith at risk. His one consolation was that his death would save her—this time, at least.

The pressure struck, jolting one leg and then the other, forcing him toward his sandals. It was the sheer physical force of Fate nudging him to play his role in events already decided. He fought every step until the pressure became irresistible. He slipped his feet into his sandals. An invisible weight on his shoulders forced him to stoop. His fingers danced wildly as he fought the urge to fasten his sandals, but his feeble act of resistance lasted only a brief moment. Cursing under his breath, he slipped on his cowl.

He was now a puppet of Fate, dancing to its whim, an observer of his own death with no means of bending its predestined course even a little. Fate bound and gagged him and marched him to his place of execution, and he could do nothing except play the brave stoic.

Pretend it's another dream, as unreal as the rest. Pretend you will not die today. Pretend you're acting in a play. Yes, you're an actor and today is your greatest performance. Your final performance.

But serene acceptance eluded him owing to a primal fear as pointless as it was desperate. He wanted to live, more than anything.

Quiescat cursed the senseless cruelty of this farcical game he must play as it swept him toward the door. It creaked noisily as Quiescat pulled it open.

Abecedar's snoring ceased. Quiescat glanced back nervously at his successor, but he appeared to be still asleep, thank the gods. The last thing Quiescat needed was to become mired in a long-winded explanation about something he couldn't change. He eased the door shut behind him and laboriously climbed the stairs up to the main deck.

The saddlemaster, Antonben, from high up in the whereabout,

roared orders through a bullhorn to her crew. Ropes squealed to the heaving of teams of drakers as the two bottom sails on two of the masts drew upward to their spars. Nobody took notice of the blind man strolling in their midst. Their efforts seemed so puny compared to the dragon's massive wings regularly eclipsing the outer sun, casting a cold, black shade over the saddledeck. Quiescat paused by the bulwark and waited patiently for his preordained meeting with Drinith. If he couldn't thwart his destiny, then he'd accept it with good grace. At least, he'd get one more chance to be a hero. And he'd get to say a proper final farewell to Drinith.

"Quiescat, what are you doing here by yourself?" she asked with alarm. To her, this encounter was no doubt unexpected, inexplicable, and worrisome, but he had seen it play out countless times before.

"Abecedar's snoring drove me from the cabin."

"You shouldn't be out here by yourself," she chided gently. "You can't see where you're going. You could trip over something and injure yourself."

"You're right, of course. It's not something I'll repeat, I promise."

She folded her arms. "I was talking to Gelasin last night."

"Oh?"

"He respects you, despite the impression he sometimes gives."

"I respect him, too. Otherwise, I'd never have entrusted your safety to him. He's a good man." He thought of Abecedar lying asleep in his bunk, insensate to what was about to happen. What were those visions he refused to share? "Have you been talking much to the new oracle?"

"Abecedar? No." She spoke with such clear reluctance. If he hadn't known better, he might have suspected her of lying.

"You should," he said. *Your survival may depend on what he deigns to reveal.* "But remember this: look foremost to your best judgment; don't let others think for you." Guilt stirred at casting aspersions on the very men he had chosen to protect her. They were no less wise than him. Perhaps they would prove wiser. "But don't ignore their advice either. Just think for yourself." Feeling feverish, he dabbed the cold sweat on his face with a handkerchief.

"I still have you to advise me," she said. "Your wisdom extends beyond your oracular power."

His gaze surreptitiously scanned the deck. The sweep and retreat of the wings' shadows across the saddledeck hampered his search for the assassin, but the pentacular must be close.

"It's very good of you to say so," Quiescat said. And wrong. He was nothing without the gift. He had depended too much on it and its loss had left him incapable of decision. Perhaps that was why he was so quick to warn Drinith to think for herself. He didn't want her repeating his mistakes. "But my wisdom isn't infallible either." *And soon it will die with me.*

The incongruity of the conversation suddenly struck him. The words and actions were so familiar, like a poem learned by heart, but the attendant emotional turbulence was a different matter entirely. Its force made him forget he had already witnessed this countless times before; every action, every word, every breath, every twitch of muscle was predestined.

"I owe you so much," Drinith said. "I have brought such suffering upon you."

Her words cut deeper than any dagger. "Not you. Magian is to blame." *And perhaps your father.* "He'd have destroyed Godsdoor sooner or later. You saved me. But for you, I'd have burned with my temple." *A martyr and a fool.* "I'd have missed out on so much." He swept his arms broadly. "All this. The Crevast. The other shards." *And I'd have never raised you. I'd have never learned to care for anyone more than the accursed Tear of Fate.* Emotion strangled the words in his throat. His ocular cavities brimmed with tears that trickled down his cheeks.

Drinith touched his sleeve. "Are you okay?"

He avoided her anxious gaze until he had his emotions in check. The pentacular would be here at any moment. "I'm fine," he said, blotting his moist cheeks. "Sentimentality got the best of me for a moment. One of the foibles of advanced years."

He looked around again for the assassin. *What delays him? At this rate, I'm liable to die of old age before he gets here.* Quiescat roared with laughter at the preposterousness of his situation.

"What's so funny?" Drinith asked, bemused.

A figure strolling across the deck, weaving unobserved between clusters of distracted drakers, cut short Quiescat's mirth. Drinith mustn't see him. She'd be sure to recognize him. "Wait here."

"Quiescat, where are you going?" she asked as he marched toward her would-be murderer, who watched his progress with incredulity. Quiescat opened his eyes as wide as he could, exposing the emptiness behind their lids, and nodded to him. Confusion, wonder, and horror spread across the pentacular's face at being acknowledged so casually by an eyeless man. A knife slipped from his sleeve into his hand. Quiescat tensed.

"Quiescat, don't!" Drinith yelled.

"Assassin!" he yelled, throwing himself on the pentacular's armed hand. He grabbed it, squeezed the arm with all his might. As frail as Quiescat was, the pentacular, for all his preternatural strength, couldn't shake his viselike grip.

"Hoy! Assassin! Get him!" Gelasin's cry rose above the fray. Quiescat had never before noticed his presence in the vision.

Drakers slammed into the pentacular until he toppled. The impact flung Quiescat clear of the assassin. Someone grabbed Quiescat's arm and dragged him across the rough deck, but his view of the drakers pummeling the pentacular remained fixed. The surrounding sounds didn't match with what he was seeing. He gazed down at the knife stuck in his belly. He had never even felt the blade sink into his flesh. Instinctively reaching for it, his hands appeared to wrap around the handle, but he clutched only air. His perspective shifted as if he had toppled over, but he hadn't moved.

The vision reached its end, and he was blind again.

"Don't kill him!" Gelasin roared. "We need him alive!"

Why am I not dead? Quiescat patted his stomach, searching for the fatal weapon or at least the wound it had made. The fabric was whole, dry to his touch. The vision couldn't have lied. A twinge drew his attention to his left side. Hot, greasy blood coated his fingers as he explored the damaged cloth.

"Let me look at it," Gelasin said. The sound of ripping fabric accompanied a chill gust under Quiescat's cowl. A hand patted his shoulder. "It's barely a nick. Looks like you'll live."

But I can't live. I'm supposed to die. Quiescat groaned. None of this made sense. Sometimes he had missed or misinterpreted details of his prophetic glimpses, but they had never erred so blatantly before.

"Is he okay?" Drinith asked.

"He'll be fine," Gelasin said. "You played your part beautifully."

"Where do you think the pentacular was hiding?" Halyard asked.

"It's a mystery, to be sure. We searched pretty thoroughly." Gelasin said. "Maybe he has been camped out on the dragon's tail since we left Thirring. Who knows what these pentaculars are capable of? Quiescat, you owe your life to Abecedar. He warned us something like this might happen."

Abecedar, Abecedar, what did you do? "Where is he?"

"In your cabin."

Pain racked Quiescat as he tried to rise. Gelasin's hand upon his shoulder pushed him back down.

"Stay," he said. "I need to treat that wound before you go anywhere. Eat this. It'll ease the pain." He shoved some reeking doughy substance against Quiescat's mouth. Grudgingly, Quiescat took it. It tasted as foul as it smelled, but he forced it down. The pain subsided and a general numbness spread through his body until all he could feel was his anger. He stewed in silence until Gelasin declared he had finished his ministrations.

"Help me up," Quiescat demanded. Gelasin lifted him to his feet. He swayed dizzily, clutching pathetically at the air. Drinith grasped his hand.

"Steady there," Gelasin said, holding his shoulder. "Take it easy."

"Take me to Abecedar," Quiescat said. The walk to the cabin seemed to take forever. The need to confront Abecedar consumed him.

"Lucky for you," said Gelasin, "visions came quicker to your successor than expected."

"Yes," Quiescat grunted.

"Do you know anything about his second vision?"

"Ask him," Quiescat snapped. "He's the oracle. I'm a..." *A living ghost.* "I'm not the oracle."

"He won't tell me," Gelasin said, aggrieved.

"He won't tell me either. He must have his reasons."

"If there's a threat to Drinith, I need to know."

"Of course." But Quiescat hadn't forewarned Gelasin about the pentacular, afraid to undermine the integrity of his vision. Evidently, his successor had no such qualms. "If it's in your interest to know, I have no doubt Abecedar will tell you."

"What's that supposed to mean?"

Quiescat shrugged. "What do you think it means? It means neither of us are the oracle."

"Watch your step," Gelasin snarled.

"What do you mean by that?" Quiescat demanded. He wouldn't be cowed by the warrior's threats.

"I mean we're about to descend the steps to the cabin."

A strange exultation gripped Quiescat as he reached the bottom. This would be his third fight of the day. The door creaked open and Gelasin led him into the room.

"You survived, I see," Abecedar said. "There's a seat to your left."

Reaching out, Quiescat found the back of the chair and gripped it tightly. "I prefer to stand."

"Should I stay?" Gelasin asked gruffly. "I need to attend to the pentacular."

"Very well," Abecedar said. "I think Quiescat would prefer to talk with me in private, anyway."

You're damn right about that at least. "Yes, Gelasin, leave us." Quiescat waited until the door creaked shut. "What have you done?"

"Saved your life."

Quiescat snarled. "You had a vision of my death and revealed it to Gelasin and the others, corrupting it and unloosing terrible consequences."

"What are these terrible consequences you foresee?"

Quiescat bristled at every mocking word. "You know I can no longer glimpse the future."

"That's right. You're not the oracle. I am. I'm burdened with the Tear's predictions and their repercussions until I yield it to another."

"You might be the oracle, but you lack the humility of your predecessors. Meddling with the gift's visions is to tinker with Fate itself."

"Are you so in love with your death that you consider its prevention a betrayal?"

The question left Quiescat stunned for a moment. Had Abecedar a point? Had he wanted to die rather than face an indeterminate lifetime of dependency and irrelevance? "You can't understand how hard it was to resign myself to the inevitability of my death, to live with the certain knowledge of how and when it would come. But I accepted my doom for the greater good."

"And how do you know it was for the greater good?" Abecedar asked. "Or any good at all?"

"My death was meant to save the princess from that assassin, for a start." Quiescat blushed at the foolishness of the remark.

"But you didn't die, and the princess still lives. Your death would have achieved nothing, but perhaps you'll find a better purpose in whatever life remains to you."

"I doubt it," Quiescat said under his breath.

Abecedar snickered. "As you yourself pointed out, you can't see the future. You will have to wait for it to unfold like any ungifted mortal. You must learn to hope."

"What do you know of hope?" Quiescat asked bitterly.

"More than I can tell you," Abecedar said. "You must remain strong for Drinith's sake. I'm not the vain fool you take me for, though I won't deny I had that potential. Though you judge me harshly, I see the value in your wisdom. But despair mustn't corrupt it. Accept life as you once accepted death. Live with uncertainty as you once carried the terrible burden of prevision. Have the humility to accept the judgment of the oracle and don't treat your survival as an affliction."

Whatever Abecedar claimed, doubt in his abilities had clearly motivated him. And perhaps love for his old master, now that ambition no longer suppressed it. A terrible sadness weighed on Quiescat. Nothing good could come of an oracle leaning on hope.

"There's no point in arguing about the past," Abecedar said. "Even if I was wrong, what I did can't be undone."

Quiescat sighed. "You're right." Abecedar needed help and Quiescat would give what little he could offer. He'd face the consequences of his successor's transgression with the same courage that helped him to walk to his death this morning.

14

______

Drinith trailed after Zin, Gelasin, and Halyard while they dragged and shoved the bound assassin toward the hatch to the lower deck. As they forced him down the ladder, he suddenly slid down the rungs and landed at Antonben's feet. She gasped and reached for her sword. He sprang up, but Zin leapt down and landed feetfirst on him, slamming him to the floor.

"You could have killed him!" Antonben chided.

Zin's crazed laugh as he stepped off the squirming pentacular made Drinith cringe. "He has the strength of three men. That blow would only kill one or maybe two of them."

The pentacular twisted around and grinned up at him.

"Oh, think it's funny, eh? How'd you like it if I made that smile permanent?" Ignoring Antonben's disapproving glare, Zin tickled one corner of the pentacular's mouth with his dagger. The villain, still grinning, didn't flinch.

Gelasin chuckled to himself as he climbed down the ladder. "He's just trying to look tough. Well, I hate to tell you, pentacular, but grinning fools don't scare me." Drinith and Halyard descended after him.

The pentacular's booted foot whipped out, knocking Zin's legs out from under him; his dagger sailed into the darkness. In a flash the prisoner was upon him, snarling and biting. While Zin struggled to push him away, Gelasin attempted to dislodge him with a series of vicious kicks. Halyard wrapped an arm around the pentacular's neck to wrest him off Zin, but the pentacular head-butted him, bucked off the dazed courtesar, and sprang to his feet. Gelasin seized the assassin in a stranglehold from behind as Zin, now recovered, came at him with fists balled. Halyard, too, shook off his stupor. The pentacular dashed Gelasin against Zin, pinning them both against the wall until he broke Gelasin's grip, and brought a foot up to kick Halyard in the chest. The courtesar grabbed his foot and yanked him to the floor, whereupon Zin pounced upon the prisoner, stomping him amidst gales of maniacal laughter.

"Smile now, you bastard!" Zin crowed as he continued to rain down blows.

"Stop!" Antonben yelled, drawing her sword. "Stop this instant!" Zin, with a disdainful glance, obliged—but not before getting in one last kick to the assassin's head. The grin, which hadn't left his face throughout the fracas, was gone now.

"Easy, Zin," said Gelasin, panting. "We don't want to kill him."

Zin snorted. "Maybe *you* don't."

Gelasin bent down level with the pentacular's face. "All right, you bastard, I trust you'll behave yourse—" A pink wad of spit struck him full in the face. Gelasin nonchalantly wiped it away with his sleeve. "Under any other circumstances I'd slit your damnable throat, but killing you is the last thing we'll do. We plan to keep you nice and healthy."

"You can plan whatever you want," the assassin said, straining against his bonds. "But I'll die soon enough. Our covenant will be honored, and my successor will kill your mistress." His murderous glance sent a shiver through Drinith. "How long do you think you can keep me alive without food and water? I haven't eaten or drunk for more than a day already."

"Don't worry," Gelasin said. "We'll hack off your jaw and pour soup down your gullet if we must. We'll make sure your life is long and painful."

A wave of nausea overwhelmed Drinith. Halyard's clenching jaw made clear that he shared her disgust. The assassin only smiled.

Antonben opened a stout wooden door with a small grille. "This is our brig. You can put him in here," she said, still livid. "There's a dragon spine sticking through the floor. You can use bunk webbing to secure him to it."

"You heard the saddlemaster," Gelasin said. "Get this piece of dung inside. Zin, you're first watch. If he gives you any trouble, I don't care what part of him you lop off, provided he's still breathing."

Zin poked his recovered dagger at the assassin's crotch. "I think I know just the spot."

Antonben slapped the weapon away. Zin glowered at her. "I don't trust this man," she said. "Two of my crew will join him."

"Whatever you say, *sir*," said Zin pointedly. "The more the merrier."

The moment Halyard and Zin bundled the assassin inside, Antonben stalked over to Gelasin. "I want to make something clear," she said. "I won't tolerate the torture of a prisoner. If you attempt to carry out your threats, don't think we won't stop you."

Gelasin raised his hands. "I was just playing mind games with him. It was all a bit of bluster to encourage him to behave. All his like understands is violence. They're like pyrates."

Antonben's eyes narrowed. "That had better be the extent of it," she said, striding away. "But I'm still posting those guards—more to keep an eye on your deranged cohort than the assassin."

Gelasin marked her disappearance through the hatch with a grim chuckle. "She has some cheek to accuse me of cruelty. I could tell she didn't like my jibe about pyrates. The gentlest punishment drakers mete out to any pyrates they catch is to make them walk their dragon's tail until they freeze and plummet to their deaths."

Two surly drakers armed with swords descended the ladder and tromped into the brig.

"You didn't mean those threats you made," Drinith said, hoping Gelasin would agree.

His mouth set in a grim line. "Princess, if you don't mind me saying so, you're making two mistakes. The first is you're assuming because the assassin's been captured, he's no longer a threat. I guarantee you behind all that talk of martyrdom he hardly took any notice of what I said because he's so preoccupied working out how he can engineer another opportunity to kill you.

"Your second error is in assuming because he looks human, he's not a monster. He isn't even a person. He's an amalgam, a blend of five men who sacrificed their individuality to kill you. After the pentaculars kill their victim, the survivors hunt each other until one remains. He lives like a deity for five lifetimes. All you are to him is a sacrifice to facilitate his temporary godhood."

"You're missing the point. It's not about him. It's about us and what we stand for." Irritation crept into her voice. "We have to be better than Magian and his ilk. Otherwise, why bother?"

The bemusement on Gelasin's face faded into dull resignation. "I wouldn't serve you if you were like Magian. But he didn't conquer Rhumgad through moral superiority. He won because he did whatever he needed to win, and he did it better than his enemies." He squeezed his eyes shut and rubbed the bridge of his nose with his thumb and finger. Looking at her again, he sighed and said, "But if it is your will—"

"It is," Drinith said firmly.

"Then I must comply. I won't harm the pentacular."

Drinith was pleased; she had rarely gotten the better of the wily old warrior in an argument. "And tell Zin if he ignores my instructions, he'll be looking for a new employer. That is a promise, not a threat!"

Gelasin's eyes flew wide. "Zin might be a bit temperamental, but he's my best man. I need him."

"Then, you had better make sure he behaves. He is, as Antonben aptly observed, deranged. If he should harm, or worse, kill the pentacular, I shall hold you responsible."

Gelasin flashed his dented grin. "I get the message, Your Highness. You've changed since you fought the first pentacular. For the better. I'll tell Zin straight away." As he entered the compartment, Epmar descended the ladder.

"Did you hear any of that?" Drinith asked.

Epmar nodded. "Most of it." She patted Drinith's forearm. "It's not easy to rein in a stubborn mule like him."

"I had to," Drinith said. "I can't be party to torture. I simply won't."

Epmar gave a subtle nod. "You've chosen a difficult path in life."

"It was chosen for me," Drinith said bitterly. "Magian chose it. He has hunted me since I was a baby. While he rules Rhumgad, I'll never be safe."

"I don't know," Epmar said. "The Crevast is a big place. You could disappear. That gem on your forehead could pay for a quiet life on some distant shard."

Drinith stroked the jewel. "Forsaking my mission might be the saner course, but it's not one I could ever take. It's as much a part of me as this gem." She had never regarded her life through any other lens.

"Of course," Epmar said. "Believe me, I understand. I've let my heart rule my head on more than one occasion. You must prepare yourself for disappointment in Gyre. I can't be certain if the meritocrats I wrote to on your behalf remain the heads of their families. Even if they are, and they deign to offer you help, it is unlikely to extend to going to war with Rhumgad. I wish I could do more..." She smiled demurely.

Drinith patted her shoulder fondly. "Your help has been a boon to me, Epmar."

Gelasin emerged, still grinning. "I told Zin he'd better be on his best behavior. To be honest, if the pentacular knew of your magnanimity, I doubt he'd appreciate it."

"I don't care whether he does or not," Drinith said.

A clarion yell reached them through the open hatch. "Dragon pyrates!"

"So much for Pinchel's talk of a smooth journey," Gelasin muttered.

Drinith's heart sank. It was too much of a coincidence. If the pyrates were servants of Magian, then she'd be the only prize they'd want from the *Surly Bonnacon*.

"I need to find out exactly what's happening up there," Gelasin declared, racing up the ladder, Drinith close on his heels.

They found Antonben on the deck staring down a spyglass at what appeared to be a bright star.

"I hear we have company," Gelasin said. "Pyrates."

"They're flying bones on a black flag," Antonben said.

"It wouldn't be a tree of bones, would it?" Gelasin asked. Magian's emblem would be incontrovertible proof of his involvement.

"No," Antonben said, lowering the spyglass. "It's a flower with a skull at the center. The notorious pyrate, Planked Shad, flies that flag. The dragon fits the description of his *Demon's Breath*."

Antonben peered again through the spyglass. "He's flashing a signal at us." She tossed her head back and laughed. "He's offering clemency if we surrender. His word isn't worth a spit over the side. If he took Surly, his promises would quickly slip his mind." She slapped her hands against the bulwark. "Where's the rest of his flock? The last I heard, he traveled with a half-dozen dragons." She shrugged. "Who knows? Maybe they got scattered by a storm or took on somebody too big for them. Or Planked Shad's crew mutinied. There are a hundred reasons a pyrate king's fleet could fall apart."

The deck tilted as the *Surly Bonnacon* banked to the left, impelling Drinith and Gelasin to anchor their forgotten lanyards with some urgency.

"Pinchel will try to outrun him," Antonben said. "See, we're already taking evasive action."

"But there was a cloud bank up ahead," Gelasin said in disbelief. "We could have hidden in it."

Antonben smirked. "It's what else might hide there that's the problem. Like I said, Planked Shad normally doesn't travel with only one dragon. Surly's fast. She can outrun the *Demon's Breath*. Trust my father. He knows what he's doing."

"But if your dragon can't, what happens then?" Gelasin asked.

Antonben grinned. "Then we'll outfight her. These aren't the first pyrates we've dealt with." She bellowed orders at the saddledeck crew. While they trimmed the sails, Drinith and Gelasin watched the distant dragon. The bright speck mesmerized Drinith. It appeared to shrink, only to expand again moments later. Hope wavered with every fluctuation until *Demon's Breath* took shape, ending all doubt that it was closing fast.

"I've never witnessed a dragon battle before," Gelasin said. "At least, not on the wing."

"You had better get below and strap in!" Antonben hollered. "This will get rough!"

"Much as I'd love to stay and watch, she's right," Gelasin said. "Come on."

Reluctantly, Drinith followed him below deck. As she descended the ladder, she stared up at the patch of sky boxed by the hatch. She had never noticed how small it was before. The sudden slap of the lid made her shudder. She was as much a prisoner as the pentacular, her fate in the hands of Surly's crew.

15

———————

Quiescat shifted on his hard seat. Outside, rigging squealed to Antonben's barked orders. The dragon's wings beat faster. Something must be happening. Abecedar had left him alone to investigate but had yet to return. How long could it possibly take him? Being blind was bad enough, but to be left in suspense infuriated Quiescat.

He'd have to discover the answer for himself. Unhooking his harness, he rose uncertainly to his feet. The dragon's sudden shudder sent him wobbling across the cabin. He slapped a hand onto an unseen wall that prevented him from falling. The exit must be somewhere to his right. He teetered toward it with outstretched hands, fearful of being thrown in another random direction. He winced as he touched the smooth, cold glass of the window. He had headed in the wrong direction. He turned at a right angle only to bump his knee against a low wooden bench. Reaching for it, he patted soft bedding. It had to be a bunk.

The door creaked open. The stench of stale puke assailed his nostrils.

"What's happening?" Quiescat demanded.

"Abecedar asked me to look in on you," Prosper said, sounding as though he might vomit again. "It seems we're being pursued by pyrates."

"Gods!" Quiescat exclaimed. Hadn't he suffered enough trauma for one day? "Can we outdistance them?"

"They are closing, but Abecedar is confident we can drive them off."

What would Abecedar know about dragon warfare? He was probably just trying to bolster Prosper's delicate nerves. "What did he say?"

Prosper gulped audibly. "He gave me a letter to give to you after the threat had passed."

Quiescat's hair stood on end. Something terrible was about to happen—Abecedar's second vision. "Read it!"

"I'm sorry, Quiescat, he said—"

Quiescat lunged and seized two satisfying balls of coat fabric. He pinned the trembling, gasping man to the wall.

"Read the damned letter, I said!"

"I made a solemn vow by the gods of Rhumgad that I wouldn't place it in your possession until the fighting had ended."

Quiescat fought the urge to punch him, afraid the little eel-like man would slip from his grasp as soon as he loosened it. The rolling thunder of cannon fire sent a shiver through both men.

"D-do you think those c-cannons are ours or t-theirs?" Prosper stammered.

As if in answer, a thunderous crack shook the walls, followed by the reports from much nearer cannons. Falling dust from the cabin's ceiling tickled Quiescat's face.

Quiescat closed his empty eyes and took a deep breath to quell his rage. He forced himself to let Prosper go. "I'm sorry. I shouldn't have done that."

"I understand," Prosper said. "I swear to you, I don't know what the letter says. It's sealed in an envelope."

"Abecedar was wrong to thrust you into this position. I understand you must not break your oath to the gods, but lives may depend on the contents of that letter. Tell me what you promised him

—the exact words." He could barely hear himself over the din coming from the upper deck. From the shouts, the pyrates might already be on board.

"I swore to deliver the letter to you after the battle," Prosper said.

"Are you sure that was the extent of your oath?"

"Absolutely."

"Then you didn't promise not to show it to others in the meantime. Give it to Gelasin or Drinith." He clasped his hands together. "Please."

Prosper bolted away, mumbling something unintelligible as the door whined open. The smoke sweeping through the cabin made Quiescat cough. The door slammed shut, deadening the noise outside again, but the smoke lingered.

Panic gripped him. Had Prosper hurried to warn the others, or had he fled in terror? What could be in the letter? If Abecedar wrote it, it could only be because he wouldn't be able to communicate any other way. If he died, the gift would die with him.

A loud bang made the cabin shudder. Falling objects clattered around Quiescat. A terrible yawning creak, like a falling tree, ended with a loud crash. The door squealed open.

"Prosper? Abecedar?"

No answer.

It had been a mistake to send Prosper alone out into that chaos. As dangerous as blundering blindly about might be, Quiescat couldn't sit here. He must seek someone, anyone, who could help him find Abecedar. Quiescat stumbled over to the doorway only to find the passage blocked with a jumble of rope, torn sail, and smashed timber. He tried to wrench a large piece of wood from the pile, but it wouldn't budge. Suddenly the room spun, sending him flying. He slammed against the floor or the ceiling or a wall, he couldn't tell which. Forewarned by the clatter of shifting debris, he threw his arms over his head as random objects rained down.

16

———————

Drinith squeezed the hilt of her sheathed knife as her cocoon of protective netting danced along to the pitched battle rocking the *Surly Bonnacon*. She needed it to cut her way out of this spider's web and to defend herself from any pyrate who might find their way below decks. She didn't trust she could undo all those clasps securing her in this tangled mess fast enough in an emergency.

Glancing about the room, every face echoed her fear. Halyard and Epmar held hands with quiet resignation. Jarma winced at every jolt. Gelasin alone smiled, but the manic gleam in his eyes proclaimed that he did so out of spite. Fear was just another enemy for him to fight and defeat.

A shadowy figure blundered through the open doorway. Drinith's damp hands fumbled to open the clasps. One jammed. She stabbed her knife in it and tried to pry it open. Halyard and Gelasin had already thrown off their nets and rushed with naked swords at the intruder.

"It's me!" Prosper squeaked, raising his hands. "Don't hurt me!"

Finally the clasp snapped open and Drinith slid awkwardly out of the net.

Keeping one hand raised, Prosper warily pulled out an envelope with the other. "Quiescat asked me to give this to you." He waved it uncertainly between Drinith and Gelasin.

Gelasin snatched it from him. "I'll read it." He tore open the envelope and stared down at the letter. "Everyone, pair up! We have to find Abecedar and Versifer now!" He leaned close to Drinith and whispered. "Abecedar predicted—"

A loud bang threw them across the room. Gelasin grabbed Drinith and took most of the blow as they slammed against the wall. The entire structure trembled and groaned. A series of loud snaps threatened its imminent collapse.

With an ear-splitting screech, Prosper buried his face in his hands. "The cinch is broken!" he wailed. "We're all going to fall into the abyss! We're doomed, doomed, *doomed!*"

"Shut up, you gibbering idiot!" Gelasin's backhanded slap dropped Prosper to the floor, where he lay whimpering. Gelasin glowered at the others, brandishing the letter like a weapon. "This says we'll all be fine. But Abecedar won't be if we don't find him. Jarma and Epmar, search headward." He plucked the cook off the floor. "Prosper, you can help them after you tell Zin what's happened. My advice is don't barf in that room or he's liable to toss you overboard. Halyard, check in the hold. Drinith, come with me. We'll look tailward."

Dodging wayward barrels on the tilting, quaking deck required fancy footwork on Gelasin and Drinith's part. Acrid smoke burned their lungs and stung their eyes. Against the cannons' roar and the creaking timbers, their shouts for Abecedar and Versifer might as well have been whispers.

Without warning a figure burst out from the smoky haze. A glancing blow sent Gelasin sprawling. A lampstone illuminated the attacker's bruised and lacerated face—the captured pentacular, somehow escaped. Drinith drew her knife as he inched toward her.

"I promise I'll be gentle," he said, grinning.

"Well, I sure as hell won't!"

The pentacular whirled around just as Zin barreled into him. The two tumbled to the floor in a heap, whereupon the pentacular shrugged off his foe as effortlessly as one might doff a cloak. Zin soared through the air and slapped headfirst against a stack of barrels with a pulpy smack. Gelasin stumbled to his feet, dagger drawn. The pentacular sprang up, grabbing him around the throat and pinning him against a wall. Gelasin stared down in amazement at his boots dangling two feet above the deck. His dagger spilled from his hand.

"Not so tough now, eh?" the pentacular hissed. Gelasin's eyes bulged; his tongue lolled out grotesquely.

"Let him go!" cried Drinith. As she closed on the assassin, his homicidal grin turned toward her. He swatted her away, delivering a stunning slap with his free hand. She stumbled backward and tripped over the insensate Zin, but piled canvas sacks arrested her fall.

"I'll be with you in a moment, Princess," the pentacular said, "as soon as I finished off this wriggly maggot."

Gelasin's double ear slap brought the assassin to his knees. Gelasin crumpled to the floor like a sodden scarecrow. "Run, Drinith," he croaked. "Run!"

His hoarse cry cut through her daze and she fled toward the hatch to the saddledeck. Already the pentacular staggered after her. If she could reach the saddledeck, the drakers up there might help her.

She skidded on the greasy floor but kept her balance. She reached the ladder and climbed. An iron hand gripped her leg and wrenched her off, banging her forehead off two rungs. She kicked her free foot at the pentacular's hand. She bent forward and swiped her knife at him but, laughing, he smacked it out of her hand.

As he reached down to seize it, a cowled figure burst from the shadows and leapt upon him, seizing him around the waist. The pentacular turned Drinith's blade on his assailant who fell with a yelp. Drinith pulled free of the assassin's grip and crawled up the ladder again. The frantic yells of Antonben and her mates promised safety if she could climb through that square of smoky sky.

The pentacular wrapped his hand around the back of her neck, his fingers digging into its muscles, and lifted her. As he twisted her around, he raised the bloody knife to strike.

A meaty crunch cut through the tumult of battle. His face slackened. His whole body shuddered. Drinith slipped from his loosening grip and landed beside the ladder. She crawled to get clear of his toppling body, but his crushing weight landed on her. Zin leered down as she wriggled from under the dead assassin. Blood gushed from where the hilt of a dagger jutted out of the back of the assassin's neck.

"Did you have to kill him? We needed him alive," Gelasin muttered as he hobbled over to them.

Zin's tone reeked of lecherous sarcasm as he pressed the dead man down with his foot and yanked his dagger free. "I'd much rather have our princess alive than dead." He offered Drinith his hand; she spurned it, clambering to her feet using a wall for support, much to his amusement. "You seem upset with me, Your Highness. Should I have let you deal with the pentacular alone?"

"Thank you for your help," Drinith said, poorly concealing her dislike.

"How in the bowels of Empyrosis did the pentacular escape?" Gelasin asked.

"The two drakers assigned to help me ran off as soon as the battle started," Zin said. "A cannonball smashed through the wall and snapped the dragon spine holding our friend here. It momentarily stunned me. The cook died trying to stop him."

"Prosper was never much of a warrior, but he was a good man," Gelasin said. "And brave."

Trembling, Drinith approached the corpse of their mysterious helper. Two empty eye cavities stared up at her. "Quiescat!" So he had only cheated Fate for a day. But it couldn't be him. The face was too young. She fell to her knees. "No...Abecedar."

Gelasin's hand rested on her shoulder. "Zin, stay here with Drinith. I'll find Versifer."

The hand lifted away. A chill shivered through her as Gelasin melted into the darkness. She risked a glance at Zin. The left side of his blood-spattered jaw was discolored and swollen. His predatory gaze bored into her, forcing her to look away.

"I hope my jaw isn't broken," Zin said. "Wouldn't want to ruin my good looks."

The whole structure tilted vertically. Drinith and Zin exchanged a last look of horror. Too late they lunged for each other's hand as they skidded down the deck, the corpses tumbling after them like rag dolls.

Her hands scrabbled against the smooth wood until she seized the jamb of a door. Above her on the opposite side, Zin hung on in a similar precarious manner as Abecedar and the pentacular slid into the smoky gloom. All she could do was tighten her grip and hope this upheaval, whatever it was, didn't fling her into the steepening darkness.

17

The snarl of debris blocking Quiescat's exit groaned as it shifted. A howling wind rampaged through the cabin, violently flapping his cowl. Objects thumped and smashed around him. He banged his shins against low furniture sliding across the room. He reached out until he touched a wall, patted it in vain for an anchor point. The door slammed repeatedly until it finally smashed itself apart.

Gradually the madness swirling around him subsided. The pull of gravity shifted, and he slid down one surface to stand on another. The wind had diminished to a cold whisper, but he couldn't tell from which direction it came. He didn't dare move in case he accidentally stepped through the window. An eerie stillness settled over the cabin, in its way as terrible as the preceding chaos. For all he knew, the saddledeck might be plummeting alone into the inner sun. Blindness might be a mercy.

No, he had no sense of falling. The fear ebbed, and an awful loneliness weighed upon him. *Might I be the sole survivor?* he wondered. *If only I had made Prosper read me Abecedar's letter. I should have never depended on him. What if he fell into the abyss before he could deliver it? Drinith might be dead now because Abecedar's warning never reached her or Gelasin.*

"Hello," he ventured timorously. "Hello! Anybody there?"

A chorus of cheers answered—rescuers happy to have discovered a survivor.

"Hello!" he called again, cupping his mouth with his hands.

Footsteps. "Are you hurt in there?" It was Antonben; he'd know her fluty tones anywhere.

"I'm fine!" As far as he could tell it was true, aside from this insufferable tremble plaguing his entire body.

"We'll get you out. Don't worry. Clear the entrance!"

He listened helplessly to the grunts of his rescuers and the scrape of the debris as they yanked it clear.

"Good to see you survived in one piece," Antonben said as she crunched across the glass-littered floor. "You're nearly the only thing in here that did. Was there anyone else with you?"

"Prosper went to find the princess," Quiescat said.

"Prosper?"

"The thin man, the one always getting sick."

"Ah, yes. He made it below deck."

"Thank the gods," Quiescat said, though the revelation brought little relief.

"I can't say what happened to him after that, I'm afraid."

"And my other companions?"

"I sent two drakers to check on them. They should be fine as long as they wrapped themselves in their webs."

Antonben was right. Gelasin would have seen to it. But the knot of tension in Quiescat's chest tightened. It wouldn't unravel until he knew the others were alive.

"Is the battle over?" he asked.

"We lost at least six of the crew," she said as she helped him onto a seat. "The mainmast and mizzen are broken, and the saddledeck is holed in a few places, but, yes, we won thanks to my father, Captain Pinchel. He flew Surly straight up. Fortunately, the pyrates took the bait and followed. Once they were below, he had the *Surly Bonnacon* dump her dung on her pursuer! Dragon dung's very flammable. That's why it's one of the principal ingredients for cannon powder. The *Demon's Breath* turned to flee, but Pinchel strafed it with Surly's flame. The *Demon's Breath* is burning now, and its crew is dead."

"That's ironic given your dragon is named after a creature that uses its dung as a weapon," Quiescat said.

"It's not a coincidence," Antonben said, her voice brimming with pride. "My father has used this trick before. There's talk of claiming the *Demon's Breath*. That's if we can catch her with only one sail, of course."

"But will the fire not kill it?" Quiescat asked.

Antonben laughed. "She might be a bit scorched and a little out of sorts because of it, but it would take all the flames of Empyrosis to kill a dragon."

A male draker murmured something Quiescat couldn't quite catch.

"I'll be back in a while," Antonben said. Quiescat felt a slight tug on his lanyard as she hooked it onto the anchor point with a click.

"Thank you," he said. "You are most kind."

"My pleasure. Back soon."

Quiescat waited. And waited still longer; his agitation increasing with every passing moment.

"You survived again." Gelasin's gruff voice made him jump. "Fate mustn't like the taste of you."

Quiescat stood. "Drinith? Is she—"

"She's fine. But we lost Prosper...and Abecedar."

All the strength drained from Quiescat. His legs turned to jelly. He clutched the air for something to hold on to. He felt Gelasin's strong hands grab him.

"Easy there," he said. "You'd better sit down."

Quiescat let the warrior steer him back onto the seat. He had failed Abecedar. If he had been a better teacher, if he had prepared his successor better, if he hadn't permitted his arrogance to come between them, Abecedar might still be alive. Abecedar had saved him, and Quiescat had vilified him for his generosity. And now it was too late to make amends. Abecedar was dead.

And the gift had died with him. Quiescat's stomach roiled at the realization. The first duty of the Oracle of Godsdoor was to preserve the gift.

"There's something else. Before he perished, Abecedar transferred the Tear of Fate."

The gift still survived! "To whom?"

"The poet."

This was good; they had been friends, and at least Versifer was a learned man of some refinement.

"Would you like me to read the letter Abecedar wrote to you?"

So Prosper had delivered the letter successfully. Fear clawed at Quiescat's throat, but he needed to know the letter's contents. He nodded.

Gelasin cleared his throat. "It begins... My master."

Quiescat fought the urge to weep as pride mingled with guilt at being addressed so reverently by his successor. He stifled a sob.

"Do you want to continue?"

"Yes," Quiescat said, blinking away tears. "Please."

"Forgive me for this second impertinence. I could not afford for you to meddle in my death as I meddled in yours. The knowledge that my successor, Versifer, has you to guide him is the only reason I have the strength to face my end. I carried the terrible burden of the gift for only a short time, a moment compared to you, and I know your wisdom will help poor Versifer more than my inexperience could ever do.

"Yes, duty made me rescue you from your preordained death, but I also rejoiced in your salvation. In the past, I regarded you as my mentor, my rival, and even my enemy, but now I look upon you as my friend and brother. I beg you to forget my many faults and failings and remember me with the same affection.

"Your acolyte, Abecedar."

"Where's Versifer now?" Quiescat croaked.

"In the saddlemaster's cabin. He seems to suffer the same

disorientation as Abecedar after receiving the Tear of Fate. Otherwise, he's uninjured."

Quiescat knew he should go to him, but he had to rein in his grief first. "Give me a few moments alone, would you? This is a lot to absorb." Tears pooled in the hollows of his eyes.

"Of course," Gelasin said.

Quiescat held his breath until the warrior's retreating steps faded. Then, he broke down and wept openly and unashamedly, letting his grief, leavened with a certain relief, wash over him in a cleansing wave. He had been so utterly wrong about Abecedar, about everything. And yet Versifer provided hope. Perhaps, through him, Quiescat might yet make amends for his past failings.

18

Drinith stood patiently beside one eyeless man as he shed silent tears over the corpse of another. "Versifer needs you," she said softly. The poet lay unconscious in the saddlemaster's cabin, in Epmar's care.

"You're right. I should go," Quiescat said, but he did not leave. He just sat where he was and wept.

Everything damaged had been removed from the cabin, leaving it bare except for the bed and chair. The smashed window had been boarded up, casting a somber gloom over everything. The only light entering the room crept through the broken door. Not much of it remained beyond a couple of planks clinging bravely to a hinge.

Antonben filled the doorway and knocked on a jamb. "Apologies for interrupting," she said, "but we must deliver your dead friends to the void as soon as we have dealt with our own."

"What sacrilege is this!" Quiescat exclaimed.

"It's our custom to return the dead to the inner sun from whence all life came."

Quiescat bolted upright. "That's not our tradition. This man here"—he pointed at Abecedar's midriff—"is one of a long line of oracles. By rights, he should be immersed in red incindar resin and returned..." He gasped for breath.

"Calm yourself," Drinith pleaded.

"He deserves more than being tipped over the side. He deserves a proper burial in a proper grave. He deserves a mausoleum."

"And your other friend, the cook, does he deserve a mausoleum too?" Antonben asked with a hint of sarcasm.

Quiescat had no answer beyond a sputter.

"Thought not," Antonben said. "We treat everyone the same way in death. You're no longer a landlubber out here once you're a corpse. If you wish to honor your friend, then treat his funeral with the dignity it deserves and make no trouble when we commit him to the inner sun."

He replied with a solemn nod, but the instant she left, he threw himself down upon the corpse, landing across the legs, and wept. He crawled up the body until he found Abecedar's forehead and kissed it.

Quiescat punched the dead man's shoulder. "It should be me lying in this bed," he wailed, "not you!"

He wasn't accustomed to such outpourings of emotion. He'd regret it later, particularly if others witnessed him in this state.

Drinith rested her hands on Quiescat's shoulders and gently guided him back to his seat.

Gelasin entered. "Your Highness," he said, nodding to Drinith. Zin and Halyard stood behind him, carrying folded sheets. "We're here to prepare Abecedar for the funeral," Gelasin said. "The room must be cleared."

"I'm staying," Quiescat said, wiping the tears from his face.

Gelasin grimaced. "It's a bit cramped for us to do what we must."

"I'm sure you can manage," said Quiescat haughtily. "Drinith, you can leave. I shouldn't need anything, but if I do, I'm sure Gelasin can get it."

"She can't go off wandering by herself," Zin murmured to Gelasin.

Halyard squeezed by them and, laying his sheets on the corner of the bed, crouched beside Quiescat and rested a hand on his shoulder.

"You have my word that Abecedar will be treated with the utmost respect. Funereal etiquette is something every courtesar understands."

"Of course." Quiescat sniffed. "I'll leave you to it. Drinith, would you mind escorting me to Versifer?"

"Gladly." Drinith guided him past Gelasin and the others toward the exit.

Gelasin said, "One moment, Your Highness. The service for the dead drakers will take place first. I thought you might like to attend. Epmar can mind Quiescat."

"I'd like to attend too," said Quiescat. "It would be churlish not to, given we benefited from their sacrifice."

Drinith led Quiescat into the neighboring cabin. Versifer lay so still on the bed he might have been another corpse. Epmar, bespectacled, looked up from her book and shook her head. "No change, I'm afraid." She vacated her seat, whereupon Quiescat sat down in a mournful hunch.

Shuffling feet and furtive whispers beyond the door disturbed the watchful silence.

"I should go and see what's happening," Drinith said, nervous that Quiescat would insist on investigating.

"No need," he said. "Halyard gave his word everything would be handled properly."

Epmar smiled.

The noise faded away and they sat again in silence. Crisp footsteps heralded Gelasin's entrance. "It's time to go."

The saddledeck looked bare, with only the foremast intact and the others reduced to jagged stumps. Jarma, Halyard, and Zin had already joined the crew on the saddledeck.

Six corpses, including Abecedar and Prosper, had been laid in a neat row, their pallid faces peeping out from cocoons of blankets. Two other drakers were missing, knocked overboard and presumed to have plummeted to their deaths. Antonben called out each of the drakers' names and invited anyone in the crew to come forward to extol their virtues. If nobody volunteered, she delivered the eulogy herself. The crew greeted the end of each speech with applause. The corpse rested in a chute until everyone who wished to had said their piece, whereupon it was dropped into the void. Antonben made a subtle signal to the whereabout. Moments later, the dragon let out a mournful roar as if it lamented the death of these fleas on its back. The crew answered with cheers.

"They had better not do that when Abecedar's turn comes," Quiescat muttered under his breath. Thankfully, only Drinith heard him. The drakers would not take kindly to his disapproval of their obsequies.

Antonben announced that in most cases, the possessions of the dead drakers would be returned to their families. There was one exception who had no blood relations. The crew would divvy up his property by lot.

"What of the dead passengers?" one of her crew asked. "Are we not going to send them to the inner sun?"

"Of course, Threem," Antonben said. "Remember, landlubbers don't understand the void as we do and consider silence the height of respect, so please don't cheer when the dragon roars, as they might find it offensive."

"Might?" Quiescat grunted.

As drakers placed Prosper on the chute, the placidity on his face was so out of step with the living man that the reality of his death struck Drinith. Falling into the void had been his worst nightmare.

"Who will speak for this man?" Antonben cried.

Drinith shot up her hand. "I will."

With Halyard taking Quiescat's hand for support, she stepped forward. "Prosper Destil had once been the richest banker on Rhumgad, but he maintained that after he lost his fortune, he became a better man. I'll remember him as great one. This is a sad end for him. Not the one he would have ever chosen. Everyone knew him to be kind, but he had courage, too, despite the impression he sometimes gave. And he was loyal. His loyalty got him killed." *How many more of my friends will die for me?* The appreciative clapping of the drakers discomfited her.

"Somebody should say a prayer," Gelasin said.

Squeezing Halyard's arm, Quiescat murmured, "Guide me to him." The courtesar gently steered them both forward. Quiescat recited a prayer to the god of pilgrims, Grinere. Prosper slid down the chute and disappeared into the void. Everybody maintained a respectful silence as the dragon saluted.

As the drakers lifted Abecedar onto the chute, Gelasin turned to Quiescat, saying, "I suppose you want to say a few words for your successor."

"It should be Abecedar standing here, eulogizing me," Quiescat said. "This is an unnatural and unprecedented situation. He was a braver man than me and history may remember him as the wiser. Certainly, more kept him in their hearts." Drinith glanced at Jarma. "He was more connected to his humanity than any of his predecessors, including me. That aspect of his character will remain with us." Quiescat raised his hand. "But we will miss him."

Jarma jerked forward. "I must speak." Her sweeping gaze brooked no refusal.

She approached the corpse and stroked Abecedar's cheek. Her every breath had a feverish quiver. "I loved him. He loved me, too, though he'd never dare say it. Duty came first." She glared at Quiescat. "His sense of duty made him sacrifice his humanity and then his life." Quiescat pursed his lips but kept silent. She trembled with such anger, Drinith readied to block her from attacking Quiescat. Jarma turned to the corpse. "Dear Abecedar, I give you freely what we denied ourselves while you lived." She kissed his lips and backed away, weeping.

As soon as Abecedar's body had been committed to the inner sun, Jarma fled to the lower deck, doubtless to find some secluded nook to wallow in her grief. Drinith moved to follow, but Gelasin blocked her. "Best leave her be for now," he whispered.

"My best friend needs me," she hissed back.

Gelasin arched an eyebrow. "Does she need Zin and Halyard observing her grief as well? Because you're going nowhere without them."

"This is intolerable."

Zin stood right behind her. Halyard, passing Quiescat's care to a draker, joined him.

"Don't blame me," Gelasin said with his most insufferable grin. "It's the fault of the pentaculars' paymaster."

Drinith watched the draker lead Quiescat back to his cabin. "The pentacular on board is dead," she reminded Gelasin.

"We can't assume he was the only one. We came too near losing you. I'm not taking any chances."

Antonben wormed through the dispersing crowd. "I must speak to you both. I've received communication from the headstall that may not be to the liking of your Gyran friends."

Drinith tensed. What further calamity was about to befall them?

"Spit it out," Gelasin said.

"As you've probably noticed, we've sustained a lot of damage, including the loss of two masts," Antonben said, folding her arms. "But our biggest source of worry is the damage to the cinch. If it breaks, we'll all drop into the void. It wouldn't be safe or wise to journey beyond Gyre in this condition. We'll have to perch there for a while, a red month or more."

"Epmar will not be happy," Halyard said.

Antonben opened her arms as she shrugged. "There's nothing I can do. I'm sorry."

"The Fire Emperor hired you to take us wherever we wanted to go," Drinith said.

"Whatever destination *you* desired, Your Highness," Antonben clarified, "not your retinue."

"But you agreed to take Epmar and Halyard to Laxur," Drinith said.

"Only if it was practical and safe. Laxur is no longer either. We must think of the well-being not only of Surly and her crew, but yours as well."

"Well, it appears we're not in a position to argue," Gelasin said. "How long will it take us to reach the Halcyon Republic?"

"Without sails, five days by my reckoning," Antonben said. She glanced at Halyard. "If you want to appeal to the captain directly, all you have to do is walk the length of the neck to the headstall." With a nod, the saddlemaster departed.

"Don't be a fool, Halyard," Gelasin said. "She's only joking."

"I had better go tell Epmar," Halyard said coldly.

"You do that," Gelasin said. He added, after Halyard's departure, "He's a big tough warrior except when it comes to his lady love. With her, he's a lapdog."

"I don't know why you put up with him," Zin said.

"Epmar and Halyard have always been loyal," Drinith insisted, resisting the urge to tell him to mind his own business.

Zin smirked. "But they are more loyal to each other."

She would have loved to contradict him, but Zin had a point. "I wish I knew why Epmar was so dead set against returning to her homeland."

"I'm sure we'll find out shortly," Gelasin said. "In the meantime, we had best prepare for our arrival in Gyre."

The bleak finality in his voice, perhaps imagined, made Drinith uncomfortable. "This will be our last chance, won't it?"

A pitted grin spread on his face. "Don't worry. You won't end up begging on the streets."

"Good," Drinith said stiffly. "I've heard Gyre isn't very hospitable to beggars."

19

———

Quiescat sat alone in his blindness, listening to Versifer's steady breath beyond the darkness. Antonben had moved them back into Quiescat's cabin. The poet now rested on the same bed Abecedar's corpse had lain upon, much to Quiescat's discomfort.

Versifer needed his help. He was the least prepared of any oracle, going back to the Larcener. Quiescat knew he mustn't repeat the same mistakes that had soured his relationship with Abecedar. He had learned his lesson in the most painful fashion. Abecedar had proved to be a worthy successor despite Quiescat, not because of him. He would approach Versifer's training with more humility and compassion.

The poet gasped awake as if rising from a great depth.

"You're okay. I'm here." Quiescat reached out a tremulous hand into the black void.

A moist hand clutched it. "Quiescat, thank the gods! Abecedar…"

"Gone. Swallowed by the Crevast," Quiescat said wearily.

"He told me he'd die. He said to tell you not to blame yourself."

Quiescat sighed. If only absolution was so easy. He tortured himself with second guesses about the myriad decisions that had brought about this tragedy.

"I had a dream," Versifer said.

Quiescat cringed. "Tell me."

"A man sits in a room with no walls. A hood hides his face. His limbs are twisted together in a great tangle. He shakes one hand as if to throw a die, but when he casts it, it's a crystal sphere that rolls across the floor. Snickering, he lifts his hood, exposing the laughing mask beneath it. Removing it, he reveals only an empty shadow."

"What do you mean by a room with no walls?"

"I don't know," Versifer said. "I just...felt it. I felt the room, though I couldn't see the walls."

Quiescat inhaled to speak, but Versifer continued. "There's more. The crystal rolls into another room full of male peacocks with shimmering scarlet plumage, the eyes of their fanned tails blood red like wounds. I watch them strut across the white marble floor, hooting proudly. Interspersed among them are the peahens—black with gold disks on their heads. The cocks hiss as they fold their trails. Feathers fly as they leap at each other, pecking and scratching, their long trains of feathers rustling behind them. The black peahens spring up onto gilded perches and emit honking laughter as they watch the fracas."

Quiescat kept silent, afraid to even breathe in case he missed a word. Suddenly parched, he patted the little table beside him until he found a goblet. He took a deep draught of its lukewarm water, wishing it was wine. "The vision ended with this fight?"

"When I realized I was dreaming, I panicked and woke up."

Versifer could have missed a critical part of the vision. Quiescat took a deep breath. The poet had undergone none of the training normally part of an oracle's preparation. "Every moment of a vision is critical, every nuance, every detail."

"I'm sorry," Versifer said.

Quiescat squeezed out a smile. "It's not your fault. I'll teach you a technique to avoid waking prematurely. You'll be ready the next time."

"I might have the same vision again."

"You might," Quiescat agreed.

"I'll endeavor not to awaken before the end the next time. What do you think the vision means?"

"It means…" *Your poetic sensibilities have infected the gift.* "I don't know what it means." How could he pick any meaning out of such phantasmagoric chaos? Who could this tangled man be? Perhaps Versifer himself. *It might even be me.* "Write it down," Quiescat urged. "Take your time and record every detail you can remember." Thank the gods, Versifer was a lettered man.

Quiescat gnawed his lower lip impatiently as the new oracle fumbled around the cabin for writing materials and scratched down his vision with vexing deliberation. A sudden sting warned Quiescat that his biting had drawn blood. He pulled out a handkerchief and pressed it to the cut until he couldn't feel any wetness when he rubbed it with his finger. Versifer's quill continued to scratch the parchment.

"Are you nearly finished?" Quiescat asked irritably.

The quill plopped in an inkpot. "About halfway," Versifer mumbled as the scratches resumed.

Quiescat sighed inwardly. The young man had none of the years of training he or Abecedar had undergone. He had the intelligence, but had he the temperament or the mental discipline? The question was irrelevant. Versifer was already the Oracle of Godsdoor. Quiescat would have to make do.

As soon as Versifer put his quill aside and declared his account finished, Quiescat had him read it. The poet paused a few times to correct an error or add a forgotten detail. Quiescat asked him to reread it repeatedly as he tried to puzzle out the vision's meaning.

He bowed his head and rubbed the back of his neck. The peacocks must represent the oligarchy of Gyre. The roosters were courtesars while the black peahens were meritocrats. Unable to make sense of the rest, he invited Versifer to offer his interpretation. After all, it was his vision. He must have some insight into its meaning.

"I don't know" Versifer admitted. "The imagery perplexes me."

The new door of the cabin shrieked worse than its predecessor as it swung open. "Apologies for interrupting," Drinith said, after a courtesy knock. "I just called to see if you needed anything."

"Drinith, please take me to Gelasin," Quiescat said, rising from his seat. "I need to speak to him. We must not disembark on Gyre."

"But the *Surly Bonnacon* will travel no farther. It must perch for a red month there for repairs."

Quiescat tottered. Drinith's hand steadied him. "Nonetheless, I must talk with Gelasin. Try to get back to sleep, Versifer. Perhaps you'll have another vision that will reveal more clues to this puzzle."

"I don't understand... Never mind. Stupid question."

"Go on—ask any questions you like, stupid or clever," Quiescat said with a smile. "I mightn't be able to answer the clever ones though."

"You were angry because Abecedar prevented your predestined death. If the visions must unfold as we see them, what use is understanding their meaning?"

"That's not a stupid question. On the contrary, it elevates you in my estimation. Two forms of vision exist. One form reveals actual snippets of the future. Until Abecedar saved me, the presumption was that they were fixed like stars in the night sky. You could only modify events around them. Of course, you can still miss details. For example, I saw Drinith's victory against the pentacular but not her wounding."

Quiescat rubbed the back of his head. "Your vision is the other form. It is a warning written in symbols. The interpretation of such visions is fraught with error and uncertainty, but if we can decode it, we can change the future." *Our lives may depend on it.*

"There's nothing I can do." As Gelasin spoke, the memory of his perforated grin nettled Quiescat. He couldn't recollect the warrior's face without it.

"Versifer's vision suggests great danger awaits us in Gyre."

"Great danger awaits everywhere. According to the drakers, the cinch won't hold much farther than the Halcyon Republic."

"Are you certain they're not overstating the danger?"

"They passed up a chance to chase the *Demon's Breath* because of it."

"I suppose I'm wasting my time arguing," Quiescat groused.

Gelasin's fading footsteps confirmed it. "We should all get some rest," he added as an afterthought from some distance away.

"Take me back to Versifer, please," Quiescat asked Drinith.

Halyard and Zin dutifully dogged their steps.

"Either of your escorts could take me back, Drinith," Quiescat said.

"Our orders are to follow her," Zin muttered.

Halyard insisted on checking the cabin before he let Drinith and Quiescat enter.

Versifer shifted on the bed. "You're back at last. I've had another vision. A different one."

Quiescat braced himself.

"Are you okay?" Drinith asked.

"Yes, yes," Quiescat said, patting her steadying hand. "Help me onto the chair, please. Then get some rest. It's not right for you to tend me like a servant. You're the future monarch of Kaplar and I..." *I'm nothing.* "Playing nursemaid is a job for Jarma or Epmar, not you."

Drinith sighed. "Jarma still grieves Abecedar. And Epmar is in a foul mood after learning she'll be forced to disembark at Gyre." The servants enjoyed more freedom than their mistress, picking and choosing their duties according to their whims. If Quiescat had been whole, he'd have never countenanced such behavior.

She gave his shoulder a sympathetic squeeze. "Goodnight to both of you."

As the door squealed shut behind her, Quiescat said to Versifer, "Well, tell me your vision, and spare no detail."

"A great cauldron simmers on a fire. Its rim is adorned with a snake swallowing its own tail. The chunks of wood beneath are shaped like dragons. As the cauldron comes to a boil, bubbles disturb its fizzing surface, each bearing a different distorted visage. There's something more: the tops of the bubbles are curved like talons. As they sink again, they whisper. I can't make out what they are saying. More and more bubbles rise until the faces become a froth, and their whispers expand into an impossible roar. Peering in, I spy a shadowy shape almost lost in the foam. It rises above the spitting churn. It is a hand and forearm, green-black, delicate and feminine. It belongs to Drinith."

"Do you know that for sure or are you supposing?" Quiescat growled.

"I'm certain it's her arm," Versifer said. "I can't explain how I know. I just feel it. There's more. The dragons beneath rise and the cauldron overturns, spilling its boiling waters across the floor. The draining water reveals a gleaming dagger. Its pommel has an amethyst engraved with a dragon's head."

"And then?"

"The vision ended and I woke up. Do you think it predicts...how Drinith will die?"

Quiescat's palms tingled with the urge to throw something. "Everything else in the vision is allegorical. Her arm must be allegorical too." The bubbles with talons had to be the meritocrats again. Yes, whatever its exact meaning, it again prophesied terrible danger for Drinith in Gyre. And Quiescat could do nothing to avoid it. Fate conspired to send her there.

———

Quiescat tossed and turned in the bed, unable to sleep. Damn this infernal blindness! It could have been any time of the day or night. This must be what it was like to be on the receiving end of the oracle's wisdom. Quiescat developed a creeping dread of every time Versifer broke the silence. What horror would he reveal next? What doom would he foretell?

"I've had another vision," Versifer declared.

Quiescat's heart sank. "Go on."

"I write gibberish symbols in red on an endless scroll. My quill runs dry. I use the wound in my chest to refill it. The sound of tearing paper makes me look up. The scroll festoons the sky, forming a gigantic web. Three shadows move across it like a three-legged spider until they settle around Drinith. Dressed as a bride, she struggles against invisible bonds. I move toward her on unseen wings. Gold symbols run down her face like tears. I rub one away, and it burns my fingers. I look around and the whole web is aflame. I turn back to Drinith but she's gone. Everything has disappeared and the Crevast stretches before me in all directions. I spot a glinting object hurtling downward. Distance makes me mistake a screaming woman for a twittering bird at first. Massive black dragon jaws emerge from the clouds and swallow her."

Quiescat sighed. "Write it down. Every word." Gibberish symbols? Three-legged spiders? How could anyone make sense of this preposterous nonsense? The rate at which Versifer had these visions was frightening. It was as if he was burning through the gift. Or the gift burned through him.

———

The next morning, Versifer left Quiescat alone to take the air on the saddledeck. Quiescat needed human contact as never before. The darkness was oppressive enough without empty silence making it unbearable. *I might as well be sitting in a tomb.*

He smiled as the door screeched open and Versifer blundered in. The chair beside him creaked as the oracle sat down. "Quiescat, I need your advice."

"Of course."

"Tell me about the power of the Tear to...bend perceptions."

Well, that was unexpected! "I'm surprised you know of that attribute of the gift. I only used it twice. The first time, a boy witnessed something he shouldn't have: an indiscretion by the King of Zadmy while on pilgrimage to Godsdoor. He was determined to kill the urchin, but I convinced him I could obliterate the memory. The king relented and I found a home for the boy." *And I never told you, Abecedar. You never knew what I took and what I gave to honor my word to an ignoble monarch long dead.*

"If it's too painful…"

"Painful or not, you need to understand. The second time happened while Drinith was a baby. I sent a man to his certain doom to save her from her pursuers, Magian's relentless hunters, the infamous Souldiviners. Both instances were matters of life and death. The subjects willingly submitted to my manipulation. It won't work otherwise. It can't be used against a person's will. Despite this, I struggled with terrible guilt over my part in both incidents, particularly the second. I forswore ever using that power again. The Tear certainly isn't something to be trifled with. What made you ask about it?"

"Jarma came to me," Versifer said nervously. "She begged me to help her forget Abecedar. I fear she's not in her right mind."

"The gift must not be used for trivial purposes."

"It's not a trivial matter for her. She's distraught."

Quiescat inhaled to object, thought better of it. "I suppose you're right. Take me to Jarma. I will do my best to comfort her and dissuade her from this dangerous notion."

"I don't think that would be a good idea," Versifer said. "She blames you for Abecedar's death."

Quiescat bristled. "Let her have a proper reason for her hate. Tell her I denied you the secret of the power."

"She won't be deterred so easily."

"Dissemble. Tell her you need time to work out how to do it without my help. In the meantime, discourage her from this course. You are supposedly a man of words. Use them."

That night, Quiescat burned with too much anger to sleep. His guilt was already heavy enough without Jarma adding her censure. Who was this maid to condemn him?

Sometime in the night, he drifted off to sleep only to be awakened by an insistent tug on his sleeve.

"What now?" he groaned.

Versifer's bedclothes rustled as he propped himself up. "I've had another vision." His voice trembled with excitement.

Quiescat nodded wearily.

"Three shadows of a man wax and ebb with the passing of three moons, but no man stands to cast them. Stars fall from the sky and become letters that litter the desert. The letters become blossoms and the flowers snap from their stems and flutter like butterflies across a shriveling landscape. They settle on the carcass of a dead mule. The air reverberates with the chitter of a million tiny jaws. When the butterflies rise again, they leave only gleaming bones and a grinning skull."

The three moons, Quiescat reckoned, must be a reference to Rhumgad. The shard had an extra moon, Bawror, a giant glass sphere that roamed above it alone. The three shadows were a motif repeated from Versifer's second vision. But what of the rest? Every vision only added more riddles. Quiescat couldn't even be sure the events they alluded to occurred in sequence. Unless they were all the products of a rambling imagination, or... "Have you taken any hallucinogens?"

Versifer guffawed.

"You can tell me. I won't be angry," Quiescat said, as if his opinion mattered.

"I admit to a past fondness for the dried petals of the hallucinogenic brine flower, palasgard—purely to enhance my verse, you understand. I haven't touched anything since I became the oracle. Things are weird enough as it is."

The missing part of the first vision might be the key to deciphering these puzzling images. "Have the first two visions repeated yet?" Quiescat demanded.

"No."

"Write it all down," Quiescat said. "Every detail. Omit nothing."

————

Versifer's visions haunted Quiescat, monopolized his thoughts. He learned their detail by heart and recounted them to himself over and over in a desperate attempt to parse their meaning. In normal circumstances that would be exclusively a task for the oracle, but poor Versifer was too bewildered to be of help.

No dreams disturbed Quiescat's fitful sleep. Mortal men dreamed, why couldn't he? Was even that scrap of comfort to be denied to him? The dead don't dream, and he had been marked for death.

Versifer had left him alone to wander the saddledeck when the door squealed open.

"Drinith?"

"Guess again," Jarma hissed. "You took the man I loved away from me and now you deny me the means to escape my grief at his loss. How cruel you are!"

Quiescat needed to be patient and gentle, two virtues that did not come easy to him. "Don't deny yourself those memories. In the end, they are all any of us have."

Jarma uttered a mild curse. "This sorrow is useless. I can't bring him back. I'm merely a maid, not a magician."

What sort of fantasy had she constructed around Abecedar? Did she think he would renounce his vow of celibacy and take her as his wife? She probably knew deep down that her dream was impossible, but she clung on to it. At least she had dreams.

"Some might have called me a magician once, but now I'm nothing. I look back upon my life and see only a litany of failures. I lost my temple. I broke hundreds of years of tradition I swore to uphold. I failed to save my successor. I couldn't even die when I was supposed to. Before Godsdoor burned down, I might have looked down on you because you're a servant, but I'm in no position to look down on anyone now.

"You're young. Your sorrow will heal, and you may love again. You have the consolation that Abecedar loved you. Why would I let Versifer take that away from you? Why would I help him change you into something less than you are? Forgetting is not the answer for your pain. Or mine, for that matter. For all my failures and disappointments, I'm a better man now than when kings and emperors knelt before me." The realization gratified him. In some small way, her loss mirrored his own. He had been in love with being the oracle. He had let his own vanity seduce him. "You and I are the two people who knew Abecedar best—"

"What nonsense you speak!" Jarma protested. "You didn't know him at all."

The charge stung. Quiescat had trained Abecedar since he sought sanctuary in the temple. He had watched him grow from a boy into a man. She knew him for only a handful of years. And yet he couldn't deny that she spoke the truth. Quiescat had been wrong about him. "All the more reason that you must remember him."

Having no better argument, Quiescat made no effort to stop her as she stormed out of the cabin.

Versifer returned soon after. "I've had another vision. It was bizarre, like falling asleep standing up."

"You didn't wake up in the middle of it again?"

"No. I don't think so," He didn't sound confident. "I'm sure I saw the vision right to the end."

"Tell me then."

"I see an endless midden. A cloaked figure so hunched I cannot see his head moves in its midst. He picks through the shells and bones and detritus. He spies a crystal eye in the rubbish's midst, he seizes it, studies it, mumbles to himself, and then throws it away. He finds another eye and tosses it away in the same fashion. The third eye he finds is set in a wedding band. As he studies it a bright light in the east makes him lift his head. In the sky, the crystal moon, Bawror, sweeps toward him, incinerating everything beneath it. He never moves, as though dazed by the approaching conflagration until it engulfs him."

Quiescat massaged his forehead. "Write it down." The presence of Bawror meant this vision must be set again on Rhumgad, but its meaning otherwise eluded him. Five dreams in three days, each one an impossible riddle. It was as if Fate mocked him with an obtuse jumble of portents. He might as well be the figure in the midden, scrounging for perception, finding only rubbish, oblivious to a terrible calamity drawing ever closer.

20

———————

As Drinith leaned against the wall of her compartment, the knotted web of rope pressing into her back shifted like writhing snakes. Even with Jarma and Gelasin on errands elsewhere, there were two too many crammed into the narrow space. At least Halyard had the grace to avert his gaze. Zin stared at her all the time. The glares she returned only seemed to stimulate his lechery. They were more like jailers than bodyguards. Gyre couldn't come soon enough. She'd get some privacy there even if she had to barricade herself into a room.

Jarma entered. Even in the dull light of the lampstone, the puffiness of her eyes was apparent.

"Is everything all right?" Drinith asked.

Jarma's red-rimmed eyes widened with feigned surprise. "Of course, Your Imperial Majesty," she rasped. She threw herself on her bunk and faced the wall.

"Leave us!" Drinith commanded.

Halyard moved toward the exit, but Zin blocked him with his arm. "Gelasin said we were to stay by your side at all times, Your Highness."

"He's not the one who pays your wages," Drinith snapped.

Zin smirked. "Funny, he's the one who gives us our coin. Not that he has given me anything other than promises for the last two red months."

Drinith's jaw slackened. She knew that they were close to being broke, but she had no inkling that she was in debt to the likes of Zin. She never wanted to owe that brute anything.

"Halyard, what about you?" she asked.

"I am owed the same."

Zin sneered. "I'm surprised your ladylove hasn't tackled Gelasin on this matter already."

"I haven't told her," Halyard said with a shrug. "What I'm paid for my service to the princess is my business. I can live off my savings for now."

Zin swore. "They've obviously been paying *you* too much."

"Come on, Zin," Halyard said gruffly. "Can't you see the princess needs some privacy? We'll be right outside, Your Highness. If you hear anyone boring through the bulkhead, call us."

With a scowl, Zin reluctantly slunk out the exit after him.

Drinith knelt beside Jarma. "Tell me what's wrong."

Jarma sat up and wiped the slivery sheen off her cheeks. "I feel a bit unwell. I need to go topside for a while."

Drinith held her arm. "Why have you been avoiding me?"

Jarma's jaw dropped. "Your Imperial Majesty, I have been nothing but polite to you."

Exactly. Nothing but. "I never said otherwise. But you must admit you've been behaving like my maid rather than my friend."

"I am your maid. That's why you pay me." She paused, adding sheepishly: "Or used to."

"How long haven't you been paid?" Drinith asked in alarm.

"Four red months. The money doesn't bother me. What would I spend it on? You provide me with board and lodging."

"That's not the point. You earned your wages. You're entitled to them. I'll speak to Gelasin about this. I promise." He had stopped paying Jarma earlier than the warriors, taking advantage of her loyalty. But Drinith knew that was not the primary source of Jarma's melancholy. "You mourn yet for Abecedar."

Jarma hid a new spasm of grief behind her hand.

"Would you like to talk about it?" Drinith asked, pressing a hand to her shoulder. "We've been friends for a long time. I hope you know you can confide in me."

Jarma smiled through her tears. "I had words with Quiescat. I wanted him to help Versifer make me forget Abecedar. His barbed truths wounded all the deeper because I could not deny them. I had been satisfied with being your maid before I fell in love with Abecedar. I was content to live in your shadow. He showed me I could be something more."

Drinith hid her dismay behind a smile. "I understand. You want to leave my service. I'll make sure Gelasin pays what you're owed, and I'll scrape together as much extra as I can to help you on your way."

Jarma grinned and patted Drinith's hand. "I would never abandon you. You're my closest friend. Gods, I've lost enough already without parting from you. Don't send me away."

Gelasin blundered in, interrupting their hug. "Hope I'm not disturbing anything."

"Just the man I wanted to see," Drinith said. "Why haven't you paid Zin, Jarma, and Halyard for months?" She led with Zin in the hope Gelasin would blame him for raising the matter.

"Because we have next to no money."

"And how do you propose we rectify this?"

"We continue to pay them with promises. Once we've secured a backer for our campaign against Magian, we can make good on our word."

"I don't want to owe Zin anything," Drinith said.

"You already do," Gelasin retorted. "And we need him. Unless your maid, who has already demonstrated her skill with an axe, intends to learn how to wield a sword."

"Jarma's no longer to be referred to as my maid. She's my companion. You can inform the others. As for Zin... Is he outside?"

"He had better be."

"I want him paid at the earliest opportunity."

"He'll be delighted to know you care so much about him," Gelasin said with a smirk.

"And if we don't secure a patron, what then?"

Gelasin rubbed his scars. "Then, we'll have to sell that jewel on your forehead."

The gem was the last bit of her homeland she possessed, the only physical connection to her heritage. It had been set in her forehead shortly after her birth. It would have to be surgically removed and the scar left by its amputation wouldn't be solely physical. It had become part of her, fused with her sense of self. "Quiescat was against selling it. He said we would never secure its true value."

"I would remind Your Highness we weren't facing penury back then. We'd get enough to keep us going a little longer. But it mightn't come to that. I've a good feeling about Gyre. It might very well change our fortunes for the better."

"I hope you're right."

Gelasin grinned. "So do I. Leave Zin to me. I'll sort him out." He strolled out the doorway.

"Gelasin made a valid point," Drinith said to Jarma. "You need to learn how to defend yourself. I'll teach you." *And you must teach me how to be a maid. The way things are going, that might become my future occupation if the pentaculars don't kill me before I go broke.*

———

The next morning, Drinith stood atop the saddledeck, staring at Gyre in the distance. The gleaming constellation on the virtual horizon gradually resolved into a haphazard pile of random-sized floating islands. Behind her, Zin's expansive yawn was a dismal reminder that he and Halyard continued to shadow her everywhere. The alcoholic reek on his breath confirmed her suspicion that he'd been sampling freely from the ruined rum barrels in the hold. He sat down against the bulwark.

"You don't want to behold Gyre in all its splendor?" Halyard asked.

Zin snorted. "I've seen it before."

"So have I," Halyard said. "But it's a sight I could never tire of."

Drinith was pleased when Zin's chin fell upon his chest, and a light snoring came from his cruel mouth. Gelasin's underling was only tolerable when he was asleep.

It was only as the *Surly Bonnacon* neared that the monstrous scale of the city could be appreciated. Pink buildings smothered the archipelago, spilling down its forbidding dusky yellow precipices. Atop a conical hill collared with smaller buildings, a gleaming white confection of interconnected towers stood.

"Is that the ducal palace?" she asked Halyard, pointing to it.

"That's the Grand Preservatory, Your Highness," he said. "The Ducal Palace and the Parliament of Merit are over there by Crimson Plaza." He indicated a cluster of palatial edifices looming over the rest of the city, dull yellow in color as though they had been hewn from the bedrock of the islands.

A web of silvery threads crisscrossing the islands resolved into aqueducts and bridges. And far beyond stretched the long, shimmery brushstroke of the continental shard, Noster, where much of Gyre's wealth was plundered.

"Pyrates founded it, didn't they?" she asked.

Halyard nodded. "The pyrate, Olmpeda Wealgiver, was its first queen. Her descendants ruled Gyre until the birth of the republic. Even today most meritorians are descended from her."

"I thought the rulers were called meritocrats."

"Meritocrats are indeed the heads of Gyre's leading families and sit in the Parliament of Merit," Halyard said, "but we refer to the other family members as meritorians."

"Are you a meritorian?" Drinith asked.

He shook his head vehemently. "I was born into the Kasjor family, but I'm a courtesar. I take no interest in finance or politics. My calling is my sword and my love."

Zin awakened with a snort. "By the gods, Halyard, you are a

windbag," he said, blinking the sleep from his baggy eyes. He rose and squinted ahead at their destination. "So we're almost there. About damn time."

"Beautiful, isn't she?" Halyard prompted.

A loud belch was Zin's only reply. Drinith eyed him with open contempt.

"Perhaps I must talk to Gelasin about your sleeping on the job," she said. "And for being drunk on duty, as well."

Zin idly dug in his ear with his pinkie, examined the foul harvest. "Do whatever you please, Your Highness. But just remember, you get what you pay for. And you've paid nothing for two red months."

Drinith ignored his raspy laughter.

Despite her misgivings, excitement stirred as the glittering city drew nearer. The chance Gyre offered might be her last, but it was real nonetheless, and she must seize it.

"We've come to join you for the perching," Versifer said as he led Quiescat by the arm toward them. Drinith could manage only a strained smile in response to Versifer's winsome grin. Before his transformation, she had been drawn to the handsome young man and delighted in his attention. She had even entertained idle dreams of taking him as a husband, though such a union was politically unfeasible while she claimed the throne of Kaplar. When she looked upon him now, she couldn't see beyond Quiescat's crystal eyes, and the memory of her former infatuation filled her with an embarrassing revulsion.

She turned her attention to the clusters of perches jutting from the cliff faces. Around them, sailed dragons swarmed, landing and taking flight. The harbor facilities dwarfed anything she had seen before. The meritocrats had the resources to help her, if not the desire.

Two black dragons with red sails flying the sunfinch emblem of Gyre swept toward the *Surly Bonnacon*, then turned to fly alongside her.

"I guess we've an escort," Versifer said.

A signal light on the dragon to the left blinked a message. It struck its sails while its companion banked to the right and sped away.

Epmar strode over to Halyard and squeezed his arm. "Home at last," she said without enthusiasm. Gelasin and Jarma joined them soon after. With exception of Quiescat, everyone stared at the nearing city with quiet apprehension. Even he looked uneasy.

Gelasin sidled up beside Drinith and whispered, "Don't worry. You won't end up begging on the streets. I know some people in the city who might help us."

She could see the ancient palaces and mansions of Gyre now, piled on top of one another. As the *Surly Bonnacon* drew close to a perch, the cliff face cut off Drinith's view. The dragon landed with a gentle bump and the air stilled as its wings folded. Its head drew back to the platform atop the whereabout, the so-called springboard. A half-dozen drakers, including Captain Pinchel, jumped down from the headstall while an equal number climbed inside it to replace them. The dragon's neck stretched out again into the distance and dipped out of view. Two platforms dropped on either side of the saddledeck and a gangplank slid down from one of them. Pinchel and Antonben summoned the drakers on deck as armored men in red livery trooped down it.

"Customs officers," Epmar whispered. Judging from the boxy springbows several of them carried, they were prepared for trouble.

"Welcome aboard, good sirs!" Pinchel said with all the warmth of an old friend as he bowed to their leader.

"I'm Senior Inspector Jyner," the officer said, lifting his chin so he could look further down on the diminutive captain. Most of his colleagues busied themselves searching the saddledeck with almost comical thoroughness while a few loitered behind him, doubtless watching the crew for any telltale hint of anxiety. "Where is your manifest?" He pinched the scroll Pinchel proffered between his thumb and forefinger and snatched it from his grasp. He unrolled the document and studied it with disgust. "According to this," he said, glowering at Pinchel, "you're traveling with little cargo. Not like your sort to travel the Crevast so empty."

"We ran into some pyrates. We had to lighten the load." Drinith was taken aback by the captain's explanation, but she remembered drakers telling similar white lies to smooth their passage through customs on other shards. Discovering that the emperors of Thirring had paid for the voyage would only deepen the senior inspector's suspicion, dragging out this interrogation, and perhaps getting the crew and passengers detained and the *Surly Bonnacon* impounded. Panic gripped her. The last thing she needed as her introduction to Gyre was to spend time in its jails.

Senior Inspector Jyner suspiciously eyed the broken masts that lent plausibility to Pinchel's excuse. He rolled up the scroll and waved it about. "Your manifest should have detailed your original cargo."

Pinchel smiled disarmingly and shrugged. "We lost the original document in the battle."

"How convenient. The date on the document suggests otherwise."

"An error on my part in redoing the manifest," Antonben said. "I was more focused on preparing a full and accurate description of my cargo and passengers than bureaucratic niceties such as dates."

"Our apologies." Pinchel bowed, pressing one hand to his chest, but as he straightened, he grinned up at the senior inspector. "I thought your function was to check what was on board, not what wasn't."

"My duty is to determine if your dragon is carrying contraband, contagion, invasive species, or subversives. And if I find any, I promise you'll be held personally responsible." Unrolling the manifest again, Jyner gave it a savage glance. "My team will search the saddle, cinch, and head. I also intend to formally interview your passengers, particularly this princess of Kaplar, a province of the Javlohm Empire on Rhumgad. Am I to understand she's a vassal of Magian the Infinite?"

"I know little about landlubber politics," Pinchel said. "My interest in any shard never strays beyond its ports. Perhaps her adviser could enlighten you." A flick of his head beckoned Gelasin over.

"My princess is the true heir of the Blood Crown of Kaplar," Gelasin said. "Magian is nothing more than a thief."

Jyner smirked. "So she's a pretender."

"You insult her, sir," Gelasin growled.

Drinith cringed. Jyner didn't strike her as the sort to forgive insolence. She stepped forward to speak on her own behalf only to be stayed by Zin's unyielding arm. Drinith shrank from his touch.

The senior inspector arched a brow. "Is that not what one calls a claimant to a throne?" He added with a simper, "If her realm awaits her in Rhumgad, why has she come to Gyre?"

"To seek the meritocrats' support in vindicating her claim."

"To beg, more like it," Jyner quipped, glancing back at the officers tittering behind him.

Drinith's chest tightened. The senior inspector must be goading Gelasin into a fight as a pretext to arrest them all.

For his part, Gelasin threw back his head and laughed. The warrior was too canny to be provoked by the senior inspector's needling. "That's a good joke, Inspector," he said. "I heard the Fire Emperor of Thirring is looking for a jester to amuse his favorite pet rat. You should consider applying."

Jyner smirked. "We'll see who's laughing by the time this inspection is over."

Several of the officers descended through the hatch to explore the lower decks.

Jyner perused the manifest again as though he had erased Gelasin from his consciousness. "I see you also have two Gyrans among your passengers. I would like them to come forward and state their business."

With an apologetic murmur, Halyard stalked over to the senior inspector, halting dangerously close to him. Was the strutting peacock about to do something stupid? Even Gelasin looked worried.

Amused, Jyner eyed him up and down. "Such bright plumage. You dress like a courtesar."

"I am a courtesar."

"An old one. Peacock feathers haven't been the fashion for some time. What are you doing wandering about the Crevast? Where is your mistress, if you have one?"

"I am here." Epmar's eyes glinted with disdain as she strode forward. "You may address me as Meritocrat Hax."

Shaken, Jyner bit his lower lip. "A bold claim."

The saddledeck rang with drawing swords as Halyard pulled his own from its scabbard. A curt wave from Epmar halted him. She smiled with malevolent sweetness. "One which only a fool would make if it were untrue. Do I look like a fool to you, Inspector?"

Wilting under her fierce gaze, Jyner took a step backward and bowed. "Forgive me, Meritocrat. Yes, I recognize you now. My apologies. I heard you left Gyre on a grand tour. I wasn't aware..."

"Your ignorance is understandable, your rudeness less so," Epmar said casually.

Jyner looked feverish as he rubbed his cheeks with a trembling hand. "All I can do is beg for your clemency, Meritocrat, however undeserved it might be."

"Being of generous disposition..." Epmar paused. She smiled as Jyner's face twisted between hope and apprehension. "I'll forget this slight this one time."

Jyner nodded. "Thank you, Meritocrat, thank you." His hands reached to grasp hers, but horrified by the errant impulse, he quickly pulled them back.

"I vouch for the princess and her entourage," Epmar said. "And this dragon and its crew."

Jyner turned and barked at his nearest subordinate. "Call back the others! We're leaving!" He bowed again so low he could have easily head-butted the deck and fled up the ramp, leaving the other customs officers to scramble after him.

Epmar pursed her lips. "I wonder how long it will take the news of my arrival to filter through the city. Not long, I imagine." She placed a hand on Halyard's shoulder. "Stay close. Drinith, it would be my pleasure if you were my guest for the duration of your stay in Gyre." She hadn't addressed Drinith as princess, a subtle acknowledgment that she was nobody's servant here.

Just behind her, Gelasin nodded enthusiastically. Had he known, Drinith wondered, of Epmar's eminence in Gyre? He must have at least suspected. This would explain his desire to come to this city.

"It would delight me, Meritocrat," Drinith said.

"Let us dispense with tedious formalities between us, Drinith, and address each other as friends might."

"Very well, Epmar," Drinith said, despite her misgivings. Aside from her bloodline, tedious formality was pretty much all she had.

"You can leave your baggage here," Epmar said. "I'll have my servants collect them. I doubt the *Surly Bonnacon* will leave for some time given its state of disrepair. To that matter..." She turned to Pinchel. "You dragged me back to Gyre—"

"Blame the pyrates, not me," Pinchel said, blushing.

"—but I feel obligated to help you in some small way." Epmar's gaze rested on the two jagged stumps of the masts. "When you are talking to the saddlewrights, tell them to send the bill for the repairs to me. Repairs, mind. Any enhancements are at your own expense."

"Of course. And would the meritocrat like to travel on with us later?"

"Perhaps," Epmar said. "Let me know when your dragon's ready again for the Crevast."

"Gladly. Any passage with us will always be free for you and your courtesar."

Epmar nodded. "Thank you."

Sweeping around him, she took Drinith by her arm. They led the others up the ramp, strolled along the pier and ascended the zigzagging stone steps up the cliff face toward the crane-crowned summit. A flock of small yellow birds flew by, gleaming in the sunlight like sparks in formation.

"Sunfinches, native to the archipelago," Epmar said. "They're much more brilliant than their mainland counterparts."

At the rear of the group, Versifer and Jarma patiently helped Quiescat.

Epmar drew Drinith close. "I wonder if the Grand Preservatory could help our friend, Quiescat," she whispered. "The preservators might treat his blindness."

"His oracular gift burned out his eyeballs," Gelasin muttered behind them. "I doubt even the preservators could cure such freakish wounds."

"Dr. Aerwig said the mechanisms of the eyes were otherwise intact," Drinith observed.

"I'll arrange a consultation," Epmar said.

Gelasin stroked a cratered cheek. "Their therapy is prodigiously expensive."

Epmar chuckled. "I just promised to pay for the repairs of the *Surly Bonnacon* on a whim. Unless my steward has squandered my wealth, I think we can safely afford the Grand Preservatory's price for two eyeballs. It's the least I could do to repay Drinith's kindness in taking me in."

Drinith found it strange to witness Epmar so casually taking charge.

"Where is your mansion?" Gelasin asked.

"Hax Plaza, of course," Epmar said with a sly grin.

"Your Highness, I'll meet you there. I have some old friends in the Blue Quarter I want to call in on, first."

"Oh? Who might they be?" Epmar asked.

"Like I said, old friends, retired mercenaries." He dashed off, but not before leaning close to Drinith and whispering, "If I don't meet up with you before nightfall, send Zin to the Gad Moon Inn in the Blue Quarter. Its owners are longtime friends of mine, fellow exiles who are sympathetic to our cause."

"I never took Gelasin as the sentimental type," Epmar murmured.

A short, sour man in black waited for them at the top. He wore a conical black helmet stamped in gold with his emblem—a wheel of rats knotted together by their tails. A yellow stripe stretched down one shoulder.

"I was wondering how long it would take you to learn of my return," Epmar said.

"It's my business to know such things." A smug grin deepened into a perpetually constipated look on his piggish face. "Is your courtesar still with you?"

"Yes."

"I'm glad to hear it. We had feared you might never return from your grand tour. I even heard the Ducalion received petitions to declare you dead."

Epmar's eyes narrowed. "And who might have sent them, I wonder?"

"Now, now. You know such matters are treated with strict confidentiality. Your good friend Thaxen Savarel stymied their efforts, in any case."

Epmar smirked. "A good friend indeed. I must write to my cousins. I'm sure they'll be delighted to learn of my safe return."

"I'm sure they will."

"Cordent General Greny Scylax, permit me to introduce Drinith, the rightful Empress of Kaplar."

Scylax executed the most pathetic excuse for a bow Drinith had ever seen. "A fine title. Kaplar is on Rhumgad, isn't it? A part of the Javlohm Empire?"

Drinith bristled at yet another reminder of her political impotency, but managed a polite smile. "For now."

Scylax's grin broadened. "Fighting words. I hope you've no intention to fight here." His piercing stare belied the lightness of his tone.

"Drinith will pose us no trouble," Epmar said. "She is my guest while she remains in the city."

The cordent general rubbed his chin. "Then, I'm sure she'll be only a positive addition to Gyre. I trust you'll instruct her and her retinue in our ways."

"A grave matter needs your attention." Epmar glanced at Drinith. "I'm afraid my friend's life is under imminent threat from assassins."

Scylax scowled. "Oh?"

"Pentaculars. The first three are dead, but the other two may come to Gyre..."

He puckered his lips and nodded his head as if weighing the import of Epmar's revelation.

"The assassins look like blue-black Rhumgadians," she said. "Their faces are identical. If you send a cordent skilled in sketching over to my mansion, I'm sure we can help him construct an accurate portrait."

"Have they any distinguishing features—scars, birthmarks, that sort of thing?"

"No. But they're likely to come here from their home shard, Thirring."

"I will send over one of our artists, of course, but I caution you not to depend solely on our vigilance. The pentaculars are skilled in subterfuge. I will make sure special attention is paid to dragons arriving from Thirring, but I fear the pentaculars are too canny to travel on them. And they are likely to disguise themselves until they are ready to strike. Stay alert and keep her bodyguards close at all times."

"Your counsel is wise, Greny, as always," Epmar said.

The cordent general snorted. "For now, I bid you both farewell."

As he strode away, two soldiers clad in yellow and black brigandines trailed after him at a discreet distance. Drinith took notice of their squat helmets with three front-to-back ridges.

"They're cordents, our local constabulary," Epmar whispered. "Well, one flavor of them."

Scylax climbed into a strange carriage, a palanquin borne by two giant black birds. Orange casques protruded like frowns above their bright yellow hooked beaks. Beside them stood a clothed rat the size of a man and shaped like one from the neck down. Its dark eyes regarded Drinith until a series of thumps from inside the palanquin spurred it to drive the birds forward.

"I didn't know there were male meritocrats," Drinith admitted. *Or birds carrying palanquins in Gyre, or man-shaped rats, for that matter.*

Epmar squeezed her hand and smiled. "There's a lot you don't yet understand about this city, but I will teach you. Never fear."

21

———

Leaning near the open window of his rocking carriage, Quiescat tried to conceive the city's soundscape. Aside from the rhythmic clang of hammers announcing a nearby forge, it was hard to make sense of the slippery stream of noise pouring around him—trundling carts, startling avian shrieks, distant dragon roars, milling crowds and their confusing babble. The city teemed with voices. Everywhere, people conversed, shouted, argued, laughed, sang, begged, hawked wares. It all must have been quite a sight.

Odors mapped the city better. Exotic aromas wafted from spice markets and perfumeries. The mouthwatering smell of fresh-baked bread thankfully overpowered the metallic scent of blood from a nearby slaughterhouse. He detected the sour stink of urine coming from a tannery long before he passed it. He breathed in the marvelous pungency of incense as they passed near the Temple District.

"We're not going to pass a dreamery?" he asked, reflexively. Dreameries couldn't pose much of a risk to him now he was no longer the Oracle of Godsdoor.

"The route we're taking will avoid them entirely," Gelasin promised.

"If only the darkness wasn't so implacable..." he said wistfully.

"You'll be able to see soon enough."

"I hope so," Quiescat said. "I tire of this shapeless night. Tell me, why did you volunteer to accompany me?"

"I worried those youngsters might lose you. Besides, it gives me an excuse to wander the city a little by myself."

"You found your friends yesterday?" Quiescat asked. Gelasin had been noticeably tight-lipped about his little excursion.

"I did," Gelasin said. "I plan to meet up with them after I have delivered you to the Grand Preservatory."

"What are you up to?" The question came out much sharper than Quiescat had intended.

Gelasin snorted. "Not everything has to be part of some nefarious plot. I can have friends who are just friends. Since you lost your gift, the burden of protecting Drinith has shifted entirely onto my shoulders. The poet is... He's a frightened child. If Abecedar had lived..."

"He'd have made a better oracle than I ever was," Quiescat said.

"Don't run yourself down," Gelasin said. "That's my job."

It felt good to laugh together. Had it ever happened before? Quiescat couldn't remember.

"I just want to forget my responsibilities a little while," Gelasin said. "After I broke my ceremonial dagger, after I grieved the life I had forsaken, I discovered freedom for the first time in my life. I discovered its joy."

"I've never really been free," Quiescat admitted.

"Then what did I do? I threw that freedom away and joined you on this ludicrous venture."

Quiescat bit his lip. He didn't appreciate Gelasin's choice of words but antagonizing him might undermine their nascent reconciliation.

"I want to taste a bit of freedom and remember what it was like."

"Did you know that Epmar was a meritocrat?" Quiescat asked. "Is that why you wanted to come to Gyre?"

"I knew she was a meritorian."

"I had assumed the same."

"I met plenty of them before who left the Halcyon Republic for one reason or another," Gelasin said. "But I never imagined she was a meritocrat. I thought the Parliament of Merit forbade its members to leave the city except for government business."

"It was certainly a fortuitous turn of events."

"Yes," Gelasin said glumly. "It was."

The vehicle shifted to one side and then the other. Quiescat pressed against the walls to steady himself as it tilted upward. "This is the most unsteady carriage I have ever had the misfortune to travel in," he complained.

"It's a palanquin carried by casquars, large flightless birds from the shard of Nemon. There's one at the front and one at the back, and our little cabin is suspended in between. Meritorians and other rich folks here use them on account of the narrow and winding streets."

They rocked gently as the palanquin climbed higher and higher. "Please tell me there are walls on both sides of us."

Gelasin chuckled. "No need to fear, Quiescat. We won't plummet into the void. Besides, we're almost there."

The palanquin halted, and Gelasin helped Quiescat out of the nauseating contraption. "We have to climb a flight of stairs. An odd choice to put them there considering it's supposed to be a place of healing."

Quiescat greeted the top of the steps with breathless thanks. Gelasin was right. How was a sick person supposed to ascend them without aid? The wealthy would have had plenty of servants to help them. The meritorians must compensate the Grand Preservatory well for its services.

Doors groaned open and Gelasin's hand gently drew Quiescat forward. After a dozen paces, they halted. Whispers passed back and forth ahead of them.

"I am Adept Preservator Zoarzi." The sonorous male voice echoed as though they stood in an exceptionally large chamber. "Please state your business."

"Meritocrat Hax sent us," Gelasin said. "She hopes you can cure this man's blindness."

"It's been quite a while since Meritocrat Hax used our services. We treated her injured courtesar if I remember right. He was near to death, poor man, but we nursed him back to life."

"The meritocrat asked me to give you this letter," Gelasin said.

Zoarzi unfurled the crinkling parchment and read it. "Hmm. I must thank the meritocrat for sending us a most interesting case. I haven't had the fortune to treat anyone blinded in such a supernatural manner before. I must invite the Grand Preservator to consult. I'm sure she would be fascinated." His enthusiasm, however restrained, annoyed Quiescat. It shrank him down to the very affliction he despised. "We will have to examine the patient first to confirm if he is a suitable candidate for our therapies. Leave him here with us. We will return him to the meritocrat's mansion when his treatment is complete."

"I have to go," Gelasin said. "People to see, things to do, and all that." He clapped Quiescat heartily on the back, startling him. "Good luck."

"Mind Drinith!" Quiescat cried. Stupid thing to say. Of course, Gelasin would give his very life for her.

"I'll take care of her. Never fear," the warrior said cheerily.

Quiescat lost the sound of his hasty retreat in the flurry of movement around him. How many preservators surrounded him? Hands gently pressed him to sit. He found himself ensconced on a wicker seat. Somebody lifted his feet onto a wooden plank. The chair rolled smoothly forward.

"I have never encountered a preservatory before," Quiescat said, piercing the oppressive silence.

"Lesser physicians, mere quacks and charlatans, slander us because the efficacy of our methods threatens their livelihoods," Zoarzi said. "It was such malicious lies that forced us to forsake our original home in Laxur. But lies can't persist forever, and the Crevast is slowly opening to us. We recently founded a new preservatory on the shard Magmel, for example. Here we are—the examination room."

As Quiescat settled on a leather couch, Zoarzi greeted the Grand Preservator.

"So this is the patient," the Grand Preservator said. Her soft, mellifluent voice possessed an unexpected youthfulness. "I understand you are a learned man."

"I am...I was the Oracle of Godsdoor on Rhumgad," Quiescat said.

"Understand that expertise in one field of endeavor does not translate to another. We only teach our ways to our initiates. You wouldn't divulge the secrets of your vocation to a layperson, no matter how educated. Here you are the layperson. Do you understand?"

"Yes," Quiescat said, repressing his exasperation.

"Good," the Grand Preservator said. "Very good. Please keep the questions to a minimum. Resist the urge to point out what seems illogical and inconsistent in our discussions, however glaring it may seem. Permit us to practice our arts uninterrupted and we will strive to restore your lost vision. The mortal sort, anyway." She sniffed. "I'm about to examine your ocular cavities. The sensation shouldn't hurt, but it may feel odd. It's important you keep as still as you can."

Cold metal clamped one eyelid open and then the other.

"Very interesting. Everything looks intact except for the missing eyeballs. The tissue looks fresh. No cauterization or scarring. It's as if some invisible film protects it. How much pain do you experience?"

"None."

"Any sensations normally?"

"When I cry, I can feel the tears pool in the cavity. I can feel the flutter of my eyelids," Quiescat said. "Otherwise..." He shrugged.

"If there's a barrier, tears must pass through it. We won't know for sure until we operate. I'm sorry, old fellow, what's your name again?"

Your bedside manner leaves much to be desired. "Quiescat."

"You may need some time to think about this, Quiescat," the Grand Preservator said. "I believe we have the wherewithal to return your sight. But as with all such operations, there are risks, both predictable and unpredictable."

"I'm familiar with the foreseeable and the unforeseeable," Quiescat quipped.

"Quite," the Grand Preservator said, or had she meant quiet? "Your case poses a special risk in that there may be some sort of invisible film over what remains of your eye. The tissue looks fresh like it was severed only today. We may have to remove more of the remaining structure to ensure success."

"I'll do it," Quiescat said. "Even if it costs my life, it's worth doing." Whatever the risks, it was preferable to being a burden to Drinith and the others.

The Grand Preservator clapped her hands smartly. "Excellent! That's the spirit! When did you eat last?"

"This morning."

"Then we'll carry out the procedure tomorrow morning. In the meantime, you must fast—no more food and as little water as possible. Zoarzi, escort our guest—Quiescat, wasn't it?—to a patient room."

Patient room—what bitter irony! Quiescat struggled to find patience, cut off from the rest of humanity, utterly alone. This might have been a much more pleasant experience in different circumstances. The preservators' other guests would have had retinues to attend them. The chamber might well be stocked with books, games, or other diversions he couldn't see. But this darkness in which he lay might as well have been a crypt.

Only the pangs of hunger reminded him he wasn't dead. Yes, hunger was a constant, nagging companion. That, and the expectancy of seeing again, and the gut-wrenching fear that his hope might prove forlorn. Sleep would not come this feverish night. He prayed to all the gods he could remember, of Rhumgad and other shards, that one might pity him and bless him with slumber.

When he ran out of deities, he turned to Versifer's visions. Under no illusion that he might solve them, he let speculation run wild. The shadowy man who rolled the Tear of Fate intrigued him. The room without walls could refer to his blindness. He had borne the Tear of Fate and given it away. He might be this tangled shadow. Then the vision must predict his death here in Gyre.

The preservators' arrival intruded on his musings. Was it morning already? He had fretted the night away. A wave of sick exhaustion overwhelmed him.

They helped him onto another bed. Something stabbed his neck like a bee sting. "No need to be frightened," Zoarzi said. "It's a general anesthetic, so you sleep comfortably during the operation."

As consciousness ebbed away, Quiescat wondered bitterly why they couldn't have given him a dose of it the interminable night before.

22

———

They breakfasted around a long table—Epmar at the head, Drinith, Halyard, Gelasin, Jarma, Versifer with his glinting crystal eyes, and Zin. Two servants in teal hovered nearby, ready to pounce at the hint of any need. Drinith hadn't slept well, thinking about what might happen to Quiescat, and even sips of her spicy yellow tea couldn't relieve her gnawing headache. She placed a small saffron scone on her plate and slicing off a portion, chewed on it slowly out of politeness. Epmar sighed exasperatedly at the chime of a distant bell. "I wonder who calls this early. My steward, Picrity, isn't due to arrive for another hour."

Her butler, Fenvar, entered. Everything from her white bowl crop haircut to her shiny black boots was so precise and proper. Even the lines on her coral pink face fell neatly. The black apron she wore over her teal dress bore Epmar's emblem, a bird taking flight, embroidered in gold.

She drew to Epmar's side and cleared her throat. "Meritocrat Trajar has arrived to renew your acquaintance. I've invited her to wait in the parlor."

Epmar puffed out her cheeks and exhaled. "Elca, eh?" Dabbing her mouth with her napkin, she rose from the table. "Drinith, will you accompany me? I should introduce her to you. The rest of you, please stay here and enjoy your breakfast."

"I'll have some tea and scones brought to the parlor," the butler said.

As Drinith rose to follow, so did Gelasin. "May I tag along?"

"I think not, this time," Epmar said. "The meritocrat might find too many unfamiliar faces uncomfortable."

Glowering, Gelasin dropped back into his chair. "Very well."

As they passed through the reception hall, Epmar whispered, "Let me do the talking as much as possible without making it obvious. There's never been a more venomous snake than—" She pushed open the parlor doors. "Elca, how lovely of you to come to visit!"

The pale luminosity of Elca Trajar's eyes was so unexpected and arresting, Drinith struggled to see beyond them. Stars dappled Elca's violet skin and bright white tipped her twisted shoulder-length cascades of black hair.

"It's a delight to see you again, Epmar," Elca purred. "And who is this young woman with the pretty jewel on her forehead?"

"This is my good friend Drinith," Epmar said.

"Ah, yes. The heir to the Kaplar Empire. Your reputation precedes you, my dear." Elca seized Drinith's hand and shook it with surprising firmness. As they sat down on separate couches, Drinith shied from her intense gaze and pretended to study the carpet. She wondered what Elca had really heard about her. Perhaps the reference to her reputation was merely a pleasantry.

Fenvar entered with the refreshments and placed them on the low table in the center of the room. Drinith took the opportunity to take in her surroundings. Women in black glared down at her from the portraits covering the walls. A large painting took pride of place above the red marble mantelpiece. A woman wearing a crown threw herself off a jutting tongue of red rock. Behind her, women dressed in black fought back warriors in bloodstained armor.

"Thank you, Fenvar," Epmar said. "I'll serve. You can go." As the departing servant closed the doors behind her, the meritocrat leaned forward and stirred the pot.

Elca glanced about the room. "I don't see your mother's portrait, Epmar."

"It's upstairs." Epmar began to pour the tea.

"And how is dear Halyard?" Elca asked.

Epmar's hand trembled, splashing some tea onto the tray. Her false grin couldn't conceal the anger in her eyes. She obviously didn't appreciate Elca mentioning him. "He is very well."

"Good. After all, his welfare was why you forsook us, wasn't it?"

"Among other reasons." Epmar placed a filled cup on a small tray and offered it to Elca.

"Indeed," Elca said, flashing a smile as she took it. "They say there's no such thing as an old courtesar. I have had four courtesars this year alone. It's in their nature to fight. They can always find an excuse—to win the favor of a meritorian, to vindicate their honor, to avenge any insult no matter how slight."

"What do you mean, Elca?"

Elca sipped her tea, savored it. "I'm saying it might be best if you plucked Halyard's plumage."

"Surely a lot of his contemporaries are..."

"Dead? Oh, yes. But he had a certain reputation in his prime, and that only magnified after his departure. What courtesar doesn't dream of running off with his lover? You have to admit, your relationship with him is unusual and rare."

"It's not unprecedented," Epmar insisted.

"No, but such dalliances rarely end happily."

"And were your four courtesars happy with their fates?"

Elca grinned, reveling in what Epmar intended to be a jibe. "The fourth is still among the living the last time I checked." She leaned back on the couch. "I can't be held accountable for courtesars' jealous natures. Halyard's return puts his life in jeopardy. It will provoke a new crop of rivals to challenge him at every opportunity. I doubt it is in his nature to refuse a challenge." She sipped her tea again. "But, much worse, he may draw admirers from among his class. The courtesars might come to see him as a leader of sorts."

"Halyard is devoted to the Courtesar Code," Epmar said. "He would never go against it."

"I'm glad to hear it," Elca said. She studied her cup. "It's good to know his experience in less civilized realms hasn't turned his head."

"What business is it of yours, anyway?" Epmar snapped.

"Haven't you guessed? I'm the current Arbiter of Courtesars."

"I'm surprised someone of your obvious talents would take such a humble position."

Elca examined her nails. "I am gratified to hear you say so. Somebody must do it. Besides, flying too high for too long makes others jealous. I hope for a promotion soon. In some ways, courtesars have an easier life. While we meritocrats are burdened with the travails of government, they get to play with their swords and honor." Elca turned to Drinith. "They are so headstrong. We can't even trust them to join our armies, much less command them. They'd lose us the Short War in a red month."

"The Short War?" Drinith asked.

"The struggle with the other great powers of Noster for dominance of the shard," Epmar said glumly. "The name is ironic as it has been rumbling on for nearly two hundred years."

"With mercenaries leading our armies, what else can you expect?" Elca asked rhetorically. "The whole conflict has taken on the aspect of a ritual. We're nowhere near losing, but we're nowhere near winning either. Which reminds me..."

"Yes?" Epmar said wearily.

"I'm holding a ducal reception tomorrow evening to celebrate our liberation of the city of Cariphas and get everyone in the mood for the upcoming Crevastival festivities. Obviously, all meritorians in the city are invited. You should bring Drinith. Perhaps she can press her case there with our beloved Ducalion."

Epmar snorted. "We'll be glad to attend."

Placing the cup on the table, Elca rose. "Now, I must leave you, I'm afraid. I've much to do today in preparation for tomorrow. No rest for the wicked."

"Of course," Epmar said. She sprang from her chair and escorted Elca out of the room. Drinith nibbled on a scone while she waited.

Returning, Epmar slammed the doors shut and plopped on the couch. "What an appalling creature! Those mesmeric eyes aren't natural, you know. She bought them. There's no feature of her appearance that she hasn't had tweaked in the Grand Preservatory."

Epmar sighed and shook her head. "I nearly damned myself there. I was about to say Halyard would never act without my assent, but I realized Elca would love to cast me as a potential mastermind for a courtesar rebellion.

"Tyranny is the greatest fear of our republic. We haven't had a monarch in nearly a thousand years. That's why her talk of putting your case to the Ducalion was a jibe at your unfamiliarity with our ways. We might pay lip service to the Ducalion's authority, but she is a figurehead, a mouthpiece for the true heart of our government, the Parliament of Merit."

"What am I supposed to do?" Drinith asked, lost and dejected.

"You need to build up support quietly among the meritocrats. You have me. I'll introduce you to others, old friends and other potential sympathizers. We'll start tonight. I won't lie: it will take time. It might take years and a lot of luck. You must be patient."

Drinith nodded despite her chagrin. How long did she have with the next pentacular hunting her? For all she knew, he had already arrived in Gyre.

"One step at a time," Epmar said. "Tomorrow night should at least be fun. One of Elca Trajar's few virtues is that she can throw a decent party."

———

Epmar's maids spent most of the next morning fussing over Drinith for the ducal reception. She disliked how Jarma had been sidelined, as if she was too uncouth to prepare her for Gyran society. Drinith couldn't make herself take an interest in their incessant chatter, however much she tried. She didn't like the cut of the black dress. It was too body-hugging, and its off-the-shoulder neckline meant she couldn't wear her mail shirt under it. The line of brass buttons down the front seemed a superfluous touch. She detested how her hair had been darkened and braided.

"You're unhappy," said Perian, the boldest of the maids.

"My hair looks so dull." The gem was the only recognizable feature upon the gloomy stranger in the mirror.

"Trust us," Perian said. "A few choice pieces of jewelry will sort everything. And I have a silk belt to match your gem. Gyran fashion is all about the little details."

Drinith greeted the entrance of Epmar and Fenvar with relief. The meritocrat studied Drinith and examined her dress.

"Bare shoulders are the height of fashion," Perian said with enthusiasm.

Epmar sighed. "But whose?" She picked at the dress fabric. She glanced at Fenvar with irritation.

The butler gave a plaintive shrug. "Perian came highly recommended."

"By whom?"

"She had a glowing reference from Meritocrat Orom."

"Ah! Dear Ecethor. Now I understand. Always so enthralled with the latest trends, she's blind to their cost. Somebody once quipped she had the dress sense of a courtesar."

Fenvar bowed her head. "I should have realized..."

Perian's face turned a deeper red as her eyes darted between them. "I'm sorry, Meritocrat. I failed you." Her fear and bewilderment made Drinith tense. What had she done that was so wrong?

"No harm done. You need a little guidance, that's all," Epmar assured her. "Everything a meritorian wears is not merely an affirmation of status. The subtle details of her attire map out her friendships and loyalties. It defines her politics. This dress..." She waved a hand at it. "I've been too long away from Gyre to be know the political nuances of its design, but it's likely to make Drinith more enemies than friends."

She stroked the line of gold buttons above her bosom. "Put her in a plainer version of my dress. I'm sure there's a spare in a wardrobe somewhere."

"Do you want her buttoned to the collar?" Perian asked with horror.

"She can decide for herself how open she leaves it."

"A dash of color is pretty much universal these days," Perian croaked. "I was going to give her a belt to match her gem."

Epmar nodded her approval.

"And the hair? It's a common style among her people."

Epmar raised an eyebrow. "You've been to Rhumgad?"

"I've visited the Blue Quarter."

Epmar winced. "Shorten and straighten it like a young meritorian's." She gave Drinith a reassuring pat on her shoulder and departed with Fenvar. For a time, the maids worked in chastened silence, but their chattering soon resumed as merrily as before. The maids had located a replacement dress by the time the dressmaker arrived. Perian gave her instructions, dismissing her misgivings that the work could be done in time with the haughty authority of a meritocrat.

"I'm sorry to intrude." Drinith caught Versifer's reflection in the mirror. He looked pained and bashful.

"Please leave us," Drinith said, seizing the chance to be rid of the maids and their jabber. Perhaps Versifer had some new insight into his visions. Quiescat had encouraged her to read them, but she could make little sense of the baffling jumble of images.

Versifer pulled up a chair and sat beside her. "I wrote you something," he said, thrusting a sheet of parchment at her. Another vision, no doubt. It must be important for him to come so urgently. She took it. "I couldn't say it, so I had to write it down."

> "Sweeter than palasgard
> Is love's immortal bloom.

> The hot sun cannot wilt it,
> Nor the Roaming Sea drown it."

She could read no further. Afraid, she thrust it back at him. "I can't accept this."

He waved it away. "Keep it. It's for you."

"It's inappropriate for me to have it," she said, casting her glance around for Gelasin in the vague hope he might barge into the room. Until recently, she had longed for the poet to show her affection in this way, but this gesture mocked that very yearning and made her feel foolish and a little scared. For gods' sake, he was the Oracle of Godsdoor. He was supposed to be beyond such romantic notions, just as she had to be.

"It's inappropriate for anyone to have it other than you," he said. "I want you to have it. Please."

"I can't return your sentiments. I don't share them."

"I thought..."

He looked so forlorn and broken, but she needed to tread carefully. Softening the blow might only encourage him to live in hope where none existed. "In the past, perhaps, but no longer," she in a firm voice.

"I shouldn't have done this," he said. "Forgive me. I had promised myself to never yield to those tender feelings I held for you. While I was simply a man, albeit one gifted with eloquence, I kept that promise. But now, when you need me most, I have capitulated to my loneliness." He bowed. "I am drowning in the inhumanity of these damned eyes."

Drinith gripped the rests of her chair as he reached for the crystal spheres. Was he about to pluck them out? No, his hands hovered near them but never made contact.

"This obscenity, this curse, this baneful sting of Fate. Perhaps if I was a worthier man, more prepared, I might be better able to endure this burden." He growled as he punched the air. Drinith held her breath. "No! It ruined Quiescat and killed Abecedar, and now it gnaws on my soul as a ghoul might until it has wasted me to naught but a living cadaver. I never asked for this affliction. Abecedar, in desperation, forced it upon me. They call it a gift, but it's more akin to a disease. Has Quiescat told you about my visions?"

She nodded.

"What use are they if we cannot figure out their meaning? Quiescat told me their cryptic nature was down to my poetic imagination. As though my imagination, the best part of me, was a poison. It's the gift that is the toxin." He covered his face with his hands. "I wouldn't be surprised if the Fate Healer let the first oracle, Agebor, have it as a punishment. What vain fools these oracles are to presume a mortal man could outsmart a goddess. This is all a game and Fate laughs at us as we play, ignorant of the rules."

Drinith leapt out of her seat. "So should I give up and wait for a pentacular to put me out of my misery? You're not the only one who must bear impossible burdens and play other people's games. I asked for none of this. You, at least, had a choice—"

Dropping his hands, he stared up at her with those inhuman eyes. "Abecedar said your life depended on the gift's survival." He spoke without reproach or rancor, which made the revelation sting all the more. He averted his gaze. "I'm sorry. I shouldn't have said that."

"Never apologize for telling me the truth, no matter how hard or ugly," she said, sitting back down and brushing down her skirt.

"I didn't mean to tell you all this—"

"Who else could you tell? Not Quiescat. He has his own troubles."

"You can confide in me as the Oracle of Godsdoor."

She displayed the poem. "Not while this exists," she said sadly.

He recoiled. "You're asking me to destroy a part of my soul."

"I need an oracle, not a poet; a confidant, not a lover." Again, she thrust the parchment at him.

He hesitated, took it. He strode over to the nearest candle with the dignity of a noble walking to his death. He touched a corner of the parchment against the flame until it spread across the vellum. He tossed it in the empty fireplace, and standing over it, watched it burn. "It's done."

"Thank you," Drinith said. "I will try to be worthy of your sacrifice." Why had she said that? She blushed.

"Your trust is reward enough," he said, his voice trembling with emotion. He limped toward the door as if physically injured. For a moment, it seemed as if he had forgotten her, but he paused at the threshold. "Goodbye, and good luck tonight."

"We'll talk again soon," Drinith promised.

"Yes."

She had no time to mull over their conversation, for as soon as he left, the maids swarmed back inside.

———

Drinith's retinue gathered to see her off that evening. Aside from Quiescat, only Versifer was missing. His absence stung. Did he merely lick his wounds, or had he intended this snub as a punishment for her rejection of his feelings? The answer would have to wait. She had a more pressing problem—Gelasin.

He paced angrily back and forth across the reception hall. "So again, I am excluded!"

Epmar regarded him with a mixture of forbearance and disdain. "Your princess was invited. You were not."

"She needs me there," he fumed. "She has no experience—"

"And you have? How many ducal receptions have you attended? You know little or nothing of the inner workings of our society. If you did, you'd understand that witnessing a man giving Drinith orders would diminish her in the eyes of meritorians."

Gelasin swatted at the suggestion. "I don't order her about."

"But your very presence would cause them to suspect otherwise," Epmar said. "You're too old to be a courtesar."

Drinith's face burned with embarrassment at the notion anyone might mistake Gelasin for her lover.

"Then Zin should accompany her, at least."

No, not Zin! Her skin crawled at the prospect of being trapped alone with him in a cramped cab. Zin leered at Drinith, as if reading her mind.

"Halyard will be with us." For the first time, Epmar's voice quavered with uncertainty.

"*You're* his focus. Drinith needs someone to protect *her*. For all we know, the next pentacular may have already reached the city."

"It's up to you, Drinith," Epmar said.

However much Drinith desired to contradict Gelasin, he was right. She would be a fool to ignore sound advice. "We should bring him."

Halyard studied the lowlander. "Should we dress him in more fitting attire? In that battered breastplate and moth-eaten tunic, he's liable to be mistaken for a rough off the street and escorted off the premises."

"But I've such lovely manners," Zin said with mock dismay. He strutted and clucked like a chicken. "How do you do? How do you do?" he cooed. Halyard averted his eyes as though the spectacle was beneath his interest.

"Knock it off, Zin!" said Gelasin, masking his amusement.

"He could certainly do with some fresh clothes," Epmar said. "But his garb mustn't be too fancy. We don't want him to be mistaken for a courtesar. Zin's presence is meant to prevent trouble, not cause it."

"A pity," Zin said. "I was looking forward to borrowing Halyard's peacock feather bustle and platform shoes." Halyard shot him a withering glance.

Fenvar announced that the casquar palanquins were ready and waiting. As Drinith moved to follow Epmar, Gelasin seized her arm. "Are you wearing your mail under your dress?"

"Of course," she said.

"Be careful," he whispered. "We don't know what game our meritocratic friend is playing."

Repressing a sigh, Drinith gently pulled free of Gelasin's grip. He was the one playing games. Jealousy compelled him to badmouth Epmar at every opportunity.

"I'll not get a wink of sleep until you're back safe," Gelasin muttered.

Drinith joined Epmar on the steps outside. The meritocrat wore a black velvet dress, a long black shawl embroidered with red leaves, and a conical black velvet hat bearing her emblem.

"Don't mind Gelasin," she said. "He can't see you're not a child anymore. Zin will travel with you." He gazed at her with his habitual sneer through the open window of the palanquin.

"Very well," Drinith sighed. It would be a long night.

23

——————

Was Quiescat dreaming? The room must be an illusion, surely. With only dim light spilling through the darkened window, the chamber was outlined in gray, as if sketched on a shadow.

Quiescat held his hands before his eyes and wriggled his fingers. He could see! He could see!

A lumpy silhouette shifted in one corner. Quiescat held his breath. His chest constricted. Could this be the tangled man foretold by Versifer's first vision?

"You're awake at last." Quiescat recognized the Grand Preservator's voice. "Good. We put you in this darkened place so that your new eyes might adjust gently to light."

Quiescat exhaled softly. She couldn't be the tangled man.

"The operation appears to be a success," she said. "The magical barrier proved to be a minor obstacle. It dissipated as soon as we probed it with a scalpel. We were able to knit the muscles and nerves easily. Your face may feel a little numb. That is normal. In time the numbness will fade, and you may experience some discomfort, particularly where we had to cut through bone. We'll give you a mild analgesic to relieve that. You're a little swollen and bruised around the eyes, but that's normal and this will heal in a few days."

Quiescat grinned so hard it hurt. "I can't believe it. The memory of sight had begun to fade into a dream, and now I can see again."

"Your blindness will become the dream."

"Indeed." Without thinking, he flung off his blanket and swung his legs over the side of the bed. He hesitated. "Should I be getting up?"

The Grand Preservator chortled. "We didn't operate on your feet."

He stood warily. His legs trembled beneath him. "How long have I been asleep?"

"A day."

A full day! What might have happened in the meantime? He grabbed his clothes off a chair and threw them on over his nightshirt. "What is the time now?"

"The late afternoon. We'll release you as soon as you have grown accustomed to sunlight outside." She pressed a button on the wall and the light through the window strengthened.

He could see her properly now. Her youthfulness shocked him. Her hair had the luster of red orichalcum, her hooded eyes were deep turquoise, her skin the color of bronze fresh from a mold. She looked a little older than Drinith, but her self-possession suggested a woman of far greater years. The prospect of being alone in a room alone with a woman, particularly one so attractive, disconcerted him. He had shared quarters with Drinith, but she was like a daughter to him. The Grand Preservator was a stranger with a magnetic and enigmatic beauty. Her amused smile alerted him that his gaze had lingered too long upon her. He stared at the door, the only means of escape from this claustrophobic little room.

"You look a lot younger than I expected," he said, instantly regretting how fatuous this must sound.

"I'll take that as a compliment," she said with a cold smile. "Being a preservator has its advantages. Our science keeps us youthful for a long time. Of course, the aging process cannot be cheated forever. It may surprise you to learn I'm nearly twice your age."

"You never told me your name," Quiescat said lamely.

"Did you introduce yourself to every supplicant at your temple?"

"No," Quiescat admitted.

She languidly picked a mirror off the table beside her and floated featherily toward him. "Look at yourself. The eyes might appear small, but they'll grow to better fit your face in time."

He took the mirror from her hand and, with sudden modesty, withdrew two steps away. As he turned the mirror, some wayward reflex made him close his eyes. He giggled at his boyish reluctance. He looked. A stranger stared back at him, a typical lowlander, undistinguished in appearance. The black eyes inset in his face looked like they belonged there. They didn't look small, in his estimation. Still, his heart sank at having diminished to a normal man, with ordinary sight. "Very nice work."

"Fortune smiled on us. We often struggle to get eyes in pairs at such short notice. We sometimes must use eyes from separate donors, leading to subtle mismatches. In your case, we convinced the donor to part with both eyes."

Quiescat gaped. His eyes hurt as they expanded. "The eyes come from a living donor?"

"Oh, yes. Dead tissue won't do. Don't worry. The donors are well compensated for their sacrifice." She spoke with a breezy certainty as if the matter was entirely inconsequential. "But I'm sure you knew that coming here."

How could he have been so naive? So dazzled by the prospect of seeing again, he had never thought to question how this miracle might be achieved. His fingers curled with the urge to rip the two abominations from their sockets. "No, actually, I didn't."

The Grand Preservator regarded him a moment with disdain. She studied her hands as she rubbed them together. "You'll be able to leave in a while and resume your life."

"I'm leaving now."

She gave the most languid of shrugs. "That is your right," she said coldly. "This is a place of healing, not a prison. We do nothing to people here against their will. Follow me. I'll show you to the door."

Outside, a young boy waited.

"Run ahead and arrange a palanquin to take our guest to Meritocrat Hax's mansion." She turned to Quiescat with a caustic smile. "I trust your moral qualms don't extend to a lift."

He had no idea how to get to Epmar's mansion. He had never even seen the city, nor had he any knowledge of its geography. Chagrined, he admitted defeat with a nod.

The sunlight stung his eyes as he followed the boy out of the building. A casquar palanquin already awaited him at the bottom of concentric, white marble steps. A recent shower had left them slippery, forcing him to descend with care. If only he had been outside during the rain that he might feel clean again. Reaching the bottom, he glanced up at the Grand Preservatory. Its white spires and domes put him in mind of a pile of bones. Somewhere inside, the owner of Quiescat's eyes might be still convalescing.

"Is there another entrance other than this one?" he asked the driver. "One where the preservatory's donors come and go?"

"The preservators paid me to take you to Meritocrat Hax's mansion," the driver muttered, his whole face crumpling under the frown of his bushy monobrow.

"Meritocrat Hax will make up any additional charges," Quiescat assured him.

The driver shrugged and pulled back the black drape over the entrance. "I'll go to Empyrosis itself as long as I get paid." His laugh exposed his jagged yellow and black teeth.

The palanquin descended the winding street from the Preservatory and entered cramped lanes. Everywhere Quiescat looked, people were hanging brightly colored bunting from their storefronts and homes. Quiescat yelled to the driver, "Is there going to be a fete?"

"Crevastival is tomorrow," the driver said, incredulous at his ignorance.

Chastened, Quiescat sat back and drew the curtain. Of course, Crevastival, when the peoples of the void made offerings to dragons. In Gyre, it was a three-day affair, also celebrating the founding of the city. How did he not know? He should have paid more attention. No, he was being too hard on himself. This was the first time he had seen the city since his arrival.

They traveled so long, he wondered if the driver had forgotten where they were supposed to be going. The vehicle halted in a narrow street so dark it was hard to tell filth from shadow. No bunting hung from the drab windows. The driver drew back the curtain again and pointed to a door across the street. It looked nondescript except for the begrimed statues of hooded figures on either side. Each figure had a palm open as if begging, while its other hand held invisible alms between its thumb and fingers. The message was clear: give, and you shall receive. But what did you get for your eyes? Was it worth the sacrifice?

The driver's cough intruded on Quiescat's daze. What was he doing here? His donor mightn't leave the Grand Preservatory for days, or he might already be gone. Delaying here wasted his time and Epmar's money.

The door whispered open. A hooded figure emerged, dragging a young blue-black boy by the hand. A bandage covered the boy's eyes, or at least where they should have been. Quiescat pressed a hand to the sudden ball of pain in his chest. The preservators had taken this child's eyes and given them to him, but Quiescat might as well have plucked them out himself.

The hooded figure shot him a furtive glance and continued down the squalid lane, roughly leading the child. Could this be the tangled man?

Quiescat leapt out of the palanquin. The driver made an obscene gesture of frustration.

"Please wait!" Quiescat called after the retreating figure. The foolishness of his plea struck instantly. How could he compensate for the child's loss? He hadn't even the basest coin to offer. He glanced at his naked fingers, the rings long since sold.

The hooded figure looked back. A black scarf covered the lower half of the face, but the visible portion was unmistakably feminine. "What do you want?" She had to be the boy's mother. She must have been desperate to submit her child to such appalling and irrevocable injury.

"Thank you," he said. Realizing how inadequate this was, he added: "Thank you for my gift of sight."

To his surprise, she took a step back to study him, her head cocked. A little gasp came from her. He knew why, of course. Her son's dark eyes peered back at her from his wizened, unworthy face. She reached a hand toward him and quickly withdrew it, her eyes, moist now, still fixed upon...her son's eyes, not his; they would never be truly his. Quiescat could not bear her scrutiny and looked down, ashamed.

"I beg you to come to Meritocrat Hax's mansion," he said, addressing his boots. "I promise that you'll be rewarded."

The spell was broken; the woman snorted derisively. "I don't need your money or your guilt. I have enough of my own," she hissed as she strode up the lane, violently tugging her blind son along behind her.

Quiescat watched, defeated, as they disappeared around a corner. Climbing back onto the palanquin felt like a chore.

"I could have told you this was a bad idea," the driver said.

"Mind your own business and take me to Meritocrat Hax's mansion."

———

Quiescat never bothered to peek through the curtain the rest of the way to the mansion. He let the sounds and smells, once so precious, wash over him without a thought. When the palanquin halted, the driver's gruff announcement of their arrival at Hax Plaza took him by surprise.

He climbed the wearying steps up to the door of Epmar's mansion and pulled the bell cord. The male servant who opened the door regarded him with murderous contempt.

"Be gone, beggar!"

"I'm your meritocrat's guest," he said, before the servant could slam the door in his face. "The palanquin driver is owed some money. I promised your meritocrat would pay."

"I'll speak to the butler," the servant said, lips curling in distaste. "Wait—"

"Let him in!" Gelasin bellowed. "I'll vouch for him!"

With a frown, the servant stepped out of Quiescat's way.

"Don't forget to pay the driver," Quiescat said as he entered.

Gelasin's eyes bulged. "Bawror burn me! You look like a normal man now." He grinned. "Though, I must admit, one who has suffered a terrible beating about the head." Darting over to Quiescat, he seized his hand and shook it enthusiastically. "It's great to see you."

Somewhat taken aback by the genuine warmth of Gelasin's welcome, Quiescat reciprocated. "Where is Drinith?"

Gelasin's smile fell away. He placed a finger to his lips. "We must talk in private," he murmured.

"What's wrong?" Quiescat asked.

"One moment," Gelasin said as he drew Quiescat into the parlor, shutting the doors behind them. "Drinith is fine as far as I know." Though they were alone, Gelasin continued to whisper. "As for how long she remains that way, I can't say for sure. Epmar is intent on taking her over. She isolates Drinith from us at every opportunity. This very evening, Epmar whisked her off to a ducal reception without any of us. The only exception was Zin, and I had to beg for him to be permitted to accompany them."

It was not so long ago that Gelasin and Quiescat might have accused each other of something similar. "She may be right to exclude us. We're barbarians to these people, foreigners."

Gelasin squinted. "No no no. There's something else under the surface. I can feel it. Epmar makes decisions without consultation or even explanation."

Quiescat smiled. Gelasin had described his own worst tendencies.

"She has some other plan for our princess," the warrior insisted. "If Drinith forsakes her birthright, then all hope of freeing Rhumgad from Magian's tyranny is dead." He massaged his forehead. "But we have a more pressing problem—Versifer."

Quiescat's heart sank. He had forgotten about his successor. "What about him?"

"He's shut up in his room, moping. Seems he shared his tender feelings for the princess with her. She refused him graciously, but he's been brooding ever since. He'd be better off peering into the future Epmar has planned for our princess than pining over what could never be."

Poor Versifer had never sought the gift, Quiescat mused. He had neither the discipline nor the sense of purpose of a worthy candidate. He was still trying to cling on to the parts of his humanity the Tear of Fate had burned away. The old Quiescat would have condemned Versifer as a feckless fool, but the former oracle saw the world through new eyes in more ways than one.

"I'll talk to him," he said.

"Do that. I'm sure you can knock some sense into him."

"I'll try." Quiescat headed for the door.

"I'll stay here," Gelasin said, fairly bouncing off the walls with nervous energy. "I won't get a moment's peace until our princess returns."

Versifer's room was on the third floor. Quiescat knocked gently on the door. Receiving no reply, he rapped again, harder.

A low moan came from inside. At least the romantic fool still lived. Quiescat turned the handle and pushed the door open. The wedge of light from the hall revealed Versifer lying asleep on a rumpled bed, blankets spilling down one edge, leaving the far side bare. Versifer shifted, moaned again.

Quiescat's shadow bit deeper into the light as he entered the room. On the bed, Versifer writhed and groaned. Quiescat hesitated to wake him. Whatever nightmare tortured the oracle might be prophetic.

Versifer's eyes popped open. He bolted upright, pulling the blanket around him. "Who...? Quiescat, it's you. I didn't recognize you with the new eyes. I must say, they become you." His cheeks turned a feverish bright blue. "I have had the first vision again." He hesitated. "But it continues on."

Quiescat took a deep breath. "Tell me."

"Amid the squabbling birds, a tantalizing gleam attracts my gaze —the Tear of Fate. I work toward it, pick my way through the frenzied combatants. I skid on the marble made slick by blood and feathers, and I fall backward. I fall through the floor, down a black shaft like a grave."

Quiescat forced himself not to turn and run out the door. The dream must portend danger for Drinith at the party, but every detail, no matter how apparently insignificant, might prove the key to saving her. "Continue," he murmured, though every instinct urged him to scream.

"The birds cease their combat and stare down at me as I plummet until the opening shrinks to a speck...and then nothing. Where are you going?"

Quiescat was already racing out the door. He must find Gelasin. They had to get to that party and save Drinith before it was too late.

24

———

Silently fuming, Drinith gazed out the window of the palanquin to avoid Zin's stare. Everywhere, smiling commoners hung bunting. Many had Nosteran heritage or at least hints of it in their features—aquiline noses, maroon complexions, rose eyes, bright red hair. Their cheerfulness vexed her. She felt naked here, alone with this lecher. If only this contraption could accommodate more than two people. If only she could afford to dismiss him from her service. He didn't strike as the sort who'd stay out of loyalty. Unless he hoped she'd reciprocate his lust. She shivered.

"Are you cold?" he asked with a cloying gentleness that made her want to screech.

"I'm fine. Thank you," she said primly. "Why do you stay in my retinue? Surely a man of your, er, talent could find more lucrative employment elsewhere."

He smirked. "Blame my romantic streak." He lifted the curtain and peeked out. "And you owe me money."

Her hand sought her knife on reflex but tonight she was unarmed. Though their escorts might bear arms, custom frowned upon the guests themselves carrying weapons at ducal reception. "Money's important to you, I take it."

"It's always important when you don't have it. I bear Gelasin no ill will. He's doing his best in a difficult situation. You're lucky to have him. If you listened to him more often, you'd be a lot closer to getting your empire back. Quiescat and his successor might be learned and all that, but they lack pragmatism. In the past, their wondrous prophecies stupefied monarchs, but now they only serve to bamboozle the oracles themselves. The Tear mightn't garble its predictions if wielded by a harder, more practical mind than the poet's."

Quiescat had hinted at something similar, but she bristled at Zin's impertinence. "Who are you to make such judgments? And what you know about Versifer's prophecies?"

A fat grin split the diamond lines on his face. "I mightn't be familiar with their detail, but I grasp their meaning as well as Versifer and Quiescat. They're stumped, that's plain. Forget them. They're a dangerous distraction. Heed Gelasin's counsel."

He certainly looked up to Gelasin. This advice Zin offered had to be a regurgitation of private conversations with the old warrior. The two were more friendly than Gelasin let on to her.

"Thanks for your advice," Drinith muttered under her breath.

The palanquin swayed to a gentle halt. Drinith moved to leave first, but Zin slipped ahead of her. He held the drape back for her with exaggerated gallantry, his smile broadening with triumph. Had she unknowingly given him hope he might seduce her? As she stepped out onto the cobbles, Epmar took her arm in hers and finally rescued her from him. However, she could still feel his eyes upon her as he and Halyard trailed after them.

Behind them, a column of other palanquins snaked across the plaza, each waiting patiently to offload their passengers. Men in gaudy clothes, alone or in small clusters, lined the fronts of the adjacent buildings. Their painted faces displayed boredom and irritation in equal measure.

"Must the courtesars wait outside?" Drinith asked.

Epmar followed her gaze and laughed. "Those courtesars have no meritorian. They are drawn here like moths to a flame. Sometimes they try to challenge their more successful counterparts to duels. Other times, they fight amongst themselves. Hopefully, nothing too outrageous will happen tonight and they'll tire of their vigil and scatter before the ducal reception concludes." She turned to Halyard. "Styles have changed, it seems. Half-skirts have replaced the bustles of peacock feathers your generation so loved, and red appears to be the most popular color."

"Fashions change," Halyard said with a smile, "but steel never does." He sniffed. "I detest red. It's the sartorial refuge of the sloven and the braggart."

"Now, now," Epmar murmured, amused despite herself. "We don't want someone overhearing you and taking offense."

Halyard grinned. "Of course. I will keep my sharp tongue scabbarded."

Elca Trajar's mansion was easily twice the size of Epmar's. Gyran flags hung from the upper windows. A gilded plate bearing Elca's emblem, a four-horned snake's head, hung above the main door. A servant led Drinith and Epmar along the concentric steps spilling down to an equally grand side entrance. Elca greeted them at the threshold. A gold medallion bearing her emblem hung across her forehead. Her black dress was studded with bright lampstone beads as if she wore night sky itself. Drinith noted Elca's bare shoulders. She must have been the inspiration for the style. She struck Drinith as a leader rather than a follower.

"I am delighted you both could make it," she declared. "Everyone worth inviting is coming except the Rat King, Greny Scylax." She shrugged. "Still, two out of three cordents general is not a bad turnout. All the foreign diplomats are in attendance"—she flashed a devious smile—"including Lysan Molyar, the ambassador from Rhumgad."

Drinith seethed at the mention. Did Elca expect her to spend the evening exchanging pleasantries with the mouthpiece of the tyrant who butchered her family and stole her kingdom?

Epmar sensing her unease, squeezed her arm. "I'm sure in the unlikely event we stumble across him in your massive home," she said diplomatically, and with a touch of sarcasm, "Drinith would appreciate engaging in a civil conversation with him."

"Indeed," Elca said. "Make yourselves at home."

"What was that about?" Drinith asked as she and Epmar ambled into the hall.

"She wanted to make sure you didn't create a scene if you blundered into Lysan."

"I would never abuse her hospitality in that way."

"I know. Be warned, Lysan may try to goad you. He's clever and dangerous."

Was there nobody in Gyre who wasn't? Drinith tensed as they wandered through the throng of black-clad women and their colorful male companions. On the podium, an orchestra kept up a steady barrage of somber music that to Drinith's ears sounded like funeral dirges.

"Are all of these meritocrats?" she asked Epmar.

"No. Only those wearing emblems of merit on their headgear or their foreheads are meritocrats. The meritorians incorporate their family emblem into their brooches or rings or pendants."

Epmar chatted with each meritocrat who acknowledged her, displaying an extraordinary capacity for remembering their names, lineages, and interests. She always addressed them by their first names, whispering their family names to Drinith only after they had parted. Their ancestry appeared to be much more varied and exotic than the people they ruled. Perhaps less than a third had Nosteran features.

"It's our pyrate heritage," Epmar explained between introductions. "The crews who first settled the archipelago were drawn from across the Crevast."

The genuine warmth of many meritocrats surprised Drinith. After her interactions with Greny Scylax and Elca Trajar, she had assumed them to be calculating and devious. The only awkwardness happened whenever they asked after Halyard. Epmar's pained smile,

the deadness in her tone and the curtness of her answer warned
them off the subject, and they quickly steered the conversation onto
something less controversial.

Halyard himself had melted into the crowd, presumably to renew
old acquaintances. His disappearance didn't bother Epmar, so
Drinith didn't worry either. On the other hand, Zin dogged her every
step like a menacing shadow. Worse, every time she glanced back his
gaze pounced on her. Epmar, sensing her tension, gave her arm a
reassuring pat.

"Zin, we're quite parched from all this talking," she said. "Would
you mind fetching us some punch?"

Zin's face twisted with irritation. "Very well." Bowing, he stalked
toward the nearest refreshment table.

Epmar giggled. "He looked as though he would have liked to give
me an entirely different sort of punch."

"Thank you," Drinith said. "It is such a relief to be rid of him,
even for a little while."

"It's my—"

"Epmar, it's wonderful to see you." The speaker was a short
woman with beady black eyes and a severe face. Her emblem was a
knotted winged snake. "Why haven't you called?"

Epmar kissed her on the cheek. "I haven't had a moment since my
return..."

"I understand. You only arrived recently," the woman said. "You
must be still settling in." Her gaze fixed on Drinith. "And who is this
lady with the remarkable jewel on her forehead?"

"Thaxen, allow me to introduce Drinith of Kaplar."

"A pleasure." Thaxen offered her hand, and Drinith shook it. Its
calllouses surprised her.

"I must talk to Thaxen in private a few moments," Epmar said,
looking around. "Wait here for me." Before Drinith could answer, the
two meritocrats disappeared into the throng, leaving her adrift,
detached from the conversations and laughter swirling around her.

"Excuse me, Meritorian."

She turned to the speaker, a pale young man with watery blue eyes. Dressed finer than any ambassador, his white hair hung in a single plait down his back.

"I'm afraid I'm not a meritorian. I only recently came to Gyre."

He made a sweeping bow. "My mistake. To whom have I the pleasure of speaking?"

"Drinith, Princess of Kaplar." His smirk made her add: "And its rightful empress."

"A fellow pretender! I am Cransome Scarlee, the rightful Great Earl of Freeg, denied my throne by the usurpers Hamvok the Merciless and his successor, Draston the Unjust."

"I'm afraid I am unacquainted with Freeg," she admitted.

His eyes boggled with a mixture of incomprehension and horror. "Freeg is one of the most renowned realms in Phule. You must have heard of Phule, the shard of a hundred kingdoms? Well, until the tyrant Hamvok conquered most of them."

"I'm afraid not."

Pity softened his demeanor. "I understand. I really do. Such ignorance is commonplace in Gyre. The learned of this city could tell you about every ruler of the old empires of Noster. They can recite the works of poets dead over a thousand years. They possess a wealth of information about Gyre and its rivals and the cities they so cruelly pass back and forth in the Short War. But of other shards, they know little aside from the goods they trade."

He glanced around, then leaned unnervingly close to her. "I have lived among the meritocrats for five years, and all that time I have worked with obsessive devotion toward one goal: to win their aid in the vindication of my birthright. Yes, five long years of begging, cajoling, and bartering. Aside from my benefactor, I have recruited five meritocrats to my cause, one a year. But, as I am sure you'll find, it is hard to move them to act beyond their immediate interests."

He spoke with pride, as if such minuscule progress was a massive achievement. Dismay seized her. In five years, would she be able to boast the same? Did Gyre care about Kaplar's fate more than that of Cransome's home? The meritocrats were too preoccupied with their own affairs to worry about some mountain realm they'd struggle to locate on a map.

Her mission to liberate Kaplar evaporated in a terrible instant, like a dream slipping from memory. She felt suddenly bereft. She had devoted her entire life to this cause. But for her heritage, she'd be no better than a pauper. She was a fraud standing among these powerful oligarchs.

"Drinith, there you are!" Epmar grabbed her hand and pulled her away. "I'm afraid I must steal her away from you, dear Scarlee."

"Of course," Cransome said without a hint of rancor. "I'm sure we'll meet again." The crowd swallowed him before Drinith could reply.

"I noticed you needed rescuing from that windbag," Epmar whispered.

"He called me a fellow pretender," Drinith groused. "Will I end up like him?"

"Like him? Never. He's a joke. Nobody even heard of Freeg until he swaggered into the city. Many question if it even exists, if he is merely a charlatan or an idiot, or a combination of both. He could fill the Crevast with his airs and empty bluster."

Epmar gave Drinith's hand a reassuring pat. "You are an entirely different proposition. There's no guarantee you'll ever reclaim your empire. You face a lot of obstacles, it's true. But though Kaplar may not be resurrected, you won't end up a ghost of a fallen dynasty like Cransome. If one destiny is denied, you'll forge another. I've observed you for some time. You have the mettle to become as capable a leader as any meritocrat here."

Drinith acknowledged the compliment with a nod, though she didn't believe a word of it. What had she ever done to be worthy of such praise?

Epmar bit her lip. "I—"

"Your drinks," Zin growled, offering them two glasses of ruby punch on a silver tray.

"You disappeared for quite a while," Epmar observed as she picked one of them. Drinith took the other.

Zin's scowl deepened. "I've been looking for *you*, Meritocrat."

Epmar laughed as though Zin had intended it as merely a witticism and not a jibe.

"I'll get rid of the tray." Zin stomped away.

"Oh, look," Epmar said. "There's an old friend of mine, Thespenilea Reiner." She nodded at a willowy middle-aged woman whose absurdly thick eyebrows were styled in the shape of a dragon's dorsal spikes. "Hello, Thespenilea!"

"Hello, Epmar! I heard you had returned triumphant after your grand tour." She turned to Drinith with an amiable smile. "And your friend...?"

"Drinith of Kaplar. A pleasure to make your acquaintance."

"I'm delighted to meet you, too, Drinith. That's a pretty bauble you have on your forehead." Thespenilea made a vague gesture to her two companions, also meritocrats. "Permit me to introduce Tomyr Pitero and Anyrim Lavise." The two young women bowed elegantly. "We've been engrossed in a debate over strategy inspired by the Tease's taking of the city of Trunyor."

"The Tease?" Epmar asked. "I haven't been following the nuances of the Short War."

"He's Ophigee's current mercenary general," Thespenilea said.

"He has won an impressive string of victories recently," Anyrim added eagerly.

Thespenilea rolled her eyes. "Anyrim and Tomyr have been trying to convince me it would be worth luring him from Ophigee so he can win the Short War for us. I've been trying to explain to them what a monumental waste of effort that would be."

"But he has won every battle he has fought," Tomyr said.

"But not every battle he ran away from," Thespenilea observed coolly. "And he's called the Tease not just for his exploits on the battlefield. He has changed sides three times already."

"The Shopkeepers of Ophigee took him back," Anyrim said. "They aren't the sort to be sentimental. They think him worth their coin even after he left them."

"They might even take him back a third time after we purchased his service," Thespenilea said. "Many generals, just like him, have risen, but the victories never last; the gains are lost, and the spark of genius is snuffed by a series of misfortunes and reversals. He has fought predominantly Laxur and Numenal. I hear both have replaced their generals. Numenal has tempted Sathorn Sawbone out of retirement." She rubbed the rim of her goblet with her finger. "Let's see the Tease win a series of victories against old Sawbone before we consider him as a possible new Emperor of the Crevast."

It dismayed Drinith to hear them speak of the whole matter as a diverting game. They would surely treat any military intervention they made into Rhumgad with even less solemnity. And yet Drinith must have their aid or Kaplar would be lost forever.

"What's your opinion?" Anyrim asked her.

Uncertainty made Drinith hesitate. The question demanded she take one side over the other without being sure of the cost of either.

Epmar leaned into her. "There's no greater curse you could put on the Tease than suggesting he had such potential."

Her quip spared Drinith from answering. Thespenilea roared with laughter. Anyrim and Tomyr tittered nervously.

Epmar stared into her goblet. "My cup is dry and talk of such matters of import makes me thirsty. If you will excuse us, we'll leave you to your strategies and refill our cups."

As she and Drinith drifted away, a trumpet fanfare drew everyone's attention to the podium. The orchestra fell silent. Two files of soldiers adorned with gilded armor and headdresses of golden feathers cut a channel through the gathering. An attendant entered, carrying atop a staff the emblem of Gyre wrought in gold. Other servants followed in myriad costumes carrying other standards.

"The vassals and clients of Gyre," Epmar whispered to Drinith. "Each standard-bearer is kitted out in the corresponding local costume."

Behind them, carrying a golden throne, trooped eight giants in black armor studded with runes. Upon it sat the head of state, the Ducalion, encased in gold and gems.

"What do you think, Drinith?" Epmar asked.

"This feels more like a state occasion or a religious celebration than a private party."

Epmar smiled. "That's why it's called a ducal reception. Your observation of the religious overtones is interesting. I hadn't thought of that before. It's hard to know whether the Ducalion is an idol or a sacrifice. Perhaps she's both."

The dais was lowered onto the podium, and the carrying poles slid away. Two attendants pulled open the casing like the jaws of a bejeweled clam, revealing the pearl at its center: the Ducalion in white silks, looking testy. Drinith bowed with the rest.

"We thank our host, Elca, for inviting us to her home," the Ducalion said, producing a small circular biscuit. "We offer this token as gratitude for her hospitality." The meritocrat approached the dais and, bowing, took the gift. Applause thundered through the hall as Elca held it aloft.

As the clapping waned, Epmar explained to Drinith: "It's hardtack—a reminder of our pyratical beginnings, and a warning not to assume this lavish wealth will last forever. Elca has put on so many ducal receptions, she must have drawers filled with the stuff."

Elca signaled to the conductor, and the orchestra finally played a lively tune. The crowd shuffled toward the walls, leaving an open space in the center.

"Time for the dance." Epmar patted Drinith's hand. "No need to worry. I won't let anyone drag you onto the floor against your will."

They wheeled around at the sound of a loud metallic bang. A prone courtesar slid across the floor. Blood poured in rivulets from his broken nose as he fumbled with an empty scabbard. Drinith followed his murderous glare to Zin's malevolent sneer. He held the silver tray in both hands, dented, its surface streaked with blood.

Drinith groaned inwardly. This wouldn't end well.

25

———

"Wait!" Versifer cried as he stumbled down the stairs, his unfastened sandals slapping against his feet. But Quiescat could brook no delay as he charged down the steps. Every moment counted. It might be too late to save Drinith, but he had to try.

Gelasin rushed to meet him as he drew near the bottom of the stairs. "What's wrong?" he asked, his face mirroring Quiescat's horror.

"We need to get to the ducal reception before Drinith dies," Quiescat panted, hands on knees. "I'll explain on the way."

"Versifer, you and Jarma can meet us there!" Gelasin yelled as he dashed for the door.

"Wait! How will we find Elca Trajar's mansion?"

"I know where it is," Gelasin said as he flung open the door. He raced down the steps and across the plaza.

Quiescat got his second wind, trotted after him. "Should we get a palanquin?"

Gelasin flicked an impatient hand. "Faster on foot."

On *his* feet, maybe. Quiescat couldn't remember the last time he had moved so fast.

"Come on!" Gelasin yelled. "I know a shortcut!"

They weaved through a maze of progressively narrower, angular lanes. Twice, Quiescat lost Gelasin when he disappeared down hidden turns at what looked like dead ends, and had to redouble his pace to catch up. At last they emerged onto a wide lip of walkway along a curtain of precipices. On the far side of the void, the neighboring shardlet floated, its densely packed buildings leaning precariously over the edges, as though they might topple into the Crevast at any moment. Through drain holes bored in the stone flags, Quiescat glimpsed the same emptiness under him.

Gelasin pointed to a slender bridge straddling the chasm. "We must cross there."

"How do you know the city so well?" Quiescat asked, out of breath again.

"Remember, I've been here before," Gelasin said as he darted toward the bridge. "Save your breath for running."

"What breath?" Quiescat wheezed. "Lead on!"

They raced up a steep, narrow stairway to the bridge, shoving their way past descending pedestrians. Gelasin came to an abrupt stop. Quiescat dragged himself up the last couple of steps. His breath burned like fire in his throat. His leg bones felt like they'd turned into water.

"The bridge is blocked," Gelasin said, pointing to the crowd clogging its width. His finger moved upward to the smooth white shaft above them. "The canal. There's a stairwell just over there. We'll cross using the canal."

Quiescat gazed up dubiously. "You're joking, right? I can barely stand."

Gelasin smiled sympathetically. "We should split up. I'll take the canal. You try the bridge."

Quiescat nodded breathlessly.

"Listen carefully," Gelasin said. "Once you are across the bridge, keep going until you pass the Sanctuary of the Silent Scream. Take the first right and then the second left. You should be on Gray Shambles Street. At the far end is the Flower Market. From there..."

The shouts of frustrated travelers drowned out the rest of

Gelasin's directions, but not wanting to delay him, Quiescat nodded confidently as if he heard every word. He'd have to ask for directions. Surely he'd find somebody who knew the way.

As Gelasin plunged down the stairway, Quiescat forced himself upward against the descending traffic, squeezing by irate men and women raining down curses and insults upon his ears. After a slow and frustrating climb, he reached the bridge to find it still blocked. A handcart had turned over, spilling its fruits and vegetables every which way. While the owner remonstrated with two cordents waving back the crowd, several of the spectators seized on the distraction to slip by them and filch what they could. Quiescat rushed after them and picked a path across the spilled produce.

"Stop! Thief!" a voice yelled. A hand grabbed Quiescat's arm and swung him around to face the flaring nostrils of the cart's owner. "Dirty Gadfly!" The two cordents pulled the man away before his meaty fist could smash Quiescat's nose and pinned him on the ground.

"I've had enough of this," one cordent groused as the prostrate man bucked and screamed under the knee of his colleague. He beckoned the crowd. "Take all you want! We won't stop you. Think of it as an early Crevastival present."

Hands outstretched like claws, the cheering crowd surged forward. Behind the scavengers trundled other traffic, intent on crossing the bridge. After wading across a morass of stooping backs, Quiescat pushed his way through the teeming mobs flowing in the opposite direction.

A wild cheer rose. "They've thrown a cart over the side!" It wasn't clear who they were—the cordents or the looters. He had weightier concerns. Hopefully, Gelasin had made better progress.

People pressed in from every direction, immobilizing Quiescat. His arms jammed so tight against his sides, he couldn't lift them. All around him wild-eyed faces cried desperately for space and air. If he sank beneath this crush of bodies, he would die.

Whistles from both sides of the bridge pierced the shouting. Male and female cordents in black and red brigandines wormed through the press of bodies, picking it apart as they barked orders to clear the way. As the crowd dissolved around him, Quiescat took a deep breath to celebrate his newfound freedom, then pushed on.

The street on the far side wound to the right and then emerged into a long avenue. Nameless lanes and streets branched off it at irregular intervals, while nondescript temples lined both sides. Which one might be the Sanctuary of the Silent Scream?

He asked a few passersby, but they either were foreigners or had never heard of it. At last, he chanced upon an old lady selling votive offerings—little straw figures wearing tiny diadems of flowers. She looked at him up and down critically. "What would the likes of you want with a terrible place like that? It's little more than a brothel."

He tingled with the urge to race on. "I'm looking for Gray Shambles Street."

"Ah, it's directions you seek." She spat something dark and viscous on the cobbles. "Both the sanctuary and Gray Shambles are just beyond the dreamery."

Quiescat's blood ran cold.

"You can't miss it. It's a huge clear globe in the middle of the street." She flashed a snaggle-toothed grin. "Do you want to buy an offering for the dragons tomorrow?"

Damn, here came the hard sell! Quiescat reached for his money pouch, realized he'd forgotten to bring it. "I'm afraid I can't afford one at present. Please, madam, I—"

"Do you have a son or daughter?"

"A daughter," he said, meaning Drinith. "Now I must—"

The woman pushed a doll into his hand. "Then take this queen in case you don't come this way again. No charge. Throw it off the Plank and ask the dragons to bless your child."

"Thank you." He meant it. "I have to go. There's an urgent matter—"

She excused him with a wave. Bowing awkwardly, he ran down the street. The doll comforted him. Surely it must be a good omen.

Was this how normal men thought of Fate? Did they assign such significance to random kindnesses? He reckoned they must. He was a normal man now. He should remember that.

The avenue turned and the dreamery glistened ahead, mocking the neighboring buildings' feeble efforts at grandeur. He had never glimpsed one before—he had never dared. He was the Oracle of Godsdoor no longer. He should be safe. He approached the sphere warily.

Some alternate route must avoid it. He should have asked the old lady, but he had been in too much of a rush. She might have given him directions to Elca Trajar's home if he had thought to ask her.

Could he feel the dreamery's tug or was it the artifice of his fear? The enormity of the upside-down image of city and sky filling it mocked his insignificance. Only the very bottom of the sphere kissed the ground. Nothing appeared to prevent it from rolling about. Might it roll on top of him? Keeping close to the adjacent temples, he eyed the sphere for any hint of movement as he circled around it. As soon as it lay behind him, he ran.

In his haste, he almost missed the Sanctuary of the Silent Scream. The archway at the entrance gaped like an open mouth. As Quiescat dashed by it, his gaze followed a tongue of red carpet up the steps to the forbidding black doors. How well was Gelasin acquainted with the sordid business that went on inside?

He turned down Gray Shambles. Great slabs of meat hung from hooks outside a row of butcher shops, attracting more fat black flies than customers. The squat butchers, their forearms as big as hams, stood in their gore-splattered aprons with cleavers at the ready, both to ply their trade and scare off thieves. The stench of blood was overpowering. Quiescat covered his mouth with a handkerchief and tromped through the dirty sawdust miring the street with head bowed.

He greeted the Flower Market with relief. Several women rushed toward him flourishing straw dolls for sale but retreated, muttering oaths, when he displayed the one he possessed. Through the stalls of varicolored exotic blossoms, he glimpsed casquar palanquins waiting patiently for customers. Dashing over to the nearest, he inquired breathlessly, "Where can I find Meritocrat Trajar's mansion?"

The female driver grinned. "I don't know where she lives, but I'm sure my casquars know the way, if you get my meaning."

"I have no money, I'm afraid."

Frowning, she scratched the back of her head. "Then it's shanks' mare for you, *I'm* afraid."

"Please! A girl's life may depend on me getting there."

The driver drummed her lips with her gloved fingertips. "Is that so? Well, you look like an honest fellow to me, so I reckon I'll oblige you." She pointed across the stalls to a gap in the encircling buildings. "Over there you'll find Treadware Lane. Turn left at the far end. Take the second right, then the third right. The meritocrat's mansion is in the next plaza."

He grabbed her hand and shook it. "Thank you." He didn't wait for her reply. Even as he followed her directions, doubt nagged. Could she be playing a trick on him? He glanced upward at the aqueducts and canals netting the sky. He should have gone with Gelasin.

A slap on his shoulder halted him. He swung around, his balled fist ready to strike his attacker. "Gelasin! Thank the gods you're here!"

"My shortcut wasn't as short as I hoped," the warrior said. "We're not far now though." As he led the way, Quiescat noted his route matched the driver's directions.

At the end of the last street, he glimpsed the plaza beyond a line of cordents. Gelasin tried to nudge his way through them only to be pushed back.

"You two Gadflies must have your fun in another plaza tonight," one of them said. "There's a ducal reception going on in there tonight."

"We have to speak to Meritocrat Hax," Quiescat said.

The officer squinted at him. "On what business?"

"Hey!" another guard said, pointing into the plaza. "They're coming out."

Quiescat stood on his tiptoes and craned his neck to see over their heads as they stared into the plaza. Gaudy courtesars and black meritorians poured out of one mansion and spilled down its steps.

"Too late," he murmured. "We're too late."

26

———————

"Zin!" Drinith yelled.

She rushed toward him, but Epmar held her back. "This is a courtesar matter. It isn't appropriate for you or I to intervene."

"Zin's not a courtesar," Drinith protested.

"Assaulting one made him subject to their code. Not even the most powerful meritocrat would dare intervene."

Damn Zin for this act of idiocy! Damn him for putting her in a position where she must defend him, for making her worry about him despite her detestation.

Amid the looks of shock, titillation, amusement, and boredom, a young meritorian's face stretched with horror. She must be the courtesar's lover.

Halyard interposed himself between Zin and his victim. "He is a foreigner in this city and ignorant of our ways."

The prone courtesar scrambled to his feet. "He assaulted me like a coward in a ducal reception." He probed his ruined nose with the tips of his fingers, pointed at Zin. "He drew blood. This insult must be answered outside with something sharper than words." He gave Zin and his tray a sour glance.

"He is a foreigner and unworthy of staining your blade."

"He stained my face and my clothes and my honor," the courtesar insisted, glancing down at the bloody front of his coat.

"Let me fight in his stead," Halyard said.

"No!" Epmar cried. "A thousand times no!"

Halyard waved at her to be silent. Epmar cursed under her breath. "Barely back two days and already the fool is intent on getting himself killed."

"I shouldn't have brought Zin," Drinith said.

Epmar's savage glare fell upon her. "That's right. You shouldn't have."

"What's your name?" Halyard asked the courtesar.

"Gwyred of Kerth. I know who you are, Halyard of Kasjor. Though it is tempting to duel a legend like yourself, tonight I will accept no opponent other than my attacker."

Halyard pointed to Zin. "This man is beneath you. He has no name, no honor. He hasn't the heart of a courtesar."

Zin dropped the tray, letting it bang against the tiles. "I'll have one when I carve it out of your chest, Gwyred of whatever."

A smattering of gasps and tut-tuts rippled through the crowd.

Epmar sucked in a sharp breath. "Insulting a meritorian family like that won't endear him to this audience."

Gwyred sneered. "Then you'll accept my challenge?"

Zin rocked back and forth on his heels. "I'm sure I issued *my* challenge when I slapped you in the face with the tray."

"Then I accept." Gwyred waved vaguely at the entrance. "Let us proceed outside and settle this matter at the point of a sword." His nose scrunched as if he smelled something vile. "I warn you, expect no quarter."

Zin laughed. "Expect to die."

Gwyred lifted his chin, swiveled around, and marched toward the door. Zin sauntered after him, looking supremely arrogant.

Halyard's shoulders slumped in resignation as he rejoined Epmar and Drinith.

"Thank the gods they've chosen to kill each other and not you,"

Epmar said. "What were you thinking? Haven't you fought enough battles without taking on Zin's?"

Halyard shrugged. "I hoped I might divert them from murdering each other."

Epmar planted her hands on her hips. "Well, it didn't work. I wish you would put away your sword once and for all. I know you think otherwise, but I would love you even more if you ceased to be a courtesar."

His smile radiated disbelief. They drifted toward the entrance, drawn by the current of the crowd.

"Do you think Zin has a chance?" Drinith asked.

"I do," Halyard said. "But that still may not save him. He's playing a game he doesn't understand. If he breaks the rules, every courtesar in Gyre will hunt him down."

"Then do what you can to help him," Epmar said.

Nodding, Halyard glided away from them, gracefully weaving through the chattering crowd until he disappeared.

Beaming with relief, Epmar took Drinith's arm. "I was unfair earlier. It's just that impossible man sometimes seems determined to get himself killed. Zin will be fine. Halyard's an old hand at this; he'll offer him some pointers."

Drinith answered with a forced smile. Why should she fret over Zin when he reveled in his own jeopardy?

The guests spilled out of the mansion, down its steps and into the plaza. Courtesars cleared a large circular space around the two combatants. Only Halyard dared to encroach it. Zin nodded along as the courtesar whispered in his ear. Gwyred chatted quietly with two other courtesars as he slipped off a glove and encased his naked hand in a gauntlet.

Window shutters swung open around the plaza, and excited heads leaned out to watch. Curiosity drew even the remaining palanquin drivers from their vehicles to observe the proceedings from a respectful distance. Duels were evidently a popular spectator sport in Gyre. The lower classes must have relished watching two pompous courtesars slicing each other to bits. But Drinith didn't share the crowd's excitement. She found no pleasure in the prospect of even Zin's life being lost.

A hand touched Drinith's shoulder. As she turned to see its owner, she and Epmar were gently pushed aside by two of the Ducalion's bodyguards. Behind them strode the Ducalion. She looked a good deal shorter than she had on the dais.

"So you're back from your self-imposed exile, Epmar," she said. "Looks like your courtesar has gained some wisdom in the meantime, but not enough to put away his sword."

"Ducalion, permit me to introduce my friend, Drinith."

Drinith bowed as the Ducalion's cool glance fell upon her.

"Have you forgotten my name like the rest, Epmar?" the Ducalion asked.

"It's not...the custom," Epmar said.

"And everything in Gyre must accord to custom or the whole city will sink into the void." The Ducalion laughed lightly, but Epmar's eyes widened with panic. She opened her mouth to speak but shut it again.

"I had better move on," the Ducalion said, "before your meritocrat friends get jealous." She waved vaguely over her shoulder. "I'm sure we'll chat again soon."

"I'll look forward to it," Epmar muttered. The Ducalion, flanked by her bodyguards, moved two steps ahead of her and Drinith and focused her attention on the makeshift dueling circle.

There, Halyard exchanged a few final words with Zin and withdrew. Gwyred limbered up and swept his sword before him. Zin spun his dagger in one hand. He drew his sword with surprising awkwardness. Gwyred licked his lips. He cut the air by his side twice, stepped forward. Zin raised his foot but kept it hovering above the ground. Excited whispers rippled through the crowd.

Zin planted his foot in its original position.

"He can only do that once more," Epmar said. "After that, according the Courtesar Code, Gwyred can attack as soon as Zin lifts his foot."

Gwyred tensed as Zin raised his leg again. The moment he

planted his foot on the cobbles, Gwyred sprang forward. Zin parried his thrust. As their blades slid together, Zin stabbed at his foe with his dagger, but Gwyred's gauntleted hand grabbed the blade and yanked it from his grip. Zin groaned as Gwyred delivered a knee to his stomach. As the warrior stumbled backward, he waved his sword to ward off any pursuing attack, but none came. The courtesar instead tossed the bent dagger away and waited for Zin to steady himself.

"You had enough yet, Gadfly?" Gwyred asked coolly.

Zin spat on the ground. "I'm just getting warmed up." He charged.

Gwyred danced clear of his blade to appreciative cheers. Zin chased him about the circle, but Gwyred dodged every thrust and swing to the delighted exclaims of his audience. The courtesar was toying with the lowlander. Gwyred could finish his opponent at any time of his choosing. Zin was outclassed.

Zin halted his pursuit in dismay. "I thought you were here to fight, not flutter about like a startled chicken!"

The crowd laughed, but at him, not his joke. He glared at them with such rage Drinith feared he would turn his blade on them.

He pointed his sword at Gwyred's feet. "Take off those fancy spring-loaded platforms and fight like a proper man."

Gwyred swished his sword thoughtfully. He slipped off his shoes. Barefoot, he looked a good deal shorter.

A murderous grin spread on Zin's face. This was exactly what he had hoped for. He rushed at the courtesar, but even shoeless, Gwyred was too fast for him. The courtesar blocked three of Zin's cuts with consummate ease, slipped back from a fourth. Blocking the downward sweep of Zin's blade again, Gwyred closed the distance between them and punched him in the face with his gauntlet, knocking him off his feet.

Still clutching his sword, Zin was too stunned to use it as he lay prone on the ground. Gwyred thrust the tip of his blade at his foe's neck. Drinith gasped, expecting Zin's death. The combatants spoke for a moment, then Zin's sword clattered on the cobbles and Gwyred stepped away. He waved his sword above his head as applause, whistles, and cheers filled the plaza.

"Zin must have accepted an offer of clemency," Epmar said.

Behind the jubilant victor, Zin sprang to his feet. He picked up his discarded blade and strode toward Gwyred, but before he could close the gap, Halyard intervened, knocked the sword from his hand and pulled him away. The surging crowd engulfed them as Gwyred's friends hoisted him onto their shoulders like some conquering hero.

Drinith glimpsed a palanquin driver just behind her out of the corner of her eye. His stillness in the hubbub's midst held her attention. What was he doing here so far from the rest of his colleagues? His blue-black skin and frizzy blue hair identified him as a lowlander from Rhumgad. Fear dwelled in those black eyes. His face was ugly with fear.

As she turned to him, he rushed toward her, lunging with a dagger. She swerved. The blade cut through her dress, scraping against the mail beneath. She grabbed his arm with both hands and yanked him forward, smashing her forehead into his face—a handy move Gelasin had taught her. Stunned, he dropped the knife and stumbled backward.

He collapsed face up onto the cobbles, his eyes bulging, his mouth gushing pink froth, his body shaking. Surely Drinith's blow couldn't have caused such a seizure. She scanned the screaming crowd for a second assassin. The Ducalion had disappeared but one of her guards pointed his sword at Drinith while others plowed through scattering meritorians toward them. Epmar hugged Drinith. "She's not an assassin. He is!" She pointed to the supine man.

The Ducalion's guards encircled him. One knelt beside him and pressed down the dead man's tongue with his knife. "He's dead. Looks like he took Sweet Silence or some similar poison. I can see shards of an ampoule in his mouth."

Drinith trembled as if a terrible weakness had sapped every muscle. She felt the exposed mail on her side. If she had been a fraction slower...

"It's okay," Epmar said. "He's dead. You're safe." Drinith didn't answer. She felt so cold, as cold as any corpse.

An unfamiliar meritocrat strode up to her. Her downturned green eyes and heavy eyelids gave her a melancholic aspect. "The Ducalion has invited you to her palace."

"There's no need, Osro," Epmar said. "I can vouch for her."

The meritocrat smirked. "I'm afraid the Ducalion insists."

Epmar answered Drinith's expression of puzzlement with a sigh. "You're being arrested."

"What!" Drinith's eyes darted back and forth between them.

"I wouldn't put it so harshly," said Orso. "You'll scare the girl."

"Use whatever euphemism you like," Epmar replied, "it amounts to the same thing. You go too far."

"The Ducalion's wellbeing is paramount," Osro insisted. "No Ducalion has fallen to an assassin in two centuries, despite countless attempts, precisely because of our meticulousness in such matters. If your friend has nothing to hide, then she won't mind answering a few questions."

Drinith stared at the corpse. He was from Rhumgad and so was she. "I'll go," she said, "if that is what I must do to prove my innocence."

Osro clapped her hands together. "Splendid!"

Epmar shook her head. "You had better not hurt her."

"I'll return her in the same fine condition she's in now. I might even get someone to sew up that rip in her dress after we've searched her." Osro slipped her arm under Drinith's and led her down the steps.

Drinith shrank from the curious stares of the onlookers, but she couldn't block out their whispers:

"They're taking her to the Inkeep for questioning."

"Foreigner."

"Gadfly princess."

"Who is that if not the assassin?"

Burning with indignation, she scanned the crowd, but the identity of this last slanderer eluded her in the confusion of faces.

A half-dozen of the Ducalion's guards awaited her at the bottom. And a coffin. Her blood froze. She turned to flee, but gauntlets seized her arms.

"Don't struggle," Osro urged. "You'll only injure yourself."

"What's the meaning of this?" Thaxen strode toward them. "Foreign agents fall within my remit."

What did she mean by foreign agents? "I'm no spy," Drinith insisted.

Halting, Thaxen arched an eyebrow. She turned to Osro. "Epmar is worried about her friend."

"The innocent need not worry."

"She questions if you have cause to arrest her friend, given she's obviously the victim of the attack, not the instigator."

Osro bowed her head and pursed her lips meditatively. "Yes, she's the victim, apparently. Her assailant wasn't particularly adept, to be honest. One blow from her was enough for him to give up and kill himself. He could have struck during the duel, but he waited until she might be alert for his attack."

"You can't blame her for the incompetence of her enemies," Thaxen said.

Drinith nodded, afraid to speak in case she inadvertently undermined Thaxen's argument.

"She's wearing a mail shirt as if she expected trouble," Orso pointed out.

"According to Epmar, she had reason. It's not the first time that an attempt was made on her life."

In Drinith's mind, the distance between her and the box expanded. Surely, Osro must listen to reason.

"Still, you have to admit it was all a bit"—Osro pulled a face—"convenient. How well do you know this girl?"

"I know only what Epmar told me." Her indifferent tone made Drinith shiver.

"True," Orso agreed. "And Epmar has only recently returned to us. How well could she know the girl?"

Thaxen flicked her wrist impatiently. "Enough prattling. Take her away!"

"No!" Drinith cried toward Thaxen's retreating back. "I'm innocent. You can't just abandon me. I did nothing wrong!"

"If you don't stop struggling, we must bind your hands," Osro warned as Drinith was manhandled into the box.

Fighting was pointless. Drinith couldn't win. She needed to save her strength for a better opportunity to escape. She lay down in the box. The soft black velvet lining teased her hair and caressed the back of her neck. *Well, at least it's comfortable,* she mused in a moment of gallows humor. But as a rectangular darkness slid across the top of the box, panic overwhelmed her. Hearing the screws squeak tighten above her, she punched and kicked the lid and screamed.

27

———————

Helpless, Quiescat watched the commotion in the plaza from behind the city guards. What was going on in there? Was Drinith safe?

The little straw doll tickled as it crinkled within the greasy pressure of his hand. It had already lost its flower headdress. Quiescat stared at the crushed figure in disgust. His hand trembled with the urge to throw it away, but a creeping suspicion that it might be unlucky to do so prevented him. He tucked it away inside his cowl.

He spied two familiar faces among the dispersing crowd. Halyard, downcast, and Zin, grim and fierce, strode at speed toward the cordon. Quiescat opened his mouth to ask about Drinith, but Gelasin shushed him.

"Drinith's obviously in trouble," he whispered. "But revealing our connection to her might land us in difficulty, too." He rested a hand on Quiescat's shoulder. "Panicking won't help her."

If she wasn't dead already. Quiescat took a deep breath to unravel the painful knot in his stomach. Memories of her as a child came unbidden to mock his failure to protect her. It would have been better if he had died on the *Surly Bonnacon*, as Fate had decreed, than outlive her.

Halyard and Zin breezed past the cordents, muttering ignorance of the situation when questioned. Halyard chopped the air sideways with his hand as a warning to Quiescat and Gelasin to be quiet. The four moved away from the barricade to the far end of the street.

"Drinith has been arrested," the courtesar said. "I don't think they realized Zin was her servant. Otherwise, they would have detained him, too."

Gelasin shook his fist at Zin. "You were supposed to protect her."

Zin raised his chin defiantly. "I did."

Gelasin's nostrils flared. "Evidently not very well. You shouldn't have taken your eyes off her for a second. Where were you, Zin?"

"Our friend here got himself embroiled in a duel with a courtesar, Gwyred of Kerth," Halyard interjected.

"I'm not your friend," Zin muttered.

"Zin would be dead now but for his opponent's gracious offer of clemency. When Gwyred turned away to bask in the crowd's adulation, Zin attempted to take a coward's revenge on the man who had only moments earlier spared him. Had I not intervened, Zin would have brought dishonor on us all and gotten himself killed either by Gwyred or a vengeful mob. Thanks to Zin's antics, neither of us were with Drinith when the ducal steward arrested her." He glanced at Zin. "Did I leave anything out?"

Shamefacedly, Zin shook his head.

Gelasin glowered at him. "A duel?" He cursed prodigiously. "You stupid—" He lunged at Zin.

Halyard stepped between them, saying, "Recriminations can wait."

Gelasin raised his open palms, "You're right. Fighting among ourselves will help nobody."

"I don't understand," Quiescat said. "Why was she arrested?"

"An assassin tried to kill her." Halyard raised a silencing hand. "Don't worry, she escaped unscathed. But the ease with which she dealt with her attacker made the ducal steward suspicious. That meritocrat is prone to seeing plots and conspiracies."

Quiescat stroked his chin. "So the pentaculars have followed us here already. At least there's one less."

"It wasn't a pentacular," Halyard said. "He was a lowlander from Rhumgad."

Gelasin nodded. "Magian, unhappy with the pentaculars' failure, must have recruited rival assassins."

"The princess is to be held in the Inkeep beside the Ducalion's palace," the courtesar said. "Epmar is doing her best to sort this mess out. She said we should await her at her mansion and do nothing to jeopardize her efforts."

A casquar palanquin halted beside them. Jarma leapt from the cab. "There you are! I thought I'd never get here. The traffic was appalling." She frowned. "Where's Versifer? He should be here by now."

Quiescat rolled his eyes. How much bad news could he take? "What do you mean?"

Jarma studied her knitted hands. "He hopped out of the cab a while ago. He said he'd be quicker on foot."

Quiescat couldn't reach the ache behind his forehead, no matter how hard he massaged it. "Why didn't you go with him?" he shrieked.

Her lower lip jutted in defiance. "I tried to, but I lost him in the crowd. I had to go back to the palanquin—he had a map we borrowed from Meritocrat Hax's study. I did my best to keep him in the cab. He kept trying to jump out. He blamed himself for putting the princess in danger."

The fault for this fiasco, as with so many others, lay with Quiescat. If he hadn't been so quick to blame Versifer—

Jarma started. "Where is the princess?"

"She's alive," Gelasin said. "Don't worry about her for now. Versifer's disappearance is more urgent." A wry smile played upon his lips. "It appears our seer didn't foresee his own vanishing."

Quiescat slapped the smugness from Gelasin's face. He covered his mouth and stepped backward, appalled by what he had done. "I'm sorry."

"You will be," Zin muttered.

Gelasin rubbed his jaw and chuckled. "I probably deserved it. I often do. My attempt at levity seems to have achieved the opposite effect."

"I'm really sorry," Quiescat said. "I've never hit anyone like that before."

"You're doing lots of new things lately." Quiescat let the jibe, if it was one, pass. He hadn't the right to quibble with anything Gelasin said after striking him.

Jarma gazed at the surrounding buildings with dismay. "How will we find Versifer in this sprawling metropolis? It's hopeless!"

"Better calm down or Quiescat might slap you, too," Gelasin joked. Blushing with embarrassment, Quiescat shied from his theatrical wink. "We'll look, simple as that. He can't be far, and this city is safer than most. Jarma, have you money?"

She nodded.

"Great. You and Quiescat will take a palanquin back to Epmar's mansion. The rest of us will split up and search."

"I'm staying," Quiescat insisted. His palm yet tingled from the blow.

"Far be it from me to disagree with a man with such a mean smack, but you and Jarma are strangers here. Zin and I have some passing familiarity with Gyre and Halyard knows it intimately. We can move faster without you."

"I have legs and I'm blind no longer," Quiescat said. "I can partner up with one of you." That way, at least, he wouldn't be sitting in a wobbly palanquin cab or pacing the floors of Epmar's home, feeling useless.

Gelasin said, "Jarma, head back to the mansion. Someone must tell Epmar what's happened when she returns. Halyard, you take Quiescat. And don't lose him. We've had enough drama for one day."

"I won't be a burden," Quiescat promised, though the aches in his calves belied his claim. Perhaps he shouldn't have volunteered so hastily.

Gelasin and Zin raced away while Halyard hailed a palanquin for

Jarma. As soon as she climbed into the cab, the courtesar turned to Quiescat. "Are you sure you won't go with her?"

"I won't delay you," Quiescat insisted, shaking his head.

It quickly became clear he couldn't keep his promise. His leaden legs couldn't keep pace with the courtesar's bounding strides, and Halyard kept having to pause for him to catch up. If only he had springs in his shoes like the courtesar, and the strength to take advantage of them. Breathless, Quiescat stopped by a small fountain, plonked down on the rim of its basin, and waved Halyard on. The courtesar stared back at him askance.

"I'll be fine," Quiescat insisted.

"Stay there," Halyard said, glancing around. "I'll be back as soon as I can." Before Quiescat could answer, he disappeared down a street.

"We must find him," Quiescat murmured as he scanned the faces of passersby. Surely somebody must have noticed a man with crystal eyes. He'd ask if they had seen Versifer. Anything was better than doing nothing. "Sorry, have you—"

A coin landing in his lap took him so much by surprise he halted mid-sentence. A second clattered against the stone rim of the fountain and rolled at his feet. He bent down and picked it up. One coin was blackened bronze, its detail worn away. The other was a dull silver wafer, not much bigger than his thumbnail. It had been minted in Thirring, but if scrapped, its metal might have had some small value.

He burned with hate for what he had become in the eyes of the public: a common beggar.

A man stood in front of him. Eyes downcast, Quiescat glimpsed his balled fists shaking in fury at his sides. "Get back to the Blue Quarter, Gadfly!" the man shouted. "We don't want your type around here pestering people, understand?"

"I..." Quiescat couldn't think of an answer. He didn't dare look up to face his harasser. He was less than nothing to this man.

"Lost your tongue, have you? Look at me when I speak to you!" Quiescat slowly looked up into the man's smirking face. "I suppose you were somebody important back on Rhumgad, some mighty lord. Hah!" He spat copiously in Quiescat's face. "You all put on airs when you arrived here. After a few months, your money was spent and now you're all living in the gutter and cadging honest people for coin and thieving and causing trouble and you still think you're better than us."

Quiescat reached for his handkerchief mechanically and cleaned his face, vaguely aware the man was still haranguing him. Presently he heard a familiar voice.

"It would be best for you to move on and leave my friend alone." Halyard. Thank the gods!

The man stood his ground. "Mind your own business, courtesar."

Halyard drew himself up. "Move along," he said, tapping his sword hilt, "or you'll face my wrath."

The man fled. In disgust, Quiescat tossed the coins into the pool. They plopped into the dark water and vanished.

"My deepest apologies," Halyard said. "In other circumstances, I'd have called cordents to deal with him properly. I should have never left you here by yourself. The city isn't safe for lone Rhumgadians at night."

"Any sign of Versifer?" Quiescat asked. If the oracle had met others of the same ilk as Quiescat's persecutor—he dared not think of it.

Halyard shook his head. "Hopefully, Gelasin and Zin fared better."

They returned to the spot where they had separated from the others. There, they waited well into the night, but Quiescat didn't complain. At least, Gelasin and Zin were still looking. The prospect of their return inspired a creeping dread. Grains of hope slipped away with every passing moment until only empty despair remained. Quiescat's vanity had caused this calamity. He had ordered Versifer around like a servant when it should have been vice versa.

Halyard kept to the shadows behind Quiescat as knots of merry courtesars in gaudy attire drifted from the ducal reception. Their banter and singing filled the night, but melancholy and dull anger lurked behind the veneer of bonhomie. These boys hadn't yet made names for themselves nor earned the admiration of a meritorian.

One of them halted and squinted as if straining to see something in the shadows.

"Run along," Halyard said. "I cannot play tonight."

The other courtesars around the squinter froze. Quiescat held his breath.

"And why might that be?" the courtesar asked.

"I am honor-bound to protect this man who stands before me."

The courtesar rubbed a finger across his mouth and winced. "My lips always chap in this dry weather. I am Myrthar of Sonet." With a flourish of his plumed hat, he bowed.

"You know my name already."

"Indeed, Halyard of Kasjor, I saw you at the ducal reception. You have quite the reputation. If you can't fight me tonight, then tell me when and where you can."

"But our appointment might force you to spurn other challengers in the meantime."

The other courtesars laughed. Myrthar's head snapped one direction and then the other to glare at them. Halyard's comment, delivered without a hint of rancor, slighted him in their eyes.

Myrthar stretched to full height. "Know, Halyard, you've made an enemy tonight."

"I'm sure we'll meet again in circumstances more to your liking."

"I'll make sure of it," Myrthar huffed as he strode away. With a few nervous titters and whispers, his audience drifted on as well.

"Do a man a favor and he hates you forever," Halyard said after the street cleared.

"You're an intelligent man," Quiescat said. "Epmar would be delighted if you put your sword aside. Why do you choose this life?"

"Why did you sacrifice your true eyes for crystal ones?"

"Touché."

Zin raced up to them. "We found him...or at least his corpse."

No, he must be mistaken. "Show me," Quiescat whispered.

He took no notice of where Zin led him. Part of him wanted to turn around, to flee the horror awaiting him in some dingy alley. Versifer was dead and the line of oracles broken.

"Are his eyes intact?" he murmured.

Zin didn't reply. Quiescat lacked the courage to press for an answer. He'd find out soon enough. Too soon.

The eyes had always been transferred as tears. The dying Versifer might have wept them into the gutter.

Gelasin, shielding a candle with one hand, awaited them outside an arched sewer. Its low ceiling forced them to stoop as they entered through a gap in rusty metal bars across its stinking mouth. The sound of rushing water came from a large hole at the back. Against one wall lay a pile of rubbish.

"Prepare yourself," Gelasin said as his candle drew near the heap, revealing it to be a corpse. He knelt and turned the dead man's face to the light. Two ruined ocular cavities stared up. The bridge of the nose had been hacked through. Someone had violently ripped the Tear from Versifer's face. Quiescat fought the urge to retch. The Tear hadn't merely been lost. Somebody had stolen it.

28

———————

A piece of torn lining tickled Drinith's cheek. Annoyed, she slid her hand up to her face and tucked the fabric away. Either she had ripped it in her initial panic or some previous captive had damaged it. She shifted about to get comfortable, but the stuffy heat of the metal box increased with every humid breath. Sweat soaked the back of her neck. Could she suffocate in this contraption? She fingered the lining for air holes. Finding a couple, she twisted and curled so she might peer through one, but no hint of light came from it. She pressed her cheek to it, feeling a movement of air so subtle she fancied she imagined it.

The rasp of sliding wood made her shudder. What was happening outside? The scraping sound repeated. A muffled grunt came from beyond the box. She gripped fists of velvet as the container swayed back and forth. A casquar screeched. Accompanied by groans of exertion, the box pitched and leveled. Metal jangled. It rocked gently to the scratch of casquar feet against cobbles.

She calmed a little to its steady swing and relaxed her grip on the lining. She closed her eyes, but try as she might, she couldn't fall asleep to its soothing rhythm. She positioned her ear close to one of the air holes and listened to the sounds of passing traffic, trying to make sense of the route. Cartwheels trundled by. Peddlers hawked their wares. A priest upbraided passersby for their disinterest in his temperamental storm god. The footfall surged and ebbed until the ring of hammers and puffing bellows drowned it out. She must be passing through some industrial part of the city, an armory perhaps. If only she knew Gyre better, she might have guessed the exact location.

The box shifted. She slid head-first against one end as the other tilted upward. What was happening? Bracing her hands against the panel to take the pressure off her head and neck, she listened. The docile scrape of the casquar's claws and the plodding steps of their driver and escort reverberated against a stone floor. Ragged breaths suggested great exertion. The climb must be steep.

"Whoa!" a man yelled. The box shuddered to a stop and leveled, much to Drinith's relief. "We'll take the prisoner from here."

"Our orders were to accompany the prisoner to Inkeep," said a second man.

"Drop your weapons," the first man said. "She's not worth getting killed for."

The familiar whisper of swords being drawn from scabbards answered. Two meaty thumps followed in quick succession. The casquars screeched. The box dropped, slamming Drinith against the lid. Outside, swords clanged and scraped, men grunted and cried. Something large made a loud splash.

Drinith punched the box in frustration. The ambushers must be more of Magian's assassins. She could do nothing to influence the battle, trapped in this contraption. If the assassins triumphed, this box would be her coffin. They didn't even need to open it to kill her. They could just toss it in whatever body of water lay nearby and let her drown. The prospect of never even glimpsing her murderers added to her sense of helplessness. All she could do was pray to the gods of Rhumgad for a miracle.

The battle fell silent.

"Hello?" Drinith asked.

Heavy footsteps punctured the eerie stillness. Metal jangled.

"Answer me," she begged.

The box wobbled awkwardly as it lifted.

"Answer me!" She might as well be dead already for all the good her cries did.

Boards creaked beneath stamping boots. The box tilted downward. It trembled as if it, too, was afraid. Water lapped against a hard surface. They were going to drown her!

If that was to be her fate, then so be it. She wouldn't give them the satisfaction of begging for her life.

The box plunged. She squeezed her eyes shut and gritted her teeth in expectation of its smack against the water, but it struck a wooden surface. Its gentle sway intensified with every heavy thud of boots against the boards.

"Careful," someone hissed. "You'll capsize the boat."

Two more of the ambushers leapt on board. Based on what she had heard, there must have been four in all. Something plunged softly into the water. The boat wobbled forward. Trickling water preceded a second plunge. The pattern of sounds repeated at irregular intervals as the boat continued its onward motion.

Her relief at not being drowned quickly dissipated. How could she be sure they weren't carrying her out to some deeper watery grave where her coffin was less likely to be recovered?

She had traveled upward for some time before the ambush. Her new captors must be transporting her on a canal. Fresh relief surged at the realization. If they intended to drown her in the canal, one point would suffice as well as any other. They must have some other plan for her. She could postpone worrying about her death for a little while.

As time dragged on, a leaden weariness overcame her. No matter how much she urged herself to stay awake, her eyelids grew so heavy she couldn't keep them open.

She awoke with a start to a metallic clickety-clack. The sound of rushing water filled her with terror. Could she be near some waterfall?

As time passed, her panic eased. The churn turned echoey. It diminished to a trickle and stopped. A tremor passed through the boat as it slid forward. "Thanks!" someone yelled.

How long had she been asleep? For all she knew, it might be the middle of the night or even the next day. She had to be still somewhere within the city, hadn't she?

The boat shuddered as it scraped against something hard. Water splashed around it. In great heaves, it was dragged up a stone ramp. Ropes slid under the box. With groans of effort, her kidnappers lifted it. The box rocked as they walked, its edges gnawing on the ropes.

The box settled gently on something soft, a cushion perhaps. The screws squealed all at once. Drinith tensed. She must seize the first chance to escape. As the lid lifted and slid away, the cold made her shiver. A ring of bland masks stared down at her.

"Leave us," a gravelly voice commanded.

The masked figures withdrew. Drinith gripped the box's sides and pushed herself upright, the air chilling her sweat-soaked back. At the far end of the box stood a veiled woman dressed in black. "I hope your journey was not too uncomfortable," she rasped.

"Why have you brought me here?" Drinith asked.

The veiled woman took a step closer and rubbed a gloved hand against the rim of the box. "I like to help the innocent. You are innocent, aren't you?"

"What about my escort? Were they not innocent too?"

"Don't worry about them. The casquars, unfortunately, had to be put down. We couldn't risk them running away with you. We left enough coin to pay for replacements so Osro won't be out of pocket. Your guards are very much alive, if a little bruised and sore. We wouldn't let a difference of opinion between two meritocrats spiral into a feud."

"And what difference would that be?"

The veiled woman pointed a finger at Drinith. "Osro suspects you might be part of a conspiracy of Rhumgadian exiles believed to be operating in our city. I prefer to give you the benefit of the doubt." She curled her finger back into a fist. "You're not a member of this conspiracy, are you?"

"No," Drinith insisted. "I only arrived in Gyre recently. I hardly know it."

The woman opened her fist, revealing a bright white stone chrysanthemum resting in her gloved palm. "And the truthstone agrees. Very good." She closed her hand again and dropped it by her side. "You're not a part of the conspiracy. On the contrary, these conspirators' distaste for you is sufficient for them to try to kill you."

"They must serve Magian the Infinite," Drinith said. There could be no other explanation.

"That's a possibility, given their antipathy for you. They must see you as a threat to them, which makes you useful to me. I'm letting you go."

Drinith arched an eyebrow. "You're just going to let me walk out of here? Oh, I see—you're using me as bait."

"No, not exactly. Hopefully, you can do more than be their quarry. Being the rightful heir of Kaplar must give you a certain prestige among many of your fellow exiles. Perhaps they can help you root out the conspirators before they hunt you down."

"And if I refuse?"

The meritocrat tilted her head quizzically. "Can you? I know you've insufficient funds to leave Gyre. Aside from the gemstone on your forehead, which you'd never be able to sell without getting caught, robbed, or both, you're destitute. If your Rhumgadian enemies don't catch you, Osro surely will, and she won't be as gentle or trusting as I am. You could hide in some sewer for the rest of your life, but where's the fun in that? You've no choice but to play the game until you win, or somebody takes you off the board."

As much as Drinith yearned to contradict her, she couldn't. "How would I go about finding these conspirators?"

The meritocrat shrugged. "If I knew that, I wouldn't need you. Try the Blue Quarter. Most of the local Rhumgadian refugees live there. You'll be less noticeable among your own people."

"Then I guess I have no choice," Drinith said. Gelasin had friends there. They might know something about this group, rumors at least.

"Good guess." The meritocrat pulled a lever. The box dropped through the floor. Dazed and lightheaded, Drinith gripped its sides and screamed. Distance quickly shrunk the rectangular gap through which she had fallen. Her descent slowed to a crawl and then halted with a sharp click. She scrambled out of the box and slipped off the table beneath, hitting the grubby, wooden floor with a loud bang. Picking herself up, she rubbed the dust tickling her face. Dizzy, she seized the edge of the table for support. A clap of laughter made her look up. The meritocrat peered down from the hole in the ceiling for a heartbeat before she disappeared.

A leather bag plummeted down, raising a cloud of dust as it thudded against the floor. Unbuckling the flap, Drinith found fresh clothes inside. She nodded with approval at the simple headdress. It would conceal her jewel. The dress was a gaudy patchwork of red and yellow reminiscent of the Aether Emperor's jester's motley. "I'm going to stand out wearing this."

"Crevastival begins tomorrow. You'll stand out if you don't," the meritocrat said from somewhere above.

As Drinith unfurled the dress, a sheathed dagger and a small pouch fell out. The pouch contained ten bronze coins, enough to keep her fed for a few days, but too little for her to entertain thoughts of escaping the city.

Fearful she was being observed by her mysterious benefactor, Drinith retreated to the darkest corner she could find and changed. Ready, she hastened through the door, stepping into a grim, empty lane. She hurried toward the bustle beckoning beyond it.

She'd head to Epmar's place, though a vague doubt plagued her. The mastermind of her liberty would surely have foreseen such a move. She must know, too, that Drinith wouldn't find there the aid she expected.

Regardless, she'd have to try, assuming she survived long enough to reach it.

29

———————

Quiescat's knees ached as he knelt on the cold, greasy floor beside Versifer's body.

He rubbed a trembling hand across his mouth. "How will we get him back to Epmar's mansion?"

Gelasin's hand rested on his shoulder. "Move away, please."

Quiescat used the slimy brick wall for support as he rose and stepped clear.

Gelasin dragged the corpse toward the hole. "Zin, give me a hand."

"What are you doing?" Quiescat's cry echoed around them.

"We need to get rid of the body," Gelasin said with shocking nonchalance as Zin helped him.

"You can't!" Quiescat cried.

"We've no choice. We can't carry him across the city without raising suspicion and we can't split up, given that whoever killed him might be still lurking nearby. We don't have the money to buy him a place in a mausoleum. We can't even afford to pay the tax to officially send him to the inner sun. Paupers don't get that luxury in Gyre. Their remains are sold in bulk to the Butchers of Laxur so they can make their undead puppets. The sewer must eventually lead to the void. The corpse will be safe from defilement in the Crevast. Just as Abecedar's was."

The name stabbed Quiescat's heart. He had failed Abecedar, too.

"The opening to the void may be some distance away," Halyard said.

Gelasin glared at him. "Then we'll carry him there."

"I'm staying put," the courtesar declared, covering his mouth and nose with a handkerchief. "It stinks bad enough up here."

"Worried you'd puke your guts over those pretty garments?" Zin teased.

"No, I'm worried I'd end up smelling like you normally do."

Zin grabbed for his sword, but Gelasin punched his arm away. "You've caused enough trouble tonight already. Cool it!"

"Are you sure we shouldn't inform the authorities?" Quiescat asked.

"Drinith has already been arrested for defending herself from an assassin," Gelasin said. "What do you think they'd do to us if we lead them to a corpse? Zin, get down the hole. I'll lower the corpse down to you."

Zin shot him an incredulous stare.

Gelasin sneered. "Think of it as a penance for your sins."

Making a vulgar gesture, Zin leapt down into the hole. His hands thrust out of the darkness to receive Versifer's body.

"Wait!" Gelasin said. He looked to Quiescat. "Do you want to perform any rite on the corpse before we take it away?"

Quiescat crouched beside Versifer, pressed a hand to his ice-cold forehead and repeated the same orison he had recited over Abecedar. Who would say that prayer when Quiescat's turn came?

After he finished, his hand remained until Gelasin gently removed it. "We can't delay any longer."

Quiescat stepped back. Gelasin pushed the corpse into the hole. The violence of his handling disturbed Quiescat. Versifer deserved better than this. Zin grunted as the shadowy mouth swallowed the body.

"I'm coming with you," Quiescat announced.

Gelasin, his face softened by sympathy, shook his head. "It's too dangerous down there. We've suffered enough today without some misfortune befalling you. Leave this to lesser men, please."

His sudden humility astonished Quiescat. He nodded.

Gelasin sat on the edge of the hole, then slipped down into it.

"They could be some time. We might as well wait outside," Halyard said. "Somewhere sweeter smelling."

They loitered outside the entrance until the overpowering malodor drove them farther away. But the stench traveled with them, clinging to their clothes. Halyard sniffed a cuff on his shirt and wrinkled his nose. "No perfume could mask that stink. I must have a bath tonight for certain."

Gelasin and Zin emerged from the sewer much sooner than Quiescat had expected. A disgusting gray slime covered their boots and spattered their leggings up to their knees.

"I need a wash," Gelasin said.

"There's a bathhouse nearby where we can clean up," Halyard said.

"We haven't time for preening!" Quiescat snapped. "Drinith is in danger."

Gelasin pressed his hands against his sides. "We can't do much to help her while she's the guest of the Ducalion. I'm sure Epmar is doing more to free her than the four of us ever could. If we go anywhere in this state, we'll be arrested. Cleaning up is a necessity, not a luxury."

Quiescat rolled his eyes. A trip to a bathhouse certainly felt like a luxury to him. Surely they could find some other way to clean themselves without resorting to this decadence.

His impatience grew as they wandered through anonymous streets.

"Are these no good?" Zin asked as they passed several gaudy buildings sporting bath brushes.

"They're not the sort of establishments a person of my standing frequents," Halyard said. "There's a place just up ahead."

He stopped before a stately building that looked like a private residence. A stone sword dangled over the door.

"I'm giving you fair warning, Zin," Halyard said. "If you embarrass me in here, Gwyred won't be the only courtesar to give you a trouncing this night."

"Keep your mouth shut!" Gelasin growled at Zin before he could reply. "You're to cause no more trouble tonight, understand?"

Zin scowled resentfully at him but kept quiet.

Inside, the proprietor, a rotund woman immaculately dressed and coifed, greeted the courtesar as an old friend.

"Halyard of Kasjor! You're a sight for sore eyes."

Halyard bowed gracefully. "The pleasure is all mine, Ganlyn. We need a bath and a change of clothes."

Ganlyn grinned. "I should say so! Would that I had a nosegay to counteract your reek. I suppose I shouldn't ask what you've been up to..."

"I would tell you, dear lady, but such dark matters should not trespass on this sanctuary. Now, about those garments. Something plain for my companions. I don't want them confused with courtesars. And for me, the nearest to my style you have."

The woman nodded. "I'm sure I might have something suitable." She rang a bell.

Serving girls in silk dresses swirled about them. Zin snatched his sword away as one tried to draw it, eliciting astonished gasps from the staff.

"No weapons are allowed beyond this reception area," Halyard explained. "And no fighting is permitted in the building. If you want to keep your sword and dagger, you can wait outside and continue to smell like a pig."

For a breathless moment, they glowered at each other. Quiescat sighed with relief as Zin slowly drew his sword and dagger and handed them to the girl.

"We want only one room," the courtesar said. "As you can see, my friends are unfamiliar with our customs."

"I'll have the room split with screens so you can enjoy a little privacy." At her sharp nod, her girls scurried up the stairs.

"It's been a long time since you graced our establishment, Halyard," she said.

He glanced at the coffered ceiling. "Yes, Ganlyn. Three years...I think. I haven't seen too many familiar faces around."

"They've mostly...moved on. Retired or dead." She bit her lip. "The life of a courtesar is brief."

"But it is glorious."

"Yes," Ganlyn said, somewhat distracted as a girl signaled her from the top of the stairs. "Your room is ready. I will show you the way."

Screens divided the chamber in four, each division containing a bath. A girl gently took Quiescat by the sleeve. Struck dumb with bashfulness, he let her lead him to the section nearest to the door. As she tugged at his clothes, he tensed. His face burned with embarrassment. Nobody had undressed him since his childhood, much less a woman.

"Perhaps you would prefer to undress yourself?"

Tongue-tied, he nodded vigorously. As she stepped away, he turned his back to her. Having stripped to the waist, he seized a towel and clutched it round him while he awkwardly removed his breeches and underpants with one hand. The scented water of the bath proved a double relief. Not only did its heat soothe his physical aches, but it also shielded his nakedness from the girl's gaze.

"Now, don't be shy," she said, sashaying toward him. Quiescat noticed how her wet frock clung to her pert figure. She picked up a bath brush and fondled it suggestively.

Quiescat gulped. "Thank you, no. I'd prefer to wash myself."

Her smile disappeared. Shrugging, she gathered his clothes and shoes and carried them away.

"Have you no blood in your veins, Oracle?" Zin jeered from the far side of the screen behind him. Quiescat was no longer an oracle, but he let it pass. He was grateful when Zin turned his "rapier wit" on the courtesar.

"Hey, Halyard," he said, "does your beloved know you hang out with pretty women like these?" His attendant rewarded him with a feigned girlish giggle. Quiescat scowled. How could anyone find that pig of a man amusing?

"She's well aware of our customs," Halyard said, a mite testily.

When his attendant returned with new garments, Quiescat dismissed her and climbed out of the bath. He caught his reflection in a mirror. He looked like a stranger. The festive red and yellow of the garments mocked him. He had nothing to celebrate. Finished dressing, he impatiently tapped his fingers on the back of the chair while he waited for the others.

He stamped in frustration. "We need to get back to Epmar's!"

Sloshing and trickling water answered him as his companions climbed out of their tubs. The pat of towels and the tap of water droplets hitting the tiles preceded the jangle of buckles and the whisper of clothes being put on. He waited for them by the door, intent to depart as soon as they were ready. Gelasin, bearing a sheepish wince, soon joined him.

Zin emerged next, scowling. "I look like a clown in this garb."

"That's an opinion I'd keep to myself if I were you," said Gelasin. "These clothes will be considered the height of fashion for the next three days. Most of the locals will be wearing something similar."

"Are you nearly ready, Halyard?" Quiescat asked.

"Nearly," Halyard said. "I just have to paint my face."

"Why do you wear that muck?" Zin snapped.

"As a warning not to annoy me."

Halyard sought Ganlyn in the lobby. "Make sure to charge everything in full to my account."

"Nonsense, there's no charge. You've already paid in sweet memories long forgotten," Ganlyn said. "Next time—"

"Ah, Ganlyn, you know better than that. There may not be a next time."

Ganlyn smiled sadly. "Of course, I do. Down the years, so many courtesars have left this establishment in high spirits, never to return. But the best recompense you can give me is to make sure you're not one of them." Two courtesars had arrived; she nodded to them. "Take care, Halyard of Kasjor." With that, she was gone.

Their weapons and a tray of shot glasses awaited them. Halyard picked up one. "Drink. It's tradition. And you never know if it will be your last."

Quiescat suspiciously eyed the clear liquid before following Halyard's example and gulping it down. Its burn stung his mouth and chest, bringing tears to his eyes, before spreading a gentler warmth throughout his body. Stepping outside, he was thankful for this blessing as the chill evening air slapped his cheeks.

The glow from the inner sun washed the edges of the shardlets and the web of bridges and canals connecting them, ensuring that however dark the sky turned, an eerie twilight hung over the city.

They trudged back through bustling, restless streets. None of them bothered to suggest traveling by palanquin. Walking was faster, and they had dawdled enough.

They reached the mansion with surprising swiftness. Epmar answered the door. "Where have you been? I was sick with worry." She scrutinized Halyard closely, apparently noticing he had changed his clothes.

"Versifer is dead," the courtesar said wearily as he gently pushed by her.

Her jaw dropped. "How?"

"Murdered," Gelasin said, following Halyard. "His killer was gone by the time we found his body."

"Come in," Epmar said, beckoning Quiescat and Zin as she retreated from the threshold.

"Any word of the princess?" Quiescat asked, lingering outside.

Epmar shook her head. "Not since she was taken to Inkeep."

Stamping feet echoed across the plaza behind him. A large detachment of cordents emerged from a side street. At their head swaggered five courtesars.

"Inside. Quick." Epmar pulled Quiescat through the door and slammed it shut. "I fear they're coming to arrest me."

"Arrest you? Why?" Quiescat asked.

"I don't know. It must have something to do with Drinith's arrest. She must have said something."

"Drinith would die before she'd betray any of us," Quiescat declared with absolute certainty.

"I wouldn't be so sure. People like Osro have ways to make people say things against their will. Gah! That's why Zizor Findol dropped by so unexpectedly. I should have known." She dashed to the parlor. Quiescat and the others followed.

Epmar threw the doors to the parlor open. The meritocrat, a small woman with large expressive eyes and a dark red complexion, jerked upright in her seat. Epmar and Halyard entered, but Gelasin blocked Quiescat and Zin from following them. The three of them stood in the hall, watching through the open doors.

"Zizor," Epmar demanded, "why are there cordents approaching my doorstep?"

Zizor lay a trembling cup on the table and forced a smile. "I'm afraid my visit is not entirely social. I've been appointed your advocate."

"I didn't know I needed one."

Zizor's smile turned more genuine. "Good. That means I'm not wasting my time. Your friend Drinith was liberated from her captors by a gang of sham cordents. The scoundrels had impeccable manners, not killing or seriously maiming anyone, and leaving ample compensation for the casquars they slew."

So Drinith was free. Relief surged through Quiescat only to wilt the next instant. She hadn't been rescued. She'd been kidnapped and the culprits likely belonged to the same group who had tried to kill her at the ducal reception. She could be already dead.

"It's assumed a meritocrat arranged the rescue," Epmar said.

Why would a meritocrat kidnap Drinith? Unless she wanted to curry Magian's favor.

"Exactly," Zizor said. "And you're the only meritocrat with reason to help her."

Epmar stared at her in incredulity. "Do you believe me capable of such arrogance?"

Zizor opened her arms. "I don't, that's why I'm here. But you must admit it looks suspicious. You've transgressed decorum before."

Epmar scowled. "That was nothing in comparison."

"True, but you left Gyre for a long time. People change. Left unchecked, harmless tendencies can become dangerous ones."

"I had no part in this crime," Epmar insisted.

"Then some enemy of yours must be responsible, someone with a grudge. Someone who lost a lover to Halyard, perhaps."

"Such vindictiveness would go against decorum."

"True," Zizor said. "But you yourself have broken with custom. What would stop another meritocrat following your example, especially when you're the one who would be blamed?"

Epmar sighed. "Sounds plausible, but it could be anyone. It could even be you. You could have volunteered to advocate so you could gloat to my face. No offense."

"None taken," Zizor said. "I understand exactly what you mean. Unfortunately, that leaves only one obvious suspect—you."

"Rather, that leaves us with no suspect at all, given I had nothing to do with it."

"I understand Drinith came to Gyre with several followers."

"They—"

Zizor made an imperious gesture. "Before you answer, you should know that Halyard and three others were observed visiting a bathhouse near where the attack happened. There was blood on their clothing."

"An unrelated matter," Epmar said. Zizor's insistent nod urged her to divulge more. "One of her companions came to an unfortunate end through no fault of his own."

"An accident?"

Epmar gave Halyard a nervous glance.

"He was murdered," he said.

"And you reported his death to the cordents?" Zizor asked.

Halyard's lips pressed into an angry line. "We thought it simpler not to, given Drinith's arrest."

Zizor crossed her legs and clasped her knee with both hands. "And where is the body?"

"We consigned it to the void."

"That is unfortunate," Zizor said. She turned to Epmar. "As your advocate, I must counsel you that your best course of action is to surrender to the cordents. I'm sure an interrogation by a pair of truthscryers will prove your innocence."

Gelasin drew Zin away from the open door. "We have to get out of here," he hissed. "Find Jarma."

Zin turned to go but halted. "She's standing on the stairs."

Gelasin twisted round and beckoned her.

"Wouldn't it better to submit to interrogation and prove our innocence?" Quiescat suggested.

"Innocence of what?" Gelasin snapped. "There's no telling what they'd ask once they had us. I've visited Gyre before, remember. It would be best to keep the city's authorities ignorant of my previous escapades here."

"Why?" Quiescat asked. "What did you do?"

Zin snickered.

"Never you mind," Gelasin said. "Old business, best forgotten."

In the parlor, Epmar scowled. "And what about the five courtesars outside? Why did they accompany the cordents?"

Zizor glanced at Halyard. "They're...a precaution. If Halyard makes no trouble, they won't either."

"The mansion must be surrounded," Zin whispered. "They'd hardly be so stupid as to let us slip out the back door."

"There won't be any trouble," Epmar said. "I'll make sure of it."

Zizor uncrossed her legs. "That is very reassuring." She rose to her feet. "I'll leave you now and talk to the party outside. I'll assure them everyone will surrender peaceably."

Halyard sprang from his seat. Quiescat tensed for violence, but Epmar's raised hand stilled the courtesar. "Thank you. I'm glad you chose to be my advocate."

Zizor shook the hand Epmar extended. "It's my privilege to help a friend in need."

"Indeed." Epmar laid a hand on the meritocrat's shoulder and steered her toward the door. "I'll show you out."

They chatted blithely about inconsequential things as they strolled to the front door. As the door shut behind her guest, Epmar's veneer of congeniality fell away. She turned to the butler, who had appeared by her side. "Fenvar, take everyone through the black passage now. Halyard, you must go with them as well. I must be the only person they find in this mansion when the cordents enter."

30

———————

Drinith pushed through the jabbering crowd. Their excited curiosity made her queasy. Beyond the line of cordents across the plaza lay Epmar's mansion and her friends. This commotion couldn't be a coincidence. It must be connected to her escape.

What was the name of the inn Gelasin had mentioned? The Gad Moon Inn. If he was still at liberty, he'd head there.

She drifted to the periphery of the mob. A hand grabbed her arm. She repressed the urge to punch its owner. Engaging in a fight here would attract unnecessary attention.

"Whash goin' on?" a man slurred. The single white tooth jutting from his gums emphasized the lack of the rest. His breath stank of cheap rum.

"I don't know," Drinith answered. "The cordents had the street blocked before I arrived."

His hand released her sleeve, his smile slackening with mild disappointment.

As he drifted away, she grabbed his arm.

"Wha' d'you want?" he snapped.

"I need to find the Gad Moon Inn. It's in the Blue Quarter."

"Find i' yourshelf. De Blue Quarter'sh na' da' big." He pulled free of her grip.

"I don't know where the Blue Quarter is."

He cocked an eyebrow. "But you musht. You're blue."

Damn this ignorant man. Could he not see she was green-black? With strained patience, she explained, "I'm new to the city."

"Den folla de shmell, Gadfly!" he shouted over his shoulder as he scurried away.

She forced her curled fists open. She'd find the Gad Moon Inn herself if she had to walk the entire city.

"Hey, are you looking for the Blue Quarter?" another man asked. He pointed down the street. "Keep going that way until you cross the second bridge. Then take the first right and second left. The Blue Quarter is over the next bridge."

"Thanks," she said, turning to leave.

"Be careful down there," he called after her. "It's a rough neighborhood."

She followed the directions without difficulty. A musty smell assaulted her before she reached the final bridge. Its parapets had been crudely painted bright blue. Beyond, the buildings were poorly maintained, worn with age, and marbled with black mold. She found it curious that buckets lined the streets.

The faces of the people she passed represented every region of Rhumgad, but their one unifying feature was their hard stares. Several looked her up and down with palpable disdain. Why should they direct such hatred at her? She was a Rhumgadian exile like them. Whether they were highlanders or lowlanders, the distrustfulness was the same.

She approached the least threatening passerby, an old woman hobbling along with half a loaf of bread tucked under her arm.

"I'm sorry to trouble you—"

The old woman jerked away from her, clutching her half-loaf tightly with both hands. "What do you want?" On the far side of the street, two young ruffians leaning against a wall snickered. The last thing Drinith needed was their attention.

"I'm looking for the Gad Moon Inn," she said sweetly.

The old woman glowered at her and then the toughs.

"I am supposed to meet friends there," Drinith explained, keeping the thugs fixed in the corner of her eye.

"If they were friends, they should have given you directions," the old woman huffed. "Leave me alone!"

The two wiry youths straightened and slipped across the road. "Hello, beauty," the taller of them said with a fat, greasy grin. "You're seeking the Gad Moon Inn? We'll show you the way."

How long would it take the two of them to lead her down some darkened alley? They were in for a surprise if they tried anything. It wasn't so long ago that Drinith killed a trained assassin. She could take these two ruffians if she had to. "That's kind of you."

"It's not far," the taller youth assured her as he strode down the street. Drinith didn't miss the shorter one's delay in following. She gestured him to walk ahead of her. He complied with a shrug.

"How come you don't know where the Gad Moon Inn is?" the taller one shouted back.

She gave the shorter one a stare to let him know she wouldn't forget him despite his friend's distraction. "I'm new to Gyre."

"I knew I hadn't seen you around before," the taller youth said. "Did you come from Rhumgad?"

"I was a baby when I left," Drinith said.

"I was born after my parents fled. My father was a nobleman in Erdabo."

"His father was a nobleman," his companion mocked with a high-pitched nasal voice. "Mine was his servant until he ran out of money."

"In all seriousness, I'd be dead now but for his parents," the taller one said. "My father gave up and died, and my mother worked herself to death soon after that. Nosdan's parents took me in. They treated me like their own son."

Nosdan smirked. "They treated you better, Jathar."

"Well, you were always so cheeky."

Drinith mustn't let this banter lull her. These two might turn on her at any moment.

Jathar pressed a fist to his chest. "One day, I'll return to Rhumgad to fight Magian. And you'll come with me, Nosdan."

"To be your servant? I don't think so."

"If we live here for a hundred years, we'll never belong."

Was this merely an idle wish on Jathar's part or something more? Perhaps, Drinith had been looking in the wrong place for support. There must be many enclaves of Rhumgadian exiles dotted about the Crevast, yearning to return home. But wishes weren't enough to win wars. She needed money.

Her guides fell silent and turned down a narrower street. Heads leaned out windows, watching. Would any of them come to her aid if these two boys attacked her? She realized with a shiver she had counted on facing them alone. They could be leading her to where several of their friends waited. She needed to escape now before it was too late.

"There's your inn," Jathar said, pointing at a ramshackle building.

"There's no sign outside," Drinith said, glancing up and down the empty street.

He snickered. "Why would they need a sign? Only locals drink in it. We would escort you inside, but the owner, the Widow, banned us. Hey, you might put in a good word for us with her."

It sounded plausible. Drinith kept an eye on them as she approached the door. No telltale sounds of merriment came from inside; in fact, all was as silent as a tomb. She wrapped a hand around the hilt of her dagger and pushed on the door.

It squealed open. A half-dozen empty tables were scattered around the room. In the brick fireplace, a pile of sticks smoldered. A battered rectangular shield was mounted above the mantelpiece. The scarred image it bore appeared at first glance to be a simple double-headed axe, but the winding handle was a snake. The shield's edges had been notched in several places and two diamond-shaped holes had been punched into it. Two men sat hunched at a narrow bar. Drinith glanced behind her, half-expecting the two youths to charge at her and push her inside, but they had disappeared.

She entered and sat at the nearest table. From somewhere behind the bar a blue-black lowlander appeared, heavyset, bald, his beard braided. One patron mumbled something, then downed his drink. He and his companion coolly eyed Drinith as they slid off their seats and sauntered out the door.

The man behind the bar dried a tankard with a raggedy cloth. "What do you want?"

"I'm here to see the Widow. I believe she's the owner of this establishment."

He theatrically studied his handiwork. "And does she want to see you?"

"That depends. Who are you?"

"I'm the Widow's husband." His hands disappeared under the bar. Beneath the table, Drinith's hand tensed on her dagger's hilt. His hands reappeared, clutching a pewter jug, which he placed on the counter.

"The husbands of widows generally aren't in a position to serve drink," she said dryly.

He sighed. "Folks call her the Widow because her previous husbands died tragically. I'm her fourth and, I hope, the last. Now, quit wasting my time. Who sent you here?"

"Gelasin." She lifted her headdress a fraction to reveal her cyan emerald. If he knew anything about her, he should recognize it.

He relaxed. "Forgive my irascibility. Royalty rarely patronizes our humble establishment. I'm Woad Glastum. Did Gelasin ever mention me?"

"Not by name, but he said I could trust this inn's owners."

He nodded as if any other answer would surprise him. He picked up the pewter jug and two mugs and lumbered over to her table. "My wife, Tazran, is out on an errand. She'll be back in a while." He sat down beside her and filled the two mugs. He slid one in front of her. "Things must be bad if you've turned up here by yourself."

"I think Gelasin may be under arrest."

He sipped from his mug. "That can't be good. Tell me everything. Leave nothing out."

She took a sip of the sour black beer. She swallowed it to be polite, nearly gagging. She recounted everything that had happened since the assassin attacked her at the ducal reception. He sipped his beer and listened. He asked a few questions about the meritocrat who had freed her but offered no opinion as to her identity.

As Drinith described the suspicion the other inhabitants of the Blue Quarter had shown her, he burst out laughing. "It's your clothes. We don't bother with Crevastival down here and those garments look as if they have never been worn before. The cordents are always sending spies to the Blue Quarter to make sure we're behaving."

"Surely everyone couldn't have noticed my attire," Drinith said.

"Most people would. It's a poor neighborhood. There isn't even a well on this shardlet. That's why there are buckets everywhere outside. The meritocrats generously open sluices in the canal that crosses the quarter at night so we can fill them. Somebody wandering about in nice clothes is bound to attract attention. And those who didn't notice immediately would pick up on others' chariness. Fear is contagious around here."

She told him about the two boys who had escorted her to the inn.

Woad grinned. "I know those two rascals. Nosdan's father is a regular here. I never met Jathar's. He was long dead before I arrived. Drowned himself in drink, I heard. They're the lucky ones, you know, the ones who made it off Rhumgad. Magian massacred the rest. Anyone who opposed him, or might. Buried them in mass graves or fed them to the Inner Sun." His voice shook with rage. He stared vacantly a moment, lost in his anger.

Presently a smile returned to his face. "You're safe here for now. Gelasin won't divulge anything under interrogation." He refilled his cup and topped up Drinith's. "It's good, isn't it? It's specially imported from Rhumgad through an unofficial channel."

Drinith gulped down another mouthful of the vile sludge and gave him a tactful smile. "How can you be so sure Gelasin won't talk?" she said, quickly changing the subject.

"I've known Gelasin a long time. I gave him that name." He pointed at the shield. "We served in the same mercenary company until he joined your retinue. He'd die before he'd betray us. Don't doubt that." The casualness with which he spoke of death made her shudder.

"Hopefully, it won't come to that," Woad added. He took a long draught that drained half of his mug.

She wet her upper lip against the rim of her mug to be polite.

The door pushed open. Woad's brightening expression quickly turned to puzzlement as if he had assumed he knew the entrant only to realize he didn't. Drinith glanced over her shoulder at the stranger, recognized that now-familiar face.

"Assassin!" she roared, lifting from her seat, flinging her mug at the pentacular. He batted it out of his way. She drew her knife.

"I want no trouble," Woad said, rising stiffly from the table, lifting two trembling hands. "You two can do whatever you want after I'm gone." He shied from Drinith's glare as he shuffled toward the door. How could he just abandon her?

"He'll kill me!" she yelled.

"Not my concern. Sorry," he said without even a glance.

The pentacular's triumphant laugh sent shivers through her.

Woad suddenly sprang at the assassin, but the pentacular moved with incredible speed, deftly avoiding his knife and knocking him across the room.

"Run!" Woad cried.

She dashed toward the bar. A hand seized her shoulder and spun her around. Her knife struck the assassin's arm as something sharp punched her chest. She toppled backward. The floor slapped the back of her head, dazing her. Shadows tangled above her. A snarl ended with one shape tossing off the other. It landed out of sight with a bang and a pained groan. The victor seized Drinith by the front of her dress, enclosing a ball of the knitted metal beneath in his fist.

"That explains why you're not dead," the pentacular said. "You have been full of surprises." He lifted her with one hand as if she was nothing. He dangled her before him, her mail constricting so tight around her torso she struggled to breathe. Plaintive groans coming from Woad somewhere on the floor roused her from her stupor. She screamed. Her wild kicks couldn't reach him. She dug her fingers into his arms until her nails broke. It only made him laugh.

"It's been a pleasure, but now—" He shuddered. As he turned to face the woman standing behind the counter, Drinith glimpsed the hilt of an axe jutting from his back. He dropped her to the floor as a second axe spun at him. He snatched it out of the air, used it to deflect a third. Drinith grabbed her knife and scurried on her hands and knees toward him, but Woad reached him first. As he yanked on the axe in the pentacular's back, the assassin swung around and stabbed his arm. Woad fell backward, pulling the axe free. Blood gushed down the pentacular's legs. He teetered. A dagger struck him above the eye. The woman mumbled a curse, but the assassin dropped to his knees and then face-down on the floor. Axe in hand, Woad slipped and slithered across the bloody tiles and lopped off the pentacular's head.

"Apologies for the ruse earlier," he said. "I hoped if the pentacular thought I was a disinterested bystander, I might catch him unawares, but the bastard was too fast for me."

"I suppose we're closed for the rest of the night," the woman said, sauntering over to the door and shutting it. Her tied-back hair added to the harshness of her long, blue-black face. A forbidding sternness chiseled its every line. "Woad, are you okay?"

He wrapped a bandage around his arm. "I've a few bruises and he nipped me with his knife. It's nothing serious. Tazran, permit me to introduce Drinith, Princess of Kaplar."

The woman nodded. "Pleased to meet you, Your Highness."

Woad grinned. "Princess, this is the widow you've heard so much about."

"I'd have been a widow for the fourth time if I had been a moment later," Tazran said.

"He was a pentacular," Drinith said.

Tazran's eyebrows arched. "The princess keeps some rarified company."

"This is my fault," Drinith said. "I brought him here."

Woad shrugged. "If he had been stalking you as you made your way here, you'd have never reached the inn. Maybe he followed Gelasin when he visited us, or somebody tipped him off. The pentaculars are as famed for their spy network as their efficiency at killing. Where in the queue did he come?"

"Fourth," Drinith said.

"The fifth won't be far behind," Woad said.

"Why isn't Gelasin minding her?" Tazran asked.

"He's been arrested, we think."

Tazran rolled her eyes. "We had better get her away from here then, fast. I don't fancy fighting another pentacular."

"I'll take her to our safe house on Wealgiver Street," Woad said.

With a sigh, Tazran picked up an axe. "You can help me get rid of the pentacular's body before you go." She glanced about the blood-spattered room. "I guess I've a great deal of scrubbing to do."

"I'll help," Drinith said, though the prospect made her queasy.

"The best thing you can do is clean yourself upstairs, in our bedchamber," Tazran said. "There's a jug and basin on the chest of drawers. And you'll find some of my old clothes in a trunk. Try not to drip blood everywhere."

Relieved, Drinith hurried upstairs. Ignoring the sound of chopping coming from the common room, she carefully stripped off her outer garments. A fire in the wood-burning stove made the room cozy. The pentacular had broken a link in her chain mail and left a large bruise over her left breast. She washed her hands, face, neck, feet, and sandals, turning the water in the basin pink. Throwing open the chest, she dug through the crumpled clothes, picking out the drabbest and most worn.

Tazran ran up the stairs. She approved Drinith's new apparel with a nod. She picked up the basin and tossed its contents out the window. "The canal rain will take care of it." She grabbed Drinith's discarded clothes and threw them in the stove.

Outside, a loud whistle preceded a sudden deluge that ceased as suddenly as it began. People rushed from every house and waded through the retreating floodwater to reclaim their filled buckets. Laughing hoarsely, Woad squelched up the stairs. "That's me, washed." Chuckling, Tazran threw him a towel. He winced as he caught it with his injured arm. Drinith gazed out the window while he changed. In the twilight glow of the inner sun, the rain's gloss returned to the quarter a little of its lost splendor.

Buttoning his shirt, Woad cautioned, "You'd better hide that jewel on your forehead, Your Highness. It would attract a lot of attention."

She glanced at the blood-spattered headdress lying on the floor. She had forgotten the gem.

Tazran pulled a wool hat from a drawer and offered it to her. "That should cover it."

Drinith put it on, pulling it down over the jewel.

"Time to go," Woad said.

"Let me dress that wound first," Tazran said.

"No time," Woad insisted. "I've had worse cuts shaving."

He and Tazran shifted the wardrobe away from the wall. They removed a floorboard beside one wall. Woad reached beneath the wall, and a large section slipped down. He lifted it away, revealing a stairwell on the far side.

"It leads up to the canal," he explained. "The proper entrance at street level has been bricked up for years. We made a new one in case we needed an emergency escape route." He and Tazran kissed. Lighting a torch in the stove, he stamped up the winding steps. As Drinith followed, the sound of the wall sliding back into place echoed up the well.

Woad was panting heavily when they reached the top. "Old age must be catching up with me," he muttered. He slid back a bolt on the door and pushed it open. A small punt—a flat-bottomed boat, long and narrow—was moored in the canal directly in front of it.

"This will take us to Wealgiver Street." Woad rubbed his wrist. "You can punt. Normally I would, but my arm is sore." They climbed on board. He released the mooring and Drinith picked up the pole. With Woad's guidance, she quickly learned how to propel and steer the boat.

The light of the inner sun didn't reach up here. Beyond the parapets of the canal, ornate buildings loomed, carving jagged silhouettes against the starry heavens. Bridges linked some to the canal.

Most of the traffic they encountered was casquar-drawn barges. Drinith shuddered as they passed a water hearse traveling in the opposite direction. She needed no reminder of death. A veiled widow, sitting at the foot of the coffin, reminded her of the mysterious meritocrat who had helped her escape. A bright coat was draped over it.

"A fallen courtesar," Woad whispered. "The meritorian mourning him might be his lover, or sister, or mother. Judging from the direction they're heading, the coffin is being escorted to a family crypt on Mount Riddle." He winced and shifted in his seat. "After I've gotten you to safety, I must find a healer and get this wound treated properly." He rubbed his forehead and studied his hand. "I'm sweating. Why am I sweating? I'm cold. In fact, I'm freezing." He hugged himself. His bushy eyebrows pressed downward. "The pentaculars must be getting anxious you might ruin their fearsome reputation."

Drinith's laugh died in her throat at the sight of Woad's grave demeanor.

"What makes you think that?" she asked.

"The pentacular's dagger poisoned me."

31

———————

Quiescat stood in the hallway, detached from the hubbub spreading through the mansion. The remonstrations of Halyard and Epmar behind closed doors in the parlor reached him as an incoherent murmur. Fenvar had disappeared through a servant door to gather the rest of the household staff. Gelasin, Zin, and Jarma had dashed upstairs to collect the group's possessions, having dissuaded him from accompanying them. He shouldn't have listened. *I should do something instead of standing here like a dead man.* But what? He stewed in his indecision, his gut twisting ever tighter.

Gelasin and Jarma bounded down the stairs. Zin with a violent scowl wobbled after them, carrying twice their burden of baggage. He dropped one at Quiescat's feet. "You can carry that much at least."

Quiescat snapped it up. Its weight dangerously strained his back. "I can carry more," he lied. Zin ignored him.

Fenvar herded sheepish servants through the narrow service entrance. "Wait here, please," she said to them as she strode over to the parlor doors. She gave them a crisp rap, halting the heated debate within. "Everyone is here." She respectfully stepped back.

Halyard burst through the doors, his face full of murderous

intent. "Follow me." He led everyone through a sequence of interconnected rooms. Quiescat struggled to keep up. The bag made him list to one side. He felt tired and weak. Dizziness threatened.

A maid grabbed the bag from his hand. "I'll take that." He didn't quibble.

They halted before a locked door.

"Open it," Halyard said to Fenvar.

"Only the mistress has a key to her study," the butler said. "One of us will have to go back and get it." Gasps and sighs rippled through the group.

"No time." Halyard shouldered the door. Dropping his burden, Zin joined him. The door groaned with each blow until it flew open with a mighty crack. Zin grabbed his bags and the courtesar led everyone into the room. He pressed a carving on a bookshelf and turned a bust just above it like a lever. A set of shelves shifted with a soft sigh, revealing a passage behind it. Halyard pushed it further open. The retreating darkness revealed a shelved recess on one side holding various jars and curios. "Everyone, down there now. There's an exit at the far end. Don't go home. Hide elsewhere until this mess has been resolved."

Quiescat spluttered, "Where will we go?"

"I have my friends. We'll be okay," Gelasin assured him.

Halyard pushed past them in the wrong direction.

"Where are you going?" Zin demanded.

"I'm getting Epmar even if I have to carry her," Halyard growled as he disappeared through the broken doorway. Zin, Jarma, and Gelasin moved to follow the servants down the passageway.

"We must wait for him!" Quiescat yelled.

"Why?" Gelasin asked stonily.

"Are you trying to get us caught?" Zin muttered, lumbering into the passage.

"Epmar and Halyard are part of us," Quiescat said. "We can't just abandon them."

Zin gesticulated at the passage entrance. "He told us to go."

"We've lost Abecedar, Versifer, Prosper..."

Zin turned to Gelasin. "This useless old fool is going to get us killed. We should leave him."

Quiescat's heart shriveled with despair. What was he without his gift? A burden.

Gelasin stared at Zin, then at Quiescat, his eyes cold with calculation as he stroked his ruined cheeks. He said with agonizing slowness, "We need him."

"But—" Zin began.

The zigzag veins in Gelasin's temples bulged as he chopped the air with his hand. "But nothing! We're all in this together. Leave the baggage down. We'll wait, but at the first sign Halyard isn't going to make it, we close the secret door. Fair enough, Quiescat?"

"I suppose so," Quiescat said, unable to muster enthusiasm. He was in no position to argue any longer.

They waited and listened. Zin mumbled something under his breath, but Gelasin shushed him.

A distant scream sent a shiver through Quiescat. "Halyard, no!" Epmar cried. Furniture crashed. A door slammed. Glass shattered. Clashing swords rang. Running feet thumped ever nearer.

"Let's go," Zin urged. "Before it's too late." But nobody moved. "Fine, I'll go myself."

Gelasin held his arm and grinned. "What's wrong? You're always looking for a fight and now when one comes to you, your first reaction is to run away."

"I can't afford to be arrested," Zin groused, resting a hand on the hilt of his sword.

Gelasin's eyebrows arched. "Then make sure you're not. But keep your nerve a little longer."

Boots pounded across the wooden floor outside. Spurred by the others readying their weapons, Quiescat unsheathed his knife. Epmar stumbled through the door. "Thank all dragons, you're here," she said between gasps as the sounds of battle crept nearer. "Halyard needs help. He can't beat five courtesars by himself."

Gelasin shook his head. "I'm sorry but—Quiescat! What in Empyr's fiery bowels do you think you're doing?"

Throwing my worthless life away to give Halyard a fighting chance. As Quiescat careered toward the battle, he had no illusion he would prove anything more than a brief distraction to the courtesar's foes, but it might be just enough to give Halyard a vital edge.

The fighting grew louder until the thunder of boots behind him drowned it out. He didn't dare look back in case his charge broke its hold over the others, and they fled back to the secret passage.

He entered the room where the courtesars fought. Backed against a corner, Halyard desperately fended off two of his attackers, while a third stood with his sword poised, ready to strike at the first opening. A fourth lay propped against a wall, rasping heavily, a handkerchief pressed to his chest failing to dam a gushing wound. The fifth lay sprawled face down in his own blood.

Quiescat rushed toward the third courtesar. Alerted by the approaching clatter of his sandals against the wooden floor, the man spun round to face him. A shove from behind knocked Quiescat clear of his thrusting blade. He skidded across the blood-greased floorboards until he slammed into a wooden cabinet.

Behind him, Zin, his face contorted with bloodlust, hacked down the third courtesar. Gelasin stabbed one of Halyard's opponents in the back. The other turned to face him, only to be run through by Halyard.

"Hardly honorable combat," he muttered.

Zin smirked and cocked a thumb at the fourth courtesar, now dead. "They're not complaining."

Quiescat accepted Jarma's help to climb to his feet. A bruise stung his arm, but otherwise, he was fine.

Epmar lurched into the room. "Thank all dragons," she said between pants. "And thank you. Thank you all so much." She frowned at Halyard. "What did you think you were doing?"

Halyard lifted his chin. "Protecting you."

"By getting yourself killed—"

"What's that noise?" Jarma asked.

Somewhere nearby, glass shattered.

"The cordents must be breaking in," Zin said. "I guess they wearied of waiting for the courtesars to finish Halyard off."

"I couldn't let you be taken away like a criminal," Halyard said to Epmar.

She rolled her eyes and threw up her arms. "So you turned me into one."

"Bicker while we run," Gelasin said. "We'll get out of here faster."

As they raced back to the study, their pursuers rumbled ever closer. Quiescat slipped to the back of the group. Heaving painful breaths, he glanced back. Cordents raced toward him, less than two rooms behind. A hand grabbed his arm, pulled him forward.

"Run!" Halyard yelled.

I am! Quiescat was too breathless to reply as the courtesar dragged him on.

The study door drew near, but a glance back confirmed the cordents had closed the gap to a single room. Halyard tugged him on. "Run or we're both dead!"

Quiescat threw every bit of strength he had into one final burst of speed. They hurtled into the study. As Gelasin and Halyard dragged Quiescat into the passage, cordents rushed inside the office.

Quiescat hardly felt the stone floor as he hit it. Every heartbeat struck him like a mallet as he struggled for breath. Epmar, kneeling by his side, turned him to face her. "Are you all right?"

Behind them, Halyard, Gelasin, Zin, and Jarma struggled to push the passage door shut against the cordents on the far side.

"I knew you'd kill us all, Quiescat!" Zin's snarl echoed down the tunnel as the door yawned a little wider.

He's right. Gods, what have I done?

32

———————

Drinith desperately looked up and down the empty canal. "There must be some healer nearby who can help."

"There is," Woad said, clutching his wounded arm. "The Grand Preservatory has an entrance along the canal, but the preservators' help costs more than either of us could afford."

"There must be someone else," Drinith insisted. "Some other healer." She punted as fast as she dared, straining her arm muscles to propel the boat.

"Given who deployed it, this poison is probably something special, beyond the skill of most healers, alchemical or spiritual," Woad said. "I should have guessed from the way the pain spread. If I had realized in time, I might have found someone who could help, but now, it's too late." He glanced down the canal. "Keep going straight until you reach a lock. Take the exit on your right—"

"Is that the way to the Grand Preservatory?" Drinith asked.

"No, Wealgiver Street. The house has a blue door. There are three moons carved on it." He winced as he thrust a key toward her.

"Never mind that. Where's the Grand Preservatory?"

"We pass it soon. You can just dump me by the door and ring the bell. The preservators are more likely to help if I'm on my own."

Drinith had no intention of abandoning him, but she'd save that inevitable argument for when they got there.

"Yes, the pentaculars must fear you," Woad said. "Otherwise they would never have stooped to poison. Normally, their skill and strength prevail without resorting to such expedients. You had killed three already, and I guess the fourth didn't want to take chances. Killing four is unprecedented. If you vanquish the fifth, it will ruin the order's reputation."

Drinith smiled reflexively, though his admiration brought little comfort. A single pentacular remained to hunt her, with the strength of five men and all the ingenuity amassed by generations of his order. Desperation would make him even more dangerous.

"Imagine his face when you beat him." A stupid grin fixed on Woad as he stared at nothing. "Imagine his surprise. His chagrin."

He jabbered on along the same theme, putting her on edge. He couldn't help himself. The poison had made him delirious. She had to find help fast. "How will I know the entrance to the Grand Preservatory?"

"Don't take him to the Grand Preservatory," Woad said. "Kill him first. Kill him and take him to the Grand Preservatory. But first, you must find him. Find him and kill him. He'll be surprised. But you're five times stronger than him..."

Drinith repressed a scream of frustration. Losing her temper wouldn't help. The entrance could be anywhere along the canal. It could already be behind her. She spotted a barge approaching. She waved to attract its crew's attention. "My friend is terribly ill. Please, where's the Grand Preservatory?"

The crew all pointed at the third bridge ahead, an elaborate arch reaching into the darkness. Hooded figures stood guard on either side of it. They might be preservators. They could treat Woad on the canal without further delay if she could convince them to help.

She punted harder, lost her rhythm, tottered dangerously. The canal wouldn't be deep, but she couldn't afford to lose precious time by falling in. She gentled her pace. She'd soon be at the bridge. She would just have to be patient.

The silence struck her. Woad had ceased his chatter. He lay slumped over, eyes closed. She couldn't spare the time to check if he still lived. She had to reach the preservators.

The two figures ignored her cries for help. They remained still—too still.

"Gods damn you!" she cried. How could she have not noticed before? They were statues!

But the bridge remained, and hope lay on the other side. She drew up beside it and moored the boat. Slipping her arms beneath Woad's, she clasped his chest and awkwardly heaved his insensate bulk onto the walkway. How could she get him up the stairs? A small punt was passing. She waved her arms at the man on board. "Please, I need your help!"

He kept his stare fixed on the canal ahead, deaf to her plea. She leapt onto Woad's punt, grabbed the pole, and stabbed it into the water in front of the other vessel. The man nonchalantly steered around the obstacle with no other acknowledgment of its presence.

Drinith waved a fist at his back. "Coward! Murderer!"

"What's this about?" A man approached on the walkway, carrying a sack on his back.

"I need to take my friend to the Grand Preservatory," Drinith pleaded. She pressed a hand to Woad's forehead. It felt cold. He might already be dead.

The man eyed them both with suspicion. "It's not contagious, is it?"

"No," Drinith said. "But if I don't get him to the Grand Preservatory, he'll die. Please."

The man put down his sack and approached warily. He and Drinith dragged Woad up the steps and plonked him by the door.

"I have to go," the man said, retreating backward.

"Thank you," she said.

He wobbled dangerously on the edge of a step, turned and fled down the stairs.

She knocked on the door. Receiving no reply, she banged on it with both fists. "I need help! Please!"

The door groaned open. A tall man, bald, in a black robe, looked down upon her.

She pointed to Woad. "Please help me. He's been poisoned."

The preservator lifted his chin. "This entry is reserved for deliveries. We normally accept petitions for treatment through either the main entrance or the one on Shadow Street."

As he shut the door, she blocked it with her foot. "He won't live long enough to reach either."

His mouth shifted to one side as he studied Woad. "He was poisoned, you say?"

"By a pentacular." She hastened to describe Woad's symptoms. The preservator listened, tapping his chin, his gaze fixed on Woad.

"We might be able to save him. I think I recognize the venom used, an old favorite of the Jemenchy Clan." He smiled at her. "Of course, there's the matter of the fee."

Drinith waved empty hands at him. "I have nothing."

He tilted his head. "Surely you can't expect me to believe that, with that expensive jewel on your forehead."

The emerald—she had forgotten about it. She reached up and touched it. Her hat had shifted, exposing it. Could she give up the last remnant of her heritage? She was nothing without it—just a girl with a sad story. She'd lose whatever chance she had of fulfilling her destiny with its surrender. But what did it matter anymore? Quiescat, Gelasin, and the others were under arrest. Any hope of saving Kaplar was gone.

"You can have the jewel," she said, "but only if you cure him." Better to spend it on saving Woad than waste it on an impossible dream.

33

"Save yourselves!" Quiescat rasped. "Run!" But nobody listened.

"Epmar, never mind Quiescat!" Gelasin growled. "Help us!" The wavering crack in the door offered a glimpse of the press of cordents on the far side. It was hard to believe that Gelasin and the others could hold them back much longer.

Epmar rose. She rifled through the contents of the shelved alcove.

"We need your help now!" Gelasin roared as the door yawned open a little more.

"One moment," Epmar said coolly as she continued to examine jars.

Quiescat had to do something. He crawled toward the door. Even the tiny amount of effort he could add might make a difference.

Strewn baggage littered his route. He struggled to push them out of his way. He had almost reached the door when Epmar jumped over him. She flung a brown glass jar through the opening. Shouts and curses accompanied its shattering. The cordents gave way; Gelasin and the others slammed the door shut.

"You sure took your sweet time," Gelasin muttered.

"I just wanted to scare them, not hurt them," Epmar said as she pulled down a lever beside the door. She helped Quiescat to his feet. The dull glow of circular disks embedded in the tunnel floor carved the darkness into recognizable shapes. "We should be safe for now," she said. "The door is reinforced and I've jammed the opening mechanism. It will take them some time to break through it."

"But they could be already waiting for us at the other end," Gelasin pointed out. "Your servants have gone ahead of us. Can you be certain of their loyalty? What's to stop a spy among them leading their paymasters to the other exit?"

Epmar grinned. "Domestic households in Gyre are often riddled with informers and I'm sure mine is no exception." She pressed a shadowed patch of wall and the alcove swung open to reveal another tunnel. "But we're not using the same exit they did."

They gathered the bags and trundled down the new passage. Epmar pulled another lever and the shelves clicked back into their original position.

"The question is, what should we do next?" Epmar said. "I find myself somewhat of a stranger in Gyre, and I'm ill-prepared for a flight from the city."

"We can't leave until we find Drinith," Quiescat said.

"The answer to both problems may lie in the Blue Quarter," Gelasin said. "I've friends there. They'll help us find her. Drinith might even head there if she remembers my mention of their inn."

It was a better plan than anything Quiescat might have come up with, but its vagueness worried him. If Drinith didn't turn up there by herself, how long would they look for her before they gave up?

"Gods keep her safe," he whispered in the darkness as they marched to an uncertain fate.

It took him a moment to recognize the woman awaiting them at the far end of the tunnel. Fenvar was dressed like a rich merchant. She bowed to Epmar. "I brought extra clothes from the servants' stock for your companions in case they also needed to change."

Halyard picked up a black cloak on top of the neatly folded pile, sniffed, and tossed it back. "I'm not wearing these drab rags, skulking around the city like a coward."

"You must and you will!" Epmar snapped. She softened, adding: "At least wear a cloak over your clothes—please, for me?"

"Very well," he sighed, picking up the cloak and flinging it over his shoulders.

"I'm happy just like this," Gelasin said, indicating his Crevastival garb.

Zin examined his blood-spattered tunic and grinned. "Damn, it'll feel good to be shed of this jester outfit!"

Quiescat couldn't resist smothering his gaudy attire with a brown cloak.

Epmar and Jarma dug through the pile for new clothes to wear. Halyard protected Epmar's modesty with his cloak while she changed. Jarma, who had to endure Zin's ogling, deserved the same courtesy. Quiescat shyly volunteered.

"Killjoy," Zin hissed, and turned to Epmar. "So, what's our plan?"

"Fenvar will go to the perches and secure our passage to another shard with some friendly captain," Epmar said.

"The *Surly Bonnacon*?" Jarma ventured.

Epmar shook her head. "She won't be ready to leave for several weeks and the cordents will be watching her given she brought us here. Fenvar will hire some other dragon. In the meantime, we must learn what we can about Drinith's fate...if she can be saved."

"There's no if about it," Quiescat insisted. "You can't just abandon her." He wouldn't, at least, whatever the cost. He stared at each of his companions, daring them to contradict him. Jarma gave a sad nod. Zin tucked his grin behind his hand, but his eyes made plain his derision. Halyard lifted his chin as if to imply that such a betrayal was beneath him. Gelasin nodded proudly in agreement.

Epmar frowned. "I don't think you fully grasp our predicament. At this moment, every meritocrat in Gyre is mobilizing her resources to hunt us. The entire city is against us."

"Nonetheless, Quiescat is right," Gelasin said. "We're staying until we find her."

Zin rolled his eyes. "Forget her! We need to look out for ourselves now."

"I would advise you," Quiescat said, "to keep your unwanted opinions to yourself, or, or..."

Zin took a menacing step toward him. "Or what, old man?"

Gelasin shoved him back. "Shut up, Zin. Epmar, I understand your situation is different. You and Halyard probably need to leave. You're too easily recognized. But the four of us are just an anonymous bunch of Rhumgadian exiles indistinguishable from the other blue faces that wander this city."

Halyard pounded his fist into his open palm. "I'm not leaving until the princess is found."

Epmar stamped her foot. "You'll get yourself killed!"

Halyard folded his arms. "The life of a coward is no life at all."

"A life with me, you mean."

Gelasin raised both hands. "Enough. We already face enough problems without you two falling out."

"You should wait for me at the perches," Halyard suggested to Epmar.

She gave a defiant headshake. "No. I'm staying with you and that's final."

"You must still have a spy network," Gelasin said. "All you meritocrats have one."

"True, but I can't rely upon it in these circumstances. The only people I can trust are in this tunnel."

Gelasin rubbed his cratered cheeks. "My friends in the Blue Quarter will help us."

"Meanwhile," Zin said, "I'll make separate inquiries with my own friends."

Gelasin's eyebrows flexed upward. "Oh, yes. I had forgotten about them. Good idea."

Reasoning that if Zin wandered off by himself he might never return, Quiescat said, "I'll go with him."

"The people I'll be meeting are leery of unfamiliar faces," Zin said. "It's best if I go alone."

"He's right," Gelasin admitted with reluctance. "They don't like strangers. Zin, you can meet us at the Gad Moon Inn when you're done."

Fenvar opened a horizontal slit in the wall and peered through it. She twisted and pushed something in the shadows and an invisible door swung open noiselessly. A shudder of recognition passed through Quiescat as they stepped through it. Had they entered the very same sewer in which they had discovered Versifer's corpse? No, the roof of the short, arched tunnel was higher, and the far exit had no bars.

"Leave your bags here," Fenvar said. "I'll organize their transport to the perches." She exited the tunnel and turned left. With a final smirk, Zin turned right. Gelasin led the rest down an unfamiliar street dead ahead.

"Supposing we never see Zin again?" Quiescat murmured to Gelasin.

The warrior flashed him an amused grin. "As nasty as he's been to you—you're a soft-hearted old fool, right to the end. It wouldn't bother me if I never see that thug again. He has caused nothing but trouble since we arrived here." His vehemence took Quiescat aback. Gelasin had always been Zin's staunchest advocate. "He'll come back to us. He has nowhere else to go."

Quiescat took little notice of their route, so that their sudden arrival in the Blue Quarter surprised him. The glow from the Crevast kept it in an eerie twilight. Long ago, it must have been impressive, but the once grand buildings were dilapidated and stained black like dying flowers. The furtive locals gave them a wide berth, some retreating into shadows as they passed. But Quiescat could feel myriad gazes falling upon him from the chinks in shuttered windows.

Gelasin led them to a nondescript door. He pushed against it, but it didn't budge. He hammered on it with his fist.

"Go away!" a woman yelled from within. "We're closed."

"It's Gelasin!" he yelled back.

"One moment!" A metal bolt slid across and the door opened. A stern woman peeped out. She gave Gelasin's companions a sour glance. "You've brought quite a delegation."

"No choice," he said. "They're all friends in need of help."

"This might not be the safest place." She sighed and gestured to them to enter. "Grab buckets on the way in."

Quiescat strained to lift one pail with both hands, while everyone else picked up two with ease. Manual labor had never been his forte. After they all had trampled into the common room and deposited their burdens, the woman bolted the door.

Gelasin pointed to the mop and bucket leaning against a table. "I see you've already had a visitor, Tazran."

Quiescat shuddered at the sight of the bloody handprints on the mop handle. The water in the bucket had a deep red tinge.

"Two," Tazran said. "The slop in the mop bucket is all that remains of the second, a pentacular hunting your princess. The princess was the other, but Woad's taken her to our house on Wealgiver Street. We thought it best to get her out of here before another pentacular turned up."

Quiescat clapped his hands. "Thank the gods! She's alive and free!"

"How did she escape?" Gelasin said, exchanging perplexed glances with Epmar.

Tazran shrugged. "I only know what Woad told me while we were disposing of the pentacular's corpse. Apparently, a meritocrat sprung her in order to root out some conspiracy by Rhumgadian exiles against Gyre."

Gelasin pensively stroked his scars. "No doubt these conspirators are comrades of Drinith's attacker at the ducal reception. If we could prove they were Magian's agents, we'd not only exonerate Drinith, but we'd also have a chance of enlisting Gyre to our cause. Any ideas as to whom the meritocrat might be, Epmar?"

"Please describe this meritocrat, good lady," Epmar said to Tazran.

"Woad said she was veiled."

"Then, it could be any meritocrat," Epmar said. "Excepting myself, of course."

Gelasin grinned. "I'll follow Woad and Drinith to Wealgiver

Street. In the meantime, everyone, get some rest. Tazran, will you rustle up some supper for them?"

She snorted. "To be honest, Woad does most of the cooking around here, but I'm sure I can find something in the pantry. Best use the secret passage upstairs to the canal. The fifth pentacular might be watching the inn."

As Gelasin moved to leave, Quiescat grabbed his arm. "I'm coming with you."

"I'll travel faster alone."

"Be that as it may, I've got to see for myself that Drinith is safe."

Gelasin sighed. "All right. But I warn you, if you slow me down, I'll leave your arse in the gutter."

"Fair enough. Let's go!" Quiescat started up the stairs. Gelasin swerved by him. By the time Quiescat reached the room, the warrior had opened the secret door to the stairwell. It gaped open like a giant crooked mouth. While he rummaged through drawers, Quiescat plunged into the darkness.

"Wait!" Gelasin called after him. "We need light. And we're going up, not down."

With a lampstone in hand, Gelasin led the way up the stairwell. Quiescat puffed behind him, his legs straining to keep up. The warrior's struggle with the door at the top proved a welcome respite.

As he pushed it shut again behind them, Gelasin glanced up and down the empty canal. "This veiled meritocrat could be our friend, Epmar."

"No," Quiescat gasped. "Why would Epmar do such a thing?" They started walking along the canal.

"She and Halyard have always been aloof. From the moment we arrived in Gyre, she latched on to Drinith and has done her best to isolate her from us."

"You're being paranoid."

"I'm not saying she's definitely this veiled meritocrat. I'm just saying it's a possibility. For all we know, the meritocrats might have ordered the raid on her mansion because they uncovered her part in Drinith's escape."

"For all we know." Quiescat grunted. "We know nothing."

"I'm sorry I brought it up."

"So am I." Did the rogue Warserk harbor similar ridiculous notions about Quiescat? Did Gelasin whisper them to others behind his back?

They walked on in silence until the warrior stopped beside the entrance to another stairwell.

"We had better descend," he said, opening the door. "You're not supposed to wander around up here unless transporting goods."

The street below proved as lonely as the canal. Gelasin set off at a run. Quiescat struggled to keep up until his burning lungs threatened to explode. "Wait for me," he pleaded breathlessly.

Gelasin stopped and glared back at him. "I told you I can't wait for you. Go back to the inn."

Quiescat glanced behind him at the unfamiliar street. Perhaps it would be better if he let the warrior continue alone. It had been a mistake to accompany him. "How do I get there?"

Gelasin rubbed his cheeks. "Come along," he sighed. "You'd probably get yourself killed if I left you behind. But you've got to move as fast as you can. Understood?"

"Of course," Quiescat said as he stumbled after him on aching legs.

They soon entered a more bustling part of the city. Sellers cajoled them to sample the wares in their stalls, offering discounts.

"Does this city ever sleep?" Quiescat muttered.

"Never entirely," Gelasin said. "And Crevastival begins tomorrow. The merchants have charms and souvenirs to offload before the holidays pass and everyone loses interest. Tomorrow morning, these streets will be empty. Everyone will be gathered in Crimson Square outside the Dragon Church to cheer the meritocrats as they make their sacrifices to the Crevast." He halted, nodding at a building across the street. "Here we are. You wait here. I'll check inside."

"Why can't I go with you?" Quiescat asked.

"Too many entering and leaving might attract unwelcome

attention. I want you to watch out for any suspicious loiterers around here. Just in case."

Quiescat glanced around nervously at the shoppers browsing the stalls. "And what am I supposed to do if I spot someone?"

"Tell me when I come back," Gelasin said, walking away.

"You're just trying to fob me off," Quiescat groused.

The warrior turned and rested a hand on his shoulder. "Look, I'll be straight with you. I don't want you coming with me because I don't know what sort of trouble I'll encounter in there."

"What do you mean by trouble?" Quiescat asked.

Gelasin glanced at the door. "The last pentacular could be waiting in there. I'm still handy in a fight, but I can't beat a pentacular who has the strength of five men, even with your help."

What aid could Quiescat give? Nothing except pose a brief distraction for such a deadly assassin. "You're right, I'll stay here. But what do I do if you don't come back?"

Gelasin pursed his lips. "Wait until the first morning bell, then head for the inn."

As he crossed the street, Quiescat prayed to all the gods he knew of that all Gelasin would find in the house was Drinith.

34

Drinith sat by Woad's sickbed, waiting, watching for the first flicker of consciousness, afraid to trust the preservators' assurances. Her forehead smarted where her emerald had been removed. She gently brushed a finger over the tender skin. It felt smooth to the touch. The preservator had assured her in a day or two, the pain would fade away. It would be as if the jewel had never been part of her.

The so-called recovery room looked more like a royal bedchamber. It had finer furnishings than either of her rooms in the Aether Emperor's palace. The silk drapes over the window would have made ideal material for an empress's dress. In a city where timber was a precious commodity that had to be imported from the Nosteran mainland, a small fortune of logs crackled and spat in the ornate hearth. Frescos of pastoral scenes covered the walls. The elaborate lampstone chandelier slowly spun, casting flying birds across the egg-blue ceiling. Everything was gilded and embellished with semi-precious stones. Unlike her former quarters, the dragon amber tiles on the floor might very well be real. Yes, the room was fit for any potentate, but this incongruous bubble of opulence within the preservators' austere temple to their science made her uncomfortable. She was a trespasser in this place, a fraud.

The preservator, Zoarzi, sat nearby, studying a book on his lap. She peered at the open pages, but she didn't recognize the script. He looked up and smirked. She turned her attention back to Woad.

His eyes popped open, wild with incomprehension. He looked around, recognized her, and sighed with relief.

"You're in the Grand Preservatory," she said.

"How did I get here?" he asked, incredulous. His eyes narrowed as he studied her. "Where's your jewel gone?"

She blushed. "It was the price to save you."

"You shouldn't have done that," he said. "You only just met me! And that jewel was worth perhaps a hundred of me..."

Drinith bit her lip. "How can I put it into words? It would not have been honorable to let you die. You and Tazran saved my life. I have merely returned the favor. A jewel, no matter how precious, isn't worth as much as a human life." She smiled slyly. "Besides, how could I allow Tazran to become a widow for a fourth time?"

Woad smiled back, and squeezed her hand feebly. "It was a foolish thing to do, but I thank you for it."

The gawky shadow of the preservator fell over Drinith as he examined his patient. "You must rest here for a few days. You were a lucky man this lady fetched you here. You were beyond the help of lesser healers. Her quick action saved you."

"Yes, that *and* her munificence," Woad said sharply. "I doubt you've often been rewarded so well for your services."

Zoarzi's chin rose. "She agreed to the price."

"Then at least reward her generosity with a little of your own by having someone escort her to her home." He answered Drinith's look of confusion with a smile. "It's on Wealgiver Street." He was talking about the safe house.

"I'll have an acolyte accompany her. I promise she will reach her house safe and sound," the preservator said with polite condescension. "Anything else?"

Woad winced as he shifted in the bed. "Somebody must let my wife, Tazran Glastum, know I'm here."

"Where does she reside?"

"The Gad Moon Inn in the Blue Quarter."

The preservator dabbed his nose with a handkerchief. "I should have recognized the musty scent on your clothes. Very well. I'll send a messenger there." He glanced at Drinith. "I hope your wife wasn't responsible for poisoning you."

Woad emitted a wheezy chuckle. "Do you imagine my misfortune resulted from some lovers' tiff?"

Drinith cast a vicious scowl over her shoulder at the preservator. "I hope you're not implying *I'm* his lover." She shot Woad an apologetic glance. "No offense." He grinned.

Zoarzi raised his hands, rocked backward a step. "I never meant to imply anything. We pride ourselves on our discretion and take no interest in our patients' private matters."

Woad attempted a dismissive wave. He let out a weary sigh as his whole body slumped from the effort.

"I'll leave you two alone to say your farewells," the preservator said, beating a hasty retreat.

"Perhaps I should stay," Drinith said. "I should be safe enough here in the Grand Preservatory."

"Don't be so sure," Woad said. "You're not the preservators' patient and you've nothing of value left to buy that privilege now. If the fifth pentacular follows Tazran here, the preservators have neither the obligation nor the ability to protect you. You'll be safe in the Wealgiver Street house, at least for now."

He gripped her hand. Gratitude shone in his eyes. "I owe you my life, and neither Tazran nor I will forget your kindness. We will help you whatever way we can, no matter the difficulty or danger."

"Thank you," Drinith said. Right now, all she wanted was to feel safe.

———

As soon as they reached Wealgiver Street, Drinith dismissed her guide.

The gray-robed girl frowned. "My orders are to escort you to your home."

Drinith couldn't afford her knowing the safe house's exact location. She gazed at the crowds milling about the stalls. "I'll be fine," she promised. "Thank you for your help!" she shouted over the acolyte's emerging protest.

"If you're sure..."

Drinith folded her arms. "Absolutely."

With a farewell nod, the girl headed back toward the Grand Preservatory. Drinith watched her stride away until she disappeared around a corner.

A hand gripped Drinith's arm. "Come look at my—oof!" The man doubled over, winded by Drinith's elbow. She had struck without thinking. As he staggered away, she hurried down the lines of stalls, hoping the crowds would hide her by the time he recovered his breath. She warded off the avaricious grins of advancing sellers with a forbidding scowl.

She recognized the door by its bright blue color and the three rings carved on it, representing the moons of Rhumgad. Glancing about to confirm nobody watched her, she slid the brass key Woad had given her into the lock and opened it. To her surprise, the hall was lit with candles. Had Tazran come here ahead of her?

"Hello?" she ventured, but no answer came. She drew her knife. Entering, she shut the door but didn't lock it in case she had to make a speedy exit. The stairs creaked as she climbed them. A pained moan made her pause. It sounded female. It grew louder, more desperate. Drinith bolted up the stairs toward it.

She swung open the first door at the top and gasped. A man lay on the floor, his back propped against the wall. Rivulets of blood ran down his cheeks from the grisly holes where his eyes should have been. The man sensed her presence and stopped wailing.

"Who's there?" he cried, his head lurching about pitiably.

She recognized the voice and then the man. "Zin, who did this to you? Is there anyone else in the house?"

"Your Highness?"

She forgot her revulsion for the lecher Zin had long demonstrated himself to be. Here was a man who had protected her, saved her life. Here was a man in utter agony. She knelt beside him. "Yes, it's me. My gods, what monster did this to you?"

His trembling hand reached out. She gently held it. "I'm here." Surely, the preservators could heal this butchery. Somehow, she'd scrape together enough money to pay for—

She gasped as he yanked her to him. Her knife slipped from her fingers. She pushed against him in vain as his arms and legs twisted around her.

"This is all your fault," he hissed through gritted teeth. He pushed her down, pressing his weight on top of her, pinning back her arms. "You and that stupid poet. If he had come peaceably as I asked, he'd still be alive, and I might have never used that infernal Tear."

His clammy breath brushed against her face with every word. She grunted as she jerked her head forward but failed to connect with his face.

"It ate my eyes," he wailed. "The sockets are raw pain, boring into my skull. Every stir in the air stabs them like a knife." As he giggled, blood wept from the two gory hollows in his face, drizzling down on her face. "You always had such pretty eyes. I wonder what the Tear of Fate would do to them?"

He drew her arms together, clamping her wrists with one hand. With the other, he produced a transparent crystal sphere. She turned away as it drew nearer her face. His manic laughter mocked her as he pressed it against the side of her head. Cold and hard, it rolled across her temple toward her eye. "I wonder how close the Tear must get to your eyes before it burrows into your sockets like a stinking grub."

He leaned near so his face filled her vision, a grimacing skull contorted by pain and hate. He drew yet closer as if to kiss her, but his aim drifted so low that one of his eviscerated sockets aligned with her mouth. With all her strength, she blew.

He howled in pain. His head whipped back and forth. His forehead butted her cheek. Her hands broke free of his slackened grip. Her wild punch struck his throat. Bucking him off her, she crawled for her knife. His pained yowl transformed into a snarl. Seizing the blade, she stabbed the arm wrapping around her throat. As he roared in agony and frustration, she twisted around. She stabbed, stabbed again, and kept stabbing until her arm hurt. A cold silence descended over the room.

Panting, she pushed and kicked the corpse off her. Thank the gods, it was over. She had no fight left. She crawled over to the nearest wall and used it to stand up. She didn't even dare glance at Zin, at the carnage she had inflicted. He must have been the tangled man in Versifer's vision. She had no sense of victory, only a trembling hollowness. Hopefully, the blood smeared all over her dress and hands was his. She hugged herself to steady her tremor. She had to get out of here. But first, she needed to get the Tear of Fate. It took a few moments to locate it, shining on the floor. It was pristine in the gore's midst as if blood couldn't adhere to it. Surely, Quiescat would know what to do with it. She picked it up and headed for the door.

It opened before she reached it. Gelasin gaped at her, at the corpse behind her, then at her again. He made a throaty gurgle, at a loss for what to say. She had never seen that stubbornly hard face so soft with concern.

"Zin killed Versifer." She opened her hand and revealed the unsullied Tear nestled in her bloodstained palm like a pearl. "He had this."

He looked her up and down. "You're not injured, are you?"

She gently rubbed her smarting cheek where Zin's head had struck her. "I don't think so."

"Thank the gods," he said with genuine relief. He punched her in the face, and everything went black.

35

What was taking Gelasin so long? As Quiescat stood across the street, arms folded, passersby drew his gaze from the door. He fancied they eyed him with suspicion, but there was no mistaking the merchants' resentful scowls. He had spurned their invitations to browse their wares politely at first, and when that failed, with stinging curtness. If he had to hang around here much longer, one of them might use his loitering as an excuse to report him to the cordents.

Surely Gelasin could determine Drinith's presence in the house instantaneously. What could delay him so long? Unless he had encountered some trouble—the pentacular or members of this Rhumgadian conspiracy might have ambushed him.

Gelasin had told him to stay put, but what did his life matter if the warrior fell? Loss of the gift had made Quiescat unremarkable and unnecessary, a burden to more able men and women. Gelasin understood this city. He had the fire and determination to save Drinith. And he might be dying while Quiescat dithered.

He walked up to the door. The clamor of the crowds deafened him to any noise within. He raised his hand, undecided whether to knock or just go inside.

The door swung open. Gelasin scowled at him. "She's not here. I thought I told you to wait across the street."

"If she's not here, where is she?"

Gelasin opened his hands. "How should I know? She and Woad might arrive here at any moment. Not every delay has to be sinister."

Everything about this city was sinister, but, if Quiescat argued, he mightn't be able to rein in his temper. "What do we do?"

"I'll wait here for them," Gelasin said. "You should go back to the Gad Moon Inn in case they doubled back there. Perhaps Tazran could shed light on where else Woad might take her."

Quiescat glanced at the pedestrians streaming past behind him. "It would be better if I waited. I'm no good at finding my way around about this city."

"No!" Gelasin smiled. "No. What would you do if a pentacular turned up at this door? You're not exactly an able fighter either."

I'm not an able anything. "Very well. I'll go. But you must give me clear directions."

Gelasin grinned. "I'll make sure you won't get lost. Who knows? Maybe you'll find Drinith safe and sound at the Gad Moon Inn."

Gelasin proved as good as his word; his simple instructions guided Quiescat back to the Blue Quarter without incident. The crowds were mostly drifting toward Crimson Plaza to join in the morning Crevastival celebrations. As he drew near the inn, he slowed down and looked about. Because he couldn't see the pentacular didn't mean the assassin didn't watch from somewhere in the shadows.

As he knocked on the inn's door, a deeper apprehension seized him. On his journey, he had held on to a fragile hope that he might discover Drinith there, but it was likely to vanish the moment he passed through that door. "It's me, Quiescat."

The bolt slid back, and the door opened. Tazran filled the doorway. "Where's Gelasin?" she asked, stepping out of his way. He entered. Around a table, the others sat—Jarma, Epmar, and Halyard —but no Drinith.

"Gelasin's at the safe house," Quiescat said. "We didn't find Drinith or your husband there."

Her lips narrowed to a slit. "They'll turn up. Woad will protect her." Tazran's solemn assurance couldn't hide the anxiety on her stern face.

"Is there anywhere else he might take her?"

Pressing her hands to her cheeks, she stared at the floor. Her trance-like contemplation ended in a headshake. "I can't think of anywhere. He'd never change his plan...unless he was forced."

"Is there some friend he might have turned to for help?"

"He has friends, sure. He corresponds with a few old comrades from his days as a mercenary. But there's nobody in Gyre."

"What will we do?" Jarma asked.

"Gelasin said he'd come here when they'd turned up." *Or when he had concluded they wouldn't.* "In the meantime, we must wait here." But Quiescat couldn't just sit around doing nothing. He bit his lip. "You mentioned correspondence. Would you mind if I looked at it?"

She eyed him suspiciously. "Why would you want to do that?"

"There might be some useful clue, some chance comment that might help resolve the mystery of their disappearance. You could look at it yourself."

She snorted. "No point. I can't read. I only need to count to run a place like this."

"Then let me look."

She shook her head.

"I promise...to be discreet. Having been an oracle, I am burdened with many people's secrets. I know the letters are unlikely to be of much help, but there's always a chance."

She sighed. "Come on then. I'll show you where they are."

Epmar rose. "I'll help."

Tazran gestured for her to sit. "He's a priest, but you're not. There's probably nothing useful in the letters, anyway."

He followed her upstairs. The secret passage remained open. "Why didn't you seal it up?" he asked.

"In case we had to make a hasty exit."

"What are those?" He pointed to the books on the desk in the corner.

"They're just ledgers. Those I can read, but there's nothing of interest in them." Tazran stepped into the secret passage and produced a second set of books. "Or these either, the real figures I'd rather the meritocrats' tax collectors remain ignorant of. That's why I wasn't inclined to let the meritocrat snoop around up here. We're all on the same side for now, but that might change." Putting them back on their shelf, she lifted down a small, dusty chest and placed it on the desk. "The letters are in there," she said, brushing her hands against her skirt. "I'll join the others. No point in me looking over your shoulder at stuff I can't make sense of in the first place."

He sat down and opened the chest. A bright red leather envelope near the top caught his eye. He plucked it from the pile. In bold draker trade glyphs was inscribed OPEN IN THE EVENT OF MY DEATH. No emblem had been imprinted in the red seal.

Opening it would be an invasion of privacy. There was no telling what personal revelations it contained. But Woad might already be dead. Quiescat stared at it, tapping it against his palm, building up the nerve to break the seal. He tugged open the flap, tearing the stiff wax blob.

Inside was a paper envelope, glued shut. Written on the front was TO BE DELIVERED TO THE DUCALION.

Quiescat glanced over his shoulder to make sure nobody had come upstairs. He slid his knife under the flap and sliced the envelope open. The single page of paper within was thin to the point of translucence. The curled edges hinted that it had been tightly rolled up in the past. His nose curled at its strong chemical smell. He laid it on the envelope. He strained to read the faint writing, apparently written in pencil. A flaw at the bottom edge caught his eye. It was the tip of Javlohm's emblem, the Tree of Bones.

A queasy horror gripped Quiescat. Jumping to conclusions wouldn't help anyone. He needed to stay calm and read the message. He couldn't read the string of meaningless symbols heading the document. Fortunately, the rest was written in familiar pyratic glyphs.

We have granted your request. We will deliver the gold to Wealgiver Street.

The site of the safe house. The coincidence made Quiescat apprehensive.

Eliminate the pretender Drinith of Kaplar as soon as she arrives in Gyre.

Aside from her retinue, who knew she intended to come to Gyre? Unless Pinchel hadn't been as discreet as he let on. Or he served Javlohm.

Her execution must be in public as a warning to all our foes that no place is safe from our beloved emperor's wrath. It is imperative that this does not jeopardize your critical operation at Crevastival. Burn upon reading.

Magian had masterminded the attack at the ducal reception. Strange that the pentaculars weren't mentioned. What was the nature of this critical operation?

Quiescat glanced again over his shoulder. Woad had to be an agent of Javlohm, but was his wife? Epmar might help make sense of this conspiracy and decide what to do next. It would be difficult to speak in private to her without drawing Tazran's suspicion. Quiescat gathered the two envelopes with the letter, rose stiffly from the chair, and headed downstairs. Tucking his evidence behind his back, he entered the common room. He repressed a curse as the others stared at him from a single table. Halyard pulled up an extra chair beside Tazran.

"Any luck?" she asked.

He shook his head. He couldn't speak. Tazran and the others turned their attention back to their drinks. He ignored their chatter as he approached the table. His hand quivered as he drew his knife. The blade shivered to the pounding of his heart as he raised it to the back of Tazran's neck.

The others, wide-eyed with alarm, drew back, knocking over their seats. Only Tazran didn't move. She slowly placed her hands on the table. "Please be careful with that knife. From the way it's scratching my neck, you're not holding it very steady."

He threw the letter and the envelopes down in front of her. "Care to explain this?"

"I can't read, remember?" She picked up the red envelope. "Though I recognize this. Gelasin gave it to Woad for safekeeping."

The knife slipped from his hand and clattered against the floor. "Sorry," Quiescat whispered, covering his mouth.

Tazran leapt up and twisted around so fast, her chair flew across the room. She grabbed Quiescat by his tunic and pressed her dagger to his neck. "Give me one good reason why I shouldn't slit your throat."

"Gelasin is a traitor," Quiescat rasped. "He has betrayed us all."

36

The rope burning like fire around her ankles ripped Drinith from her stupor. Her wrists jerked helplessly against the knot fastening them to a post as she flopped about the floor. Laughing, Gelasin retreated beyond her reach. "Thank the gods. I worried I had hit you too hard."

She filled her lungs and screamed. He sauntered over to the window, threw open the shutters, and, folding his arms, leaned against the wall, smiling unconcernedly. The din of music, singing, laughter, and cheers filling the street outside was too loud for anyone to hear her. She stopped.

He shut the window and squatted before her. "Where's Woad?"

She spat at him. "There's your answer, traitor!"

He smiled with amusement as he rubbed the spittle off his face. "I suppose I deserve that for punching your lights out."

"You betrayed me," she hissed.

"Princess, my fealty was never yours to betray. I warned Quiescat as much many times, but he never listened. I joined your service in the hope you might become the savior of Kaplar. But Quiescat surrounded you with incompetents, cowards, and fools. Every shard would have toppled into the Crevast by the time you had mustered enough support to take on Magian's armies. I took matters into my own hands and devised an alternative plan.

"I identified Gyre as our best prospect for aid long ago, but Quiescat knew better, preferring to squander your life and his fortune pursuing the likes of Numenal and Thirring, smug little worlds onto themselves. Their rulers might entertain beggar princesses, but they'd never go to war for them.

"As his oracular power waned, I set my scheme in motion. Fortunately, he was too spiritual and pure to delve into the sordid matter of our finances. Otherwise, he might have noticed I have been diverting funds to pay for my operation in Gyre for some time."

Drinith had listened to his account with appalled fascination. "But how did you know the elemental emperors would expel us from Thirring after the pentacular's attack?"

"I didn't, but I knew winning them over was close to impossible and we'd eventually have to leave." He shrugged. "If by some miracle, we succeeded in securing their support, I'd have canceled my operation here. The timing of our expulsion, delivering us to Gyre a few days before Crevastival, was certainly fortuitous, even if it forced a hasty rejig of my plans."

"You never believed my slaying of the first pentacular would persuade the elemental emperors to help our cause," Drinith said. "You were testing me."

"You needed to be blooded. Gentleness doesn't win wars. I needed to know you truly had the stomach for fighting." He rose to his full height. "I'm sorry about the assassin at the ducal reception. I needed to establish you in the minds of the meritocrats as an implacable foe of Magian. It was hard sending the boy to his death. I should have known I couldn't trust Zin to protect you. He was too bloodthirsty. He couldn't resist getting into trouble. When I sent him to make the poet temporarily disappear, I never imagined Zin would murder him."

"Why did you want Versifer out of the way?" Drinith asked, horror-stricken.

He gave her a blank stare. "Because I couldn't have him helping Quiescat foil my scheme. I'd have released him after it had come to fruition, but Zin said the poet had put up a fight and he had to kill him. I find that hard to believe. Only the gods know the truth. Zin still smarted after losing that duel. Perhaps he had intended to steal the Tear of Fate from the start. He had always been an ungrateful pup, and ambitious, too." He stroked his cheeks and gazed at the shrouded mound across the room. The blood had soaked through the white sheet. Two red blotches had formed where Zin's eyes should have been. "Unfortunately for him, the Tear didn't want him." He shrugged. "Maybe it took Zin's eyes out of vengeance. Only Fate knows."

Drinith's body shook with mounting anger. "And just what do you think you'll achieve via this skulduggery?"

Gelasin took a deep breath, exhaled luxuriantly. "To the Gyrans, Rhumgad is the desert rock where rain comes from. The meritocrats treat its exiles with contempt. Why would they shed blood and treasure to win back your kingdom, an empire in name only, on a shard of no strategic interest for a people they disdain? Because you beg so prettily?"

Cursing, Drinith strained against her bonds, which seemed to only grow tighter. Paying her no heed, Gelasin went on.

"No, they'd need a more compelling reason than that. I intend to give them one. Death will rain down at the Crevastival celebrations in Crimson Plaza. I've made sure Magian will be blamed. Gyre will be forced to retaliate. Your mission will transform from an irrelevance to a critical instrument of that retribution."

"The surviving meritocrats may not react as you hope," Drinith countered.

"The meritocrats are careful and shrewd. Their greatest imperative is the perpetuation of their Halcyon Republic. Even the death of a great number of them mightn't prove enough to stir them to act against Gyre's strategic interest. But my attack will target the general populace, not their rulers. The meritocrats will have no choice but to heed the baying of the crowd for vengeance in case it turns on them."

"But what about the other Rhumgadians in Gyre, our compatriots?" Drinith demanded. "As you pointed out, they're already pariahs in this city. They'll all come under suspicion for this crime. You'll condemn gods know how many of them to persecution, dispossession, torture, and even murder."

Gelasin waved away her charge. "They've already turned their backs on their shard. They've forgotten where they came from."

"And you've turned your back on reason."

He raised a finger. "No, you're the one ruled by sentiment. Rhumgad can't contain Magian's monstrous ego forever. Eventually, he'll strike beyond his shard when some calamity, either natural or contrived, weakens those who might oppose him. How many will die then? How many shards will fall to Magian's patient genius? How many wonders of civilization will be ground to dust in the mill of his outrageous ambition? As terrible as my crime may be, in scale it is a trifle compared with the prodigious carnage he will work."

"So to stop a murderer, you become one."

"From the time I earned my honor tattoos, I've been a murderer." Gelasin rubbed his scarred cheeks. "I was lauded for being one. They hailed me far and wide as Kragan the Staunch. Even Quiescat had heard of me. But I no longer kill to serve the whim of an unworthy emperor. I act for a higher purpose."

"Keep telling yourself that," Drinith muttered. She had stopped struggling. All the feeling had gone out of her feet and hands.

Gelasin drew a knife—hers. She stared at him, mesmerized by the blade, as he strode toward her. She sucked in a shivery breath and closed her eyes. A woody thud made her open them.

He had stabbed the knife into the post above her, too high for her to reach. "The best thing you can do is wait here for Quiescat to rescue you. He'll come here, eventually."

He stroked his cheeks and headed for the door. "We shan't meet again. This will be my final service to Kaplar. I won't risk being taken alive and interrogated by truthscryers. Good luck, Your Imperial Majesty. Make my sacrifice count."

His rapid thuds down the stairs ended with the front door slamming shut. She stared up at the knife, an impossible distance away. She had to get free. She couldn't wait for Quiescat. He'd arrive too late to stop Gelasin.

37

The others stared open-mouthed at Quiescat as if he had shouted some insanity.

"But why would Gelasin betray you?" Tazran asked. "Or us, for that matter?" Her grip loosened as she stared back at the letter. She released Quiescat and lowered her blade. At least she grasped the significance of Gelasin passing the letter to Woad. Such material would incriminate anyone caught possessing it.

"Maybe Gelasin intended it as a means to expose Javlohm's activity in Gyre," Jarma ventured.

"Or to blackmail one of Javlohm's agents," Epmar said.

"You sound unconvinced," Quiescat observed.

Epmar pursed her lips and glanced at the red envelope. "Why did he keep it a secret from us all? Why didn't he even tell its bearer?"

"We don't know he didn't." Jarma's gaze darted around the circle, pleading for confirmation. "Don't we? He might have told Tazran's husband."

Tazran shook her head emphatically. "If Gelasin told Woad, I'd know."

"Then we have no time to waste," Quiescat declared. "We must head to the safe house. Drinith might already be there, in Gelasin's clutches."

"First things first." Tazran snatched up the letter and dashed over to the hearth.

"No!" Quiescat cried, too late. It dropped onto the flames, flashed, and disappeared.

Tazran stabbed the fire with a poker. "No point in keeping it. Its discovery would damn all of us. I'll get my springbow and then we'll go to Wealgiver Street. We'll head through the Blue Quarter. It's the faster route."

The dawn bells rang across the city as they left the inn. The Blue Quarter's eerie emptiness extended to the neighboring districts. But distant cheers and the tinny babble of intermingling tunes traveled from a distant part of the city. The majority of Gyre's inhabitants must be attending the Crevastival's opening festivities.

"We're being followed," Tazran murmured.

Quiescat fought the impulse to glance over his shoulder. "Have you any idea who he might be?"

"He's hooded. I can't see his face."

If their stalker was the pentacular, Quiescat couldn't afford to lead him to Drinith. He sped up and led the group down a side street.

"Do you know where you are going?" Epmar muttered as they turned a corner.

"Do you?" he asked, voice quavering.

"I'm not too familiar with this area," she admitted.

"He's gaining on us," Tazran said.

This time, Quiescat couldn't resist a glance. The hooded figure closed fast despite the apparent leisure of his gait. It had to be the pentacular.

"Perhaps we should split up," Jarma suggested. "He can't follow us all."

Quiescat knew the pentacular would follow her. Her resemblance to Drinith doomed her. "No," he said firmly.

They turned another corner only to face a brick wall. A dead end in more ways than one.

"Try to climb up there," Halyard said, pointing to a low balcony. "Tazran, stand with me." His cloak fell away as he swung around, sword drawn. Tazran aimed her stumpy repeating springbow at the approaching figure.

Jarma leapt for the balcony and grabbed two of the balustrades. Quiescat and Epmar pushed her feet upward until she scrambled over the parapet. She offered a hand to help them up.

"Never mind us! He's after you!" Quiescat cried. "Run!" As Jarma plunged into the darkness between the ajar shutters, he and Epmar drew their knives.

The pentacular halted, threw back his hood, and laughed. "Are you foolish enough to believe you can stop me? I have the strength and speed of five men."

Halyard smirked back. "You have five times the strength but not five times the blood."

"We shall see who runs out of blood first." The pentacular moved forward. Bolts from Tazran's springbow flew in quick succession. One glanced off the side of his head, another grazed his shoulder. Two more bounced off his chest, eliciting only a wince of irritation. His skin must have been tougher than the hardest metal for him to shrug off such an onslaught.

Quiescat jumped as he backed into the wall. It took all his resolve not to drop his weapon and try to climb to up to the balcony. Candlelight lit up the shutters above him and poured down the balcony. From inside, panicked voices rose in a babble.

"Run, Jarma, run!" Quiescat cried.

Tazran's glance at Halyard screamed uncertainty.

"Stay behind me," he said, breaking into a run toward the pentacular. "And keep shooting."

"No!" Epmar yelled, moving to follow. She'd get herself killed if Quiescat didn't stop her. He grabbed her wrist. A sharp pain shocked him into letting go. Her blade had left a thin bloody line across the back of his hand.

As she raced toward Halyard, the pentacular's laughter echoed through the lane. He danced by Halyard's sword thrust and shoved him to the ground. Rolling across the cobbles, Halyard sprung to his feet, his sword trained on his foe.

Epmar's dash was cut short by Tazran's outstretched foot. "Stay out of it!" The meritocrat sprawled on the cobbles. Tazran growled as she aimed her springbow again. "Unless you want to kill him."

Epmar rose to her knees and watched, trembling, her eyes engorged with horror.

The pentacular's dagger flashed and twanged twice. A third bolt knocked the weapon from his hand. Halyard charged. His sword struck the pentacular in the ribs, but it sank only a fraction. The pentacular's fist snapped it in two. Halyard fell forward and drove the jagged remnant of his blade at his foe's neck. The pentacular ducked the thrust and punched Halyard's torso, tossing him across the lane.

A whistle shrilled behind them. Another answered from somewhere beyond the balcony. A dozen courtesars rounded the corner. A half-dozen more slipped from the balcony to land around Quiescat. The lane filled with the ringing of drawn swords. Thank the gods! Help had arrived. Jarma must have raised the alarm.

The pentacular's triumphant smile faded as he scanned the circle of warriors. But they didn't move.

"Help him!" Quiescat cried, pointing to Halyard.

"We're here to arrest Meritocrat Hax and Halyard of Kasjor," one of the cordents said.

"That man he's fighting is an assassin!" Quiescat roared.

The pentacular listed. He yanked out the dagger stuck in his thigh. He stared, perplexed, at the blade, his own weapon. Snarling, he stomped toward Halyard. Screaming, Epmar crawled on her knees toward him, too. Halyard rose unsteadily, still clutching his broken sword, pressing his free hand to his injured side. As the pentacular thrust his dagger with surprising slowness, Halyard leaned into him. The two of them entered a shuddering embrace. The pentacular slid down Halyard onto his knees. With a pained smile, Halyard stepped back, and the assassin flopped face down onto the cobbles.

Epmar rose to her feet. But as she opened her hands to embrace him, he toppled over sideways. She fell on him, clutched him to her, but his dead eyes stared beyond her. The whole lane resounded with her cry as if the city itself screamed *"No!"*

Gradually, the courtesars closed around them like a shroud being drawn over her grief. Quiescat drifted with them until Tazran's insistent hand pulled him away. "For the sake of your princess, we had better leave while they're still too distracted to ask us awkward questions."

"We can't..." He knew the sentiment was futile even as he began it. Tazran was right. Nothing he could say or do could comfort Epmar, and Drinith's life remained in danger. Jarma must already be arrested, and Epmar might as well be. He and Tazran would be next if they didn't get out of here. He followed her out of the lane as the courtesars formed a respectful ring around the weeping meritocrat and her dead lover.

They found Wealgiver Street all but deserted. Only a few merchants lingered around their stalls. They eyed Quiescat and Tazran with predatory intensity as they hurried by.

They soon reached the blue door. Tazran took a step back and kicked it beside the lock.

"What are you doing?" Quiescat cried.

"I've no key," she said as she continued to strike it.

The merchants in the vicinity turned and stared. Quiescat grinned back at them and shrugged. "We lost our key." Thankfully, none of them yelled for the cordents, but they didn't look away either. Quiescat continued to smile at them until the jamb shattered, and the door flew open. He and Tazran dashed inside. As they raced up the stairs, a bloody figure appeared on the landing.

Drinith stared at Quiescat with incomprehension and terror. His heart sank as she pointed her blade at him in warning.

"Drinith..."

Relief softened her face. She lowered her weapon. "Quiescat, I didn't recognize you with your new eyes."

He bounded up the steps and hugged her, looked her up and down. "Are you okay?" He glanced through the doorway. A post had been broken in two, its fragments jutting at angles from the floor and ceiling. Rope lay strewn on the bloody floor.

"I'm fine. Gelasin—"

"We know, we know," Quiescat assured her. "Gelasin's a traitor." Thank the gods she was alive and, aside from a few scratches and a bloody nose, free from injury. Noticing her shiver, he slipped off his cloak and threw it over her shoulders. She thrust something into his hand. The Tear peeped through the opening of the pouch. He gasped and closed his fist around it.

"Gelasin will murder half of Gyre if we don't hurry," she gasped. She pushed by him, down the steps, acknowledging Tazran with a nod. "We have to get to Crimson Square."

"Wait!" Quiescat pleaded. He closed the pouch and started to tie it around his neck. He could think of no safer place on his person.

"Hurry up!" Drinith urged.

"I am," he said as he fumbled with the strings. The knot secured, he rushed down the stairs to join them. Would this nightmare ever end?

38

———————

A wall of brightly colored backs greeted Drinith and her two companions at the Crimson Plaza. The fortified Parliament of Merit and gilded intricacy of the Ducal Palace loomed above the sea of people, but everyone's attention was focused on the Dragon Church, a massive yellow edifice prickled with spires. Its portal arch yawned like an enormous mouth; the statues of dragons adorning it looked like rows of teeth. In front of it, a large dreamery shone like a pearl in the morning light. The meritocrats in black trooped out of the building by the dreamery and toward the red tongue of polished rock jutting into the void at the far end of the plaza. Each one carried a baby-sized straw doll. At the rear of the column, the Ducalion sat on her mobile throne, held aloft by lumbering giants. Two lines of bodyguards flanked the dais. Behind her, two guards carried a massive straw figure in a sumptuous dress and adorned with exotic fruit and flowers.

"They're heading for the Plank to sacrifice for a gentle rainy season," Tazran said.

Rain of a different kind preoccupied Drinith. Gelasin had promised that death would rain down...

She climbed up on the nearest statue to get a better view. Gelasin had to be hiding somewhere in that mass of people. A shadow cutting across the crowd drew Drinith's attention to the canal high above them. She caught a fleeting glimpse of Gelasin before he disappeared behind the parapet.

She jumped down from the plinth. "Gelasin's up there! I saw him!" she yelled, pointing to the canal. "Quiescat, warn the cordents! Tazran and I will try to stop him!"

They plowed through the press of onlookers and raced through empty streets until they found an access well. Two scowling cordents blocked them. "Nobody is permitted up there during the celebrations," the older man warned.

"There's a plot to attack the spectators at the Crevastival festivities," Drinith said. "The people behind it are up there."

The cordents' exchange of glances made Drinith uncomfortable. The younger man's armor looked too big for him. It couldn't be a coincidence that both were Rhumgadian lowlanders.

Drinith dodged clear of the older man's dagger thrust. He gurgled as he clawed at the knife Tazran lodged in his neck.

"Go!" she yelled, yanking the blade free as the second cordent closed on her. "I'll deal with this one."

Drinith had already shoved past the dying man and bolted through the door. On the floor lay two dead men stripped to their underwear.

She raced up the coiling staircase. Why hadn't Tazran followed? Surely she must have dealt with the second man by now. Drinith resisted the urge to turn back as she took the steps two at a time. Gelasin and his fellow conspirators might strike at any moment. How many of them might wait up there for her? A dozen or more, perhaps. But, if she didn't stop them, countless innocents would die. As she reached the landing at the top, the sound of ascending boots echoed up the stairwell—too many to be Tazran alone.

Drinith dashed through the open doorway and slammed the door shut. She glanced up and down the canal. A barge was moored some distance further down. Beside it, Gelasin stood, one foot on the parapet, staring down at the crowd below, a flaming torch in his hand.

Drinith raced toward him. "Don't do it!" she pleaded. "The people down there are innocent!"

He slowly turned to regard her as if awakening from a dream. His wry smile of recognition quickly died. "They did nothing as Magian destroyed our people. They mocked our suffering. Our ruin to them was nothing more than a topic of polite conversation. Our people didn't deserve to be broken beneath Magian's yoke. We weren't perfect. We were flawed. We did terrible things and terrible things happened to us, but we didn't deserve to be subjugated by that inhuman monster."

She paused a short distance away, fearful that drawing too near might spur him to set off whatever explosive the vessel held. "What's in the barge?"

"Barrels of cannon powder and dragon dung," he said. "Enough to blow this section of the canal to smithereens."

Below, the crowd prayed in unison, thousands of voices woven into one pleading for the blessing of dragons, oblivious that their individual fates were being decided far above them.

"There are women and children down there," Drinith said.

Cordents spilled out of the access door. Gelasin threw the torch onto the barge and drew his dagger. "Then stop me."

He leapt at her, leading with his left arm. Dodging his stabs, she stepped inside the arc of his sweeping blade and pinned his arm against her at the elbow. She stabbed a second dagger out of his right hand as it came at her under the knot of arms. She drove the knife at his throat, but he lurched away and it struck his shoulder. He grinned at her as he dropped to his knees. How many times had they practiced that sequence of moves in preparation for the first pentacular? He had trained her well, too well.

Pushing by him, she leapt onto the boat, seized the torch, and flung it into the canal. It hissed as it hit the water. But the fire had already spread and gnawed the bottom of the barrels. She took off the cloak Quiescat had given her and brushed it in the water. Flinging it over the flame, she stamped on it until all that remained of the fire were a few wisps of smoke.

She turned to face Gelasin, but he had dragged himself onto the parapet. He flashed a pained smile at her. "I did all this for you. Don't waste it."

As he pushed himself off the parapet, she dashed to catch him. She reached out over the edge, but Gelasin had already fallen beyond her grasp. The screaming crowd opened a gap beneath him as he shrank to a black dot. He burst like a red tear on the ground.

Arms seized her, pulled her back from the parapet, shoved her to the ground. A knee pressed against her back as her wrists were bound together. "You're under arrest," a female voice growled. A gag stretched across Drinith's mouth before she could answer.

39

"There's going to be an attack!" Quiescat roared at the top of his voice, waving his arms about in frustration.

The cordent pulled a face and pointed to her ears. The throng of entwining voices deafened her to his pleas.

Screams pierced the prayerful drone. Quiescat's gaze followed pointing fingers upward. A silhouette disappeared into the scattering crowd with a meaty thump. As the plaza filled with excited whispers, Quiescat pushed his way toward the fallen figure. A circle of dazed, blood-spattered faces stared down at the smashed corpse. At least it wasn't Tazran or Drinith. Quiescat shuddered on recognizing Gelasin's battered armor. Before he could draw closer, cordents swooped around the dead man and brandished their swords to force back the press of onlookers. As he retreated with the rest, Quiescat glimpsed Drinith's bloodstained knife lying beside the corpse. She must be up on the canal somewhere. He had to get to her.

He steered with courteous persistence through the shifting, chattering mass of humanity. He had closed to within ten paces of the nearest access tower when the crowd surged toward it, forming an impenetrable wall of backs before him.

"Lay off, you old fool, before I break that finger!" a burly man snapped as he swatted away Quiescat's insistent tap on his shoulder.

"What's happening?" Quiescat pleaded. He spotted a slender gap opening nearby and dived in. He wormed his way through, shrugging off dismayed yells, retaliatory shoves, and the occasional flying fist.

Cordents led a bound woman out of the tower. A sack hid her face, but Quiescat recognized the blood-stained dress. "Let her go!" he cried, arms reaching toward Drinith as he wriggled free of the crowd. "She's innocent!"

But before he could draw beside her, cordents seized him and forced him to the ground. A boot pressed his head against the cobbles while his hands were tied behind his back. Hands rummaged about his person, turned him over, rummaged again. The Tear of Fate hanging in the pouch around his neck—they mustn't take it. Tucking it under his chin, he writhed about to distract them. A black sack covered his head, a cord at its mouth constricting around his throat. As the cordents hoisted him to his feet, he ceased his struggle, feeling the reassuring tap of the pouch against his chest.

The mesh of the sack reduced the extent of his vision to crude, shadowy outlines. A sea of featureless heads, reveling in his humiliation, pressed in from all sides, threatening to engulf him. Where were his captors taking him? Darkness swallowed him as he was bundled into a palanquin and plonked down on a hard seat.

"Don't try anything," a silhouette at the door warned.

"There's no need for threats, Gartson," said an imperious female voice Quiescat didn't recognize. "I'm sure he'll behave. Remove his hood."

The cord around his neck loosened, and the bag lifted away. Drinith sat beside him, none the worse for wear. "Drinith! Thank the gods you're safe!" She embraced him.

A woman sat across from them, a tight smile animating her angular features. A lanky man with shoulder-length receding hair and an imperious disposition stood outside. At her gesture, he leaned in and snipped Quiescat's bonds.

"Thank you, Gartson," she said. "I'm sure there are matters

elsewhere you must attend to." The man took his leave with a bow. As the vehicle shuddered forward, she turned to Quiescat. "I'm Meritocrat Thaxen Saveral. I'm afraid the cordents have been a little overzealous in their duty. Put your fears aside. You're in no danger. You've done the Halcyon Republic a great service by exposing Javlohm's machinations."

"What about Tazran, the other woman your cordents arrested?" Drinith asked.

"They're not my cordents to command, but rest assured, I have already interceded with the relevant cordent general to secure her release. She's on her way to the Grand Preservatory to see her husband, who is currently recuperating there."

At least, for now, Quiescat and Drinith appeared to be safe, but he couldn't quite bring himself to trust the meritocrat's smile.

"Are you the meritocrat who freed me?" Drinith asked.

Thaxen's eyes narrowed. "You don't know your liberator?"

"She wore a veil," Drinith said.

"She spoke to you, yes? How did her voice sound?"

As Thaxen politely interrogated Drinith on every detail of her encounter with the veiled meritocrat, a creeping dread sent a shiver through Quiescat. Thaxen assumed they had foiled a plot by Magian's agents, but when she scrutinized its details, she'd quickly discover Gelasin's involvement, particularly given Drinith wasn't the sort to lie. And now wasn't the time for her to practice deceit, either. Thaxen would quickly see through any obfuscation or reticence.

"So, how did you uncover this intrigue?" Thaxen asked.

"I'll answer," Quiescat cut in. "If I may," he added, patting Drinith's hand. "I discovered a letter spelling out the plot. It led me to a house on Wealgiver Street. You'll find one of the conspirators dead there, the same man who murdered my successor, Versifer, Oracle of Godsdoor."

"And where is the letter now?"

"We burned it, I'm afraid, lest its possession condemn us. We were already on the run, you see."

"Of course," Thaxen said. "But how did you find the letter in the first place?"

His throat tightened. "One of Versifer's visions led us to it."

The meritocrat arched an eyebrow. "The same Versifer who's dead."

"The same," Quiescat said.

Thaxen leaned back in her seat. "That's unfortunate. He can't corroborate your story."

"Unfortunate! My successor is dead, my order destroyed, my life's work in ruins, and you dismiss it all as unfortunate."

"I meant no offense," Thaxen said.

He pounded the roof with his fist. "Stop the palanquin! We're getting off!"

The moment the vehicle halted, he threw back the curtain and dragged Drinith out of it.

"Calm down," Thaxen urged.

"We'll be at Meritocrat Hax's mansion," Quiescat said. "We've had enough misfortunes for one day. If you want to ask more stupid questions tomorrow, you know where to find us."

Thaxen leaned out of the cab. "I doubt Epmar will be in the humor to entertain anyone. Stay the night with me. I promise no more questions until tomorrow."

"Thank you, Meritocrat, for your kind offer, but no." *You might pause your interrogation, but you won't stop listening to our every whisper.*

She bounced a jangling coin pouch in her hand, then threw it to Drinith. "Take this and I'll see you tomorrow." She signaled the driver and sat back into the cab. The four casquars jerked forward. Quiescat and Drinith watched the bulky vehicle lumber down the street.

They found a nearby tea shop and settled into a table.

"What teas do you have?" Quiescat asked the proprietor, an aged woman with striking green eyes.

"I have a range of soft and hard teas for any occasion," she said.

"Give us whatever you think is best for a trying day."

She winked and waved her finger. "I have just the one."

They sat in weary silence until she returned with a pot of fragrant tea and two cups. The hot red liquid tasted like a scorpion sting on Quiescat's tongue, but it instantly reinvigorated him. Hard tea, indeed. He sipped it as he listened patiently to Drinith's frank account of her liberation and the subsequent revelations about Gelasin.

"Are you sure Thaxen couldn't be your mysterious rescuer?" he asked.

Drinith shrugged. "The voice was different, much lower."

"There's no certainty that your rescuer addressed you in her normal speaking voice," Quiescat said.

"I feel guilty," Drinith whispered. "Pretending Gelasin served Magian."

Quiescat stroked his chin. "Gelasin was a traitor and a murderer. He deserves no better."

"You misunderstand," Drinith said. "I feel I'm rewarding him for his treachery. He didn't care about his reputation. He wore the scars of his previous betrayal with pride. I...we are abetting him in achieving his goal."

"But it's our goal too," Quiescat said. "It's the method, not the aim, that should appal us." Yes, it was obvious in retrospect that Gelasin was the tangled man of Versifer's first vision.

Drinith rubbed her hands down her lap in a shuddery stretch. "Can good come of a lie?"

Quiescat fingered the pouch dangling from his neck. "Hopefully. Let's head on to Epmar's."

They followed the tea seller's directions to Hax Plaza. Epmar's grief-stricken wail reached them before they had crossed the plaza. Quiescat wondered if Epmar would ever really get over the death of her brave, flamboyant lover.

Jarma and an ill-looking Fenvar greeted them at the door. Jarma threw her arms around Drinith. "Thank the gods you're okay." She acknowledged Quiescat with an awkward nod.

He replied in kind.

Another wail came from upstairs.

"The meritocrat told me to bring you to her as soon you came," Fenvar said to Drinith. Drinith looked to Quiescat.

"Go and comfort her as best you can," he said.

As she started up the stairs, Jarma called to her. "I'll follow you up in a moment." She gazed down at the floor, rubbed her hands against her dress.

Fenvar bobbed her head. "Excuse me." As she hurried after Drinith, Quiescat searched in vain for some pretext to call her back to ease his discomfort.

Jarma looked up, eyed him with icy ferocity. "I owe you my life. Thank you."

"Thank you," Quiescat murmured, taken aback.

Her eyes glistened as they shook hands. She headed for the stairs. Climbing onto the first step, she cleared her throat and turned again toward him. "I blamed you for Abecedar."

Guilt squeezed his heart.

"His death wasn't your fault." Coming from her, that meant something. She had loved Abecedar and hated Quiescat because of it. She still harbored resentment toward him. He knew it took a lot of effort to reach beyond her hurt. He nodded in gratitude for her precious absolution, but she already rushed up the stairs.

Quiescat waited until she had disappeared, then headed to his room. The wailing stopped before he reached it. He sat on the bed and stared at his reflection in the vertical wall mirror. He looked haggard. Crescent bags had puffed up under his eyes. Those eyes—he hated those eyes. They made him less human than the Tear of Fate ever did.

He strummed the nightstand to relieve the silence. He opened the pouch and, removing the Tear, placed it on the stand. It appeared to be a glass sphere, indistinguishable from any huckster's bauble.

He picked it up again, rolled it in his fingers, savoring its reassuring smoothness. It looked so safe and inert. It was hard to credit the damage it had wrought on Zin, but then again, he had murdered its rightful owner. It must have acted out of vengeance. Quiescat and his predecessors, depending on a superficial understanding of its magic, had turned to ritual to compensate for their ignorance. Only the Fate Healer knew the true extent of its powers.

Had the trauma of Versifer's murder irrevocably transformed its nature, or could it be used to create another oracle? The only way to know for certain was to try. He was the obvious candidate. A lifetime as the Oracle of Godsdoor had familiarized him better than any other mortal with the nuances of the Tear's powers. And he was expendable.

He perched it on a tripod of his fingers and thumb. Yes, a final act in Drinith's service, or perhaps the first of many. This might be the real reason Abecedar saved him.

Holding open his fluttering eyelid, he pressed the Tear to the corner of his right eye. Nothing happened. The Tear was dead.

He repressed the urge to fling it away. He squeezed his fist around it, feeling its unyielding solidity. Versifer's four cryptic visions were the only dull embers that remained of the gift, and Quiescat feared that, like his first vision, they would yield their meaning too late.

Drinith burst into the room. Quiescat leapt to his feet. "What's wrong?"

She hesitated. "Epmar wants to adopt me as her successor."

Quiescat sat down. "What?"

"She wants to make me Meritocrat Hax," Drinith said. "I told her I need time to consider her offer. What do you think I should do?"

This could pose a huge complication to their goal of freeing Kaplar. It would drag them into the politics of Gyre in a way he had never imagined. He spied the straw doll lying on the floor, flattened and frayed, almost shapeless. He picked it up and put it on the nightstand beside the dead glass sphere. At the same time, Epmar's act of generosity would secure Drinith's future. She would have a country at last.

"Epmar has suffered a terrible loss," he said at length. "It may be sorrow speaking. We must give her time to reconsider when she has had a chance to grieve. If the offer still stands then, I say you should accept."

EPILOGUE

Airships beaded two invisible lines from the archipelago to Noster, a distance too short to be worth the effort of dragons. High above, a spiked aqueduct stretched across the same void to lance the snowy mountains that supplied Gyre with water.

Drinith admired the view as she stood with Quiescat and Epmar in the shadow of a small dirigible. Woad hovered at a discreet distance, keeping watch for potential assassins. Thankfully, the pentaculars no longer formed part of that threat. News of their failure had broken their aura of invincibility, emboldening their many enemies to band together to eradicate them.

"Are you sure you want to leave?" Drinith asked Epmar yet again. Three red months had passed since she had declared Drinith her heir, a red month since she formally handed over her emblem of merit.

"Absolutely," Epmar replied. "A quiet life on my country estate beckons, Meritocrat Hax."

"Don't call me that," Drinith gently chided. "We'll always be on a first-name basis. You know that, surely."

Epmar grinned. "I should hope so. From the moment I knew I

had to return to Gyre, I had made up my mind to adopt you as my successor. I had hoped to take Halyard away from here one last time and retire with him on Noster." She bowed her head. "But I couldn't save him. I failed him."

"You did your best to shield him," Quiescat said. "You lived the life of a vagabond to protect him."

"At the start..." Epmar's gaze darted between her and Quiescat. "Be wary of Thaxen. Remember, she's not your friend."

"She had some sort of hold over you, hadn't she?" Quiescat asked.

"Aye, I acted as one of her agents abroad. It was the only way out of Gyre. All Gyran meritocrats live on the archipelago rather than their mainland estates for a reason. Everyone can keep a close eye on each other here and make sure nobody poses a risk to our state. I needed to be useful to the Meritocracy to leave without being regarded as a threat."

"If Thaxen is forcing you to leave again..." Drinith said, immediately embarrassed by the emptiness of her offer.

Epmar sighed. "No. It's Halyard's ghost. Sweet Halyard. Loyal and brave beyond measure. The same men who would have slain him now sing of his victory against the pentacular. They ape his fashion. His peacock attire, once dismissed as passé, is now all the rage. I almost fainted with shock the first time I encountered one of his imitators. Their appearance taunts me. But that infernal ballad in his honor is a thousand times worse! It echoes on every street, from the mouths of minstrels and drunkards alike! They sing not of my Halyard but an exaggerated version of him, a hollow mockery of all he held dear and all I held dear in him."

She dabbed her eyes with a handkerchief. "One other piece of advice. Don't be too forthright in your advocacy of the Blue Quarter. Work through other sympathetic meritocrats." She hesitated. "Don't give them any reason to doubt your loyalty." She hugged Drinith, nodded to Quiescat, and approached the dirigible. With a last farewell wave, she disappeared into the gondola.

Drinith watched the dirigible float clear of its mooring and steer into a gap in the traffic heading to Noster. Part of her wished she was the one leaving. "There goes another friend," she said sadly. "I'll miss her advice." She and Quiescat would have to manage on their own now.

As they strolled through the docks, daunted workers cleared out of their path. It didn't matter to them that she was a foreigner. They didn't see beyond her emblem of merit. If only the same could be said of her colleagues in the parliament. Her sudden elevation had drawn ire in certain quarters.

At least, nobody suspected the truth about the attack she had foiled. She had convinced the meritocrats that Gelasin and his dead henchmen were the extent of the conspiracy, sparing the Blue Quarter from punitive raids. Of course, that didn't mean the Rhumgadian refugees escaped renewed scrutiny.

"What did you make of Epmar's last counsel?" Drinith asked.

"She's right to urge caution. We must build our support in the Blue Quarter discreetly. We mustn't lose sight of our ultimate goal. The best way to help the exiles is to liberate their homeland."

They reached the edge of the docks. Across a narrow chasm, perches scarred the cliffs on the neighboring shardlet. In each one, a dragon nestled, part of a vast armada readying for war with Rhumgad. If Drinith did not yet possess her birthright, at least she had won the instrument of her vengeance against Magian. Now she must learn to wield it.

A WORD FROM THE AUTHOR

Want to find out what happens next? The best way to learn about future releases in this series and my other works my email list at https://photocosm.org/.

It would mean so much to me if you could leave an honest review wherever you purchased this story.

Feel free to email me at noelcoughlan@photocosm.org to ask any questions or share any comments you have about this book. I love to hear from readers.

Best wishes,

Noel

facebook.com/photocosm

twitter.com/noel_coughlan

goodreads.com/noel_coughlan

amazon.com/author/noelcoughlan

bookbub.com/authors/noel-coughlan

GREATER EVIL

A lie made Drinith one of Gyre's rulers. It secured the city state's support against her enemy, the tyrant Magian the Infinite. Now it threatens to destroy her.

Drinith voyages to Gyre's bitterest rival, Ophigee, to convince its Diarchs to join the campaign against Magian. But her audience with her hosts turns into an ambush. Her reluctance to share the truth about the Crevastival attack condemns her to death.

Quick thinking wins her a reprieve from the execution block, but the route to salvation may well prove more treacherous than anything she has faced before. Everyone who attempts the journey she must undertake vanishes without trace. Can she succeed where they failed and uncover the secret that threatens not only Ophigee but her adopted homeland?

Greater Evil, the second book in the **Champions of Fate** epic fantasy series, is ideal for readers who love fast-paced action, intriguing characters, and imaginative world-building.

THE GOLDEN RULE

Elf. Warrior. Saint. Heretic. Monster. Despised by two peoples, this pariah might yet prove to be the savior of both.

AscendantSun serves a dead god no longer. Adopting the religion of his human enemies, he haunts their mountains hoping to make amends for his violence toward them. Now, a figure from his past threatens to restart the ancient conflict he has struggled so long to put behind him.

War is coming again to the mountains, but this time he'll fight the legionaries he once commanded. Prophecy is against him. Numbers, too. But the greatest peril is the distrust of his human allies. Can he forge an effective alliance before the bright power rising in the east destroys them?

A Bright Power Rising and *The Unconquered Sun* compose **The Golden Rule**, a two-part epic fantasy for readers who enjoy unique and intriguing world-building.

SHORT STORIES

Fantasy:

No Escape

A desperate warrior carries a baby girl across a foreign desert. Although truth and honor are tattooed on his face, Tharo has abandoned both virtues in his quest to protect his charge. But it's only a matter of time before he fails her. Another man stalks them, a hunter no prey can escape, the dreaded Souldiviner.

(Prequel to *Fatal Shadow*)

The Parting Gift

Certamen's god is dead. His people, the Ors, are broken and enslaved. He finds consolation in the knowledge that they are safe... But not for much longer. Their masters, facing decimation by disease, are growing desperate. Desperate enough to kill.

(Prequel to *A Bright Power Rising*.)

The Fate Healer

Draston's master, Hamvok the Merciful, craves a royal ancestor or two to legitimize his tyranny. But every avenue of Draston's research has come to a dead end. To save himself from the tyrant's violent displeasure, he commits himself to a path of forgery and sacrilege, risking the wrath of not only the gods, but a far more terrible entity, the dreaded Fate Healer.

Science Fiction:

Alienity

Four short stories about aliens ranging from humorous to deadly somber.

Horror:

The Murder Seat

Dr. Herbert Marriott has a problem that only murder can solve. Luckily for him, the perfect weapon is locked away in his rundown museum, one too incredible for any court to accept. The cursed chair kills all who rest upon it. But will Herbert's victim be so easily drawn to her fate?

ACKNOWLEDGMENTS

First of all, I must thank Marilynn Cooper who emailed me several years ago to ask if I had any plans to write more stories set in the same world as No Escape. When I originally wrote that short story, I never imagined that it would be anything other than a standalone work. It has become the germ of a pretty elaborate universe.

I want to thank Nick Lloyd for his trojan beta-reading. Also thanks to Evan Coughlan and Ian McInerney for their valuable input.

I want to thank the good people at MIBLart for their fantastic cover.

Lastly, I want to thank Pamela Cangioli and Kevin Cook from Proofed To Perfection for their editing work. Kevin in particular went above and beyond in his editing and helped take this book to another level.

ABOUT NOEL COUGHLAN

Noel lives with his wife and daughter in the West of Ireland. He writes epic fantasy, science fiction and horror.

From a young age, he was always writing a book. Generally, the first page over and over. Sometimes, he even reached the second page before he had shredded an entire copybook. And you couldn't even recycle all that wasted paper back then.

When he finally wrote and published a book, it took him fourteen years. *The Golden Rule* became two books so let us be generous and say he averaged seven years per novel. He has gotten a little faster since then. Honest.

His hobbies include writing, reading, and reading about writing. He has written about reading in the past, and he still writes about writing. He would happily stay at home all day writing, but the family dog, Ruby, insists on taking him for daily walks.

His pet hates include writing his biography and referring to himself in the third person.